OPERATION SNOWDROP

OPERATION SNOWDROP
A THRILLER

JAMES DOUGLAS

Welcome Rain Publishers
NEW YORK

Operation Snowdrop

Library of Congress Cataloging-in-Publication is available from the publisher.

ISBN: 978-1-56649-406-9

First U.S. edition: December 2020

OPERATION SNOWDROP

PROLOGUE

Tehran

Air Force General Hassan Nassiri pressed his back against the hard seat of the uncomfortable, post-Soviet commando vehicle, bracing his legs against the floor plate to absorb the impact of the potholes of the uneven access road. His gaze glanced over the pipes and voluminous tanks belonging to the large refinery, stopping on the larger-than-life portrait of Khomeini upon the grandiose, arched entrance. This afternoon, however, Nassiri's thoughts were not concerned with the bearded, long-faded Great Ayatollah. General Nassiri was focused on the future. His country was on the brink of becoming a regional atomic power. He would learn more in the conference that was scheduled to be held in half an hour.

His driver shifted into higher gear as he reached the paved section of the roadway. The First Sergeant drove past the parking lot of the refinery, without paying any notice to the austere gaze of the revolutionary leader on the portrait. In a good temper the General made a symbolic gesture of a telephone receiver near his ear. "So, Ali, do you have one?"

The driver looked over at him. "A cell phone? Sure, General."

"One of the new ones?"

Ali turned onto a concrete runway as he thought earnestly about this possibly loaded question. Was the General trying to trick him? He had served as the dedicated driver to the Air Force Chief for four years, and had always been treated well. The high-ranking officer was demanding, as was to be expected, but also gracious. He showed concern over Ali's family, for which his driver credited him highly. They talked about all manner of things on long official trips, including army routine and pressing troop concerns. Ali had never had the impression that the high officer was politically engaged. Once he had made a comment that politics may have precedence over the military, but no way would he stroke the mullahs' beards.

"Well? Yes or no?"

Ali glanced over, nodding keenly. "Yes, General, I do...I..."

"Alright, Ali." The General grinned, producing the shimmering, silver *corpus delicti* from his breast pocket. "What do you think of this?"

Ali remained cautiously neutral. "Those things were dropped everywhere from the sky. Latest satellite technology. Who could have done that?"

"Probably the Americans," the General laughed, "the evil ants."

He swiped across the newspaper on his knees with the back of his hand. Kayhan, the conservative paper, railed against foreign-influenced rascals and crooks who swindled the people. The Ministry of Information denied that unknown aircraft had infiltrated Iranian airspace. "Who else? This devil's gadget is going to liven things up, Ali, what do you say?"

An avenue of green, white and red flags led to the entrance of the air force base. Ali shifted to a lower gear to slow to the speed limit of twenty-five. "We do what we can, General. We make do. It's just a shame about the jets. We don't have spare parts. Many planes are grounded because they need repairs. That needs to change."

He sought the General's eyes, maneuvered carefully over the speed bumps, and circled the car-bomb-resistant road block.

"We won't be able to get parts for this joke of a car either. You should apply for the new Toyota cross-country, General."

The General grimaced with regret. "I know."

Ali felt emboldened. "We are isolated. The boycott is bad. If we were an open society, I mean…"

"I know what you mean, Ali. Watch out, the checkpoint."

The IRIAF grounds were now in full view. The runway shimmered, the sharp contours of the command center rose distinctly from the plain. The General relaxed, placing the worn briefcase on his knees. He dug a page out, skimmed the illustrious participant list. He mentally rehearsed his speech, going through key phrases, with which he intended to open the briefing. All the while the old fox was well aware that everything could go counter to plan. Like war. Even as the first shot sounds, the best battle plan may no longer be worth the paper it is written on…

Iran, gentlemen, is on its way to becoming the preeminent regional power, he murmured, aware of Ali out of the corner of his eye, who maintained a disciplined silence, eyes forward as he focused on steering past the obstacles.

It is not enough, gentlemen, to be merely a potential atomic power. While it is true today that we could manufacture atomic weapons within a short period of time without any foreign aid—then a poignant pause for dramatic effect—*Am I right, Colonel*...What's-His-Name?—*just as Japan or Germany currently could; Iran must no longer allow itself to be deterred from becoming a nuclear power. As a military man, I know that our forces will have a far different standing once the first Iranian atomic explosion has shocked*...*perhaps brought panic upon*...*the world. Today we will go one step further: a step that will yield a very attractive increase in prestige and power. Once the international community is forced to take us seriously because we are in possession of the A-bomb, trade embargoes will topple like*...Like what? He caught himself contemplating an amusing analogy. *Like these cell phones dropping out of the clear blue sky*...At which point I will dramatically pull it out of my pocket...No, better not. That could backfire...*But everything hinges on the atomic bomb. It is the key that will set everything in motion.* He flashed on the cell phone analogy again: *Just like these cell phones, the A-bomb has the power to bring about an open society*...Better not say that, either...*We will be able to restructure our air force, modernize our armed services. Countries like*—I'll just mention France—*like France will be clamoring for our orders, everything will take a turn for the better*...

Having successfully mastered its obstacle course, the Soviet version of a Jeep came to a standstill in front of the massive entry gate. The lightly armed air force soldiers guarding the gate recognized their commanding officer. A flurry of activity ensued, the gate was set in motion, an officer appeared on the scene, snapped to attention, saluted, shouted orders.

They waved the Big Brass through; Ali drove forward, after a few meters the nose of the all-terrain vehicle dipped, rolled down a ramp toward a second steel gate, which opened on time with a grudging squeak.

The General arrived at the reception bay, alighted with dignity, reciprocated the greetings of the troops with a sharp raising of his hand. He crossed the spacious loading dock with an energetic stride and one of his charismatic smiles. He stepped into the elevator, exiting two stories below ground seconds later and stepping into the Air Force Command Center of the Islamic Republic of Iran...

PART I

Sonoma County, north of San Francisco

The afternoon sun casts a golden glow upon the coastal landscape of Sonoma, across the picturesque hills of Glen Ellen, to the endless, glistening reaches of the Pacific Ocean a few miles west. The man with his shoulder-length silver mane, of robust stature despite his age, known to many powerful people as Cosmo, is slanted casually behind the steering wheel of his comfortable hybrid. He is enjoying the northern inland vista of coastal hills, enjoying the light playing on the spear-shaped eucalyptus leaves, allowing his face to be caressed by the gentle breeze as he drives. A small, wiry Jack Russell with intelligent, sparkling eyes is seated next to her owner, chest puffed proudly. She hears, feels, smells—the world is hers, because she is allowed to accompany her benefactor and master. Cosmo reaches out with a bear-like right paw and absently scratches the little dog's head.

"Beautiful day today, huh, Feedback?"

The creature answers by pressing her head into Cosmo's hand.

"You and me," the man continues, "we're just..."

There is a yellow flash behind him; a short, sharp siren sounds. The heavy, dusty Highway Patrol cruiser is practically tailgating them. Cosmo pulls over to the side and comes to a halt. Nothing happens for a few heartbeats. The leaves of the old, majestic trees rustle in the afternoon stillness. Feedback gives a little sound to indicate that she is ready to challenge any troublemaker. Cosmo smiles at this indulgently, watches the officer slowly exit his vehicle in the side mirror, sees him nudge his broad, department-issued belt up and commence his stiff-legged approach.

Cosmo can hardly contain a grin. The man is alone, which is against regulations; he also looks a bit drowsy. Probably been taking a nap on the gravel road back there. He looks up calmly at the young man's face. "*Yessir, officer.* Something wrong?"

"You could say that. Do you always drive so slowly?"

Cosmo has to smile. "Slowly? I was driving too slowly?"

"You were, sir. The unrestricted minimum speed on this stretch is twenty-five miles per hour. You were doing less than twenty."

"I am sincerely sorry."

"So am I. I see your dog doesn't have a tag."

"Correct."

"Correct? Your driver's license, please."

Cosmo calmly picks his license out of his pocket, holds it out to the officer.

"Take it out of the cover, please, sir."

Cosmo takes the license out of its plastic casing, hands it over. The officer reads the name, drawing it out deliberately, then repeats it.

"Jack A-bram-ian."

"Indeed," says Cosmo with a grin.

"American?"

"As apple pie, sir. If you toss in a handful of Armenian sunflower seed."

"Funny man, huh?"

The officer, plainly annoyed, turns on his heel and marches briskly back to his cruiser. Dropping into the passenger seat, he hits a button and starts to enter the information on the license. It doesn't take ten seconds for the voice of the officer in charge to respond through the intercom.

"Chip, are you nuts? Do you have any idea whom you just snagged? That's Jack Abramian."

Chip responds, a little perturbed by his colleague's tone. "Abramian. Yeees. So what?"

"So what? *So what?* Jack Abramian owns half of the county—along with about a quarter of the entire state of Nevada, is what. Your piece of shit car is parked on his land. He as much as clears his throat and you're out of a job. Anything else you need to know?"

"I understand."

"I can't hear you," the voice croaked, "are you still in range?"

Chip is already hustling toward Cosmo's SUV, handing the driver's license back through the window. "I'm sorry, Mr. Abramian, sir, my mistake, I'm new, just started last week. I didn't recognize you right away, sir, the sun was in my eyes…"

"It's all good, boy," comes the magnanimous response, "you're not the first that's happened to."

"Have a nice day, sir."

"You too," Cosmo says, smiling and starting up the car. The hybrid takes off, throwing up a bunch of sand and gravel in its wake that rains against Chip's legs. Feedback decides that this is the moment to have the last word with her best blood-curdling attack-yowl. Abramian smiles amused.

Three minutes later he is steering the car into a narrow avenue, lined by California oak trees, at the end of which awaits a somewhat understated, rustic estate. He leans across the seat, throws open the passenger door. Feedback leaps out, legs already running even in mid-flight. She is ten, twenty feet ahead as the car and its driver catch up with her, just before she reaches their destination.

Cosmo

The dim glow of the California evening sun found its way into the study, discreetly decorated in shades of beige and brown, lending it an almost romantic air. Jack Abramian's fingers scratched his loyal companion Feedback's silky coat. "So, little one, what do you say to our new president?"

Feedback looked up with sparkling eyes. She understood quite well. After all, he spoke to her intimately and often. She also knew that people moved their mouths when they spoke—so she, adorably, moved her little black lips. The effect was astonishing—the little Jack Russell terrier truly looked as if she was answering back. Abramian clearly had no difficulty understanding her imaginary words. And so he repeated them out loud. "Him? Oh, I think we'd better wait before we judge. Beginner's luck doesn't count for much in politics. He'd be a bit off base if he wanted to signal a global retreat. It's all about Iran. That's where the new beginning lies."

Feedback rubbed her muzzle against her master's silky, white sleeve. "You don't believe me, huh?"

He laughed. "Of course I do. Only, when it comes to Iran we are going to let our charismatic friend steal the show. Trust me." He looked up to the high ceiling, and the emblem intricately crafted of ivory and redwood. *Orbis Unum*. "What do you say now, you little charmer?"

The answer from the terse little thoroughbred resting on his lap, and enjoying getting her neck stroked, was something between a whimper and a yowl. "Andy!" Abramian called with a confident boom.

The lanky figure appeared in the room before the sound of his voice had faded. The young, curly-haired man moved as though he had just randomly drifted in to shoot the breeze with his boss about unimportant trivia. Feedback jumped from Abramian's lap in a high arch, then up Andy's legs with a further two bounds.

"She is clearly infatuated with you, Andy. But now, please, our man in Zurich!"

"Sure, Jack."

Fending the dog off with one hand, he conjured a small device from his pocket with the other, deftly entering a numeric sequence. Abramian stopped him with a gesture. "Just a moment. Tell me, Andy: I sometimes ask myself what you do with yourself when you're not hanging around here, driving Feedback nuts."

Andy grinned enigmatically. "What do you mean, boss?"

"Well, there's got to be something you're attached to...that you enjoy...there has to be some old car you're fixing up, yes? Don't you ever go to San Francisco with friends to watch a Giants game? Yell until you're hoarse? Your girlfriend...Kim? Is it Kim?"

Andy's grin broadened. "Kim went back to L.A. She wants to get back into her acting career. I just got myself a parrot. That's about as good."

Cosmo's laughter filled the room. "A parrot—like Churchill's? Do you remember? No, no. Of course, you're too young. 'Fuck Hitler...' is what Churchill's little alter ego used to say. What does yours say?"

Andy rolled his eyes innocently. "He just croaks, 'Oh, shit! Not the boss again!'"

The mighty man waved his hand in amusement. "Alright, alright, I understand. You have it good, Andy."

"I do, sir. I have the perfect boss."

"Oh, stop! You have your little friends. That counts in life, Andy. What do I have, except for Feedback?" He sank his head toward the dog, who had begun to calm down.

Andy allowed his casual frame to assume a new, possibly even more relaxed posture. "But you have everything, Mr. Abramian. Everything a man could possibly want in the world."

"Money and power?"

"Plenty of both, sir. A family clan in Armenia. And you have a mission. *E pluribus unum.*"

Abramian gazed contemplatively at the ceiling, before abruptly shaking his head. "You're yanking my chain, Andy."

"Well, sir, my Latin's a bit patchy. That's what it says on the dollar bills."

Abramian's eyes flew open as he let out a loud bellow of a laugh. Shaking his head, he slapped his knees. What would he do without this kid, who always managed to bring him right back down to earth with a few words? "Andy, *my boy*, you're worth every cent I pay you. If you don't ask me for a raise soon, I might have to give you one anyway. *E pluribus unum*—my ass. *Orbis unum* is what it says up there. You've only read it a hundred times, you comedian."

"That would fit just fine on a dollar bill, Jack. We could print them ourselves if we felt like it," Andy said with an impertinent expression on his face.

Abramian smiled in a part patronizing, part appreciative way. "I can think of something better than dollar bills. Something really fun."

"Yes, sir?"

"To give certain people a run for their money. Our neighbors in Armenia, those bearded mullahs." He grinned boyishly, like a kid who has just played a successful prank. Andy lifted his long arms, stretched and yawned unabashedly.

His boss chuckled, amused. "Girls love dolls, Andy. And men

8

all over the world can hardly save themselves from all the pussy, haha... They're always all over each other, the girls, the boys. They flirt, call each other on the phone, make dates, text each other. That is the ingenious prank, Andy. What I have to teach is historically valuable. My archive will re-write history."

There he goes, speaking in riddles again. Pussy, dolls, history—whatever.

"Just like the presidents and their libraries, sir."

"Ah, yes. The Presidents," Cosmo smiled a bit absently, "what would we be without them. And they without me!"

A cell phone buzzed.

"The man from Zurich," said Andy quietly, suddenly thrust back into the role of an assiduous employee, his California Dreamin' T-shirt notwithstanding. He handed his employer the phone.

"Yes? Hello? Shuky, my friend, how are you?" He heard the old man drone as he left the room stealthily, on quiet soles.

"The infiltration protection is in place," Nachman said, speaking of wide-range ground surveillance performed by an Israeli company.

"Good, Shuky."

"An eye and an ear in every last corner," the Zurich man reported.

"I know, I have eyes in my head," Cosmo interrupted, touching a symbol on the display of the tabletop. Instantly a topographic global map lit up on the wall.

"Armenia," Cosmo commanded. Instantly the globe began shrinking to focus on the country between Azerbaijan and Turkey, while the blinds on the broad windows closed noiselessly to shut out the golden evening light on the coastal elevations.

"Street map!" In short order, routes and settlements, and their identifications, appeared as scattered by an invisible hand across the southern topography of the mountainous terrain bordering Iran. A spider's web of traffic arteries spanned the capital, Eriwan, in the central plain. Further north, the border to Georgia could be seen.

"We are still doing test runs. The second installment of the payment is due," suggested Zurich from the speaker hidden in the tabletop.

The map now also showed a strip to the southwest, near a river. The pre-programmed zoom honed in on a city-like industrial complex that stretched far into the almost uniformly brownish-looking landscape, focusing on a number of long, aligned buildings on the edge of a long airfield. Large helicopters and large cargo planes stood off the runway in front of a row of hangars.

Cosmo hit the speaker button. "Zurich? You still there? I am presently looking at the new landing strip to my techno park."

His Alpine voice came over loud and clear: "The strip is a fixed operational base. It is under constant surveillance. No one is going to get in there, like the Russians into Georgia."

"Oh, the Georgian experiment was merely a little dress rehearsal; foreplay, so to speak. It was meant to up the ante a little. The Russians stomped right into the trap." He laughed smoothly. "What is the nicest thing about foreplay, Shuky?"

The Zurich contact was silent. "Listen, old boy, everything is foreplay, because all of our actions have a single, unified aim." A barking laugh followed. Andy materialized with a smile on his face and a bowl of food in his hand.

"The oil, the pipelines, the petroleum gas, the natural resources—the crux for Armenia's future..." he heard his boss lecturing. "What is in the way are the bearded numbskulls in Tehran." Andy set the bowl down gingerly. *Was Abramian speaking to the dog or to Zurich? Best not to disturb him!*

"Okay, Shuky, we'll stay on it. Keep your eyes open. I'm still interested in buying the bank in Zurich. Will I see you at the conference in Eriwan?"

The partner in Zurich said: "Jack, it's better if we meet the day after at your techno park."

"Okay, Shuky." Cosmo ended the conversation, pushed the phone away. Like triggering a military attack, he yelled into the anteroom: "Andy! Enough of the California dreams! It's time to fly."

Feedback started from where she had been enjoying her Stroganov.

Warmth flooded the room along with the light as the window shutters to the west side of the annex opened to reveal the helipad. Behind it, hills rolled to where they would meet the gentle waves of the Pacific Ocean.

We'll be in Santa Rosa in ten minutes, Cosmo considered. He smiled at the thought of his flight crew, which following Andy's call must have raced to the airfield, where the latest model Gulfstream awaited him. The trip would take him over Nevada and Canada, via the North Pole and the Ukraine to Armenia. To Armenia—home! What could be greater than being at home in two worlds!

Zurich, Bahnhofstrasse

The name of his raw tobacco trading company Trinexint AG on Zurich's Bahnhofstrasse, sounded more like a purveyor of pesticides. Certainly one would not have assumed the commercial enterprise to be a cover for big armament procurement contracts. Nachman, who had years ago selected vibrant Zurich as the hub of his international dealings, was originally from Israel; in fact, he was a highly decorated veteran of one of his homeland's many wars. He sat at his antique desk in his corner office, looking out at the pillared entrance of the major bank. A blue tram droned by, people paused to look with worry at a row of monitors showing the quotes of the stock exchange, which were following a bearish trend.

Nachman, who had invested in gold and cash at the right time, had an image in his mind's eye of the bank's massive pillars growing unsteady, and turning into crutches. Smiling to himself, he looked away and directed his attention to a small screen with a running news ticker displayed along its bottom edge... *Pentagon confirms troop withdrawal from Germany...*

His assistant, Tabah, stepped in, clearing his throat. "The Hornbachs are here, Shuky, they are on their way up in the elevator."

The heavy-set, broad-shouldered all-rounder nodded. The upcoming meeting was going to be, to put it mildly, pretty volatile. His network had provided him with the pertinent information. The Swiss Federal Justice Department had opened proceedings against the Hornbach brothers, based on a legal assistance request from the U.S. Attorney General's office. Prison time loomed. It seemed to be only a matter of time before the police would make arrests.

His trained bodyguard had picked the prominent engineers up and driven them directly to the entrance located in the underground parking level of the building. But the old fox was under no illusion that intelligence circles would ascertain sooner rather than later that the hot construction blueprints had been handed over clandestinely in the Bahn-hofstrasse. Time was of the essence.

"Bring them in!"

"Please, take a seat, we can speak German."

The two engineers, who smiled nervously as they sat, were leading experts in nuclear technology—Swiss nationals, who had been causing quite a commotion in Washington and Tel Aviv. The reason lay in two cases, attached to their wrists with steel chains, and guarded by them like the apple of their eye.

"Rabbi Shmuel sends his regards," the brother by the name of Ruppert opened in a servile tone, the aluminum case clasped firmly on his knees. He sported a shiny bald patch, and a light red tie that was a poor match to his olive sports jacket. His brother Roland, whose eyes looked out from behind thick, horn-rimmed glasses, carefully placed his black briefcase on the tabletop. Nachman was stunned by the stupidity. "You told the Rabbi you were coming to see me? Who else have you been blabbing to?"

The Hornbach brothers looked visibly uncomfortable. "He would never tell anyone, a man of God."

Eyes narrowed, Nachman took account of whom he was dealing with here. Roland had to be the genius, the tinkerer and inventor, while Ruppert posed as the businessman. He was just this minute taking the security chain off his case and opening it with an air of importance. "These are the printouts of the plans."

His brother extracted a black laptop from his case, and pushed it theatrically toward their host, who still appeared angered. "And this contains all of the sensitive data, securely protected on its hard drive."

The Israeli contained his impatience. "Are these the only copies?" he asked rhetorically.

The men nodded emphatically. "There are no duplicates."

Nachman fingered his golden pen. He believed not a word.

"You are receiving the complete plans, as agreed, Mr. Nachman. Israel could take these and start constructing the warheads tomorrow," Roland ventured eagerly. "It's all there." He gestured enthusiastically with both hands. "You see, a collision must be created between two subcritical masses of uranium-238. Then we need to radically accelerate the resulting mass..."

Nachman furrowed his brow disdainfully. "And what is supposed to be new about any of that? Any physics major can put together an atomic bomb these days."

His partner raised an index finger to intervene. "What is new, for instance, is the compact and energy efficient method by which we create the acceleration. The space required is not much larger than a pocket calculator, the absolute latest in nanotechnology!"

"We will review the drafts. What else is contained in the plans?"

"The formula that will allow for the compact, light design." The man actually giggled. Like a kid playing with Lego blocks. "And the detonation mechanism, of course. This application of miniaturized building components reduces our showpiece to the size of a sixpack. The warhead itself is tiny, not significantly larger than the space required to contain the subcritical masses. All in all, our product is half the size of previous, obsolete models, but it packs twice the explosive force, because it holds far more fissionable material. About as large as..." He stared at Nachman's broad skull. "A melon." The man gave another slight giggle and began spreading the precisely folded documents on the desk.

Nachman's face remained expressionless. "Fine. I assume that everything we have here in printed form is saved on this laptop." He reached over and pulled the device toward him, opened it.

"Exactly as you wished. The data is vectorized, which means..."

"I know. The data will fit onto the microchip without difficulty."

"A USB stick or CD would also work," Roland confirmed, peering over his horn-rimmed glasses.

"And where is the security backup?"

Both men froze and looked perplexed. "Look, Mr. Nachman, we no longer want to be in possession of anything, for our own protection," the other brother replied. "You know that we are being followed. If we are interrogated by intelligence, we can be quite relaxed about it all." He glanced at the cozy sofa in the anteroom. "You understand? If we don't have anything, we don't have anything." He spread his arms as if grasping for a final, winning argument. "The lie detector will have nothing on us."

"Except that you sold," Nachman grumbled, bending over the black, angular Notebook with multiple, colored folder icons illuminated on its gray screen. He carefully stuck one end of a yellow USB cable into the black laptop, while Tabah approached and connected the other end to the office server.

With his rimless glasses perched precariously upon the bridge of his nose, Nachman carefully maneuvered the mouse and clicked. The explosive plans, for which any secret service agency on the planet would have blackmailed, dropped millions, even killed, started to shift—as indicated by a blue conveyer graphic expanding toward the end of its frame.

"Who else knows that you are here?" It was a senseless question.

For a moment, the crackling of papers that Tabah was spreading on the floor was the only sound in the room.

Roland wiped his horn-rimmed glasses with the end of his tie.

"You are the crazy professors, I'll take care of security, understood? So, who else?"

"No one else, Mr. Nachman. This deal means everything to us!"

"And the old man?"

They looked at each other sheepishly. Roland blushed and began to stammer. "Well, eh, the family...Friedrich, our dear father...He is one of us."

Nachman had good reason to be suspicious. Friedrich Hornbach had worked for the Pakistani Khan, engaged with Libyans, and word in the industry was that he had switched over to the CIA. If the old man is used to trickery, who was to say that his sons were angels?

"So, what I am hearing is that there is someone," Nachman

grumbled. He didn't like this whole thing one bit. He glanced to assure himself that the data transfer was complete.

"Is it done downloading?" Tabah asked, then saw his boss nod silently.

Roland arose and stepped over to the window, boyishly light-footed in his movements. With a short glance onto the Bahnhofstrasse he said, almost casually, "Would you be so kind as to arrange the money transfer now, Mr. Nachman?" His brother beamed, but the Israeli was in no mood to beam back. His countenance was foreboding. "I will pay when everything is in order. That is the agreement, gentlemen."

They followed his invitation to the conference room, where the assistant had spread the plans on a long table, and began their work. For the better part of an hour they checked the original documents against the electronic data, sheet by sheet, following the numbered pages one at a time. The Hornbach brothers had taken off their jackets, rolled up their sleeves, and were not holding back on technical explanations, or references to context. This was their baby, which they were handing over for good money, and they were working themselves into something resembling a euphoria, which Nachman did not disapprove of. Somehow, their dedication spoke to the fact that the material was legitimate.

Nachman ultimately did not doubt that the plans he would be purchasing were complete, meticulous, and ready to be implemented. Still, something was nagging at the back of his mind. Their behavior when they had first arrived, the conspiratorial glances he had seen them occasionally exchange, revealed insecurity to the experienced negotiator that he did not like. He would need a little more time.

"It was agreed that you would immediately put the plans through the shredder and then burn the paper," the older Hornbach said, as the work came to a close and Nachman's assistant appeared with a tray of water and glasses, which he began to fill.

"And we will. You can be there to witness it."

"The plans are the only proof. Once they have been destroyed, there will be no more evidence that could be held against us."

Nachman put on a casual front. "You don't need to worry. Your problem seems to me that you should disappear as soon as possible. The Americans, the Russians, and the Swiss are all coming after you. They won't find anything here."

The shredder started up in the corner of the room, where Tabah's hunched back could be seen. Ruppert said, "The International Atomic Energy Agency in Vienna has also been pressuring us."

Nachman seemed to weigh what he had just heard. Even as they worked together, feeding the perilous manufacturing instructions for the latest atomic warheads into the maw of the shredder, Nachman's intuition was persistently warning him that something else was going on here. The Hornbachs were not being completely forthright.

"I have a check for the down payment, follow me, please," he said, once the rattling had ceased and Tabah had removed the basket containing the shreds.

Nachman found himself gripped by a sense of unease. At this point, he was in the line of fire! The delicate data was located, unprotected, in his office. The Swiss Intelligence Agency was not to be taken lightly. They had quite possibly been shadowing these two eccentric oddballs, and could be aware that this is where they could expect to hit pay dirt. He had to get rid of the Hornbach brothers as quickly as possible. Nineteen million U.S. dollars was not a negligible sum, but paying was not the issue.

Back in the office, the Hornbach brothers took their seats. "Let's get this over with," said the bespectacled one with barely contained excitement.

Nachman had arranged for the delicate transfer of funds with the Zürcher Handelsbank. The proprietors of the conservatively run financial institution looked back upon a long history of dealings in Swiss arms manufacturing. Their bank initially served a closely held machinery and arms manufacturing concern, before a decision was reached to take on private clients. The executive board focused investments on productive businesses, which created added value and also invested personally in an airplane manufacturing plant. Nachman had found favor in this solid business model, and not just since the global financial crisis. He had

known his banker, whose number he had just dialed, for years, and trusted him as a rock personified, with whom any storm could be weathered.

The Hornbachs sat quite motionless in their chairs, looking at the
nineteen-million-dollar check. Legs crossed, their faces as miserable as sin.
Tabah stood in the doorway, a cigarette dangling from his lips, eyes fixed
intently on Nachman, who waited, cordless phone to his ear.

"Providenciales," he read aloud from a yellow note. "Turks and
Caicos Islands. I had no idea that deepsea fishing was one of your hob-
bies." The two Hornbachs smiled as if on command, a strange sparkle
in their eyes. "We bought a boat. We could sail you around the island."

Nachman did not sway from his topic. "The money will be going
to this trust, correct?"

The two nodded, a little disappointed, before confirming the transfer details that the poker-faced Israeli read back to them one more time
for assurance.

"We have residence permits for the island," the one with the red
tie said, then, with a similarly self-congratulatory air, the other, "A nice
bungalow on the beach."

"Bretscher!" The bank came on the line. Nachman's features relaxed
into a warm smile. His cordial greeting was followed by the precise instructions to transfer nineteen million dollars. The banker acknowledged
and confirmed, inaudible to the room, that he was up-to-date on the
details of the transaction.

"Good. That's done!"

The Hornbachs stood, somewhat stiffly, gesturing their gratitude all
the while. On the way to the door, Ruppert hesitated. "As we have said,
Mr. Nachman, if anyone is to have our plans, then only Israel. You are
our guarantee that everything should go as discussed."

Nachman silently, yet emphatically, hustled the Hornbachs out.
What was discussed? The two oddballs had another thing coming. As far
as Nachman and his client were concerned, the deal was done. They wanted to do what was good for Israel, they had assured him. But he thought
it was safe to assume that these guys were decidedly more interested in
money than world peace… This was where Nachman's cynicism set in.

This is why he had made an arrangement with his banker. No need to teach your grandmother how to suck an egg.

"What would the Ayatollahs in Iran give for these documents," Nachman laughed as Tabah served him his drink.

"Presumably, they would give a damn about their prophet," his assistant said with a grin.

Nachman rocked his head matter-of-factly toward the desk. "Come, we should get going." It was time to transfer the secret data onto a micro CD. Tabah grimaced. "My gut tells me, Shuky, that something else is going on here."

Being the old hand that he was, Nachman rarely climbed on proverbial rotten branches. This time, too, he had left nothing to chance. "I have taken my precautions." He took a deep swig of the golden, glistening Scotch. "Just what the doctor ordered."

They went up to the apartment, which was reachable only via a spiral staircase located in the back office. Having arrived upstairs Shuky fell onto the couch in front of the fireplace. The whiskey had revived his spirits. He excitedly fingered his cell phone and discovered that he had a missed call: Sophie Kramer. A pleasant sensation flooded his sturdy frame, which was in a constant battle against excess weight. Oh, Sophie... *If you lose your sexual drive, you lose your daring, your energy, your imagination,* he muttered his favorite quote, emptied his glass, walked up a few steps up to the studio.

As always, he looked wistfully at the photograph that hung on the wall above the steps. It was with an inward sigh that he regarded a bold, dashing Shuky, dressed in a major's combat uniform, about to embark on a mission. How time flies. What am I still doing in this shitty business after all these years? Ensuring world peace? Yes, perhaps... He stood still, looked back on the large, blue and white triptych, portraying objects in flight against the sky. *Chaos and order.*

Sophie Kramer would not leave his mind. For several heartbeats he felt as if his life were ebbing away from him... *Call her, invite her over? Stay put, let things go? As that great maxim had it: When in doubt, do something! Bring order to chaos.*

"Okay, Tabah," he called, putting himself in gear with some determination, "time to get to work, you old bum!"

On the Flight to London

On the very same evening after their meeting with Nachman, the Hornbach brothers had boarded a British Airways City-Flyer to London. The plan was to continue their journey on flight BA0207 from Heathrow the next morning. The two frequent flyers knew the best connections from the past, and were looking forward to their comfortable, first-class seats on the gussied-up Boeing 747, with which British Airways served the overseas destination daily. After a layover in Miami in the afternoon the plane would land at the airport of the British protectorate of Turks and Caicos Islands shortly after eight.

The crew had just begun serving dinner shortly after cruising altitude had been attained over France. *"Banker on Russian Billionaire's Yacht,"*...Ruppert read yawning, pushed the tabloid aside, poked at the lukewarm roast beef, took a sip of red wine. Next to him, Roland had pushed up his horn-rimmed glasses and was studying a glossy magazine; already chewing absently on a piece of sausage, he stuffed a piece of bread in his mouth and wondered whether he should treat himself to cigars, chocolate, or maybe the Swiss luxury watch at the Flight Shop in the terminal.

Ruppert was done with dinner quickly, pushed his tray and the folding table out of the way, and leaned back. Worn from the strain of the stressful negotiations, he closed his eyes. Once again, he was treated to images that visited him quite regularly. His thoughts wandered with the monotonous drone of the engine, and he reviewed the familiar images of his life, ending with a new highlight: his double sale of the instructions for manufacturing the latest type of atomic weapon. It all began with Friedrich —the good, no, the best, who had made everything possible for his sons...

...Engineer Friedrich Hornbach, somber Swiss man through and through, had always advised his son Ruppert to err on the side of caution.

"Stick with the Americans, my son," had been his words to him one hot, humid day in June on the beachside terrace of the luxurious hotel The Chedi in Muscat.

The deep blue Indian Ocean had spread before them, while somewhere diagonally across the waters lay the endlessly long coastline of Iran.

"We could make a whole lot of money with the Libyans, and you should discreetly let the Americans be aware of this. This is your reinsurance."

Friedrich Hornbach's white mane billowed in a sudden gust of wind, standing in stark relief, for a split second, against the black robes of a slender Omani woman passing by silently.

"I cannot do that, Father," Ruppert had objected later, as they were walking along the wide, light gray beach. "Mr. Khan is paying us royally, you know that. It would not be right to deceive him."

Ruppert Hornbach's career had found its beginnings under the strict auspices of legendary atomic scientist A. Q. Khan. It had been a tumultuous time in chaotic Islamabad—an entirely new world. After a short time learning the ropes, the talented Swiss engineer had supervised the secret construction of the centrifuges as division manager for the Pakistani organization, and later even offered complete construction capabilities, along with the requisite training and full service, on the black market.

"You are working on the black market of terror," his father had warned him that day, on the beach of Muscat. He had come to a halt and impressed the words upon him. "We are experts in vacuum technology and the manufacturing of atomic weapons. We do not let undue scruples stand in the way of our business."

"But I cannot serve two masters," Ruppert had insisted, agitatedly picking up a fistful of pebbles.

Old Friedrich had remained silent, combing through his thick head of hair. When they headed back to change for dinner, he raised a tanned arm toward the gently rolling waves of the ocean. "Over there, Iran, is where we may find our next goldmine."

Ruppert stared at him intently. The mullahs? Of course! According to all of the rumors that had made their way to Khan's laboratory in Islamabad, the Iranians were working tirelessly on achieving the bomb.

As they continued to stride silently over the firm sand, Ruppert flicked his wrist tossing pebbles—one by one...

*

The French had ultimately been the ones to give the impetus for a turnaround by framing him with the crime of brokering rockets of French origin to Iraq without the required permits. The accusation was only partially correct, but the French, who were smooth customers when it came to arms trading, were not about to let a Swiss yokel cook their goose. But they had miscalculated. They had not counted on the mightiest secret service in the world to come to good little Ruppert's aid...

...Eyes half closed, Ruppert could see himself, years back, arriving at the posh hotel in Dubai, casually tossing the keys to his meticulously polished Porsche to one of the valets, throwing himself onto a comfortable lounger at the bar, under the shade of a large umbrella.

"Mr. Hornbach?" A female voice piped behind him. The exciting notion that his contact could prove to be a woman, and possibly adventurous, was however quickly destroyed. The attractive female, who turned out to be of Syrian origin, directed him to a dark corner of the bar, further exciting his erotic fantasies. But then she left him there with a huge man, who arose to six-foot-seven from the leather sofa to shake his hand. "My name is Jim Kidman."

It was 1999. The CIA agent had a fully developed plan up his sleeve on this hot and humid afternoon. He placed his identification badge on the table, announced in an almost offhand manner: "The French will drop the charges against you. I will see to it that you are fully rehabilitated."

Ruppert shifted nervously back and forth in his seat. His shirt was drenched and clinging to him despite the powerful A/C. He was at a loss for words—he had not expected to encounter a CIA agent. They told him about the usual suspects, who may be interested in Khan's services. First contacts, such as they were, mostly took place in a conspiratorial atmosphere. Ruppert had thus come rather laid-back to the confidential meeting, expecting not much more than to sound out his party.

Now he nervously fingered Kidman's badge with the prominent CIA emblem. "What do you expect from me in return? You people aren't exactly known for your charity."

Jim Kidman grinned broadly, took a drink from his Daiquiri. "Don't worry. The agency will remain in the background. You will be working with the Dyna Corporation. It belongs to us."

"I don't want any difficulties," Ruppert composed himself, ordered a beer from the waiter who had appeared next to him.

"You already have difficulties, Ruppert. The French will put you on Interpol's wanted list, and you'll be in the shit up to your neck. My offer is a fair one."

Ruppert raised his brows expectantly.

"As a little return service you will be working with me from now on. Call me Jim." He raised his glass. "To our collaboration."

The young waiter served the drink. Ruppert reached hesitantly for the glass filled with the appealingly refreshing beer. "You know where I work, Jim, right?" He paused. "Exactly. I am a loyal man. The Pakistanis pay very generously and..."

He stopped when Kidman slapped a piece of paper onto the table, with a condemnatory look.

Ruppert spoke French as well as his mother tongue. He recognized the document at first glance: *Mandat d'Arrêt*.

"The arrest warrant issued in Paris," Kidman said in an unctuous tone. "If we can agree, it will never have existed. You understand, Ruppert? One call to Paris will be all it takes." He looked pointedly at his wristwatch. "You should know, by the way, we like the Swiss," he added, without batting an eye. "I worked in Bern for a long time. It has a certain tradition for us. The Swiss are reliably neutral. They are accustomed to accommodating themselves with all sides."

Half an hour later the deal with the CIA was sealed.

What Jim had put to him casually, as if it had been a suggestion to meet for lunch, was really not an offer at all. It was extortion. Later Ruppert Hornbach was in no doubt about this. But the conditions worked—and how had father put it? *We do not let undue scruples stand in the way of our business.*

London, City Airport

I never regretted it, Ruppert mused as he sank into the soft armchair cushions over the English Channel and placed a moist towelette across his balding forehead. "You have always trusted me, Roland, and you were right to do so. This time will be no different—it will all be fine. After all, we are experienced double-agents." He chuckled.

"What do you mean?"

"You assured Nachman that nobody else had access to our secret plans. That was true. We turned down the Russians. They are probably pissed off."

The Russians had been a no-go because they simply could not win their favor. The lack of sympathy had a lot to do with their language. Their tongue-twisting rasping turned the Hornbachs off even more than the communist background of these parvenus. The billionaire oligarch and syndicate head Oleg Nedjew had coaxed them onto his luxury yacht in vain, despite tempting them with almost obscene offers. They resisted, in the brave tradition of their distant forebears at the victorious battle at Morgarten against the Habsburg cavalry. The two wise guys, however, would surely have shuddered to think that smart Nedjew had been having them shadowed for some time, with every intention of seizing the secret plans from them by applying some old-style KGB method. Ruppert cheerfully chewed his food. "If someone is going to be pissed off, it will be Jim if he gets wind of it."

"Kidman? I think we should leave him in suspense for a while." Of course the Hornbachs had no intention of letting down the CIA ally, given all of their common, lucrative dealings in the past.

Roland raised his brows. "Agreements must be honored—*pacta sunt servanda!*"

Both laughed jauntily. Ruppert raised his glass, Roland put the back of his seat in an upright position. "The family has always held together," he said. And it was true. The three Hornbachs had dedicated themselves with every fiber of their collective being to the fascination of technology; had perfected the vacuum technique required in the building of centrifuges. Their expertise was key to being able to enrich uranium in a closed circuit. Everyone knew it. Including the CIA.

"We prevented the Islamic bomb, that counts for something," whispered Ruppert, as if to appease his conscience. "We deserve what we have made on this."

"Why Islamic?" asked Roland. "Is the American bomb, Christian? The Israeli bomb, Jewish? The Chinese, Confucian?"

"Easy, brother. No need to start with politics. As father keeps saying: we are neutral." He fiddled with his Blackberry. The collaboration with Jim Kidman following his Dubai recruitment had been intense. The Hornbachs had swiftly adjusted to the new situation and faithfully passed all intelligence on to the CIA agent. The events in Zürich would not change that.

"You remember...?" Ruppert wanted to ask his brother about the previous Christmas Eve in their Appenzell vacation home, but Roland had nodded off.

"The German freighter was anchored in the Italian harbor of Tarent," Ruppert remembered his father saying, as if it had been yesterday. "Everything on board was arranged and packaged with German efficiency. The boxes and bags were addressed to Good Looks Tailor, Islamabad, to feign a harmless clothing delivery. The entire cargo consisted of Kahn's gas ultracentrifuges, a construction kit for the assembly of a bomb, and the remaining components we know of. It was about three in the afternoon..."

Roland had been perplexed. "You were actually on board? Personally?"

"Only briefly. I wanted to assure myself that everything was in order. I was working for the Pakistanis. Following my orders I went to the harbor master under a false pretense, it was like in a movie…"

…An oppressive heat lay over the ancient historic district of Tarent, located on a small island. The Italian flag hung listlessly from a mast atop the massive walls of the fortress that looked over the harbor. Friedrich Hornbach pulled the cap he was wearing down over his face and stepped into the shade of a palm tree. He raised the small binoculars to his eyes. The freighter was moored in the new harbor beneath a crisscross of crane booms. The white lettering on the black stern read *BC China*. The ship siren sounded twice. There was much activity on deck. Behind the vessel the deep blue sea stretched into the far distance, just as it had thousands of years ago, when the Greeks had built their temples along this shore. A small trawler chugged by swiftly, drawing white waves in the black-blue waters in its wake.

Then the peaceful contemplation came abruptly to an end. Speedboats appeared seemingly from nowhere, their howling sirens joining those of police vehicles racing toward the dock. "Carabinieri," Friedrich muttered, directing his binoculars once again toward the freighter. The men on deck of the *BC China* appeared to freeze.

The Guardia di Finanza boats with their mounted submachine guns had blocked the harbor entry. A swarm of dark figures charged terrifyingly up the landing stage and onto the deck of the ship, followed by commandos in compact formation. Judging by their gear, they appeared to be anti-terror units. Friedrich was impressed by how swiftly and precisely they strong-armed their way onto the vessel and took control.

There had been no resistance. The surprise had been completely effective. He pulled his cell phone out of his pocket and quickly keyed in a number. Only now did he notice the sweat dripping down his body.

"We can't sail. The police are inspecting the ship," he laconically told an answering machine somewhere in Islamabad, then strode to a bar with a functioning air conditioner. He ordered an espresso. Nobody paid any attention to him. They were all puzzled about what the hell was going on at the harbor. Minutes later Friedrich drove on the freeway through Apulia toward Bari.

The intercepted cargo meant for Libya had put an end to Gaddafi's plans for hegemony.

"My good deed for the day," Friedrich nodded to himself in the rearview mirror—and found it appalling, how old and tired his unshaven face looked…

…The jet touched down on the wet runway of the City Airport punctually at a quarter past eight. Ruppert grumbled contentedly when he found that his cell phone had bars again. Smiling faintly to himself, all he was interested in now was a well-deserved nightcap at the hotel bar. They had booked a double room at the Travistock near Oxford Street.

While they waited for their suitcases at baggage claim, Ruppert busied himself with his Blackberry. As he had hoped, he got mail. It was from Meridian Trust Bank to which the Israeli had transferred their millions. With pleasant anticipation he opened the mailbox, then stopped short.

"Your suitcase," Roland called, but Ruppert continued to stare at the small display.

Roland had retrieved the baggage from the conveyer belt and now stepped next to his brother, visibly impatient. "What is it?"

Ruppert raised a shaking hand. "Here look at this. I think we've been played."

Roland muttered, stared blankly at the tiny screen that his brother held before his face.

"The bank on Provo… this is from Keith… he says…"

"What does he say? Does he confirm Nachman's transfer? Is the dough in the acc…" Roland stopped. His brother's ashen complexion spoke volumes.

Either of them would barely have noticed a fist to the face as they wordlessly dragged their suitcases to the exit. They looked dazed, suddenly somehow helpless. Practically paralyzed by shock. Their deeply rattled spirits lusted for nothing as much as sympathy and security. They would gratefully have thrown themselves into the arms of any stranger, had one appeared to be willing to ease their woes.

The two men who stepped forward from the line of waiting

limousine drivers approached the Hornbach brothers with amiable smiles. The older one politely tipped his cap.

"Mr. Hornbach?"

The brothers nodded in unison, confused.

"Welcome to London. We will take you to your hotel." Ruppert kept staring at the device in his hand, as if it would surely—any second—kindly tell him that it was all a mistake. The younger chauffeur took their cases. "Is this your first time in the city?"

Ruppert shook his head, willingly handed over his luggage. "Travistock Hotel, right?"

"Yessir, it's just a short drive." The older man pressed a tourist map into Roland's hand. "Always good to have one of these. How long will you be staying in London?"

To Roland's surprise, the men headed toward a large black Range Rover, which seemed to him to be a bit of overkill for a two-star hotel. Had this made him suspicious, however, it would have been too late at this point.

The rear door opened, the men jockeyed the Swiss brothers into the back seat, and the door was shut. Ruppert looked at the figure seated opposite him and found himself looking down the long, black barrel of a heavy pistol.

"Welcome to London," the armed man said, not impolitely, while the man on the passenger seat hefted himself around to face them, holding identification up in front of his roundish head. "New Scotland Yard, sirs. You are under arrest."

The vehicle started. Tailed by two unmarked police cars, it went on to thread its way into the busy city traffic. The discreet arrest of Ruppert and Roland Hornbach in the middle of downtown London had taken all of perhaps ten minutes. Shocked though he was, Ruppert could not help but treat the British officers to an admiring smile. These people had style! No, he quickly corrected himself. They had class. Had he been able to pick the country of his arrest, only England would have done. *Here, where even a serial killer could expect to be treated fairly according to all the rules of law.*

Zurich, Bahnhofstrasse

A misty veil drifted gently across the lake, the last rays of sun bathed the screened roof-terrace in a golden light as the three men stepped into the dining room with their drinks and took their seats at the set table. Muffled appreciative murmurings persisted, accompanied by the gentle clinking of silverware.

These men had found each other amidst a fight for their country, forging an iron band shared only by brothers in arms. Their beginnings together lay in the distant past, but the sacrifices, the struggles to survive, the discipline and fortitude that had been demanded of each, along with the knowledge that they could rely on each other in the face of any danger, even death, bonded them enduringly.

The legendary threesome consisted of Shuky Nachman, Nir Barak, and Mendi Meron.

Their common destiny continued to mean as much to them now as it ever had; even if their demeanor was composed and businesslike, they would never allow insult or injury to one another. In later years, their endeavors included bold ventures, business interests—all of this had only served to further strengthen their heart-felt friendship.

Nachman raised the bottle of Beychevelle to the light, noting that it was almost empty. He signaled his wiry assistant, Tabah, to bring another.

Mendi Meron stepped away from where he had been standing at the window, running his fingers through his gray hair. "You wanna drink us under the table, don't you?"

"Nah. There wouldn't be enough time to try that on you. And we're all at an age where we can appreciate a good bottle of wine."

"True," Barak grinned, "it's not every day I get offered Château Beychevelle."

Meron sat down again. "Okay. I might as well have another one."

Nachman inspected the bottle that Tabah held out to him like an experienced sommelier. "What shall we drink to? To the big coup? Or to the big mess? No. To the old days. To daring and vision—the qualities I miss most in the generations of late."

"I'll gladly drink to that," laughed the somewhat younger Barak. "But back to Tel Aviv and the Hornbachs."

"We have to risk it, we've come too far," said Nachman. He raised a forkful of jerky to his mouth, chewed noisily.

Nir Barak gestured with his knife. "It may have been a mistake to negotiate with the Hornbachs in the middle of Zurich."

"No risk, no loss."

"This thing didn't go down well, Shuky. It wasn't smart to have the Hornbachs parading into your office for all the world to see."

"Damn it, Nir, have you lost it? We talked about all of this. Your boss, the Prime Minister, agreed. These new nuclear warheads belong to Israel, and no one else. We were on the same page."

"Still. It wasn't right. The Russians found out, and now those old Pushkins are insulted." He chuckled. "Death before dishonor—that's a Siberian saying."

"What's up with you, Nir? Any concerns?"

"Bernoff's daughter was brutally murdered in New York."

"Mad Bernoff? The broker?"

"His lovely daughter was one of ours."

"She worked for Mossad?"

Barak's brow furrowed. "Only sporadically. My New York contact sent me a crime scene image."

"Show me!"

"You're looking to throw up some fine wine, along with that jerky you've been snacking on. It's not a pretty sight." Barak waved the letter-size black and white print.

"Oleg Borisowich Nedjew is behind this, if you ask me. The killer carved the emblem of a crane beneath her navel. Look!"

He held the image in front of his eyes. Shuky cast a brief look at it, turned his face away.

Holding his napkin against his mouth, he looked again. The contorted face of the young woman looking back at him could have been his daughter, judging by her apparent age.

"The emblem? The stylized crane? Are you sure?"

"Absolutely. We know this guy inside and out, from his cuff size to his sexual perversions. We've been on his heels ever since he threw his fancy party in Eilat."

Nachman tapped the photograph with his finger. "Why New York?"

Barak raised his brows. "Brutal revenge for financial losses that he blames on Bernoff. Monstrous. Whoever is capable of dumping a naked body like that in the middle of Central Park, or anywhere else on earth for that matter, is pretty much capable of anything. That is the message."

"You think this is just the beginning?"

Barak nodded. "You should have brought us in on this."

"The Hornbachs would never have agreed. They wanted to do the deal in Zurich. With me, and no one else, Nir."

"We would have taken the brothers out—the Russians would have been clueless. As it is, you may as well have shouted the whole business from the rooftops. Look, even the Austrians have been able to find out what is going on. This Russian thug now knows exactly where to start. He will do anything to get a hold of those plans. And I mean anything."

"You're nuts, Nir," Shuky retorted.

"Sure. And the earth is flat, Shuky. Always plan for the worst case. What happened to your military thinking? Are you in need of some drilling—or what?" His brusque challenge was met with laughter. Nachman became lost in thought. Nedjew remained the topic on the forefront. Barak, who had dealt with the Russians for years in his homeland, had much background information to contribute. He started his lecture...

"When the Soviet Union imploded and the economies of its border states fell into utter chaos, the future was looking grim indeed. Gangster capitalism thrived in Moscow. The outskirts of the former superpower, particularly the Caucasus, was ruled by criminal gangs and the law of the jungle. People were afraid to venture into the streets. If you wanted to buy something, you had to run the gauntlet between mobs shooting at each other. Or at you...

"The Chechens, the Georgians, and especially the Armenians, with their inherent self-reliance and rebelliousness, had never been part of the Russian core to begin with. These communities developed a legendary talent to cleverly survive in the miserable twilight of economic scarcity that was the Soviet periphery. Radio Yerevan famously parodied their ingenious ways of overcoming bureaucratic hurdles and covertly arranging necessary goods. They organized every conceivable material, the most elaborate tools. In time they developed their own flourishing shadow economy. They were called *tolkachi*, these wily wheelers and dealers—rascals and scoundrels for whom nothing was unobtainable in these hard times.

"In a system designed to kill any inkling of personal initiative, the *tolkachi* proved to possess unbelievable entrepreneurial vision. By contrast, the Soviet bureaucracy in Moscow was utterly ham-fisted, inasmuch as it ever actually reached as far as the rough Caucasus.

"The nooks and crannies, in which economic initiative thrived, fast provided fertile soil for criminal gangs, who would later use their experience to navigate the Russian post-Communist economy.

"It was no coincidence that many of the powerful oligarchs and gang leaders originated from Georgia, Armenia and Chechnya, where they had honed their trade as *tolkachi*. And many of them were Jewish."

Barak paused, for once pouring himself a glass of water. As he drank, his eyes scrutinized his audience. Commanding the undivided attention of his friends gave him a certain sense of satisfaction—not that they weren't just as familiar with the content of his address as he was.

"The Jews of the former Soviet Union were surprised by a singular privilege in 1989—suddenly, they became eligible for Israeli naturalization and citizenship. Thousands, tens of thousands in the Caucasus, Belarus, Siberia, wherever, packed their belongings, collected their coveted passports and took off in a mass exodus, without any questions being asked of them. Eventually, it became hundreds of thousands. A scant ten years later, about a million Russian Jews were living in Israel—over fifteen percent of the population.

"To pious Jews, the move was *Aliyah*: the return to the homeland. But most were simply glad to turn their backs on uncertain developments in the former Soviet Union; glad that their new passports allowed them visa-free access to Western nations, a mild Mediterranean climate that let them forget the nasty Russian weather. Unnoticed at first, the Caucasus gang leaders, too, settled in Israel."

Barak smiled in anticipation of his punch line.

"So, I'm on the flight from Tel Aviv to Zurich. Next to me there's a Russian, who speaks good English. He's wearing a three-thousand-dollar suit, carrying a Louis Vuitton bag, a gold Rolex on his wrist and Allen Edmonds shoes on his feet.

"He tells me that he runs an export company, and is interested in expanding his business in the West. Who do you think the guy is?"

Holding up his hand, four fingers spread, Barak immediately proceeded to answer his own question. "Well, first of all, he could be who he says he is. Second, he could be a Russian agent pretending to be a legitimate businessman, or, third, he could be a Russian crime syndicate boss."

"And fourth?"

"The fourth possibility is also the most interesting one. I believe he was all of those things, and that none of the three branches will have a problem with it."

The others laughed, relieved. This was their good, old Barak—tough as steel, clever as a fox. Mendi Meron spoke up. "This Nedjew also immigrated to Israel, didn't he? Does this crook really have an Israeli passport?"

"Had," Barak corrected. "Like many other Russian fat cats. Of course, Nedjew has as much to do with Judaism as I do with the research of the common ant. Once the Russian mafia in Israel could no longer be overlooked about ten years ago, the police began to take an active interest in him. Shuky, do you remember the conference of the godfathers in Tel Aviv?"

"Of course. You don't think I'd forget having to dress up as Vice Director? At the...wait...Dan Panorama Hotel...Never."

"Exactly," Barak responded, "Nedjew was one of the new power players, who brought the others to declare Israel neutral ground—no more shootings or gang warfare."

"Are you saying all of this to tell us this gangster isn't exactly fond of us?"

"Shuky, you couldn't put it more mildly. Nedjew hates Israel like the plague. And us along with it. He will harm us wherever and whenever he can."

"What idiocy! Just because of a passport!"

"Not just that," Mendi Meron interjected. "Nedjew's son was killed before the cease fire—in a feud between families. A fragmentation bomb meant for Rosenstein tore half his head off. The Crane raged about the Israeli police, who focused only on Palestinians instead of controlling crime in the city. And here's the best: Nedjew's youngest, she is sitting in prison in Haifa, on suspicion of smuggling."

"Weapons?"

"Yes, almost certainly for Hezbollah. Although there doesn't appear to be any evidence. The savage shrew shot a cop in the knee. That's enough to serve time for a few years. Are you noticing something, Shuky?"

Nachman cleared his throat. "The Russians have always been up to their necks in weapons and drugs, and then laundered the dirty proceeds in Tel Aviv. His interest in weapons of mass destruction is new to me, but I'm not surprised."

"We estimate that the Russians have funneled over ten billion dollars through Israeli banks in the past twelve years," Barak added. "To Switzerland, in large part. To a bank by the name of Ponter."

"Sophie," Nachman muttered.

"So, there is a kind of Caucasian—Israeli—European axis?" Meron concluded.

Barak drew in an enormous volume of air, exhaling with great satisfaction. Finally they understood!

"Yes, friends. That's the way to look at it—Armenia and Georgia, then Tel Aviv. Finally Geneva or Zurich." He raised his wine glass. "Cheers, gentlemen."

Haifa Harbor, Israel

The sun beat relentlessly on the broad pier in front of the clubhouse of the Carmel Yacht Club. It was noon, and the unusual heat held the level of activity at Haifa's new yacht harbor well in check.

The harbor master and his staff, who were wearily following the news of a captured Polish vessel from their seats in an air-conditioned lounge, were in no way inclined to move their collective asses even one inch for the *Bastion*, whose docking they could comfortably follow on their monitors.

Meanwhile, Natan Eran plodded unnoticed across the hot concrete to his Jeep, which was parked next to the clubhouse. The massive, white yacht, the *Bastion*, which measured a good hundred and sixty feet from bow to stern, glided slowly through the large basin of the new harbor facility, turned elegantly, and began to reverse into the landing between two already anchored boats. *A regular customer*, the harbormaster would have said. *Comes in from Cyprus a good dozen times a year.*

Natan steered the white Jeep steadily on the pier. If he turned to face left, he was able to see the magnificent Shrine of the Báb high above the old city. In the past, when filmmaking had been everything to him, he had often shot up on the Carmel. The bronze cupola shone at the end of a long stairway that disappeared behind a bank of pointed cypresses. Muffled clanging occasionally drifted over from the industrial harbor.

The tall, slender man with hard, tanned features stood at the outer controls next to the English skipper on the *Bastion*'s bridge. He looked across the water, watched the white Jeep approaching.

His servant brought a filled glass on a silver tray. During tranquil hours at sea the man, whose face had an almost boyish look thanks to the art of cosmetic surgery, often contemplated the power that had afforded him all of this wealth and luxury. He, the Crane, had worked his way up all the way from the bottom.

From a little shithole with a furnace and straying dogs, Nedjew had crossed oceans to reach the capitals of Europe and beyond, from Manhattan to the Côte, London to Switzerland.

He took the glass, added a few chunks of ice, and brought it to his lips. His contented gaze swept calmly over the nested, white houses of the coastal town. The vodka instantly revived his spirits, the familiar smell sharpening his senses, like the smell of blood readying a predator for the kill.

Even after years of routine, large quantities of money made his heart beat faster, like today as he was about to bring from the *Bastion* under British flag ten million dollars in one-hundred-dollar bills. This was not chicken feed, not even to Oleg Nedjew. The massive bundle of cold, hard cash excited him physically. The sheer lust that overtook him was equal to anything he might feel when he was about to seal a hot deal with a woman. As exciting foreplay was to sex the transportation of cash was the sensual climax and his excitement was only mitigated by a hunch that something could go wrong.

Shiny aluminum containers waited at the stern of the *Bastion*. A casual observer may easily have mistaken the randomly stacked boxes and objects for the gear of a film crew. Tripods, rolls of film, sacks and bags surrounded a few handy containers, secured with black straps, which were not particularly conspicuous. The white Jeep approached the jetty. Natan opened the hatchback. Above, Nedjew donned dark sunglasses. The handover went smoothly, just as scripted. Nedjew was in his element, thanks to his cinematographer's feel for suspense and drama. Natan Eran stood as if on a set, gave a few dramatic gestures. He knew exactly which of the small containers was meant for him, personally.

Nedjew loved the ocean, the smell of salt, warm winds and powerful waves; the endless freedom. He had his lieutenants drop smaller amounts, generally a million, at Ben Gurion in a private jet. Official Israel was rather relaxed when it came to the Russian's financial transactions. One did not want to impede the flow of cash with pedantic regulations. But every once in a while, the border officials launched random investigations of private aircraft in search of drugs. If they were to find suitcases of money, this could definitely be awkward. Nedjew preferred the sea route.

Boxes and rolls securely stashed, Natan cast one more short glance at the dark silhouette of the man. He nodded, got in behind the steering wheel. The Jeep, which bore the label of Sunset Productions in red script, rolled slowly toward the clubhouse, then on to the red and white barrier, which opened automatically.

Although security at the Haifa-Kishon yacht harbor was rigorous, Natan Eran, whose face was not unknown in Israel, exited unchallenged. The entrances by land and sea were under constant surveillance—anyone attempting to enter the harbor facilities was subject to strict inspection. Even Natan Eran, who was known for filming in the harbor and on the water, was almost always checked damn near to his underwear. Exiting was another matter entirely. Here, at best, customs and drug enforcement may be on the lookout for specific clients.

And since Natan was not one of those usual suspects, he was soon making good time down coastal highway 2 to Tel Aviv, humming a tune to himself. He planned approximately three hours for the three hundred and thirty kilometer drive, getting to the bank in the business sector before closing. Not that he had to worry about opening hours—Dan Halpern, the director of AAA-Israel-Bank would welcome him with open arms at midnight, if need be.

Natan patted the briefcase with an affection that was usually reserved for the voluptuous thighs of his sweet Yael.

One hundred thousand dollars down, three hundred thousand upon successful delivery...A day's work for Nedjew earned him more than all of his feature films combined over the past twenty years! His phone rang.

"Natan, did everything work out? Where are you?" It was Mama Olga, his wife, daughter of a Russian immigrant, who had him well under her thumb.

"Hello, my dear, I am still at the harbor. Working hard. Don't wait up for me, I'll be back a bit late."

"Be sure to shower before you come near me, you mangy dog," Olga started on him, "or at least buy your stinking whore a decent bottle of perfume, but of course you're too much of a cheap bastard for that..."

Zurich, Bahnhofstrasse

The loyal gang—Shuky Nachman, Nir Barak, Mendi Meron—met for a second time the following day, this time at Nachman's well-appointed penthouse. Rain fell outside. They appreciated the comforting warmth of the crackling fireplace as they took their seats at the table. Nachman took a sip of wine, leaned back stretching his arms wide. Nir Barak helped himself to Greek salad. Both guests and Tabah regarded their host expectantly. Shuky indulged in a little banter about motorized yachts before letting the cat out of the bag.

"Jack Abramian wants to flood Iran with cell phones."

Mendi raised his arm in protest.

"No, Mendi, not our RADs. I'll come back to that, if you'll allow me to continue."

Shuky had encountered Abramian about two years ago at a security conference in the London Lanesborough. Supported by security experts of Aeronautics Tel Aviv, he had presented him with the concept of an integrated surveillance installation for his industrial complex in southern Armenia. They were on a first-name basis. It had been a good start, which soon developed into a respectful fondness.

"Every Iranian man, woman and child, veiled or not, students, housewives, bazaar traders, taxi drivers, every poor devil in the most remote corner of the land will have their own cell phone. Can you even imagine the ramifications of this concept?"

The objection came from Barak. "With all due respect for this dreamer, but I don't believe the mullahs will allow that."

Nachman measured the group thoughtfully. His friends did not know Cosmo—he had means almost beyond reckoning. There was that time when he had sent the Pentagon a check for half a billion dollars to improve protection of GIs in Iraq. Rumsfeld allegedly called and asked, *Who the hell are you? No,* had been the answer. *The question is who the hell are you, to send our troops into harm's way without the protection they deserve?*

Nachman's posture took on a military rectitude. "Cosmo's concept is ingenious. Also insane. But in the end, insane ideas have always been those that have helped get the job done. He reminds me of Howard Hughes—one of those creative, eccentric California types. Well, this is how it is going to go down—Cosmo doesn't need the mullahs. The signals will be coming from his satellites and a few other facilities, which will remain secret of course."

He was enjoying their undivided attention, raising the suspense by pausing to take a sip of water. "The phones are simple and solid. They can be used to make calls, text, receive images. No more than that, nothing fancy. Good battery life. And they will literally be falling from the sky for free. A gift from Allah, so to speak."

"Allah is good!" Barak declared, poker-faced.

They all started to talk at the same time. "How is it supposed to work?," "Details, please!," "Pure fantasy, that's what this is!"

Shuky raised a conciliatory hand. "It gets even better. The SIM card is already in place. Whoever picks up the phone can call and read messages that very instant. Just imagine it."

His friends furrowed their brows, collected their thoughts in an attempt to reach a critical mass of insight. Only Barak smiled, as though he was able to imagine it with little difficulty.

"A brilliant, subversive offensive. Cosmo will probably be sending his messages daily. Down with the dress code for women, or being gay is not a crime..."

"How about to hell with the executioners, or peace with Israel?" Mendi suggested, warming to the topic.

Nachman nodded encouragingly. "Thousands of messages will be circulating every day. Any concern of the people can be put to a popular vote by phone. The mullahs would be powerless in the face of this technology—they would end up basically having to concede everything that was already settled among the populace. It would be unparalleled."

Meron doubtfully raised his hands, a look of skepticism on his face. Nachman was prepared for his objection and parried it before it was even uttered: "Do you remember how Reagan weakened the Eastern Bloc with the fax? That was in the beginning of the eighties, when the fax was revolutionary in communications technology. The Soviets were unable to curtail the flow of information behind the Iron Curtain. Cosmo envisions that the cell phone will be to Iran what the fax was to the Soviet Union: the beginning of the end, a peaceful revolution for an open society, with freedom of opinion and religion."

They debated, queried the expense, as well as the motives of this insane Jack Abramian, otherwise known as Cosmo. What did they call those California boys in American politics, people like old Jerry Brown? Moonlight, moonshine, moonbeam? That was it—moonbeam! That's what he was: another one of those California moonbeams! "You can be sure he's not doing it for the love of his fellow man," Mendi Meron sneered contemptuously.

Nachman felt in his element. "Look, there are rich people who set up foundations to end hunger, send foreign aid to third world countries, donate to the fight against AIDS—think of Bill Gates, Clinton, Warren Buffett...your typical kind of charity work. But Cosmo—for him, it's about freedom of thought. Okay?"

"Give us freedom of thought, Ayatollah!" Barak mocked.

"Make fun all you want," Shuky cautioned. "He is many times richer than the five hundred richest people listed in that glossy magazine..." He forked some artichoke into his mouth, spoke around it. "...and he has way better ideas."

He liked the quote from Schiller's *Don Carlos*, but of course Jack Abramian also had some concrete interests. Nachman expanded further, "He wants to force Iran to see reason in a peaceful manner. Not with bombs and rockets, not with economic sanctions, not to mention an Israeli attack on their atomic facilities. He wants to flood the country with free phones, with news and images, and cause the dams to burst that way."

Barak was pragmatic. "And what does he get out of all of this?"

"Plenty, Nir. Having a worldly, open neighbor in Iran would allow Armenia to become a booming hub overnight. Jack Abramian is Armenian, don't forget that. His country is surrounded by hostile neighbors.

The Turks to the west, Azerbaijan to the east. They are boycotting Armenia, even Georgia has joined in."

"Armenia is orthodox, they have no issue with us," said Mendi.

Barak poured himself a glass of water. "Exactly—quite to the contrary. Armenians are dispersed all over the world, where they are either beloved or despised, very similar to the Jews."

Nachman nodded sagely. "No one is officially on the Armenian's side, only expatriates like Cosmo. But his plan is viable, of that I am convinced."

"It's worth a shot, if nothing else. I can just picture the mullahs in Tehran, dancing on hot coals, their beards growing longer by the day…" They all laughed at Barak's conjured image, and for a moment the conversation turned to reminiscing about old times. Mutterings, teasing, broad grins, the familiar sounds and voices of now mature men, solidly bonded through adventurous enterprises and successful dealings—it was a backdrop that Tabah, who was straining pasta in the open kitchen for the next course, knew well.

Although all four of them had invested quite heavily into raw tobacco as a commodity, they only smoked sporadically these days. News images flickered across a TV screen in the corner. "I got Cosmo hooked up with the integrated surveillance system," Shuky informed his friends. "Protection against infiltration, terrorism defense, internal crime prevention. The day after tomorrow I'll be flying to Armenia to meet him at his enormous techno park.

"I take it the RAD business will be concurrent," Barak said. Nachman gave a short nod. In principle, he did not keep many secrets from his friends. There were anyway only a handful of men who knew their way around the tumultuous maze of Israeli secret and counter politics like Shuky Nachman did. Sometimes he simply preferred to spare his old compatriots unnecessary brooding and headshaking. The fact was that the aforementioned RADs, Radiation Detecting Cell Phones, had absolutely nothing to do with Cosmo's visionary plan. They did, however, have plenty to do with the security of his facilities. The Israelis had developed the devices in order to enable their agents in Iran to clandestinely detect atomic sites. The spectroscopic detectors, a cutting-edge technology, were even able to distinguish between benign and malignant radiation. Potassium 40, for instance, was a naturally occurring radioactive beta isotope found in bananas, whereas uranium and plutonium, which were used for nuclear energy and atomic weapons, emitted dangerous gamma rays. The minuscule detectors within these devices, which looked like cell phones in every respect and also functioned as such, were able to locate dirty bombs and nuclear weapons as soon as the bearer of the phone came into their vicinity.

But Barak was not quite so easily mollified. "You mean that the Iranian resistance is in possession of the RADs?"

Shuky motioned with his shoulders. "The goods were shipped weeks ago. The boats reached Black Sea harbor of Poti in Georgia as planned."

Meron couldn't help a good-natured jibe. "We do know where Poti is, Shuky."

The men had eaten, smoked a last cigarette and were getting ready to call it a night when Shuky beheld an image of the Armenus Corporation techno park in south Armenia in his mind's eye. A thought hit him. "Somehow I think that Cosmo wants to return holy Mount Ararat back to Armenia."

The friends paused and looked at him with wide eyes. For several heartbeats, the only sound heard was the voice of the television commentator: ... *Russia is massively restricting the gas supply to the West ... Germany has been most affected ...*

Aboard the *Bastion*, before Latakia, Syria

The deep, blue Mediterranean waters rippled with white strips beat against the Syrian coast of Latakia. The *Bastion* slowed as it approached land that lay golden brown in the evening sun. The skipper headed toward the unimposing harbor that served the Romans as far back as Septimus Severus. The nearby chain of brown hills and foothills reached all the way down to the town, with its tall, white apartment buildings.

Further in the distance the dense forests of the steep coastal mountain range loomed dark green against a cloudless, pink sky. The last time they had approached Latakia, the skipper had handed him the binoculars. On the steep forested slope Oleg Nedjew was able to make out the ancient Saladin Citadel, of which it was said that it could never be taken uphill.

Today, however, the oligarch in chief, as he self-confidently called himself, had no time for sightseeing.

The skipper shut down the engines as the barge came into view. Nedjew had never planned to navigate the Syrian coast, and certainly not to anchor in Latakia. But the head of the Party of God, that hothead Nasrallah of Hezbollah, had categorically declined a meeting in Lebanon.

The skipper dropped anchor. Shortly thereafter, the rusty heap of a barge landed portside. Every man standing against the guardrail was cloaked in a headscarf, AK 47s with mounted grenade launchers on display. A figure in a black T-shirt stood on top of the wheelhouse, casually swinging the barrel of his machine gun back and forth, while the leader, dressed in a white robe, hopped easily onto the *Bastion*'s low, flat stern platform.

The Crane had inspected the martial escorts with his binoculars and understood the message. Nasrallah stepped into the cabin lounge, holding a gift out to his host with a charming smile. The Russian brusquely pushed the package away across the mahogany table and came straight to the point. "Can we close this?"

Nasrallah used both hands in a circular gesture that was hard to interpret. "You Russians are patient people. You have giant land from Ural to Siberia, great space that even Napoleon and Hitler could not succeed in taking. Time fills the space. Why the hurry? Thank you very much for coming to Latakia. May Allah be with you." Nasrallah pointed to the spurned package. "A little gift for the pipe smoker. Good Latakia tobacco, you will like."

Frowning Nedjew waved at the butler. "Open it carefully, there could be a bomb in there. Something that our friends have great experience with," he said sarcastically.

After a moment, during which Nasrallah unconcernedly stirred his tea, the Russian ordered the servant to leave them alone. He regarded his counterpart challengingly. Nasrallah was the brother of the Iranian Minister of Defense. That was an immutable fact. The delegation they had sent him was conservative and of high rank. The fan hummed, from outside occasional, sharp noises entered the *Bastion*'s finely furnished deck saloon, with its precious woods, gilded knobs, and luxurious upholstery. Nedjew's eyes narrowed to slits. "I am waiting for an answer."

The Iranian nodded, producing a bound document from his robe. "My government agrees. Here is the plan."

"The down payment?"

The Iranian patted his plump briefcase in answer.

"Too small," Nedjew determined callously.

Nasrallah rapped on the contractual documents. "Rest is on boat. You will receive once you have signed."

The two men leaned over the documents. The Russian committed himself to delivering twelve rockets, equipped with two hundred kiloton atomic warheads, ready to use, to Iran's northern border. In return, the buyers would pay seventy-five million dollars per rocket, as well as a non-refundable, guaranteed payment of one hundred million, due immediately.

"A billion is cheap."

The mullah shrugged. "If you say so, must be true."

"According to the Russian Security Service, my people… ," Nedjew slapped his chest, "…if Iran wants to make its own, it will take five years until they have one that works."

"Two," Nasrallah corrected nonchalantly, "two years. Even the KGB was mostly wrong about my country. When is delivery?"

The Russian knew very well that the ruling mullahs in Tehran wanted to impress with the bomb before the election. "The goods are ready, of course. Only Iran will have them. You have read the description?"

"Good. Minister of Defense wants option for more warheads from Russian stock. Our Ministry of Intelligence knows they exist. In Caucasus, Kazakhstan, maybe."

Nedjew allowed himself a wry grin. "Okay, my friend. The Iranian Ministry of Intelligence is maybe not so intelligent. Caucasus, shitcasus—I have the most modern rockets, and I have warheads from Soviet times. Me. The Crane." Again, he slapped his chest. "Maybe a bit old, maybe in need of a bit of retro-fitting, but they work. Russian precision."

"I hope better than your submarines," Nasrallah grinned right back.

Over several hours they discussed all of the details. The butler refilled their tea cups, served hummus, eggplant, and other Middle Eastern delicacies from the galley.

The transportation from Armenia, across the Iranian border near Tabriz, in particular, required seamless coordination with Iranian troops. Nedjew and Nasrallah agreed that their deputy officers would meet for a briefing at a predetermined point in time.

"Winter is convenient," Nasrallah said once they had signed the papers. "Plenty of clouds and gray skies, difficult for satellites to localize the transport."

"Do your mullahs still have the cash? Oil prices are down. Below basement level, I would say."

"No need to worry, infidel."

Nedjew accepted twenty million in cash and allowed the remaining eighty million to be transferred to an account in Switzerland. That took care of the guaranteed payment, without which he would not have lifted a finger.

Nasrallah stroked his beard approvingly. "Ponter Bank, good bank. May Allah protect it."

"Certainly," Nedjew nodded, folding the document. "Allah and the Swiss government."

A half an hour later, the *Bastion* hoisted anchor. The silhouette of the militant Hezbollah barge was slowly lost in the dusk. As if to bid the strongman farewell, the first lights began to shimmer along the coast.

After much Champagne in celebration of the day, an opulent meal served at an elegantly decked table, the best caviar, lobster, and other delicious seafood, an elated Nedjew stands at the guardrail searching the firmament for stars. The billowing silk of her airy, ivory-colored caftan allows a fleeting glimpse of Natascha's captivating shape, her firm, round breasts, the mound of pubic hair between her legs. A glass of Champagne in hand, she turns to him with a lascivious smile, nestles against him. He pushes her away, raises his vodka glass toward a small, blinking light high up in the distance that is crossing the Milky Way in a straight line. "Russian space station," he slurs boastfully, knocks back the vodka. "We have the best rockets, the best…"

"Oh, you do," Natascha whispers, grabbing between his legs, where an erection is beginning to stir. "Super rocket, come kiss me!"

He grabs her rudely, drags her inside falteringly, bottle in one hand, down the stairs into the saloon, which appears in a reddish shimmer, and toward his flight of private rooms.

Wild with desire, he rips open her silken gown, kisses her nipples and neck then, briefly, her mouth. She deftly slips out of her caftan, drags the passionate lover onto the blood-red Bokhara.

He rears up abruptly. "Wait!" He takes a swig from the bottle, goes to the antique desk, opens the bulging briefcase left lying there, grasps a few stacks of bills, rips off the currency bands and strews money wildly across the soft red of the precious rug. "Come, let's do it on the bucks!" With a giggle Natascha throws her robe aside.

"First I will lick you, then I will fu-fuck you," Nedjew panted.

"I hope you keep your word, darling." She presses against him expertly, breathes words into his ear, pulls him over to the dainty piece of furniture with the crystal box. She playfully lays his stiff member on the edge of the table, takes off the silver lid.

Oleg grabs at her, lustfully, as she bends over to scoop a handful of pure Colombian coke out of the box.

He grunts as she sprinkles it onto his throbbing, red phallus, massaging it in. "Do you have a gun license for that, lover? Lie down."

As he sinks backward onto several thousand dollars, she falls on top of him, grasping the perfectly shaped head of his penis between her full lips. She looks up: "Oh, that tastes so good, it wants to be inside."

"Ahh, that's good, the snow is making me rock-hard, oh…"

She swings around, pushing him inside herself. "Oh, oh, you are go-ing to rip me apart…" She moves up and down ecstatically, kisses, tongue writhing, feels the white powder taking hold of her, making everything more urgent, more intense.

Suddenly she slides off him, onto her back. Feverishly, he penetrates her, thrusts harder. The intertwined lovers are in a trance, say filthy things, forget themselves. "Only we Ru-Russians fuck with coke on our di-dicks." A scream of pleasure fills the room. Panting, Nedjew lies on top of Natascha with his entire weight.

Yerevan, Capital of Armenia

Rising from the gilded Bedouin roof of the magnificently restored palace, the pink tuff façade with its light blue turrets stood out like a jewelry box against the hillside in the misty dusk.

The man behind the soundproof window lowered his gaze from the blindingly white ice caps crowning the holy mountain, down to the gray haze of the city of Yerevan. Lost in thought, he ran his fingers through his wavy, white mane.

The first limousines arrived. Jack Abramian took a few steps back from the window. The city with its million and a half inhabitants and its innumerable, picturesque fountains occupied his mind only tangentially. Even Ararat, Noah's mountain, the eternally white tips of which shone reliably with each first light of dawn, only meant something to him inas-much as he had financed the Turkish generals to the tune of one hundred million for the construction of a radar and satellite receiving station up there, five thousand meters above sea level.

"Loyalty doesn't just grow on trees, right, Feedback?"

The dog in question raised her little snout and licked Cosmo's great hand, with its massive signet ring. "Of course, Master," the animal seemed to be saying, "Not without the fertilizers of power, money, and women. The guests are arriving. Shall we?"

As always, whenever he had brought his plan another step forward, he kissed the blueberry-sized lapis lazuli in its heavy, gold setting with the artfully veined emblem: *Orbis Unum.*

The Turkish general was the first to arrive, punctual down to the minute and accompanied by a diminutive, lackey secretary of the Foreign Ministry. Cosmo waited at the top of the stairs; Feedback sat on her haunches scrutinizing the arrivals along with her master.

Shortly before the conclusion of the polite diplomatic quarter hour, the Armenian president arrived with his attractive wife, in ornate national costume. Keeping a great distance from the Turks, he stepped toward the stairs and waved a greeting upward as his white-haired host began stepping down toward him.

The reception hall was soon alive with visitors. The American ambassador, her military attaché in Marine dress uniform, a Georgian—likely the energy minister—with entourage; then a group of burly men from Azerbaijan, recognizable by their signature bushy hair. Finally, the group of Israelis streamed through the side entrance, gesturing in a lively manner. The Russians, on the other hand, were conspicuous by their absence. No one at this conference would have been pleased to see them there.

A servant offered tea, which only the young wife of the president accepted.

Cosmo casually lifted his left hand: a gesture he had been fond of using since his student days at San Francisco State University. The left was his artistic hand. Even closed in a fist, it communicated confidence without aggression. It was the hand of friendship, the hand of peace.

The babble of voices quickly subsided, then went silent. At a discreet nod from Cosmo, the doorman opened the double door to the grand hall. The leader of the Israeli group by no means missed the bulge under the man's jacket just beneath the arm.

The guests started moving at a leisurely pace. The Armenian president politely touched the arm of the stylishly dressed U.S. ambassador. "Madam, I hear you are learning Armenian."

As the president led her chivalrously across the oak floor to a stone tablet, the ambassador admitted with a slight blush that she still needed practice.

"Seven hundred and eighty B.C., Madam Ambassador," he proclaimed with pride. "The tablet was discovered beneath the city during an excavation. You see, the inscription refers to the building of Erebuni Fortress—not far from my official residence, as it happens."

The ambassador nodded, impressed, donned her glasses, and leaned closer. The antique symbols were illegible to her, but she had learned during briefings for her post in Yerevan that the modern alphabet had been found to have its rudimentary beginnings in Armenia several thousand years ago. She stood upright, bestowing the president with her most generous, official smile. "We are standing before evidence of the cradle of human civilization, Mr. President. What an unprecedented honor!"

Her clearly sincere observation impressed the president tremendously. In answer, he gently squeezed her firm arm, then steered her toward the massive, oval table, where the guests had started gathering with polite patience. Cosmo, holding the dog that still eyed the guests intently, took his seat at the upper end of the table in a high-backed chair with intricate carvings on its arms.

"Ladies and gentlemen," Cosmo began, "we are gathered today to bury the hatchet, as we like to say in the States. The ancient dispute between proud people...Armenia," he briefly lowered his head, causing strands of hair to fall onto his forehead. "Excellence, Madam President, thank you for extending your hospitality in these historic walls...and Turkey. We also thank the brave people of Turkey, General!" Only a brief nod this time. "All of the old conflicts shall be buried here, today."

His words were met by a swell of enthusiastic applause.

"Armenia is a great nation." Cosmo paused. He considered the enormous investments that he had made in Yerevan and the south, on the Iranian border. "Great, indeed! Armenia extends its hand to its neighbor. And Turkey, in the best tradition of their great Atatürk, is prepared to reconcile." He looked at the general. *They had better play along!*

Their willingness to cooperate has cost me the better part of half a billion dollars. "I will make a start today by offering you two gifts, and one condition."

The silence in the hall was absolute; one could have heard a mouse sneeze. The general clenched his fists. The first lady discreetly lowered her gaze to her politely restrained décolleté.

"First the good news—we will be doubling our investments. In arms, to spoil the Russian's appetite for the Caucasus..." More swelling applause. "...In pipelines, along with the necessary infrastructure, to give us international parity."

"The old man's butler is ex-CIA," the tall Israeli whispered to his neighbor. "This thaw between archenemies started in Geneva," another Israeli murmured into his beard. "Secret accords. We have the transcripts. The old man had to invest billions to get a foothold here."

"At least we're part of it," the first whispered. His comment referred to the Israeli delivery of border protection surveillance systems. "By the way, what does he mean by parity?" He pressed his finger to his lips archly.

"The second gift is a woman," they now heard the leader of this gathering announce in his rough, always somewhat hoarse, always some-what condescending-sounding voice.

"What next?" the first Israeli muttered.

All eyes followed the outstretched arm of their white-haired host. A hidden door opened, and the woman with wavy, black hair stepped forward and walked with confidently erect posture toward the empty chair. All present immediately recognized the former American secretary of state. Their faces registered a variety of mostly surprised reactions, the shocked raising of eyebrows, several mouths agape. The general stood, gave an almost parade-worthy salute.

"My greatly experienced moderator will lead you through this con-ference. Thank you very much, Madame Secretary."

Smiling and accompanied by polite applause, the former secretary of state took her seat.

"And now my condition. Following events in Georgia I see the need for a new political platform in the Caucasus. Armenia, Turkey and Azerbaijan must work together in solidarity." His sharp gaze swept the room. "You are aware why. My country, the United States, my homeland, Armenia—we will open a new chapter in this beautiful part of the earth. Woe to the enemies who try to stand in our way!"

"Bravo…exactly…woe to the Russians…"

"Tomorrow at midnight the clock will run out for you gathered in this hall. None of you will leave before the contract for economic and military cooperation is signed by all. Should this accord not come to pass, the gifts of my investment will be null and void. Am I understood?"

His words were rewarded with vociferous agreement, earnest nodding, and spontaneous applause.

"Good. And do not forget the most important clause—all decisions between the nations pertaining to mutual cooperation are subject to my approval. Is this also clear?"

When there was not the slightest hint of dissent, and even the general was seen to raise a fist in approval, Cosmo deposited Feedback on the floor, stood, and strode deliberately toward the door. Before exiting, he turned one last time to face—it appeared to him—the shell-shocked assembly.

"Well, Ladies and Gentlemen—to work!"

Feedback let out a short bark, zipped straight toward Andy who was standing, as discreetly as his casual attire allowed, in a corner, waiting for Abramian to finish his speech. The lanky Californian sported well-worn Nikes, threadbare jeans, a belt decorated with silver Navajo ornaments and colorful beads, and a T-shirt with the faded words Thanks, But No Thanks. Along with—likely to mark the special occasion—an allegedly handmade, all-weather jacket of very real-seeming snakeskin, acquired by Andy at Bangkok's Gucci Market for a proud twenty bucks. He and Feedback now followed Abramian, albeit at a tactful distance, so that a casual observer would not necessarily—and certainly not immediately—have seen them as belonging together.

Armenus Corporate Headquarters, Southern Armenia

On the late afternoon of the same day, the Sikorsky C-76 circled over the halls and offices of the massive industrial park a few hundred kilometers south of the capital. This allowed the three passengers a good view of the newly built complex, which measured the size of a moderate town. Feedback on his lap, Andy looked down, with what appeared to be mild interest at best, at shapes and structures that harmonized in remarkable fashion with the landscape. The third passenger, Jack Abramian, was congratulating himself on the decision to award the contract for this major project to the famously restrained Swiss architect, rather than the presumptuous French.

Masses of light-brown soil testified to recently finished work, while farther up well-watered, and thus luxuriantly green lawns were a feast for the eyes. There, along the eastern border of the techno park, gentle hills arose, which gave way to inhospitable, forested rock formations. Bedded in these hills were apartment buildings and, in the forefront, guest bungalows were arranged in circular fashion around the commanding conference center, with its vaulted, wooden roofline. Farther down, on the plain, stood the production and maintenance facilities.

Toward the river, a generous runway led to an airfield with hangars, the distribution center and the facilities for freight handling.

In the far distance, on Turkish soil, stood the snow-capped, omnipresent Ararat, where Noah's Ark may have come to rest after the subsiding of the flood; majestic in the pure light of a deep blue sky. The Turks called the mighty Ararat, which they had wrested from the Armenians, *Mountain of Pain*.

Abramian shook his head. *Such childishness!* "Mount Ararat is Armenian," the Armenian president had murmured in his ear. "One day it shall be returned to us."

The pilot landed the machine in front of a low reception building on a freshly paved oval with white lettering: ARMENUS CORPORATION.

Andy nimbly hopped out on his side, as did Feedback, who moved so quickly that she managed to land even before he did. On the other side, Abramian alighted in a more dignified manner, taming his flapping, white mane with one hand. A tall man with salt and pepper hair and bright face stepped from the group of attendants and trotted, ducking slightly, toward the guest.

Nico Strom's greeting was swallowed by the noise of the slowing helicopter blades, but his enthusiastic embrace left no doubt that the two beaming men were on exceptionally good terms.

They headed to the limousines, a wagging Feedback running circles around them, and Andy following behind with the luggage. The flags suspended on high masts were set flapping by a gust of wind—the Armenian flag in red, blue and orange, the blue flag of the Armenus Corporation, and the red and white *Orbis Unum* banner. Strom's pilots—earnest young men wearing brown flight jackets—saluted briskly before they all stepped into the waiting vehicles. The immaculately polished Mercedes limousines started up quietly, glided past the high halls, in front of which maintenance teams were working on a heavy transport machine.

In the first vehicle, Strom raised two fingers against the side window. "This is the C-130 we will be flying on today. The other aircrafts are in the hangars."

"Ten, as planned?"

Strom nodded affirmatively. "Ten business jets."

Abramian regarded the Swiss man approvingly from the side. Strom, who was slowly getting on in years, had earned himself a legendary reputation in the field. Whenever a need presented itself for special maintenance, difficult repairs, urgent improvements on some heap, in whatever God-forsaken hole, Strom was your man. He had flown every craft in existence, had brokered deals, contributed expertise. The Arabs appreciated him, the Americans depended on him, and the Russians were intent on winning the brilliant, adventurous engineer for their purposes. Word had long been out that Strom was the epitome of reliability. What he said, went. His opinion was incorruptible.

The small convoy approached the low pavilion of the corporate headquarters. Next to it, a long, gray hall extended into the slope of the hill that lay behind it. Alighting in front of the office pavilion, Abramian took in the wide terrain with blatant pride. His Armenus Corporation was the perfect base for the impending operation. His gaze wandered across the gray hall, which showed no obvious entrances. Strom guessed what he was thinking. "There are almost eleven million pieces in there, ready to go. We are prepared."

"Good. Let's go to the conference room." Abramian turned away from the hall, strode toward the open entry of the pavilion.

In the room, the pilots had already arranged themselves in military single rank, standing with erect postures in front of an enormous projection screen. Cosmo inspected the parade, shaking each man's hand after he had introduced himself.

"Clifford Matoyan," the last of the rank said, head held high.

"Do I hear Armenian there, Cliff?"

"My grandparents on my father's side, sir."

"Very good, Cliff," Cosmo smiled. "I am pleased to have you with us. Where are you from?"

"Nyack on the Hudson, sir."

"A pretty little town. Not far from West Point. You're not one of those special cadets, full of airs and graces, are you?" Cosmo jokingly raised is left hand.

"No way," the young pilot said with a grin. "That's the army. I graduated from the Air Force Academy in Colorado Springs."

"And why didn't you stay in the service?"

"The pay's not that good, sir. And there wasn't a lot happening. I like it much better here."

Cosmo patted Matoyan on his shoulder with his flat hand, then turned away. They all sat down on benches, turned curious gazes toward Strom, who now projected the first slide on the big screen.

Abramian leaned back casually in the last row. His trusted sources uniformly reported that the Swiss man was in a class of his own. He had worked his way up to the rank of captain in the armored infantry of the Swiss Reserve Army, knew his way expertly around weapons and explosives, communications engineering and tactical operations. That was certainly a good place to start. Then he had proven to be quite the daredevil, supplied Unita rebel troops in Angola with goods by airdrop. Night after night he had gone up in a civilian Hercules C-130, his cargo bay filled with weapons, gear, and explosives. He had flown similar missions over Uganda and Somalia, and the devil knows where else, before putting his many talents to use in a less treacherous manner.

As he began getting along in age, he had channeled his expertise into logistic concerns, the structural layout of airport facilities, until the Emirates made him their technical advisor for the entire field of civil aviation. Strom sourced the best equipment lying about unused, restored it, and sold it in like-new condition. Abramian knew that Angolan generals had, fueled by megalomania, acquired U.S. Hercules transporters, which were soon grounded, rusting heaps, thanks to a lack of qualified personnel. This had been right up the Swiss man's alley. He had made use of his African network, contacted the chief of the air force, revived the machines, and sold the old junkers to his Arab friends... "good as new."

Abramian was particularly impressed with Strom's experience in nighttime operations over hostile territory, the tried and true infiltration techniques that he used so successfully, his knowledge of drop techniques and just about everything related to covert operations.

"We will be heading for Tehran and ten other towns," he heard him brief. He was now sweeping a red laser pointer from Tabriz in the north over Hamadan to Isfahan.

"We will deploy the business jets according to flight distance. Long range for targets like Shiraz on the Gulf, or Bandar Abbas in the south. Take a good look at this plan."

The pilots muttered, took notes.

The machines listed on the spreadsheet all had sonorous names, like Falcon, Embraer, Cessna, Cirrus, Learjet. Superficially, they were in no way immediately distinct from examples of the same models, which were in use around the globe. The structural modifications that Strom and his crew had undertaken over the past several weeks were evident on the inside, in the cabins. The passenger spaces lacked seats. In place of these, the men had installed chutes for the airdrop systems, which would allow the efficient dropping of any manner of goods or gear—maximum take-off weight being the only restriction on the nature of what could be delivered.

Strom had calculated an average load of 150,000 cell phones per business jet. If the ten machines flew two missions a night, they could collectively drop a good three million devices.

"We will be flying by night, without transponders or position lights." Strom paused, eyeing his men. Their alert features were absolutely motionless. "Now, please consider your flight routes and border approach."

Maps rustled, heads were bent forward. The tension in the room was tangible. Strom wore a satisfied smile. He was in his element.

Years ago, they had penetrated Somalia in a C-130. He had the job of flight engineer and airdrop operator. Even today, he relished the memory of this episode, which had proven to him that nothing was impossible...

..."You have entered Somali air space with no prior authorization," the announcement had come over the radio about an hour in. "If you do not turn back immediately, we will send up a fighter!"

The English pilot had looked back with a grin, selected the air traffic control frequency, answered calmly: "Roger that, ground control. Send the fighter. Over."

It had been practically impossible for aerial surveillance to find them in the night sky. Ten minutes later, they looked for the fighter, which had started as promised, on radar. They had been amused to pinpoint it, a tiny speck almost three hundred kilometers off from their position...

Abramian was impressed with the men's dedication. He stood, strode through the benches, inspected the sketches, exchanged a few words here and there.

The Hercules C-130, which was standing outside of the hangar with seven million cell phones on board, had been chosen for the flight to Tehran. If everything went according to plan, Strom's men would be dropping a total of ten million devices over Iran on the night in question. Ten million...Jack Abramian studied the clearly laid out diagram of the resource schedule: ten business jets destined for ten mid-sized cities, the massive Hercules for the capital. It made perfect sense.

A good hour had passed when Strom, after a short cigarette break, had the pilots present their flight plans.

Abramian studied the projected map, upon which the men had plotted their colored routes. Iran bordered Azerbaijan and Turkmenistan to the north, the broad, blue Caspian Sea separating the two. Armenia bordered on the northwestern tip of the neighboring country. To the east lay Afghanistan and Pakistan. Turkey and Iraq comprised the western border, but were inconsequential in the context of this mission.

Richie, an Englishman, spoke up. "There are at least four uranium enrichment facilities in the vicinity of Tehran. One of these nuclear plants is near the coast." He pointed to the city of Chalus. "There is a subterranean complex here, where Chinese and North Korean scientists are working on the nuclear weapons program. There is also an army-operated missile research center in Tehran itself."

Abramian placed a hand on his chin. "Meaning what?"

"Sir, the airspace over the capital is likely to be tightly controlled. The mullahs may have intermediate-range missiles there. Those are coveted targets for the Israelis, so they are on guard."

Cosmo nodded thoughtfully. Richie remained focused. "Defenses against Israel are oriented to the west. But we will be coming from northeast, over the Caspian Sea. Turkmenistan. A region they pay hardly any attention to. Nevertheless, we are still checking those routes."

Abramian turned to Strom. "Do you have any alternatives, Nico?"

All eyes turned to the man addressed. "Yes, I do. There is a way to get to Tehran undetected." He did not divulge more than that, and prompted the men to continue working on their planning. "Dinner is at eighteen hundred and thirty hours. I will see you then!"

The chauffeur drove them up to the guest bungalows. It was now time to discuss the sensitive part of the operation.

Abramian nodded with satisfaction. "It's always good to hear an old pro, Nico."

Strom felt genuinely flattered. "And this old pro is always happy to have another old pro in the audience, who knows what he is talking about, Jack."

Munich

The intense-looking Chechen with the flat nose dropped onto the red, upholstered chair. The waitress, who approached the guest with the copious, black hair and fiery eyes with a smile, was shooed away with an ill-tempered gesture.

The lobby of the Four Seasons was excellently suited for confidential meetings—it was filled with a bustle of activity at all hours of the day and night, the tables were well occupied, no one concerned themselves with the dealings of anyone else.

The Chechen loved Munich. The city was well situated for travel to the east, to Georgia, even direct flights to Tajikistan. His people, who venerated him like a demigod, had settled here. They called him Lord, knowing that his loyalty was not to the Queen of England, but to one who had achieved very worldly forms of power and fame. That was what counted. They never spoke the man's name. That was an iron rule. Only the Lord was allowed to utter it. Only the Lord had access to Oleg Nedjew, was allowed to call him. In the eyes of the loyal Chechen foot soldiers living in exile, this privilege alone lent him an almost divine status.

The hunchback sitting across from him was the exact opposite of the Lord: diminutive, with a narrow chest and rimless glasses. A worm of a man. But a crafty one, nevertheless, who could be useful in challenging situations.

"We found nothing at the Hornbach engineers' residence. It was empty. The birds had flown away...absolutely nothing."

The Lord's lips were drawn to a narrow line. "That means you got there too late then, doesn't it? You messed up."

"We did find two CDs, but they contained a lot of chicken scratch. Completely illegible."

"Do not tell me that you were not capable of doing anything with them!" The accusing outburst cut the hunchback to the core, yet he protested defiantly. "No. The issue is that the Hornbachs built in a vicious, time-delayed virus."

"Is the unreadable chicken scratch then not perhaps code?"

"I wish it were so, Mr. Lord. The virus on the CD was activated at the very moment that we attempted unauthorized access. We had no idea. And that was that—Bingo! A stroke of fate."

"Fate? A steaming pile of shit is more like it. So you have no idea how the chicken made it across the road, or why it started scratching. Wonderful. Why were you idiots so unprepared?"

"The thing was expertly programmed. It went off like a Stalin rocket launcher."

The Lord gave a resigned wave, sank back into his chair like a boxer ready to be cared for between rounds.

The hunchback drew his head down even further between his pointy shoulders. "What happens to the Swiss now? Do we string them up by the balls?"

The Lord had long recognized which way the wind was about to blow. He had, after all, accounted for the worst case scenario. His first tactical principle was never allow yourself to be taken by surprise.

"Time for plan B," he croaked. "You can go. Send Antoni to me."

His followers were accustomed to him holding court at the Four Seasons. They hung around at cafés in the vicinity, hoping to be summoned and entrusted with a task.

It took less than two minutes for Antoni to appear in front of the Lord, waiting to be asked to take a seat.

"Sit! Stop standing around like an idiot! We're not alone here!"

The bald man measured a meter ninety and was built like a generously sized armoire. The Lord's concern was that schooled eyes, which could always conceivably be present in the lobby, could recognize the bulges beneath the beefcake's arms as something other than poor tailoring.

"Did you have to come carrying, damn it?"

"Being prepared is everything!" Antoni grinned, flashing a gold canine.

"Okay, Antoni, you know what this is about?"

"Fixing something?"

"We will get the data from the Jews in Zurich. Tell Irina. It has been arranged with her boss. We have to be faster than the Israelis."

"What do you mean?"

"Putting ten thousand Jews in chains and sinking them to the bottom of the ocean would be a nice start, but never, ever underestimate Mossad. Don't even think of it. Or you'll be the one who ends up as fish food. Listen, Antoni, the Jew Nachman will not just have this information lying around. Find out where he is hiding it. Then make contact."

"I will. With Petrova."

"Yes, she is in Zurich. But take care that she doesn't castrate you with her bare teeth." His unearthly, rough laugh caused the reception clerk to stare over in surprise. The meeting was over. Antoni departed with a rolling stride. Lord waved the waitress to his table. This time he dignified her with a smile that caused her to blush. "Coffee with cream, please." His lecherous gaze wandered over the lovely, firm bulges beneath her spotless, white blouse. Eyes half closed, he imagined how this stark white would contrast with the soft pink of her breasts...

Zurich, Bahnhofstrasse

A door creaks downstairs.

The ghostly sound startles Nachman's assistant out of a doze. He listens intently. A muted thud...the creaking again. He places the thin Tolstoy volume on the lamp base, stands up. The sound is familiar to him, at least subconsciously. The hinges have needed oiling for a long time. Then a cracking sound of breaking wood. Tabah's heart begins to beat in his throat. He has resigned himself to listening to sounds in the haunted attic, just as he is accustomed to the magpies who lurk on the summer terrace, waiting to pick silver spoons from the breakfast table. But this is not morning, and the noises are not coming from a ghost above.

He holds his breath, tiptoes toward the kitchen. He is alone, and afraid. Yorini Nachman, the kid, had gone off to his lodgings on Zurich's ETH campus. How he despises being alone. It is dark downstairs. Stepping gingerly toward the landing, he is acutely aware that he is missing something—the weapon. It is downstairs in the office. Tabah sets off to get it. Starkly illuminated by the cone of the small, halogen lamp, the cube-shaped, golden clock on the glass table shows the time to be half past one; it is pitch dark outside. His boss must have arrived in Budapest long ago. Usually he calls when he lands. A scraping sound, rustling. *Had he not closed the door properly?*

The lines on the face of the burly Israeli appear to deepen. He takes the first steps with resolve. What a joke, to be nearly pissing himself like this.

Then he notices a shadowy movement at the bottom of the stairs. His breath catches. In these seconds, he feels exactly the same sickening tension that he felt in the Sinai. Young Tabah, lying in position at the front of the ditch.

Like ghastly toads, the hostile tanks had rolled inexorably forward, tossing up giant clouds of dust. It was nightmarish... The requested fighter jets were nowhere to be seen! In seconds it would all be too late, over... He clasped the rocket launcher, searching for a target... Then the cries of salvation... The fighter jets descended in a flash of silver, raining destruction, the nightmare was swept away... Then a misfired rocket hit just a few meters away from him...

... The sharp bang from the hallway deafens Tabah. It is just like then. A searing, unbearable pain. The bullet hits his knee, shatters the bones. The shooter runs up the stairs, two masked figures right behind him. Tabah looks up, face contorted, blinded by rage. The barrels of three pistols are aimed at him.

"Where is the information? Atomic information. Spit it out, cripple." The masked man has a Slavic accent.

Tabah clenches his teeth. The other masked figure steps out of the lounge. "The house is clean. Come, get started."

A woman recognizable only as a vague silhouette gets to work on the computer. The first masked man waves his pistol erratically. "Hurry up, man. The information for the atomic bomb!"

"Fuck you."

"You do not have good manners." The pistol hits Tabah in the face, hard. Blood streams from his panting mouth. "Fuck you...you...bastard!"

The third man catches the masked man's raised arm. "Enough!" The woman with sharp features steps out of the office, states tersely: "There's nothing there." Together they force their groaning torture victim roughly down the stairs.

Judging by her demeanor, she was in charge, used to giving orders with a hard, implacable look in her black eyes.

In the large billiard room, two of her henchmen hold Tabah brutally against the white, now bloodstained, wall. One of them tears off his stocking mask—a bald head, pushes the pistol under Tabah's chin, uses it to ram his head viciously back against the wall.

The woman nonchalantly retrieves a dart from the dartboard, faces the Israeli with a wide stance, the edges of her mouth turned down in an angry grimace. "Where is the information, you little shit?" Her fingers play with the dart.

She is met with a look of bottomless contempt. "Why don't you go fuck yourself, you desperate cunt!"

The dart suddenly finds itself buried in his nostril, the wench rips her hand upward, almost screams, blood spurts.

Expressionless, she buries the dart in the other nostril. "Talk!"

That was only the beginning. They beat him, ripped his pants off, pushed him facedown onto the pool table. The woman tied his arms to the turned table legs, pressed his head onto the hard, green surface while her buddies spread his legs. The third man tore a cue from the rack, positioning its thick handle against Tabah's anus. "If you tell us everything, we'll stop."

Tabah grunts, the attacker rams the cue home fiercely. It penetrates him deeply before breaking in two. Tabah's body quakes, spasms. The torturer takes a red ball, positions it with his fist, pushes with all his might.

Tabah must have lost consciousness for a moment. His entire body burned with the fires of hell as he came to. His eyes welled over. The satanic bitch now held a black ball under his bleeding nose. "You may want to appreciate this little thing, because after it, we will be getting the hot poker from the fireplace. Are you sure you aren't ready for a little chat?"

Tabah was a broken man. Suffering unbearable agony, he began to talk, so that it would all finally end. Surrender came as a relief.

He told them almost everything, named the names, divulged details, let his swollen tongue loose. As long as he talked, they didn't touch him…no more torture…he talked about the Hornbachs, the micro CD, that his boss walked away with it, planning to fly to Bucharest…

When the torture commando exits the penthouse about an hour later, the leader knows everything she needs to know in order to obtain the plans for the Hornbach brothers' miniaturized nuclear warheads. She has completed her mission brilliantly.

Before the night is over, the Lord receives her call in Munich. Irina Petrova tells him of the brilliant hiding place, gives him the rest of the blood-soaked information.

The Lord is on the phone to the Crane just a few minutes later.

"The Swiss plans for the nuclear weapons are stored on a microchip that the clever shit of an Israeli took away to hide it safely somehow on his plane."

"And where is the damn plane?" Oleg Nedjew asked.

"Scheduled to fly to Armenia, to the Armenus Corporation. A technopark. I will send you the details. It will be in Bucharest tomorrow, then Yerevan." The crime boss grumbled for longer than usual, which the Lord interpreted as approval, then hung up.

In Zurich Irina Petrova had, prior to leaving the billiard room, put her pistol to the side of Tabah's forehead and—without batting an eye—pulled the trigger. The bullet had ripped through his brain, torn through the table, and lodged into the Bolivian hardwood floor. *Pity about the table, really*, she had remarked almost casually on her way out, a sadistic grin on her pale face.

PART II

Zurich, Paradeplatz

"Our little world is a stage. So, of course, good drama is of the essence," John Ponter, a banker accustomed to being smiled upon by success, lectured. Sitting back in a self-satisfied manner, he puffed on the Churchill cigar that he always smoked in the afternoons. In the evenings, he was partial to long Havanas, along with delightful women, who captivated him with a mixture of classic beauty and lascivious peril. Just like Sophie Kramer who, sitting across from him, demurely turned her knees and straightened her skirt.

Four deep furrows lined his high forehead as he looked up with large, dark eyes. His long nose was slender, straight, and the focal point of a symmetric face, accentuated by two perfectly straight lines leading from his nostrils to the sides of his mouth.

"Think of our clients as the extras, if you will," he continued. "They stand around, not really knowing what to do with themselves, watching us—the actors—as we masterfully pull the strings, achieve enormous earnings, and deal with losses effortlessly, without batting an eye."

Sophie Kramer had only signed on with Ponter as a risk officer a few months ago. John Ponter had been quite dramatic, as well as perfectly clear, in his explanation of what the job entailed. "You see, Ms. Kramer, may I call you Sophie?...Listen, Sophie, I run great risks in what I do, and your job consists of shifting those risks on to the clients."

Leaning forward slightly, his expression was alert, eyes wide open, appearing to critically take in every detail around him. His eyes skimmed her wavy hair with interest, grazed her lips, finally came to rest on her eyes.

"Clients are greedy for growth and profit. We oblige them, and we also stake our bets on that greed. Their greed is what we have going for us. If and when losses come rolling in, they are the ones to feel at fault; they now understand—with a little help from us—that they were the ones who got too big for their boots and didn't realize…it's psychologically ingenious. As I said: it's all theater!" He paused artfully before continuing somewhat disparagingly with the orders for the day: "You will play a round of golf with Quadrini today. Nine holes at the Dolder. Quadrini's handicap is twenty-five. Yours is sixteen, right? Let him win. Then, for the evening, agree to meet him at the bar of the Dolder Grand and…" He smirked. "If the man still wants to go out, well, then have dinner with him. Everything else, I will leave up to you. I just want one thing: You will see to it that he signs off on the performance sheet."

"What are his assets like?"

"He has around sixty million with us. A tidy little sum. Tell Kleiber to give you a quick brief on the investment structure of his portfolio, okay?"

"And if he refuses to approve the performance sheet?"

"He won't. Can't afford to. Also, he was up eight percent, but then he took a hit on American mortgage securities. Too bad, that."

"How am I supposed to tell him about the losses, if he asks?"

"Well, that would really be your very personal, teeny-tiny problem, Sophie. But you'll see. A game of golf can work miracles. A good drive or perfect putt can put a person in a surprisingly forgiving mood. You'll be able to have a casual little chat about everything. Then later, at the fancy bar, you'll pull out that sheet with a charming smile, hand him the gold pen…Surely you don't need me to teach you these things!"

John Ponter laughed, blew smoke toward the ceiling, watched it rise contemplatively. Suddenly he lowered his head again, turning to face her in a flash, eyeing her forbiddingly. "I don't like that skeptical look I see creeping onto your face, Sophie. That one, right there. What do you have a problem with? It does not make me happy when you do not share my views loyally and completely. I have no need for your moralizing mood, unless…you want things to get very uncomfortable, very quickly. The twenty thousand I pay you every month can certainly increase, perhaps significantly, but also drop to zero point zero…have I made myself clear?" He closed with a conciliatory gesture. "Go on. Time to get to work, girl."

Sophie felt a flush coming on, and was angered by the betrayal of her face. Her sternly furrowed brow and pinched lips now signaled earnest compliance. She may as well have clicked her heels and saluted. *He wants drama? He can have drama!* She turned in the doorway, "What is your handicap, Mr. Ponter?"

"I have several, my dear. But I don't play golf."

✳

Manfred Kleiber was not in his corner office. Sophie sat down in the leather armchair in front of the elegant table with the black-and-gray-checkered stone top and looked around. The sparse furnishings otherwise consisted of a bookcase, which stood out from the wall next to a brownish row of windows like a foreign body. Its shelves were a yawning void, except for a worn out handbook on banking and the stock exchange.

A thin laptop lay next to the sleek telephone. Restless, she stood, stepped to the window, looked down into the courtyard. A highly polished stately vehicle stood at the center of the yard that was bordered by glass facades on all sides. As she watched, the chauffeur strode toward the car and began polishing the windscreen. For what? It was all theater... Ivanovic had driven her from the airport to her first meeting with Ponter. Sophie had felt an urge to open the window. There was no handle; it was all hermetically sealed. She turned.

A matte-yellow, finger-thick file lay on the desk. It was unlabeled. Sophie had never really spoken to Manfred Kleiber. What kind of a man was he? There were no photographs, such as one would usually expect to find gracing a manager's desk, no personal objects to convey a sense of the familiar, no digital clock to count the interest-accumulating hours. A letter opener stamped with the droll words *It'll get done tomorrow* lay forlornly next to an empty, dirty crystal vase. Sophie picked it up, weighed it in her hand, and was just putting it down randomly on top of the file when Kleiber stepped in. "What are you doing here? Snooping around?"

Not waiting for an answer, he stepped around the desk. Visibly annoyed he snatched up the file, dropped into the high-backed chair.

"I'm here to talk about the Quadrini portfolio. I'm meeting him to-day," Sophie said curtly. She found there was something quite off-putting about Kleiber. The man was anything but relaxed, avoiding eye contact, clutching the file as if to protect it from her.

She gestured toward it with her head. "The Quadrini file?"

Shaking his head, he opened the laptop. "It's all online. Look."

He turned the screen for her to see once the main menu appeared. "Here is the breakdown of assets. Sixty percent stocks, then bonds and cash. About sixty million."

"And which currencies?"

"Mostly Euros, over half, then Swiss Francs. Unfortunately, he also has some collateralized debt obligations..."

"Why? Aren't those junk?"

"Now, maybe. But they were great at one time. Really high interest. It was the cream." He let out an oddly high-pitched giggle. "Then the crash of the American real estate market hit us, and...yes, the bank did some creative re-distributing among its client accounts."

"Is that legal?"

"Legal? How quaint. Of course it is. We have power of attorney and are authorized to conduct transactions. Including structural ones."

Kleiber put the file on the desk, only to immediately place his hand on it. "We make good money on these clients, as long as they let us do what we need to do."

Sophie was certain that she had heard a hint of disapproval in his tone. "So, you're on board with all of this, are you?"

She was met with a silent stare. Then he gestured for her to come closer, said in a whisper, "What I am about to tell you, you did not hear from me. Can I rely on that?"

She returned his gaze, nodded.

"The bank makes a ton of money in commissions and broker's fees. Whenever we purchase anything—stocks, bonds—the client pays us for doing so. We make our profit on the margin."

"Meaning?"

"Here is an example." Kleiber moved the mouse, clicked. "Here we purchased General Electric bonds in U.S. dollars. Five million worth of what their going rate was at the time. We charged Quadrini a higher rate and came out with a profit of eighty basis points."

Sophie wrinkled her brow. She was very proficient at doing calculations in her head. "Eighty basis points—that's a whopping forty thousand dollars…that's…" Fraud, was what she wanted to say. "Not right," she mitigated.

Kleiber shrugged his shoulders. "Business politics. Orders from the boss." He made a gesture of resignation toward the ceiling, above which Ponter's commanding office took up half of the entire floor.

"The rates are public record," Sophie demurred. "Mr. Quadrini could have them checked."

"Except, he won't," Kleiber jeered. "We also make profits on the margin when we invest cash—as in fixed term deposits."

For a while, they both pored over the screen filled with number-strewn tables and colorful bar charts. Sophie pursed her lips. A question was brewing on her mind, but Manfred Kleiber beat her to it.

"Clients like Quadrini are at our mercy. Just like the newly rich from Eastern Europe, Russia, Kazakhstan. You know?"

The pretty woman looked at him, wide-eyed.

"Illegal earnings, unreported money. Quadrini is German, but he only taxes part of his assets. His real money is earned without the knowledge of the fiscal authorities. If that gets out, he will be ruined. We protect him. He knows that he can count on our silence and discretion. We make his assets invisible by investing in certain structures—it's referred to as asset protection. There is no way that anyone will be able to get their hands on them—not the tax authorities, not people he may owe money to, not an unhappy wife wanting a payout in a divorce. Safe as Gibraltar, silent as the grave."

"So, what's the catch? There must be one."

"Not that I know of," Kleiber said with a smile. "Except if someone blows the whistle on him."

"Which would be a punishable offense," Sophie added.

"Of course." Again, Kleiber displayed that patronizing grimace, which he seemed to consider a friendly smile.

"The client refrains from anything that could lead to conflict with the bank. He will put up with quite a bit in order not to provoke or risk anything. You understand?"

"I don't know," Sophie mumbled. Her counterpart moved his shoulders as if to indicate that there were other angles.

"Our clients are cautious," he said, turning his eyes upward again. "He uses their fear of being caught to his advantage."

"Why are you telling me all this?"

Kleiber looked perturbed. "Why? Well, there are many things that clients aren't aware of. It doesn't matter anymore now."

"What do you mean?"

"It doesn't matter," he erupted. "You wanted to know, didn't you? And, anyway, as I said..." Kleiber ruffled aimlessly through the pages of the matte-yellow file, holding it to his broad chest like an infant.

"Anyway, what?" Sophie was taken aback by Kleiber's erratic movements as he suddenly rose, as if transformed, leaned forward, saying, "You heard nothing from me, remember? We have an agreement."

When Sophie failed to respond, he jammed the laptop and yellow file under his arm, strode toward the door. He turned before exiting and said, quietly: "Quadrini is one of those tax evaders who couldn't care less about laws. His money is as dirty as it gets."

"I think," Sophie interrupted, "if merely having a Swiss bank account makes tens of thousands of Germans criminal, then there really is a problem with Germany, not with Switzerland."

"Whatever," Kleiber brushed her remark aside. "He will be very wary of causing waves just because of a few padded invoices. Good luck, Sophie. In case I don't see you again."

Sophie turned her head slowly back and forth, as if searching for the proverbial penny, which simply was not dropping. In case I don't see you again...?

And so she decided, first things first, to start with a round of golf. As Ponter had said so succinctly: that might just help things take care of themselves. "Well, let's see about that," she spurred herself on, extracting her cell phone from her plump purse and entering the number of the man whom this entire conversation had been about.

Pullach—Headquarters of BND, Germany's international intelligence service

The atmosphere was heavy in Pullach, in the idyllic Bavarian Isar Valley south of Munich. If not in the little town itself, with its charming old gabled rooftops, then certainly all the more at the headquarters of the Federal Intelligence Agency Bundesnachrichtendienst. Or, more precisely, under the roof of one of the building's wings, which had been chosen to house a secure, soundproof coop of sorts.

The director of procurement was painfully aware that one more slip-up would mean the end, not just for him as boss, but also for many of his subordinates, who worked in various areas of mobile and operative signals intelligence. The subdivision for Logistics, Interception and Monitoring (LIM) had set everything up with great care.

German troops had been deployed to Afghanistan on a combat mission—reason enough for Frank Steiner, decorated paratrooper major, to be cautious. Intelligence gathering had always been key to preventive operations as far as he was concerned. Only idiots believed that a combat mission could be sufficiently prepared with operative reconnaissance alone.

This was why Steiner had not hesitated when he had caught wind of the liaison between the journalist and the Pakistani minister of defense. He had immediately had the spy software implemented—it had been no issue for his LIM people. They were certainly equipped with the latest technology, and had been trained in covert operations. If anything, Steiner lamented that his people had too little opportunity to employ their perfidious tools. Frustration threatened to undermine his best agents' motivation. Idleness had always been a horror scenario to the battle tested commander. Given the circumstances, the Hindukush affair had seemed like a gift from heaven. The Beauty and the Minister—the affair was loaded in a way that could prove precarious to the troops. He recalled with bitterness the sensation fueled revelations of a French reporter, who had thoughtlessly exposed an infiltration of French Special Forces in the logistic hinterland of the Taliban. The insurgents had promptly used this information to launch a massive, bloody retaliatory attack on French troops stationed nearby.

He still felt the shock, which had given way to frustration and rage in his very bones when he learned the details. He had sworn back then that nothing of that nature would ever happen on his watch, no matter what it took. To his mind, nothing was worse than betrayal. There were certain journalists who were simply without conscience, as far as he was concerned. The type eager to publish a disclosure for money, fame, awards, and perhaps a few women who like to bask in the media limelight of whoever was their action hero.

LIM secretly released a Trojan into the network of the Ministry of Defense. The well-programmed spyware burrowed into the computer and worked silently, behind the scenes, sending the content of the hard drive to Pullach. Soon, Frank Steiner was privy to everything that was going on within the ministry in black and white.

His specialists recovered a whole treasure trove of confidential data and classified documents, as well as numerous email addresses and passwords. Among them—Bingo!—the electronic mailbox of the minister himself: *Firearm48*.

And then things started coming thick and fast. Pullach discovered via the Trojan that Firearm48 was using a Hotmail account, for which they were also able to retrieve the password. Steiner's people could simply log on and follow the correspondence. The German journalist did not reveal much, to Steiner's disappointment, but he was not about to let up—the surveillance continued unabated.

One day the agents discovered two emails that really got things rolling. The subject line of one read "Engineer Kidnapped, Ransom." In it, the reporter relayed details pertaining to the kidnapping of a weapons expert, and a demand for ransom. The second mentioned the name Khan. If things had been relatively uninteresting up until that point, this had certainly changed things. What did the German woman, who according to Steiner's finely honed instinct was almost certainly just pretending to be engaged in a harmless affair, have to do with the Pakistani bomb tinkerer?

Steiner called his men in for a brainstorming session. While the intercepted emails had been a stiff morning breeze ending the calm for the bobbing ship of the department, there were also concerns. Someone asked whether it was actually legal to monitor the press. Frank made it clear to the doubting Thomas that German troops in the field of course had absolute priority. What if Firearm48 was working for the Taliban, about to betray German troops abroad? That did the trick! The men nodded in unison, appearing relieved to have their doubts allayed. The crisis of conscience was over.

But then there had been an anonymous letter. Someone had ratted them out to the director, and dragged the in-house lawyers into things. They found that Steiner's department was violating article 10 of the constitution, which protects the privacy of telecommunications. Emails were not to be read—end of story.

Steiner was forced, albeit with clenched teeth, to halt the surveillance of the minister abroad. The fact that the affair had assumed the proportions of an earnest scandal that reached as far as the chancellery was not necessarily a bad thing, as far as Steiner was concerned. As an old hand in the business, he knew all too well that a hype such as this could be overcome simply by stubbornly sitting it out. In truth, the seasoned fox welcomed a bit of distraction. Let those bureaucratic assholes up there officiously scramble and fall over themselves to come up with new directives to obstruct his agency. Meanwhile, he would be working away unimpeded, bringing ever more opacity to the gray zone by effectively screening the explosive operations, blurring connections, using the mantle of data protection to make it impossible to discover his daring enterprise. As far as Steiner was concerned, rules were there to be intelligently circumnavigated. In any case he had learnt his lesson from the Pakistan affair.

Particularly in regards to Operation Alpine-rose-dust.

Now, Steiner gazes over the rim of his reading glasses at the large monitor and is annoyed at the thought of the amateurs, whom he has to contend with. Bureaucrats who see their life's purpose in pulling the rug from under my people out in the field, who are in the line of fire. With their legal opinions to protect targets they are just effectively aiding terrorists.

"How different the young American is, who recruited me," he mutters to himself. Clearly the guy is a completely different caliber. Totally professional, enviably efficient, presumably gifted with everything the CIA has to offer. Impervious to agency bullshit. Thinking about it... was he young? Judging by the resonant, strong voice in which he delivered his German with a slightly Texan drawl, he thought of Garp as being in his mid-thirties; a maverick, like himself.

Frank and Garp... it had a good ring to it! In fact, when he had met the almost uncomfortably attractive man with defined features for the first time at Munich Airport, he had perfectly fit his image of a dynamic hot shot.

Operation Alpine-rose-dust could under no circumstances be allowed to fail. There was too much on the line. This wasn't about a couple of dusty legal paragraphs. It was a matter of life or death. Steiner was responsible for handling the source. He alone. This time, he kept his circle of insiders so small that he remained as invisible as a speck of dust when it came to intrigue or snooping. This time none of these legal shitheads stood a chance of finding out what was going on!

Steiner turned to his counter, a dark figure—slender, large, dark glasses on his face. Then he turned up the amplifier as an added precaution, just in case the walls had ears that needed neutralizing.

"How is everything, Zack?" he asked the man opposite him through in the harsh droning of a bass.

"We're all good. The seedlings are planted. We have a sample of the first delivery."

"Volume?"

The shadowy figure crosses his legs. "Billions, by the look of things. We are currently waiting for data on over three thousand accounts. Kleiber has already delivered a small sample."

"How many of us?"

"Germans?" The shadow shrugged its shoulders. "The analysis will tell us once we've run it. Several hundred, for sure. We are being cautious. Ongoing, around-the-clock surveillance will be necessary."

"Potential for trouble?"

"The human factor. Manfred Kleiber, who is fleecing the Ponter Bank in Zurich, will be receiving six million Euros and will then be assuming a new identity. He'll be out of the picture. I think he's safe enough. If he talks, he knows he'll be digging his own grave."

"The others?"

"If everything goes according to plan, that big fancy bank will spread her legs for us like an old whore."

Steiner raises a hand. "Let's keep it matter-of-fact, please. We need to stay focused. Any questions on your end, Zack?"

"Since you ask. Are tax sinners considered public enemies?" The shadow of a man stands from his seat, raises his hands behind his head and throws back his elbows to crack his back.

Steiner snorts: "Tax sinners? The Federal Central Tax Office isn't God, Zack. The problem is not the oasis, or the jungle for that matter, but the desert all around, if you catch my meaning. The matter of tax evasion itself is not our problem. When did you start questioning the mission? Are you losing your grip? There are bigger things at stake here."

Steiner's eyes sparkled menacingly. The meeting was over. The shadowy figure gave a casual salute and disappeared in the dark.

Frank Steiner grunted, entered the password, opened the file: Gregor Zack, Berlin. Born in Leipzig, 1959. Served with the Special Forces of the National People's Army. Stasi until the wall came down. Debriefing and training with the CIA.

Steiner entered a note, then closed the file. He suddenly felt chilled. Alpine-rose-dust was no ordinary foreign operation. It was an attack on a neighboring ally. As Garp had explained to him: *Business as usual had to come to an end—bank secrecy, capital flight. We will bring the world's most powerful fiduciary custodian to its knees; hit its financial center at its core. We will destroy them! Not with bombs and tanks, that didn't even work in*

WWII—no: with secret electronic weapons… They're clueless. Completely off-guard—standing around talking about defense in terms of fighter jets and tanks, without knowing that an attack is being leveled at the computer systems of their key corporations and financial institutions.

The guardians of Swiss liberty are defenseless when it comes to electronic warfare against the substance of their research and development, and their economy.

Steiner heard the words in his head, as if the voice had only just pounded them into his ears. I don't give a shit about politics, he thought. As a soldier my job is to be committed to the mission, and not to care about the reasons why. This is the only way to ensure the job gets done, no matter the crisis. Because there will always be a crisis, sure as hell.

Frank Steiner closes his eyes. He knows this will work. It's a matter of justice and ethics the clueless fiscal policy wonks are saying. Of course they are lying. They had absolutely no clue about MADOF: the MONETARY AGENCY FOR DETECTING OFFSHORE FRAUD. What a comforting name for one of the most clandestine of U.S. agencies—as Garp had put it. Steiner chuckled to himself. Most conniving, more like it!

It's all about the economy and political power. That much is clear. Deficit-running countries with high tax rates, like good, old Germany with its insolvent politicians, would like nothing more than to have a go at Switzerland.

They had strolled through the wide corridors at the Franz-Josef-Strauß departure terminal. Garp, wearing a long coat and a weird knitted cap with a short visor, rambled along, his speech keeping time with his long stride—it was something between sharing information and indoctrination.

"The Swiss are about to go down for aiding and abetting corrupt fat cats and power brokers, Steiner. We planted some of the best assets in the industry. Their names don't matter—let's call them Buchenfeld and

Eichin. One is in Geneva, the other in Zurich. Both are highly qualified financial advisors.

"Buchenfeld was ripe for the picking. He quit his job, testified before a court in Miami and started a landslide. Tens of thousands of U.S. banking clients were exposed. That's billions in taxes and fines that we're bringing in from Switzerland. It was an ingenious move. Eichin continues to work very much undercover in Zurich—a winning card for us; a time-bomb for the major bank in question. Informants like Buchenfeld and Eichin, those are today's true heroic agents."

Garp had stopped in front of a food stand, grabbed a can and held it up, smiling. "The U.S. has always been in the business of exporting three things in particular: Coca-Cola, jeans, and jurisdiction. That's what it's all about, Steiner—we enforce our laws ruthlessly, be it at home or abroad. Hell—especially abroad!"

Whatever, Steiner told himself. *MADOF is on course to destroy the Swiss financial market, and it's going full-steam. We Germans may be feeling like the captains of a great crusade for justice, but really, we are merely obediently following along in the wake.*

Steiner duly noted whatever his spymaster from the other side of the Atlantic spewed at him in terms of justifications. He did not express views about politics as an iron principle. I am the best-paid double agent on earth! Never forget that, Frankie-Boy! Garp couldn't resist constantly rubbing that under his nose, either. Along with the polite, terse warning: the tiniest misstep, and you're done, Frank Steiner. Everything you have achieved, the perks, the millions in a secret bank account, the villa, the girls . . . the air you breathe, the light of day—it would all be gone.

"We will foster, breed and nurture insecurity, until no one trusts the Swiss any longer," Garp had continued his lecture as he neared passport control. "We need the income. What we can get our hands on at home isn't enough anymore. We have to broaden our net, and our MADOF agents are going for the jugular. It will bring us billions that we are in desperate need of.

"Many are repatriating their hot assets simply because they are afraid that the Swiss will inform Internal Revenue anyway. Hysteria will break loose, loss of confidence will seal the crisis, and we will inherit it all—the business, as well as the billions." He dug the blue U.S. passport from the depths of his coat. "Now, about Ponter…"

…Yup. That had been a few days ago. Steiner turned off the light, stepped in front of the tinted security window, the dynamic Garp still in his mind's eye. A fresh voice reaches him just moments later via a cell phone that has been secured with special encryption software. "We just hit pay dirt, Frank. Kleiber's sample file from the Ponter bank in Zurich may show a connection between Nedjew and the mullahs."

"Oleg Nedjew, the Crane?"

"That's the one."

"Analysis?"

"Money laundering, as far as the bank is concerned. But that's completely irrelevant."

"Get to the point, Garp."

"Arms trading. Judging by the sheer amount of money, it can only be one thing."

"Nuclear? With the mullahs? Iran?"

"I'm convinced of it. That clever darling-of-the-Kremlin mob boss is the only player in that league. He's the only one who can pull something like that off."

Steiner feels the ground being yanked from beneath his feet. He had focused all of his energy on Alpine-rose-dust, he couldn't possibly go full steam in two different directions. His voice wavers. "Alpine-rose-dust…"

He gets no further. The voice that comes back across the line sounds youthfully energetic and quite unburdened. "Hey, this couldn't have gone any better, Steiner. We expose the scandal of a real live nuclear weapons deal, with a little side of money laundering. This kind of development will break the necks of the holier-than-thou Swiss once and for all."

We meant Frank and Garp. It meant nothing other than the fact that Steiner was working under deep cover, for the U.S. MADOF agency.

"Nothing will be what it was, Steiner. Alpine-rose-dust will still be our top priority, but we are expanding to the international level, understood?"

Steiner was, in fact, beginning to understand. If things blow up down there, because the mullahs are playing with their bomb, we will all be in shit up to our necks. According to Garp, it would be revealed to the world that the most terrible of all dirty deals was processed via Zurich. When the mortifying mushroom cloud rose over the Middle East, the fallout would definitely bury the Swiss world of finance.

"Yes, understood. Mission acknowledged."

The connection breaks off. A visibly exhausted Steiner stares at the file, lifts it, lowers it into the drawer of the armor-cased desk. With a deep sigh, he carefully locks it.

"Zack!" he yells. "Where the hell is Zack?!"

No one hears his racket. Steiner gets a hold of himself, takes a deep breath, reaches for the cell phone and starts to type on the miniature key pad. The text reaches the special agent instantly: *report immediately.*

Then Steiner has an almost poetic vision that arises in his mind's eye. *The Crane and the Mullahs*... is spelled out in glowing lights. Almost as titillating as The Beauty and the Minister... And Garp's words echo: *This is modern warfare, my friend. Cyber-attacks, hacking into computer systems, spying, data theft—those are the new forms of ambush. No army, no matter how fit for combat, can do a damn thing against them. MADOF had opened a new dimension in the global war for wealth.*

Zurich Airport

Sophie Kramer is in excellent spirits as she parks her Mini Cooper behind the airport hangars the morning after her meeting with Kleiber. She hums to herself, almost yelps a little cheer into the morning air, but is stopped short by the loud drone of a machine over the vaulted roof of the hall. Squinting with an open mouth into the bright sun, she tries to detect the identification on the Dornier, with its characteristic superficial wing design. Was that the machine flying her boss to Belgrade? She is still blinking as the elegant bird turns away without having revealed its identity.

Sophie retrieves her skates from the back, flops onto the seat and stretches her legs into the air, strips her beige running shoes off with her feet.

"You're Beautiful" is playing on the radio. As she holds a skate up to her raised foot, she nods in time to the music, as if acknowledging that this song must be playing just for her on this beautiful morning. When a speaker interrupts James Blunt with breaking news, she disappointedly reaches to change the station, but then pauses to listen almost despite herself: *. . . as announced by a speaker of the Pentagon yesterday, plans to withdraw American troops from Germany have been confirmed. . .*

Sophie had it all, or pretty close to all, at any rate. Her job was interesting. It allowed her to pursue her passion for flying. On top of all that she was fit and—if the appraising glances of the opposite sex were anything to go by, attractive.

. . . The German chancellor did not comment on American plans to reduce troops in Western Europe prior to her departure to Moscow. . .

She runs her hand through her dark blond hair, squeezes her other foot into the skate, ties it up and stands to test her balance. You're beautiful, she sings as she pockets her car key, slams the door shut soundly, then rolls at a leisurely pace toward the street.

Flying was in her blood, her instructor had said early on. She had not even been twenty when she had first flown across the valley to the Albula Pass in Engadin, the soothing hum of the engine in her ears, and elated at having discovered an unbelievable sense of freedom.

Presumably her father's genes drove her constantly to new horizons. Indelible memories of the lovable if strict Paps often caught her off guard. He had been a renowned pilot, who had died in a fatal accident during a rescue mission on the infamous Eiger north face. She had been just ten years old at the time, and remembered holding her mother's hand as they followed the coffin. She saw herself from far above, as if it had been yesterday, as she resisted looking down into the grave. Instead, she had looked up toward the sky, where the blanket of clouds had torn apart to reveal a beautiful clear sky, in the shape of a plane. Papa was in heaven now, the adults had said consolingly. So why should she stare into a deep, dark hole in the ground?

Sophie had reached the start of the concrete track, which had been built as a tank training runway for the nearby barracks, and was open to the public for bicycling, running and roller blading when not in use. This morning she was met by a freshly hosed down raceway, not a soul ahead of her; the troops would presumably not show up with their caterpillar monsters until later.

She moves evenly, swinging her arms rhythmically, gradually gaining speed. Her breath is regular, her thoughts begin to wander...

Le Bourget, Paris, a year ago... How old might he be? She had tried to do the math once.

He had fought in Lebanon... Yorini, his son must have been about twenty-five... Who cares. What did it matter? He wasn't old as far as she was concerned. Shuky Nachman could have been her father. Why not? Teenagers flirt with their fathers. She had missed out on all that.

There was that story, which no one wanted to believe when she told it. Cinderella? What an imagination, right?

But the whole thing really had been like a fairy tale. A hard rain poured down on the runway, pounding on the ugly Russian helicopters and the elegant Pilatus machines, dripping from the sagging tarpaulin sheets of the tent that Sophie was racing toward. Futilely holding a little umbrella against the wind, she tripped on a cable that had been torn loose. She lost her footing, was barely able to catch herself, then finally reached refuge under one of the tarps. She backed up against the huddle of tightly packed men, who were also trying to get out of the rain. It was something that she would only otherwise have done if she was trying to squeeze onto an overcrowded subway in Manhattan, to get in just far enough to evade the closing doors. She was soaked, her blouse clung to her skin, her skirt to her thighs. Her feet felt nothing but the wetness of this rather miserable day. Four Gripen fighters touched down in short succession. The announcements over the speakers were lost in the heavy downpour. As the last plane of the show formation rolled past in a spray of water, he had suddenly been standing in front of her.

His blond hair was streaming with water, but his smile had been warm.

"They're really too pretty to throw away, madam."

"I beg your pardon?"

"You do have lovely feet. I understand that you don't really need shoes."

She stared at the shoes, which he now held up to eye level—her expensive, burgundy moccasins. Then her astonished gaze had dropped to her bare feet.

She blushed. That darn cable. How embarrassing! "Oh…thank you so much…that was…I mean." She threw her hands up, looked at him with big eyes.

"I have a car, come," the gallant helper had said, saving the situation. With a winning smile, he had convincingly wrested an umbrella from a pilot who had been standing there. Ignoring the protest, he had gently grasped her arm and guided her forward. Protected by the large golf umbrella, they had waded across a strip of lawn toward a black Citroën, the locks of which opened automatically. She glimpsed the light leather of the seats and asked herself with a start whether she was being completely insane, getting into a stranger's car.

Then she looked over at him from the side. Rakishly handsome, she found. With a disarming smile, he placed her shoes in her lap. "Shuky. My friends call me Shuky."

The tank track now lies completely dry before her. The mountain snowfall has not yet reached the plains. Carpe Diem! Yes, she has every reason to enjoy her carefree, independent lifestyle…*pourvu que ça dure,* she calls out boisterously—only to look behind herself, a little amused at her own silliness, just to make sure nobody has heard.

Then she spots him—tall, in skintight blue-and-white workout gear he is coming up behind her. Sophie hates being passed, picks up her pace. She pushes off powerfully, her whole body in tune with the movement. She is only wearing tight shorts and a top, no helmet or pads. She feels as safe and comfortable on these skates as she does in the air with a control stick. She skillfully commands every technique, every muscle in her body, yet the man is catching up. She feels him on her heels; feels his eyes on her back.

Order within chaos, she remembers Shuky Nachman's maxim, as she rounds a turn and the sports planes, business jets, haulers and biplanes come into view. She now senses her pursuer drawing level. He pulls past almost effortlessly, briefly raises his hand in a greeting as he does—and leaves her behind. Without even catching her eye—in true skater fashion. To add insult to injury, appearances indicate that he is not exactly the youngest. Annoyed, she redoubles her efforts to pick up the pace, but she simply cannot catch up with the damn guy. Breathing hard, she gives up, falling back into her more natural rhythm.

Sophie arrived back at the square to cool down after her forty-five minute workout, pretty exhausted. Mr. Lightning was there, acknowledging her this time, with glinting oval eyes. Was the insolent louse mocking her? *Ha, I left you in the dust!* A cloud moved over the sun, and put an end to the glint.

Sophie really was in great shape, had always placed among the top in public competitions. She had even made it to the top ten at this year's inline marathon—and then this guy just comes and . . . Still fuming at the hammering, she stepped into the pilot's room in the hangar, threw her sports bag onto the bench in front of the lockers. Standing under the hot shower, she finally couldn't help but grin about her anger. Forget about it!

The Swiss Jet dispatch manager looked up in surprise when Ms. Kramer turned up behind the monitors with slightly damp hair, wearing an elegant dark red blazer and black trousers.

"Hi, Carlo, good morning. Mmm, is that fresh coffee I smell?"

The man in question grinned from ear to ear, stroked the memory of hair on his bald head. "The smell of coffee is as wonderful as the scent of a lovely lady."

Serving herself, Sophie gamely responded: "And one can never get enough of either, right? Tell me, who left on the 328 early this morning?"

Carlo raised an index finger admonishingly. "Passenger information is confidential, Ms. Kramer."

"I know, but it would be good to know if my boss was on there."

"Ponter? Are you in trouble with him?"

"No, but he asked me to look into his invoice. Where was he headed?"

The dispatcher sighed. "Vienna."

The golden-brown coffee poured into the little cup. Sophie added a bit of sugar, stirred with a miniature espresso spoon and quickly took in the data that Carlo had caused to appear on the screen.

"I really came to book a training flight. I was down on the runway, working out." She motioned outside with her arm.

"Any time. You don't need a reason to drop by. How about the P68?"

Sophie nodded and held the cup gingerly to her raspberry lips, sipped contentedly. She was only too happy to go up in the twin engine Vulcan Air.

"Day after tomorrow, after eight suit you?"

She took another sip, smiled and nodded in agreement.

Air traffic had picked up outside. Phones buzzed in the dispatch room, messengers delivered mail.

"Didn't you have Nachman's plane under contract at one point?"

Carlo looked up from his monitor with mild interest. "Shuky, the Israeli? At least he can still afford his machine. A ton of business jets are up for sale right now because of the financial crisis."

"Are you servicing it?"

"Not yet, of course." He laughed a bit sourly. Adding, in response to Sophie's look of puzzlement, "We haven't been able to agree on the cost. You know his type, always haggling, everything for nothing—typical."

His grin died back with the change in Sophie's expression. "Typical how, Carlo?" she asked archly, annoyed by her own tone the moment she said it. She just really liked Shuky, didn't care for anyone speaking ill of him. His manner captivated her.

Shuky was so kind in his approach to her, so cuttingly cold and ruthless in his dealings with adversaries. He didn't look Jewish. His sophisticated lifestyle was pleasantly refined. His versatility, combined with a kind of charming shrewdness, made him unique in her eyes. This Swiss Jet guy had better watch himself! Wait! Why am I getting all worked up over him?

"Well, you just ask yourself how he makes his money. No one can earn that much honestly. People like that always stick together . . . but what do I care?"

Sophie adopted a wide stance, hands on her hips. "If you don't care, Carlo, then it might be good to just shut up about it, I would say. Nachman is . . . Nachman is a good man. If you don't want his business, I'll be glad to tell him for you." She turned on her heel and strode out.

Did I offend her with my big mouth? The chastened dispatch manager moaned as the glass door slammed shut behind Ms. Kramer.

Ken Cooper, who was no longer a spring chicken, stood, unceremoniously panting his lungs out. He really deserved a slap on the head, he felt; exerting himself like that just to catch up with that tantalizing chick, to get a closer look . . . to get past her and prove that his old bones were still in shape. Laughable. On the other hand, he could imagine that the woman, whom he had been watching for a while now, was involved in criminal activity.

Grimly rubbing his aching thighs, the CIA agent in the blue-and-white outfit watched her disappear between the hangars.

About a year ago, he and Marcel Dulliker, who headed the Services for Analysis and Prevention (SAP), in the justice department had agreed on the new assignment and been given a team of six men for support.

The secret service mission targeted a John Ponter—a confirmed criminal, according to the police.

The banker, who had grown successful in Zurich, was mysteriously linked to two brutal murders in Frankfurt and Lausanne. Evidence pointed to a connection between the cases. For one, both victims had been involved in weapons trading; for another, they both owed the Ponter Bank significant amounts of money.

The agent drank greedily from the green water bottle, sat down on a low wall and removed his skates. It had not taken him long to conclude that the murders had been planned by the same individual, and professionally executed. Being an intelligence agent, his interest in this case focused on different facets than those that were of most concern to the colleagues conducting the criminal investigation. His job was to establish the nature of Ponter's ties to politically connected individuals, who threatened stability and security in the Middle East with illegal arms deals.

He had effortlessly established that Sophie Kramer's life had been both tragic and straightforward. Having grown up without a father, she had been independent at an early age, before suffering a second blow—the mother had died of an insidious disease. Cooper reckoned that Sophie, as was so often the case, yearned for a father figure. It seemed plausible that she could be vulnerable to subjecting herself to a macho character like Ponter, and follow him blindly.

One of the men on Cooper's team had traced her brilliant academic career—starting as a physics student in Zurich, then going on to study economics in St. Gallen, and finishing with a year at Columbia University in New York. There was also mention of a study visit in Moscow. The report did not mention how much of her time she may have spent cavorting through the skies instead of keeping her attractive bottom obediently glued to a lecture hall seat.

Cooper had learned of her passion for flying in an aviation magazine, which routinely published articles by a certain Sophie Kramer on the topic of daring test flights.

She has to be in good shape, he mused, kneading his calf. *So, why hadn't she caught up with him? Probably just feminine tactics. The woman was not to be underestimated. What had they warned him about again? Ah, yes. Close combat. Apparently she also practiced one of those Chinese martial arts—Gong Fu, Qui Gong, Tai Chi?*

After earning her post-graduate degree in New York, Kramer had ended up first on the Russia desk, and then in the Middle East department of a large bank, where her job had been to research economic developments in Arabic countries. Then she had suddenly taken on a leading position at the Ponter Bank. Cooper shook out his aching legs, limped back to his car. Why Ponter? Cooper wanted to know the answer to this, and two other questions: How long had they known each other, and did this woman who was proficient in martial arts also know her way around knives and pistols? Should she be considered a suspect in the murders? He privately hoped that the latter was not the case. Somehow it didn't seem to fit in with her background . . .

The parking lot was at a bit of a distance, where it was screened from the runways by an earthen mound. At first, Sophie was not conscious of the three guys who stood with their heads together next to a van. She opened her hatchback, threw her gear inside, placed her neatly folded blazer next to her sports bag. As she closed the trunk, then turned toward the driver's side, keys in hand, they were suddenly there: standing around her in a tight semicircle, stupid grins on their faces.

Sophie immediately sensed the danger. How often had she imagined situations like these? An assault in broad daylight, a stone's throw away from monitored buildings, not a soul in sight. One read about these things all the time.

But a gang rape in the middle of a populated area, here at the airport?

"Hi there," the tall one grinned. He was wearing a baseball cap back to front. "We're going to have a little fun together, aren't we?" He wet his lips, grabbed his crotch and gave it a firm jerk, causing his buddies to giggle.

"Yeah, a nice little threesome, you know," his much shorter, pudgy friend next to him grunted, then clicked his tongue and stepped closer. Behind him, a dark, bald guy leaned against the side of the van, making obscene gestures with his hands.

Sophie remained calm, raised her chin. "Get out of my way and go home to your mommies, boys." She opened the driver's-side door.

"Sorry, little lady, that's not going to happen," the tall one said mockingly, pressing the door shut with his knee. He grabbed Sophie's blouse and tore at it until buttons came undone. Sophie swatted his hand off. Her eyes blazed as she said, now in a sharper tone: "Don't touch me, you little shit. Now get out of here like good boys."

The dark-skinned one tore open the side door to the van. "Come on, get the little whore in here."

Now was the time. Sophie saw the sequence: it was crystal clear. She knew what would happen next. She had often practiced for situations like these. Been drilled for them. She felt each of her tensing muscles, the warm, powerful rush of adrenaline.

When the tall oaf roughly grabbed her arm, slurring something she was unable to catch, she landed a solid punch to his solar plexus, followed it with a palm strike to the chin. It was pretty classic stuff, but effective— the blows sent him reeling back into a parked motorcycle, which he fell on as it went down.

She grabbed the chunky one's arm as he grasped at her hair, and sent him crashing into the gravel with an expert shoulder throw. Turning swiftly to face the third, she found the dark-skinned one was holding a shiny blade in his fist. He waved the knife menacingly. There was no doubt that he knew what he was doing.

Sophie jumped back, was on the hood of her Mini in the blink of an eye, then on its roof.

She had managed to startle the bald guy, who now approached, poking at her legs with the knife. Suddenly, she took off and launched a kick straight to his face, sending him back against the side of the van with a scream. His head made solid contact, and he sank to the ground, dazed.

A second round followed. The guys angrily picked themselves up, cursing, all three of them at once. The fight was rough, Sophie's blows were harder, her kicks hit their targets, two of their skulls cracked against each other...Sophie was prepared for more. Having gotten in the swing of things, she resumed her stance, scanning for the next target, breathing heavily. The tall one was crouched down, holding his crotch. The fat one lay whimpering in the dust; while the dark-skinned one was awkwardly attempting to crawl into the back of the van. Was he going for a gun?

Sophie picked up the knife and threw it across the mound in a high arch. She got in her car and drove off. Her wrists ached a bit—apparently she was a little out of shape.

Zurich, Dolder Golf Club

The longer Sophie Kramer pored over the file at her desk the next morning, the firmer she grew in her determination to help the likable lord of an Engadin castle out of his predicament. Radovan Suvorov may well have lost his wife's fortune on unfortunate speculations—he had encumbered their real estate too heavily during the good times. Now that banks across the globe were calling in debts in order to maintain their liquidity, he was faced with financial ruin.

She approached the clubhouse quite engrossed in her thoughts. Her recovery proposition would help both sides—the bank would receive cash, and Suvorov would be able to hold his castle property.

It did have to be said that she was better versed in matters of aviation than of real estate. Of this, she understood only that its value generally remained stable, and that good locations, such as St. Moritz, had become almost unaffordable.

Having reached the clubhouse, she swung the golf bag from her shoulder, rubbed her wrists. Not a whisper of an ache. Yesterday's brawl would not be affecting her handicap. She had decided to report the incident to airport security at some point. For now she inspected her golf attire, picked up the bag with the shiny clubs.

She had really imagined Klaus Quadrini quite differently. On the lookout for an older, graying gentleman, she had already walked straight past him on the small club house terrace.

"Ms. Kramer?"

Sophie turned, startled, to find herself looking at the rather youthful face of someone in his late forties. "Yes?"

"Quadrini," he said as he clasped her hand in a strong handshake. "I'm here a bit early. Wanted to hit a few balls before our game. Pleased to meet you."

"Likewise, Mr. Quadrini." She examined him in a way that women sometimes do, when their minds have already moved on from matters at hand to those of a more sensual nature. Quadrini seemed to sense this instinctively. He smiled in a friendly manner, his eyes briefly resting on her full lips.

She extracted herself from his magnetic appeal with a jolt. "Almost time to head out."

A little later as he readied himself for the first drive, Sophie took the opportunity to discreetly check out the man who had entrusted Ponter with his millions. Over a meter eighty tall, she guessed, short, blond hair, a little ashy around the temples, tanned face. The green-checked material of his pants stretched rather pleasingly across his trim, firm bottom.

Sophie's eyes remained fixed as Quadrini shifted his hips to optimize his stance. Suddenly he turned, as if he had felt her gaze.

"I'd prefer if you stood here. Across from me." He pointed to the other side of the ball.

"Of course." Sophie complied. The man looked pretty good from this angle, too. Sadly, he hit the ball a bit too high. Not a perfect shot. The trajectory was off, sending it into the tall grass adjacent to the next green, where it disappeared from sight. Quadrini wasted no words on his poor start.

Sophie felt a bit uncertain as she teed up to take her shot, slid back and forth on the short grass to optimize her stance. *Oh, what in the hell does it matter?* She swung back high, connected solidly with the ball. A light, dry sound confirmed this. Indeed, the ball followed a beautiful, long curve and landed directly on the green, close to the red flag, where it rolled to a halt.

"Good shot," Quadrini noted a bit dryly.

They made their way toward the green. "Thank you. Have you played here before?"

"Years ago, when the Dolder still had its original splendor."

With a hint of regret, Quadrini looked beyond the low club house and up at the hotel, with its newly added wings that framed the venerable stone building with its charming turrets like a pair of stylishly cropped ears.

"It's a lovely hotel," Sophie said with a smile. They had quickly settled into the kind of banter that serves mediocre golf players as a band-aid for moments of awkwardness in their game. Continuing the pleasant small talk, Quadrini made up for his initial blunder on his second drive, which he sent on its way over the undulating fairway and toward the forest edge with a tremendously powerful swing. The two watched its flight intently. Too far?

"Not out of bounds, I hope," Quadrini grumbled.

The caddie raised his hand to signal that the ball was in play. Sophie kept up, scoring a bogey.

"This is the oldest course in the region. It first opened a hundred years ago," she mentioned as they were contemplating the view of the city and lake before the next drive. Quadrini nodded appreciatively. "It's nice to have a golf course practically in the middle of town."

Should I broach the subject? Sophie pondered at the beginning of the fourth. What she had to do now was get her ball onto the green and as close as possible to the hole with a short approach. She was hesitant about barging ahead. The client was visibly content, and if Kleiber was right, he would blindly approve anything she put in front of him. Better to let sleeping dogs lie, she decided, and promptly shanked the shot. A botched hole.

She didn't win a hole until the fifth, when Quadrini put his ball clear across the water hazard and into the tree line, earning him a penalty.

"The land we are playing on is municipal. The club has merely leased it. When the contract eventually expires, the city might open the golf course to the public."

"I hardly think so. That would really be the height of stupidity," said Quadrini, looking appraisingly up at the beautifully renovated Grand Hotel.

They were speaking less now, concentrating on their game. Their shots took straight lines, landing more precisely.

"It's all downhill," Quadrini established as he reached the beginning of the eighth hole and looked down a slight slope toward the hole.

"Do you see the sand trap?"

Quadrini turned around, smiling. "I'm not talking about the golf course. I'm talking about my investments. Which are doing very poorly."

He placed the tee along with the ball, straightened up. He swung without much preparation and hit the ball with an angry force that belied his pleasant expression. The shot was perfect. Straight and true. Sophie stepped forward, stretched her neck to follow its course, watched it land in the middle of the green, where it came to an almost immediate halt. She was slightly dazed by the suddenness of this confrontation.

The man clearly knew what was going on. Not surprising, really. It had been naive to believe that she could simply pull one over on him. How dumb of her to take Kleiber's talk at face value. She swung hard, her iron making an impressive divot, but not the best contact with the ball, which had too little drive and landed far short and off into the bushes.

"Sorry. I put you off your game. Take another shot." Ever the gentleman, Quadrini smiled charmingly, as if nothing had occurred.

"Okay." Sophie repositioned herself, took a deep breath, took a practice shot. This time she swung too high, Quadrini thought, and was far too hasty on the follow-through. Sure enough, she hacked into the ground once again, even harder this time, sending clumps of earth flying impressively. The ball, on the other hand, hopped just a few meters, then rolled over an embankment into no-man's-land. The caddie signaled "Out." How exasperating.

But Sophie did not lose her cool. No excuses—that was rule number one. It was gauche to whine about poor performance in golf, just as it was to whine about injuries in tennis.

"Sorry," she said breezily. Quadrini made an understanding gesture.

"Please. It happens to everyone."

She smiled mischievously. "I wasn't talking about my shot, Mr. Quadrini. I was talking about your investments."

They looked into each other's eyes. He gave a smile of recognition. The tension dissipated somewhat, allowing Sophie to find her game. "No one could have predicted what happened in America," she reckoned as they approached the next hole.

"We have a proposition on how we can make good on the losses with some interestingly structured products."

She had barely uttered the sentence that Kleiber had fed her when she felt an almost overwhelming urge to bite her tongue. It had sounded utterly specious. And it didn't take Quadrini a New York second to start poking.

"The bank has blown a good twenty million of mine. You'll never make good on a fraction of that. And do you know why they refer to these new products as structured?"

"Structured products are financial derivatives," Sophie said. "Capital protection coupled with returns."

"But in reality, the structure is a pretty box that contains a product. You sell the client a box, but they are really buying the content. The content is what it's all about—just like the core of an atom. That is where the bank makes its killing."

"I can't see that there is anything illegitimate about that."

"Only if everything is transparent. Not if the structure is actually a smoke screen. You count on us clients to be impressed by superficial appearances, unable to really able to grasp the entirety of the concept. Because it's so sophisticated...or complicated we think it's all legit. But it's all artful deceit."

"Aren't you a bit unfair, Mr. Quadrini? Ponter products are good. Our financial experts are top of the line, we offer our clients innovative investment opportunities, and..." Sophie stopped talking as Quadrini took his club and approached the tee. Then it was her turn. The thread of the touchy topic appeared to be mercifully lost with the sharp ascent of her ball.

"I'm changing banks," he said at the twelfth hole. His voice was calm, but clearly audible. "There's no point in discussing it later. Not that I'd mind a drink at the hotel bar, quite to the contrary, but our business is done. I'm done with Ponter. I'm sorry, Sophie." He paused adroitly. "Although I could certainly picture having a structured evening with you."

"Now, now..." She wagged her finger at him teasingly. Rascal, she wanted to say. But that seemed a little bold.

"Does the bank know of your decision? I mean, apart from me?"

He shook his head, looking at her pensively. He had better keep what he was thinking to himself. He wouldn't put anything past Ponter. She sank a ball from fifteen meters, but brushed aside her golfing companion's praise.

"I don't feel like playing anymore. Shall we head back?"

He nodded. *The whole thing had taken a not-so-good turn,* Quadrini mused. *In the end, she would probably be the one to suffer, this refreshing, professional young woman.* But he was left with no choice. Ponter had to be dealt with. Did Ms. Kramer know about the precious artwork housed in the bank's vault? The German businessman was struck by a sense of foreboding.

At the clubhouse he promised to call her to make further plans for dinner.

"Around nine, if nothing comes up," he promised with a warm smile. Really, he had already decided that he was definitely having dinner with her at the Dolder Grand Restaurant. And then let the chips fall where they may...

Castelberg Castle, St. Moritz

Baron Radovan Suvorov of Castelberg walked slowly across the dark, creaking wood floor, his figure stooped. He paused, looked dimly up at the painting of the blessed General Suvorov, who gazed into the distance with a look of bold determination. Radovan had inherited his distinctive long nose. He, too, had once worn rebellious locks. But Radovan had long ago lost the adventurousness that marked his legendary ancestor's refined, lively features. Outside, the icy west winds rattled Castelberg Castle's old shutters and swept relentlessly across the frozen lake. Baron Radovan believed he also saw a hint of something roguish in the portrait. If he could have spoken, the general looked as though he probably would have treated Radovan to one of his pithy dictums.

"Prepare with diligence, fight with ease," Radovan said out loud, quoting the great commander. He took a seat at the same desk upon which Chief of Staff Rosenberg had spread a tattered map in Glarus, October of 1799, and proceeded to explain to his commander the desperate situation.

General Suvorov, who had never yet lost a battle, had stood erectly, listened carefully, his hand draped—just as it was depicted in the portrait—in his signature, casual fashion, over the back of a chair. The French general Masséna had cut off his retreat. There had been no other option than to brave the impossible route across the Alps and into the Rhine Valley.

Baron Radovan sighed and rubbed the fingers of his hands, which had become gnarled with age. The precious ring was as it had been on the large painting—only the general's hand had been slender and unmarred, lightly holding a pair of white gloves. In contrast to the decorated hero on the painting, Radovan had lost almost every battle of his life. Lydia von Castelberg had firmly held the marital reins and controlled the family fortune just as tightly. If indeed it deserved to be called a family...

She had utterly despised him. And when she had finally told him that she had fallen pregnant, after all those years, her eyes had held a glint of cold, mocking triumph that he would never forget. He knew all too well, of course, that he could not have been the father.

There had been no sex between the married couple for years, but he did remember how he had amused himself wondering who the hell would actually have gotten into bed with her—if it had even been a bed! Who had played the cavalry captain to ride her, and what might the hairy matron have paid for the pleasure? Radovan shuddered at the thought. But the grotesque comedy had ended in tragedy. His wife had lost the baby in the third month of her pregnancy.

Now Radovan held the elegant black fountain pen, inspected its silver nib. He scratched a few practice lines on a scrap, then positioned the cream-colored, hand-crafted paper, cleared his throat, and wrote in a flowing, dark-blue script…VON CASTELBERG CASTLE…added the date. A warmth suffused his chest as he wrote her name:

Dear Sophie, finally I have found the time to write…He paused, looked pensively up at the portrait. The old general had taught his soldiers to attack decisively and without hesitation. *Advance fearlessly, with a thrust of cold steel!*

He had often imagined it in his dreams—the thrust of a cold blade—and had never been daring enough. But when Lydia had faltered at the top of the landing, had fallen down the entire length of the hard stairs, he had been gripped by a curiously pleasant paralysis. He had done nothing. Instead, he had turned ever so slowly and retired to the library…this, the one and only battle he had finally won in the end. A darkness resided within every soul.

There was a knock on the door. Without turning his head, he called: "Yes, come in."

The woman stepped timidly to clear the tray with the glass and empty plate. Her voice had a pleasant tone. "Do you desire anything else, Mr. von Suvorov?"

He looked briefly at her warm, comely face, considered the white, starched blouse stretched over an ample bosom, the dark blue skirt with stitched lace and silver buttons.

"Samantha," he flirted, "you are a sight for sore eyes, as always."

"Sir, you are too kind."

He smiled meaningfully. "The sum of all vices is constant."

Teasingly, she raised an admonishing finger. "Oh, you and your little sayings," she said and walked out, hips swaying, knowing that his eyes would be following her.

He continued to write, contentedly…*I very much enjoyed our meeting. You opened my eyes. Much has changed following the death of my wife. She bequeathed most of her share of the estate to charity. She had no children. I was left with the burdens inherent to owning the castle which, exceptionally located in the magnificent Engadin, is nevertheless a bottomless pit in terms of upkeep. My deceased* . . . How should he put it? Dragon? Xanthippe? Chuckling to himself, he continued . . . *wife had let things go for too long. Of the art, I was at least left with the Rothko, certainly a gem, and the Suvorov portrait. Mark Rothko and Alexander Suvorov, two Russians. I have now decided to proceed as discussed. Samantha, my housekeeper, has the contact information of my daughter, who* . . . how to put it? . . . was born out of wedlock? . . . Natalie had remained his secret, Lydia had never known about the affair . . . *I wish to* . . .

It seemed he had heard a creaking of floorboards. He sensed a cold draft around his legs. Samantha? Why hadn't she knocked?

He looks up and sees her standing next to him. He has never seen this woman before. She is wearing heavy winter boots, a broad belt around her waist—a modern young thing. She is smiling a smile that doesn't want to suit her face. Her wiry body is transmitting a very different signal: I'm here to have some fun with you, you old fossil. Now he sees that she is holding a kitchen knife.

"Who the devil—"

She grabs his chin with lightning speed, pulls his head over the back of the chair with great force. Radovan punches upward, as hard as he can, trying to hit her in the face, to dig his fingers into her eyes. The woman jumps easily aside, tightens her grip expertly. She yanks his head up brutally, rests the cold blade against his neck. In the surreal moment of mortal fear, the expression on the face of the general in the painting appears as one of sudden horror. Cold steel . . .

With a single brutish motion, she severs his windpipe. The old gentleman falls forward, gasping his final rattling breaths. Before she leaves the room, she callously lifts his flaccid arm. Not, however, to feel for a pulse. There isn't one.

She straightens Suvorov's ring finger onto the antique wood of the desk, leaving the others bent against the edge. She positions the blade, leans the entire weight of her body forward, and severs what she wants.

Near Vaduz, principality of Liechtenstein

Manfred Kleiber drove his Audi across the Rhine Bridge into the principality of Liechtenstein.

His phone rang once again on the hands-free Bluetooth connection. He glanced at the caller ID: Ponter Bank. His office. He let it ring. They were looking for him, and they'd just have to keep looking—because they would never find him. He chuckled inwardly as he pulled into the parking lot on the other side of the Rhine. He got out, took a few steps toward the riverbank, clambered down toward the water on thin soles. The fresh air felt good on his face.

"Fresh air, new life," he called out to a heron, which startled, spread its elegant wings and rose above the water in flight. Kleiber took the battery out of his phone and tossed it, along with the casing, in a wide arch into the river. Conscientious as he was, he would have preferred to recycle the battery. A sense of duty defined him, had been his life. For a long time—too long—he had given best years of his life to the bank, served his boss loyally, arrived punctually, worked through the night compliantly when the quarterlies were due—had always been the good, subservient sheep.

His mother had probably caused the change in him. She had invited him to come along to a mission community prayer meeting one dreary Sunday.

"Manfred," she had said with fervor, "the right way is often stony and circuitous."

It was out of love for her that he had not disagreed. Mother was deeply rooted in her faith. She often let him sense her anguish over the fact that he had sold his soul to Mammon.

"You worship the golden calf, Manfred." She had never understood his choice to work for a bank. And what she didn't understand, she deemed as sinister, not what God wanted.

He had ended up nodding off during the prayer gathering of the sect. The soft mutterings, the gloomy incantations, the musty, mothball odor of the room: all of this was certainly not his thing. His mother elbowed him in indignant fright when he let out a sharp snore.

What do all these little people bowing their heads in humility do in their daily lives? He surreptitiously looked to his left, then to his right. Stooped figures, deeply lined faces, grim lips; beaming eyes, and also eyes filled with dejection.

Blessed are those who believe—the church is certainly blessed with their funds.

The contrast to his luxurious working environment, in the golden temple that was the bank, could not have been starker. He felt nauseous, and it wasn't the stuffiness that was causing it. These people lurked in the shadows of life, and at the end of it all even their priest would take advantage of them. The knowledge made him feel a sickening kind of guilt. He imagined them toiling their lives away, accepting—always accepting—hardship, giving their meager savings to their preacher, while on the other hand wealthy dirt bags like Ponter aided other obscenely rich dirt bags to hide their money from the tax authorities. Quadrini, Nedjew, and their ilk. If that all didn't scream injustice, then he just didn't know.

The sermon had finally ended. Only one message remained, and rankled:

…*Children, for those who place their faith in worldly gains, again I tell you: It is easier for a camel to pass through the eye of a needle than for a rich man to enter the kingdom of God.*

So annoying, always the same sanctimonious crap.

Kleiber balked at the thought that wealth should be bad, and why should someone who had earned his wealth not be allowed into heaven? *The poor are the only ones who are just in this church that exists but for the grace of the rich.* As the final hymn droned to a finish Kleiber was relieved that the torture of sitting still on the hard bench was over, and that the grinding millstones of faith were ready to spit him back out into the fresh air of a now brighter Sunday morning.

He had found himself plagued by a thought the next morning—one, it seemed to him, that the Sunday preacher had planted like an insidious seed inside his brain. Had it been a seed, for which his mother had dragged him to the prayer meeting—was it now sprouting because she had been right all along about him needing to turn his life around?

According to his mother, all things had a deeper meaning. Thus one should not judge, and take them as they come. Well, Kleiber was still a pragmatist who believed in arranging things so that they would come as he wanted to take them. This is what had helped him to reach his decision to finally make the call.

It had not been an easy decision, nevertheless. He had waited until the evening. It had taken several attempts to key in the number, which that nice guy had handed him at the Rimini Bar at an after-work party after a few beers...

"Hi, Manfred, how are you? Good to see you."

Kleiber flinched as the reality hit. There he was, in the flesh: the nice guy, standing right there on the bank. Just as he had at the bar, Gregor Zack quickly anesthetized his apprehensions with a warm smile.

They sat in Kleiber's Audi. The smile had now left Gregor's eyes. Their talk had turned to business, and Kleiber distinctly felt that he saw malice in Gregor's hard features.

"We checked the data. Fantastic, I would say. Do you have the rest?"

"I do. But I want the money we agreed on first. And the papers."

Gregor pursed his lips derisively. "Of course. One thing at a time." He reached into his jacket pocket, produced an envelope. "A Namibian passport, completely authentic. Be sure to remember the name and details."

Kleiber pored over the document, studied it, the picture, the information, dates. "Peter Miller..."

"Many Namibians are of German heritage."

"What else is in there?"

"Your booking, an electronic ticket. You'll be taking a flight via London to Johannesburg, as agreed."

"Good." Kleiber heaved his bag onto his knees and dug out a carefully wrapped package. "Here, the remaining data. A complete listing of accounts over the past two years."

"Hmmm." Gregor was suddenly holding a switchblade. The knife sprung open, and he waved it in front of Kleiber's face warningly.

"What the hell are you doing?" The threatened man shrank back in his seat, shocked.

"If you try to pull one over on us, I will find you. Always. Whatever rock you crawl under. I want you to understand that." With a mocking smile, Gregor used the knife to slice open the package. He pocketed the contents without a word, placed a slender case on Kleiber's knees. "The remaining money, Manfred. Take care of yourself. And remember, we will always know how to find you."

He heaved his large frame from the vehicle. When Kleiber turned just a moment later, Gregor had already disappeared. He let out a sharp breath. His shirt clung to his skin. He carefully opened the case with trembling hands. It was filled to the rim with neatly packed bills. Pink five hundreds, green hundreds, old and new, just as agreed.

Everything was now going according to plan. He would return to Sargans in Switzerland, give mother the case, drop the rental car off at the airport a few hours later, then board the flight to London.

Feeling a good deal lighter, he typed the number into his new cell phone, waited for the call to be picked up, burst forth: "Mother, every-thing went well... yes, listen..." He told her that he would be leaving now, and to meet him at the train station, as arranged, in forty-five minutes.

In the white van, behind which BND special agent Gregor Zack had disappeared, an improvised cell phone antenna had received Kleiber's call; the data had been instantly captured, saved, and conveyed to the provider's server.

Steiner's people of the LIM subdivision weren't in the least interested in the Swiss man's blathering. They noted the number of his new phone, as well as that to which the call was made. From now on, they would know with whom he spoke, and where he was.

Manfred Kleiber had almost forgotten the white envelope. He drove into Vaduz, stopped in front of the post office, got out, and dropped it in the box. But not without first running a tender hand across its surface, and checking once more the recipient's address: Sophie Kramer... 8008 Zurich.

Zurich, Main Station

Around the same time that Sophie Kramer was sinking her fifteen-meter shot on the golf course, a tall, athletically slender woman with high cheek bones and a brush-cut was exiting the small hotel just a short distance behind Zurich's main railway station. The overcast weather was to her liking. The streets glistened with rain. People scuttled by, tucked beneath their umbrellas. Nobody had the time or inclination to notice her rather imposing frame. Nobody saw her deftly toss her cell phone under the wheels of the passing blue and white bus. She had made her contacts, received her new instructions—and now she disposed of the phone as always. Her golden rule was: Leave no trace!

The listless young man at reception had taken down her details on the registration form around midnight without question. Ms. X, Lausanne address, Swiss nationality, had given him no reason to ask for ID—the law mandated official identification from foreign nationals only.

If the need had arisen, the lady had been prepared to show an ID with the name X. As always, she was well prepared.

She stopped in front of the display of a store that sold cutlery, which was located in the railway station's underground shopping passage. She browsed, went on to look at the high leather boots in a neighboring boutique, strolled past the bookstore, making sure all the while that she was not being followed. Only then did she return to the shop with the knives and enter. She took an interest in the military models, checked the blades of carving knives then finally settled on something that suited her purpose.

"We offer complimentary sharpening on all of our knives," the gaunt salesperson informed her, as he extracted the fitting box and placed it on the counter. She laid down a few bills. "No box, thank you. Just wrap it."

The clerk eyed the trim figure as she left, cocked his head appraisingly, wouldn't have minded doing that hot little number, who evidently had an eye for a good blade. She, on the other hand, was perfectly aware of his body language, of every thought on his mind, for that matter. A crude little idiot with big ideas. Out of view of his covetous stare, she deposited the long blade in the usual place in her corduroy pants, took the escalator back up to the bustling street level, and disappeared in the crowd.

Zurich, The Dolder Grand

The woman with the brush-cut and the large sunglasses that hid her impenetrable eyes averted her face as she handed the taxi driver the money. Not waiting for change, she got out beneath the taxi awning and stepped toward the door. She did not wish to be delivered to the ostentatious main entrance of the Dolder Grand, preferring the discreet rear access. From here, a bright passage led past the long wall of windows of the great ballroom to the elegantly curved spa wing.

The woman had little interest in physical improvement measures of the type that were available here. She was in exquisite shape. Her taut cheeks gave her face a sharp predatory look. Her well-trained muscles were prepared to meet any type of athletic demand. She calmly strolled past the jewelry and purse displays to the elevators, descended silently to the bright spa lobby.

She looked at the large, black marble pool with obvious admiration, before casually making her way to the reception desk.

"What lovely facilities you have here," she said, not removing her glasses.

"Welcome, ma'am. Is this your first time with us?"

A lurid smile flashed across her features. "I have just arrived. Quadrini." She commandingly motioned her chin to the monitor behind the desk. Julia, the young German clerk, promptly keyed in the name.

"May I bring you a robe and slippers, Mrs. Quadrini?"

"Yes, please..."

She waited, took the proffered bundle, started toward the changing rooms.

"Oh, Julia, one more thing..." she remarked, turning abruptly and almost bumping into an older gentleman. "Oops, pardon. My husband isn't back yet. He was not sure if he was quite happy with our room and was thinking he might want to have it changed. I don't know...perhaps you could check for me?"

"No problem, Mrs. Quadrini."

The employee tucked an unruly strand of her blond hair behind her ear, focused on the screen. "We have you in room 225 and, no, it doesn't look like any changes were made."

"Thank you, yes, that's fine then." A malignantly determined look settled behind her dark glasses as she turned away, leaving Julia to assist the gray-haired gentleman.

In the hotel room Klaus Quadrini held his cheek with the finger of one hand, with the other he meticulously drew the razor down through the thick layer of shaving foam. He stood, bare-chested in the bathroom as he did this, occasionally squinting at the bearded face of the Iranian president in the flat-screen television inlay of the mirror, then repositioning the blade against his cheek to continue his ritual. The television now showed pristinely clear images of a military parade. Generals greeted him from the long stage, upon which the haggard president sat in statesman-like boredom, his face grim behind a scraggly beard.

The only weapon Quadrini was familiar with was a hunting rifle. He would never have been able to identify the rocket that was being driven past the first dignitaries as a Shihab-3. Just as he would not have known that this monstrosity was capable of reaching Turkey, over 1,300 kilometers away, as well as any other country in the Middle East. The heavy, camouflaged rocket transport vehicle did somewhat catch his interest. Out of habit, he counted its wheels. Eighteen. As the cab, which was decorated with the national flag reached the end of the stage, the image switched to a pretty face.

Quadrini reached for the small, universal remote to turn up the volume, in order to understand what the attractive speaker had to say. Judging by her animated expression, it had to be a sensational piece of reporting on the show of force being conducted by the mullahs. Quadrini really could hardly have cared less about the Iranian fanatics and their machinations. He was fascinated by the television spokesperson; her intelligent face reminded him agreeably of Sophie Kramer. A pleasant anticipation of their mutual dinner rose warmly in his chest.

He poked at the tiny volume control with a wet finger.

"...that Shihab-4 rockets are now being developed, which will have an estimated reach of at least two thousand kilometers. According to NATO..."

He set the volume back to mute, dabbed the remaining shaving cream from his face. The ringing of the doorbell sounded.

"Yes?" he called over his shoulder. No answer. Another ring.

Somewhat annoyed, Quadrini slapped the shaving utensils onto the counter, padded out of the bathroom, and through the short hallway of the tower room to the door. Had someone said "Room Service"? It couldn't be time for the turndown service, and he wasn't even dressed. Still wondering, he opened the door.

The knife was her weapon of choice—the last thing that Quadrini would see on this earth, was a flash not unlike that which a victim of a Shihab-4 might behold if that weapon was ever deployed...

Zurich, inside Ponter Bank SA

The following morning, Ponter irately banged the streamlined phone down in his penthouse office, stared through the glass façade, across the rooftops to the gray lake that defined the edge of the city.

"Where is Kramer?" he yelled out to Rebecca, heatedly.

She stepped in gingerly. "Mr. Ponter, this gentleman insists that he has a personal delivery. He..."

A gangly bicycle courier, with a skewed cap and inane grin, pushed right past her without a care in the world, tossed a large envelope onto the desk. "I need a signature, please."

Ponter grumbled, signed, waved them both off irritably. He proceeded to carefully open the envelope, looked inside—the sight of the dismembered finger sent shockwaves through him. Albeit not entirely unpleasant ones. He deposited the envelope in the drawer with a taut smile.

Suvorov! Mission accomplished. I'll take a good look at the old general's ring later.

Two floors below, Sophie Kramer stood, receiver clenched between her head and shoulder. She arranged the Milan file, gathered her passport, credit cards, and travel itinerary and placed them back in her purse. Her mind was on Klaus Quadrini, however. She had found him very likable, so—why?

She had spent quite some time readying herself in her stylish loft the night before, in pleasant anticipation of dinner at the elegant restaurant. More than once, she had squinted over her bare shoulder into the mirror. The little black number looked good on her. Or was it a little risqué for a business dinner? She had resolutely banished the prudish concern. Then she had kicked her heels off again, slipped out of the dress and plopped, with a resigned sigh, on the side of her bed. For the second time that evening, she had dialed the number of the Dolder Grand. "Mr. Quadrini, please."

The front desk had put her call through to the room both times, but to no avail. Her dinner partner, key account customer and secret admirer, did not answer. The voice mail suggested she leave a message...

Now sitting in her office, she stared at the bare, gray wall. The little red light flashing on the phone signaled that her boss had tried to reach her. What had she done wrong?

She dialed Ponter's extension.

Monday mornings could be tricky. She had to pull herself together, be sure to somehow get the week off to a good start. The boss tended to be particularly coercive and fussy as the week began. Almost as if to reestablish dominion over his peons after any illusions of freedom that they may have harbored over the weekend, to bring them back to heel with a taste of iron discipline.

He stood me up, she would tell him. Ponter rudely preempted her. "Kramer. My office, immediately."

Kramer! That was not a good sign! She checked her hair, took her laptop under her arm, set herself in motion with a complete lack of enthusiasm.

Disappointed, she was still asking herself how Quadrini could have left her in the lurch that way. *How could he? Everything had been going well enough. Like a pathetic teenager, she had damn near called a third time!*

As she stepped into Ponter's office, he immediately started in on her, asking when she had last seen Quadrini.

The banker was seated at his document-strewn desk, fists clenched. Next to him Schindler, the bank's lawyer, sat sunken into a visitor's chair, strands of gray hair hanging listlessly on his brow. The far wall was dominated by a large, frameless oil painting featuring several enormous dollar signs depicted with dollops of paint against a rough green background. In spite of the apparent hopelessness of the situation, Sophie opted for a carefree tone. "On the golf course. Why?"

Ponter's face sagged like a week's worth of bad stock market news. "See for yourself!" he bellowed.

He gestured at a document Schindler placed on the desk. Sophie would not give him the satisfaction of seeing her looking at it. Ponter's voice sounded like the rumbling of ominous, distant thunder. "Quadrini has severed all business relations with the bank. Did you know anything about this?"

She lowered her gaze to her pointy shoes in an attempt to portray innocence, or at least virtue.

"Why did you not inform me of this?" Ponter's voice sounded terribly accusatory.

"I...I...Well, I wanted to see how the evening would go. He wanted to meet me. I hoped that I could...well, avert the worst."

Ponter slammed his fist on the desk. She jerked obligingly, once again proving the worth of her experience as an amateur actress.

"I, only I decide what should be done in a situation like this," he hissed. "You neglected your duties in the most unforgivable manner, Ms. Kramer." He nodded curtly at Schindler, who immediately rose to his full height and, with a subservient smile, produced a multi-page memo, which he now held up between his thumb and forefinger. "And then there is this, Ms. Kramer."

It was her written petition to allow Baron Suvorov of Castelberg Castle to sell his precious Rothko painting valued at sixty million, in order to enable the hard-pressed debtor to repay what he owed on his landed property in Engadin with the proceeds. The somewhat unfortunate thing was that she had not waited for Ponter's approval and, instead, had opted to clear the precious painting for sale on the bank's behalf.

Sophie crossed her arms mulishly. "The petition I submitted was very well-reasoned."

"I never received it," Ponter shot back, glancing quickly at the closing market rates.

"I sent you the memo by email."

"Perhaps you did," snapped Ponter, "and perhaps you didn't. What is certain is that your behavior is unacceptable. I deny ever seeing your alleged memo."

"Please, Mr. Ponter, there is a copy of it in the file with a handwritten note from you on it. My suggestion made complete sense. The sale of the Rothko will leave Suvorov with more than enough liquid assets to pay back the original loan along with all any accumulated interest. I am convinced that—"

Schindler pushed a sheet of paper toward her across the desk with a stiff gesture. "Your notice of termination."

Both men stared at her in silence. The game was over. She knew that this was the end of the line.

Pressing both hands flat on the desk, Ponter leaned forward. "Listen carefully, Kramer. I did not read your memo. I repeat: not ever. However, memo or no memo, what you did violates all of the rules of conduct adhered to at this bank."

An eerie calm had settled over Sophie. She felt it all the way down in her fingertips. "Speaking of violation, Mr. Ponter, what you are violating is the penal code. You appear to be quite clueless, but Mr. Schindler here will agree with me. It is a criminal offence to coerce an employee to deliberately betray her fiduciary duties to defraud a financially illiterate elderly client of the money which he has entrusted the bank and..."

"Out!" Ponter screamed, pouncing out of his chair and raising himself up menacingly in front of Sophie. "Out! Before I throw you out myself!"

Sophie rose slowly, turned her back on the men, and stepped out in a rather dignified manner, all things considered. Schindler's enraged screams echoed behind her. "Your termination is with immediate effect and without further recompense. All data... you listen to this... all data you have come in contact with during your employment is property of the bank! You have exactly fifteen minutes to clear your office with a security escort. After fifteen minutes, they have been instructed to physically put your little ass out on the street."

Brawand, the head of security, was already waiting in the hallway with a suitably grim expression to accompany her to her office. Susan, her secretary, was nowhere to be seen. Curious though it was, the thought occurred to her that this entire eviction seemed as though it had been planned well ahead.

She packed her few personal belongings into her black shoulder bag, opened the slim drawer. "You're not allowed to take anything that belongs to the bank," Brawand snapped.

Sophie rewarded him with a provocative smile. "Mr. Ponter should hardly be interested in my toothbrush, I would imagine. Now, the perfumed panty liners, on the other hand... There I'm less sure..."

The hallway leading to the elevators was conspicuously empty. Word of Ponter's outburst had made the rounds like wildfire. They could all picture what had happened. Sophie shook her head with a rueful smile. *People in these parts had enjoyed a good public execution five hundred years ago—apparently tastes had changed.*

She found the chauffeur waiting as she exited the bank through the service entrance. Petar Ivanovic took a step back from his vehicle, polishing cloth still in hand. He looked at her face, then the bulging bag. "Can I take you somewhere, ma'am?"

Well, there's one person not completely devoid of humanity. She shook her head. "Thank you, Petar, that really won't be necessary." Gathering the remainders of her dignity, she kept walking, head held high.

"I'm here if you need me," he said discreetly as she passed.

No, the Ponter Bank chapter was now definitively closed. A chill wind touched her still heated face. Black clouds over the rooftops seemed to confirm the forecasts—heavy snowfall was expected in the higher elevations. It was the perfect backdrop to the turn Sophie Kramer's life appeared to have taken.

Police Station, District 7

Special Agent Sergeant Max Rösti looked up as Hofer stuck his grinning mug through the door. "Vegetarian or tuna?"

Eleven o'clock…the hours are passing slowly at Hottingen Station this morning. District 7 at the foot of Zürichberg hill is not known for skirmishes, bloody criminal gang retaliations, or other violent inconveniences. Those being issues more confined to the areas around the central railway station and the west side, where drug gangs were ruthless in their territorial struggles. Rösti and his team dealt mainly with traffic violations, lost dogs, and noise complaints. The winter months usually saw an increase in break-ins, as Romanian burglary gangs swarmed the villa district.

Rösti opts for the tuna sandwich. He indulgently pats his sizable gut. "With onions, on whole wheat."

Hofer smiles. "No Black Forest cake today? I'll be going to Huber's anyway."

Rösti makes an attempt at pulling in his stomach, sighs. "Oh, well. May as well. Get yourself a piece, too. And coffee, while we're at it."

Hofer gives a mock salute, disappears into the hallway. The phone rings on Rösti's desk. "Schmid here, Dolder Grand. I'm afraid you will need to get over here as quickly as possible."

He listens to what the anguished hotel director is telling him, shoots up from his seat, and snatches his jacket. *Finally some actual, honest-to-God police work!*

"We are on our way. Under no circumstances is anyone to touch or move anything," he says commandingly. "Block the entire floor. What? Fine."

He hangs up. "Hofer!"

The officer sticks his head back in. "Cancel the Black Forest cake?"

Rösti buttons his uniform jacket, straps on his duty belt.

"Forget lunch. We have a call. At the Dolder."

"Ah. A Bentley parked on the walkway?"

Rösti eyes the man challengingly. "How about a man with a slit throat parked on an expensive rug?"

Hofer's chin drops a good way down toward his starched collar. "Holy mackerel! I'll get the car."

Zurich

"We have a situation," Ponter stated, impatiently eyeing his wristwatch as he tapped the elegant Japanese fountain pen on the glass tabletop. All the while, Schindler paged through the file, which he held awkwardly and almost effeminately balanced on his knees. "Klaus Quadrini's accounts have been temporarily frozen, as per protocol in case of demise. We will have to reach out to his legal heirs…"

Ponter slapped the table with his open hand. "We will do nothing of the sort, Schindler. His heirs will keep their damned mouths shut. The entirety of Quadrini's assets is tainted. You can't possibly be too thick to get the point here. No one will want to raise a stink. We will just be following our fiduciary duty in keeping the family fortune safe from the German tax Nazis, get it?"

Of course, Schindler had gotten it a good while ago. It was Ponter's intention to funnel much of the Quadrini fortune, creatively and bit by bit, into various covert accounts—all under the guise of dutifully securing the man's assets. But it simply wouldn't be that easy. Avoiding Ponter's devious stare, the lawyer objected boldly: "The examining magistrate can demand information under these circumstances. This is a case of murder. Banking confidentiality doesn't apply here."

Ponter's patience had definitely worn thin. He stood abruptly, stood gloweringly over the lawyer, who sank further down into the upholstery.

"We will proceed with the preliminary transfer into our special account, exactly as planned. You know the details. You are to liquefy all assets. This is an urgent, protective measure. And don't forget the artwork in the vault. No one knows about that. You will do this in a way that is one hundred percent clean and airtight, Schindler. By this evening, you will have taken care of this matter for me—are we clear?"

"I was on my way to Basel…"

The phone sounded a short ringtone sequence. Ponter picked up. "I'm busy," he huffed, but then his expression relaxed. "Well, why didn't you say so? How much? Good, good. Yes, put it all into fixed assets. At the official discounted rate." He now grinned at Schindler, momentarily mollified. "The Israel transfer."

"Israel?"

"Yes, Israel! What is wrong with you? A hundred million have just been transferred, a further two hundred million to follow. Ringing any bells?"

Schindler, whose face was now beet-red, struggled for words: "Yes, ehm, Oleg Nedjew…the oligarch…of course…I thought…"

His voice withered under Ponter's cold stare. "Schindler, I expect you to be on top of things. See to it that Kleiber does his job. We will not release the payment for one week. He has the documents. Where is he, by the way?"

He opened the lid to a decorative box, extracted a large cigar. "At least the Russian business is running smoothly."

Schindler cleared his throat. "About Basel. We urgently need to get our hands on Mr. Quadrini's plane. I have filed for an injunction to seize it."

"Oh, for pete's sake. And stop with the *mister* bullshit…just fix the issue with his portfolio."

In the hallway, waiting for the elevator to ascend to the director's level, Schindler dared one more objection. "The trust in Vaduz has to sign off on the transfer. Quadrini was the sole beneficiary and now…"

"Why am I forced to listen to your blathering, Schindler? You're the expert here. The people in Vaduz will do exactly what you instruct them to do, or not? As they've been doing for years. Have they once given a toss about our doings? We are…"

He stopped when the elevator door opened. They got in, remaining silent on their way down. *Of course I can find a way to arrange things,* Schindler considered as they stepped out into the courtyard, where the Maybach stood waiting beneath the awning. Ivanovic had been busy banishing imaginary specks of dust from the shiny hood with a red duster. He now jumped into action, hurried around the back of the car, opened the trunk.

Why should the police even know that Quadrini had business with us? the lawyer mused.

He was determined to execute everything exactly according to the wishes and specifications of his boss. With just one, small caveat—he would arrange for several million to be disposed of in a manner that he would later be able to shift the money to a non-taxable account whenever he desired…perhaps he would use a sham company in the U.S. state of Delaware as cover. His research had informed him that this was a very reliable way to protect one's anonymity.

A soundproof screen separated the driver from the two passengers in the back.

"We have a situation," Ponter stated again, getting back to his original point in a most circuitous way. "Kramer has turned into a problem."

Schindler did not want to believe his ears. "Mr. Ponter, the dismissal went without a hitch. She signed. The conditions are airtight. She has waived all rights to any further compensation or damages. There is even the clause that she agrees not to work within the banking industry for three years."

"Okay, Schindler. Fine." Ponter regarded him appraisingly through narrowed eyes. He shouldn't put the lawyer under too much pressure. The Sophie Kramer thing was really a matter for a different department, the machinations of which the legal department should have as little knowledge of as possible.

For a while, silence fell between them as Ivanovic conducted them through moderate traffic. Ponter rummaged through papers, made several phone calls. After a time, he remarked in a somewhat conciliatory tone, "Well, you know Schindler, I was just thinking of all of the data that Kramer might have saved on her private laptop..." Thus bringing the conversation to a less precarious conclusion.

Schindler immediately made it understood that he would take matters in hand and be sure to resolve everything in the interest of his boss. Ponter was barely listening. It was really time to put an end to this conversation. Ivanovic was steering the Maybach up the driveway, pulling in just perfectly in front of the elegant Dolder Grand entrance.

"Right, get to work, Schindler!" And with this barked command, Ponter heaved himself out of the luxurious interior of the vehicle. Schindler was just taking a measured breath when the boss stopped short. "One more thing. Suvorov's Rothko. I instructed Zebrowski in St. Moritz to have the painting delivered to us in Zurich. See to it that this is taken care of without any mishaps. That Rothko is mine. I hope we are perfectly clear on that!"

Ignoring the respectful greeting of the porter, he strode resolutely through the majestic stone reception hall. The hotel's opulent floral arrangements, too, were as pearls before swine; he continued on through the lobby and headed straight to the library.

The city and lake lay beneath them, gray against gray. Inclement weather appeared to be drawing in from the west. The golf course was deserted as the chauffeur drove the bank's lawyer back down the hill.

Schindler retrieved his cell phone, staring steadily ahead. Angela picked up—cordial and professional as always. Schindler interrupted the pleasant voice. "Get me Kleiber!"

He waited. As ranking portfolio manager, Kleiber was the best-informed resource on this delicate file.

"I am unable to locate Mr. Kleiber at this time," Angela finally responded.

"What is that supposed to mean? I expect to see him in my office in half an hour."

"It seems that he is not in the office, and…well…I am told that his office has been completely cleared. Is he on vacation, perhaps?"

"Nonsense!" Schindler spat, disconnecting the call in disgust. He stared as if hypnotized at the black phone, as if waiting for it to oblige him with an answer.

At this point irate, he next dialed the number in St. Moritz. Valerie, Zebrowski's industrious right hand, announced effusively that she had just been about to call him, about the shipping of the painting. It had been picked up from Castelberg Castle as instructed."

"Right. So proceed to send it to Zurich, as discussed."

"Of course. Shipping has been arranged with a delivery to the bank scheduled for the day after tomorrow."

"Let's hope so." Schindler hung up without bothering with a farewell.

A short while later, Ivanovic parked the director's vehicle in the courtyard's open parking lot. Nobody paid him any mind. The end of this month would mark his five-year anniversary working as Ponter's chauffeur. The job paid well, and because he was willing to be on-call and ready to serve at all hours of the day or night, the boss valued his services as driver and fleet manager. No one dared to tell him his business.

Ivanovic opened the driver's door, leaned down to where there was a hidden compartment on the front end of the seat. He entered three digits, opened the hatch. Reaching in, he found the digital recorder. Pressing a latch, he gently removed the chip and placed it in his jacket pocket. With equal dexterity he locked a new chip in its place, closed the hatch and stood.

He now went about softly wiping the console with a deerskin cloth, as if his entire life's work had been, and always would be, to lend further polish to the already spotless interior of the Maybach.

St. Moritz

Snowflakes are fast collecting on the windshield as Sophie Kramer stops at a phone booth coming into St. Moritz. It has been snowing for hours now. She gets out, pulls up the collar of her jacket, ducks beneath the small cover. She feeds the phone a few coins, calls the office number she knows by heart.

"Ponter Bank, Patrizia Vincenz, good afternoon."

"Dr. Schindler, please."

"Right away. One moment, please."

A patrol car rolls by slowly. The officer in the passenger seat signals with his hand, points back to where Sophie can see the bright warning signals of a large shape becoming vaguely apparent in the wet, almost uniform grayness. She understands, nods at the officers in acknowledgment several times, looks at her watch. It is half past five.

"Dr. Schindler's office." Sophie swallows. Coughs. She lowers her voice, asks in English: "Can I talk to Mr. Schindler, please?"

The heavy monstrosity of a vehicle, covered in snow and ice, is making a gradual, ominous approach.

"Sorry, madam, Mr. Schindler is not in the office this afternoon. Can I take a message?"

Sophie hangs up, stomps back to her Mini. She throws her arms up, feigning surprise at the sudden discovery that her vehicle is blocking road-clearing efforts.

"I'm coming," she calls out at the behemoth that is sweeping large, gray piles of sludge up into its maw, only to spit them out into different large piles, slightly transposed. It comes to a standstill just behind the Mini. She waves the driver, who is perched high up in his cabin, an apology, responds to his thumbs-up gesture with an expression of solemn gratitude, gets into her car, starts it and skids back onto the road.

She had a six o'clock appointment with Valerie at the Zebrowski Gallery. The task at hand was not going to be easy—she needed to make use of the fact that Valerie still considered her to be a Ponter employee. As instructed by Ponter, Sophie had discussed the shipment of the Rothko with Zebrowski several times. Objects of this caliber required packaging in a special, secured container, and Sophie had ensured that the painting was ready. Of course Valerie assumed that it would be picked up by Ponter's shipping partner.

Sophie makes a turn off Seestrasse toward the station. As the Mini's engine begins to rev with the strain of the considerable incline, she considers that she is glad that she had the people at the gas station put snow chains on her front tires this afternoon.

Farther up she carefully passes a Mercedes that is stuck with its rear end in the middle of the road, wheels spinning uselessly. Her windscreen wipers are working frantically. She takes the corner, accelerates slightly, and recognizes the towering silhouette of the Palace Hotel up ahead. The Zebrowski Gallery enjoys a prime location, directly adjacent to the luxury hotel.

Sophie turns into the hotel drive, exchanges a few words with the young porter wearing a fur cap, hands him a bill. As she is getting out, she gives him instructions.

A short while later, she enters the gallery, takes a deep breath. Valerie, the middle-aged, sophisticated assistant sporting an impeccable, black pantsuit, is standing in front of a large, colorful abstract with a client.

Sophie casually walks over to a tall, metal sculpture created by David Smith, according to a small, white sign. She mentally rehearses what she wants to say in order to convince Valerie of her plan, one last time.

At last Valerie says a friendly goodbye to the client at the door, turns to face Sophie.

"Hi, Valerie, I'm so sorry to barge in on you like this, but I'm afraid it's urgent. The Rothko has to be in Zurich by tonight, so I thought it would be best if I simply took it myself. My car is parked in front of the hotel next door."

"Goodness, you are completely out of breath, my dear. Allow me to offer you an espresso."

Sophie looks at her watch conspicuously. "No, thank you so much— but I had better not."

"Well, this is all so sudden...I'm a bit surprised, I must say. The instructions were quite different only yesterday, but...well, my boss will be here in half an hour..."

Sophie feels ready to collapse. She is sweating profusely and can only hope that Valerie does not notice. "Of course, Valerie—I understand completely. You know what my boss is like, once he sets his mind on something, there's just nothing to be done about it."

Valerie contemplatively rubs her narrow chin. "My boss is exactly the same, Sophie. I fear that he is not going to like this. Shouldn't we rather wait for him to get here?"

"I can't, Valerie. I'm really in an awful hurry. They're sending a driver to meet me halfway then we'll be transferring the painting to his car. Please call Schindler; he'll explain everything to your boss."

Valerie gives a dismissive wave. "No, no, that won't be necessary, I believe you."

"I insist, please do verify with him." She takes out her cell phone, dials the number, hands it to Valerie.

"All right, then. As you wish." Valerie listens for a moment, nods, asks to speak to Schindler. Rolls her eyes. "They're looking for him...Yes? I beg your pardon? Aha, yes, that will be fine...no, Zebrowski Gallery. Correct, yes. Thank you." Valerie hands the phone back.

Sophie manages to keep her voice neutral. "And?"

"Schindler is not in the office. They will have him call back." She steps from one foot to the other indecisively. The door alert chimes. Two women in thick fur coats burst through the door.

"Mr. Zebrowski is here?" one of them barks at Sophie.

Valerie steps in with a professional smile, leads the ladies into the room with a gracious gesture.

"Please. We take picture there. The big Smith one," the other woman manages in broken German with a husky voice. "We buy right away if is for sale." She points at the abstract that the other client had shown an interest in only a short while ago.

"I will be happy to assist you, if you would bear with me for just one moment, madam," Valerie chirps politely as she rushes to the phone behind the desk. Receiver pressed against her ear, she throws Sophie a meaningful look dramatically emphasized by a pair of artfully sculpted, raised eyebrows. Sophie interprets the silent message as *What is a person to do? That's the Russians for you—God bless them!* Sophie feels a huge sense of relief. Valerie is clearly in her element now, doing what she does best.

"Giovanni, bring the Rothko upstairs, please! Yes, right away."

She is all business. "I have to attend to my clients," she says to Sophie with a wink. "Giovanni will help you load it. Just promise me one thing…"

Sophie feels her heart sink to the pit of her stomach.

"Drive carefully, for heaven's sake. That Rothko is worth sixty million—at least. That's nothing to sniff at. So be safe!" She has already started to walk backward, waving cheerfully, then turns briskly on her heel to face the fur coats, charming smile already in place—on to the next item on the agenda.

Sophie mutters something incomprehensible, then pulls herself together and calls out: "Thank you, Valerie. See you."

The item that the young man wearing threadbare jeans and an unbuttoned shirt rolls over on a trolley, which Sophie eyes with concern, turns out to be a flat aluminum container with reinforced corners. Giovanni comes to a halt, wiping his forehead with the back of his hand. "*Buongiorno, signora.* Where I bring this for you?"

Sophie is already holding the door open then has a thought.

"Just a moment, eh, Giovanni? Let's have one quick look, just to make sure it's the right painting, okay?" She watches Valerie out of the corner of her eye, notes that she is having an animated conversation with her tarted-up Russian clients.

"Okay, no problem." The assistant turns the lock, opens the container with a few quick motions—a flourishing gesture. "Here you are, Signora."

Sophie looks reverently at the transparent bubble wrap, beneath which she recognizes Mark Rothko's iconic *Endgame*—dark rust and deep charcoal rectangles with blurred edges. She had first seen the austere work of art in Suvorov's study, and it had instantly captivated her. Similar to Beckett's approach to theater, Rothko's paintings expressed a great deal with very little. She runs her hand admiringly across the protective wrapping. "That's great, Giovanni. Just perfect."

She opened the door as the Italian closed the container, pointed out the direction in which the car was parked. Together they pushed the trolley through the sludge on the pavement to the dry forecourt at the hotel entrance, where luggage was piled. Giovanni blew into his hands. "Cold...uh...where is car?"

"It's coming. Right over there." Sophie was glad that Valerie was not able to see the spectacle of her little compact car among all of the stately vehicles.

Giovanni stretched, then, catching sight of the Mini, pointed to it with a large grin. "*Grande macchina,* eh? *Mamma mia*! You drive up mountain?"

"Come on, Giovanni, we need to get this loaded."

The porter opened the hatchback while Sophie leaned in to fold down the rear seats. Much to her surprise, Giovanni appeared carrying the container on his back. "Like backpack, Signora, is easy. Look!" He fastened the strap around his waist, lifted his arms and turned in a little circle. "Is easy, fifteen kilos, good to carry!"

He seemed as if he were auditioning for a sales position selling camping gear. Sophie laughed. "That's great, but I'm sure I won't be climbing any mountains with that particular backpack."

The two porters, sharing the moment of amusement, looked on as Giovanni placed the container into the trunk.

"That's just about perfect," Sophie said, lending a hand. She was right—the space fit the container like a glove.

"Here, signora. For open." Smiling, he handed her the note with the combination for the lock. "No lose, or *disastro*!"

"Thank you, Giovanni, here, take this. *Un po' di benzina!*"

He looked down in amazement at the folded hundred in her hand. "*Tante grazie, signora.*"

She put her finger to her pursed lips. Giovanni nodded solemnly. "*Capito, grande macchina!* Bye-bye, signora."

Sophie drove off with a sense of relief. The snow chains were gripping nicely, keeping the newly minted fine-arts transportation vehicle steady on the way down to the Seestrasse. Falling snowflakes continued to whirl densely in the headlights.

She felt lighter the further she distanced herself from the gallery. The tension had mercifully dissipated; the lumps at the pit of her stomach had dissolved. Instead, she was beginning to appreciate a new, incredibly strong urge. Keeping an eye out for a public restroom, Sophie reached a roundabout, decided to head for the bridge, across from which she had spotted a restaurant.

The news came on the radio. It was half past six. She hastily parked the Mini in front of the restaurant and ran inside.

Stepping into the snowdrifts a short while later, and very much relieved, an irresistible smell of grilled meat wafted out of the kitchen to meet her. She was almost overcome by a ravenous hunger. She hesitated. *Have to eat, no, can't, no time, have to make it through the pass—a sandwich maybe, no shops around, maybe the gas station.*

She hurried back to the sanctuary of her car, drove off. At least she had some water. She opened the plastic bottle, took a few sips. After passing a dimly lit gas station, that did not give the impression that it would be serving anything at all, night surrounded her. She drove as fast as the winter conditions allowed. A short stretch of ever-evolving white lane showed clearly in her headlights. She held the steering wheel with outstretched arms, heard the end of a report on traffic conditions… *Rhine Bridge shut down in Basel.*

She caught up to the municipal snowplow, visible from afar thanks to its yellow warning signals, just before Silvaplana. She rode close behind it until they reached the town, then turned off onto the road leading to the pass. She checked the gauges for gas and battery life, decided to trust the reliable little engine.

As she reached a narrowing of the road lined by old, Engadin houses, a man wearing a fluorescent traffic vest stepped into the street waving a warning light. "Good evening, ma'am." He said in a friendly voice, addressing her through the crack that she has opened her window.

"The pass is closed. We are very sorry. Where were you heading?"
Think! You need to come up with something! Buy some time!
"I'm not surprised, with this weather."
"Exactly—you should get back indoors, where it's nice and warm."
She nodded knowingly. "You're pulling the night shift, aren't you?"
"We're used to that around here. We'll tackle the pass in the morning, at daybreak." The flashlight cut through the wet darkness like a saber. "You can turn over there."
She shook her head, frustrated, rolled her eyes. "It's just...I have to pick up my dog, at the Chesa Corvatsch."
"Well, why didn't you say so?" He laughed. "That won't be a problem."
He stepped away from the car. She waved at him, careful to appear quite carefree and casual. "Thank you very much."
Wow. That had actually worked! Chesa Corvatsch! Was there even one up there? An exuberant slap of her thigh led her to skid in the first hairpin turn. Shocked, she caught herself and proceeded the climb toward the pass, now with razor concentration, and at a very controlled rate.
The snow on the road was ankle-deep and continued to fall steadily, in thick flakes. If they weren't going to be doing any clearing through the night, there would be half a meter or more by dawn. Once the sharp turns had been navigated, she kept a confident speed.
Despite all of her courage and sharp focus, the reality was that she felt acutely defenseless in the face of Mother Nature. Utterly alone on the deserted mountain road, blanketed in unruly snow flurries, heading for a pass at over two thousand meters—what the hell was she doing here? Still, her small, well-heated car was like a coat of armor. Everything will be fine! She searched the radio channels for music, received only unnerving static.
Given what she had told him, the watchman down in Silvaplana had not seen any cause to warn her of the currently severe risk of avalanches beneath the pass. Ample experience had given the helpers manning the road crews tremendous respect for unpredictable snow slides—which is precisely why they had asked the police to shut the pass to all traffic.

Locked in the specious security of her car, which was equipped with excellent snow chains and humming reliably up the road, Sophie had no idea that a pair of watchful eyes had spotted the headlights in the distance, and were following them intently as the Mini Cooper tackled the first curvy incline of the long approach to the pass.

Uli Stark had barely pulled his Hummer up in front of the garage and gotten out to open the door. At first he noticed the sound of what, to his ears, was typical for an engine revving at high speed. He found this quite perplexing: the road crew vehicles—mostly heavy four by fours, or trucks with rotors, or snowplows—made lower, rumbling sounds. Not at all like this noise, which sounded more like a sports car. Then he vaguely saw the hazy beam of light. It looked like someone might actually be driving up to the pass! And this particular someone was driving quite fast. It was not at all likely that this was a member of the police or street crew.

Uli stomped back into the shed, to the phone.

EXPERIENCE, a creased poster next to a snow shoe frame read. It was an advertisement for his event management company. A certified mountain guide and skiing instructor, Uli had led ski tours and expeditions in Canada for a number of years before he had been drawn back to his home, here in the Grison Alps.

He hesitated, receiver in hand. His independent and obstinate mountaineer nature did not easily allow him to get others mixed up in what he considered to be his affairs. He had always been accustomed to taking care of business, when there was business to be taken care of. He was perfectly confident in his ability to master damn near anything—mountains, weather and all. His instinct had never yet failed to lead him safely through any dangerous situation.

You'll fall flat on your face one of these days, colleagues, who envied his easy self-assurance, would scoff.

He put the receiver back in its cradle, went outside to retrieve the night vision glasses from the Hummer, which still sported California license plates. Winter nights in the mountains were never entirely dark. The snow reflected the light of the stars. Uli focused the infrared binoculars onto the dark gray face of the mountain just ahead of the Julier Pass, where he judged the road should be. Of course, even his highly effective device didn't give him much, thanks to the snowdrift. Contours were not apparent, shadows swallowed outlines; but then he was able to pick up at least that lonely beam of headlights. Adjusting the dial between his thumb and index finger, the object suddenly shot into focus. Yes! The light was definitely moving forward at a steady pace! He swore under his breath. Some madman is actually driving up there!

Whoever it was, the guy was either very bold, or completely insane.

"Clearly a bit of both," Uli muttered into his three-day stubble and proceeded to check the snow chains on all four wheels of the Hummer.

Scratching the back of his bushy head thoughtfully, he entered the sanctuary of the one-story hip-roofed house.

Of course he could alert the police down in St. Moritz. He immediately dismissed the thought, prudent though it may seem. They would only ask useless questions, and that was if they believed him in the first place. They would put everything off until the morning, because you could barely see anything in this weather anyway, let alone do anything. They'd ask him if he was sure it was a car, tell him that they'd ask around in Silvaplana whether anyone knew of anyone, and on, and on...

In the kitchen, he opened the refrigerator, poured himself a glass of local farm milk, sat down at the sturdy, worn wooden table. Finishing his glass, he wipes his mouth with the back of his hand with a grunt. His decision was made. He had brought a maxim back from Canada and California that had spoken straight to his Swiss mountaineer soul: *When in doubt, act!* A broad smile spreads across his face. Yup. *It was really quite simple.*

Sophie on the Julier Pass

It seems to her that the snow is coming down harder. The headlights illuminate a mad swirl of icy particles. The road ahead is buried beneath a soft layer of virgin white. It was insane to try and brave the pass in this blizzard! Sophie focused on the tall, reflective delineator posts on either side, to avoid becoming completely disoriented. These crucial markers would help the plows find their way to clear the path under the precipitation, which was often over a meter high in these parts—early next morning, for example.

Sophie had turned off the radio. She needed every scintilla of concentration to keep the car on what she suspected was the roadway. She prayed that the tall markers would continue to appear, one by one.

Sophie is acutely aware of the sound of the engine, hands clenched on the steering wheel. So far, everything has been fine. The sounds coming from beneath the hood are steady. The front wheels are gripping well, pulling the Mini onward at an even speed. Every now and then she startles violently when a clump of snow hits her windshield.

She has traversed the Julier Pass often enough, even in winter. She knows the approximate course of the road. Her thoughts race ahead to the summit, where she could, at least conceivably, seek shelter in the solid stone guest house. There would be several inclines and turns to overcome until then. Sophie longingly pictures the warm friendly glow of light behind windows encrusted in snow and ice. She considers whether or not to allow herself to interrupt her journey. It would make sense to pull in at a rest stop. She could check her chains, scrape her windows—perhaps the inn would be open, the innkeepers did live there, after all...

She reaches back with one hand, groping, feels the reassuring cold of the metal container that houses the sixty million dollar Rothko. Everything will be fine. Her plan was simple. The thought of Shuky Nachman was comforting. She felt drawn to him. Perhaps her sentiments had something to do with their shared love of flying. There had been several instants of powerful mutual attraction since the Paris air show, where she had lost her shoes. Sophie felt a tingling at the base of her spine when she thought of this, knew that she would be willing to go further than they had so far. Shuky, a gentleman through and through, had never pressured her. It was as if he was calmly certain that the ripened fruit would fall of its own accord when it was perfectly ready. There had been plenty of opportunity to get her in bed after any of many dinners at the city's most elegant restaurants. Should she simply take the initiative next time? She honestly wanted nothing more than to be bedded by him. On the other hand, prudence was essential when it came to doing business. She had no desire to jeopardize the relationship with this captivating bon vivant.

The Rothko was too rich for the palates of most collectors. Sophie had resolved not to accept less than its valued sixty million. This price would definitively allow Baron Suvorov to extricate himself from his predicament. Ponter Bank would be completely reimbursed for its services and expenses, and would not be able to impede this legal repayment with the covert intent to seize the far more valuable asset. Otherwise Sophie would make sure her former boss was visited by the regulating authorities, the federal prosecutor, the Sunday press, and possibly the televised media. Not only was Nachman the ideal buyer, but also the perfect advisor and confidante when it came to devising a strategy to save her own behind. The fact that the transaction would be private also allowed for discretion, whereas commissioning a gallery with the sale at auction would pose unacceptable risks. Ponter could challenge outright ownership, claiming that the bank had a prior claim—that would block the sale right then and there.

I will convince Shuky to buy it, she swore to herself. *I know I can do it. Such a unique work of art…and when I fill him in on the background…Just the mention of the name Suvorov should be enough to spark his interest.*

She was in no doubt. Nachman loved to talk about history, and yes, General Suvorov, his Alpine passage…the snowstorm, the rockslide…Sophie is shocked back to the present.

The car suddenly falters. She accelerates gently, takes care not to oversteer. The engine abruptly picks up, resumes its familiar hum. *What just happened?* She instinctively checks the rearview mirror. Nothing but the black of night. The drive continues.

Sophie is in the process of taking a deep, controlled breath when the Mini lurches again. A large mound of snow appears suddenly in front of the nose of the car. She steps on the brake in fright and the Mini slides to a halt. Wanting to drive on, she once again accelerates, but the car merely jerks a few times before coming to a complete standstill. Patiently, with bated breath, Sophie puts the car in first, uses the hand brake to aid her efforts, releasing it ever so slowly as she accelerates again—to no avail.

The wheels turn futilely in the snow. She feels the car sinking deeper and deeper.

Finally, she puts the car in reverse. *Try a running start, you can do it!*

Nothing! She is able to maneuver the car backwards, but is unable to gather any forward momentum from her new position. On her third attempt to back up and take a running start at the mound of snow, the rear of the Mini slips and skids outward.

Despite all of her desperate attempts, she could now no longer move at all. The car was definitively, utterly stuck. *Shit, shit, shit!*

She bit her lip, shoved the door open, got out. The white night did not reflect enough of the headlight's glare to illuminate the jam in its entirety. Attempting to get closer to the back of the car in order to assess the situation, Sophie promptly sank up to her knees into the fresh snow. The back of the car was angled. She wasn't able to tell what had gone wrong. Damn it!

She clambered back, tilted the driver's seat forward, looked urgently for the kit. Typically cautious, she always carried a few practical items in the car, things that would be useful in case of an emergency. She found the scrunched-up pouch beneath the passenger seat. Tearing at the Velcro with icy, wet fingers, she unfurled the pack and grabbed the flashlight. Now she was able to survey the damage. By the bright beam of the lamp, she could tell that the back of the car was tilted seemingly off the road—*a damn ditch*, she proclaimed. A roadside marker pointed askance from beneath her bumper. Worse, the rear wheel appeared to be pushed up into the fender. This was not looking good. The snow continued to fall, silently. Relentlessly. She could not give up. She tried again to get the car to move in either direction, playing carefully with the gas, willing the wheels to gain traction. It was hopeless.

Getting out with the flashlight once more, she was finally forced to concede defeat. She was stuck. The body of the vehicle was essentially jacked up on a solid mass of compressed snow. No amount of maneuvering would change that.

Sophie brushed the snow off as best she could; returned, shivering, to the relative warmth of her vehicle and shut the door. *What to do? How could she find help?* She retrieved her cell phone from her jacket pocket. *Who could she call? The police? Roadside assistance? She shook her head irritably. Someone down in the valley would have to come to her rescue... Ivanovic in Zurich? Impossible. Zebrowski? Definitely not... The guys at Samedan Airport? Yes. That's it. They'll totally come and help. They'll know what to do.*

"I'm calling Heinz," she said out loud, as if to bolster her decision, and dialed the number for Air Engiadina. She waited for the familiar "Reber" of the officer in charge. Shit... She stared at the display with a sinking dread: *No signal.*

She was finally starting to panic. Where was she, even? Suddenly, she had an idea. She turned on the navigation system, relieved to see the little screen on her console slowly come to life.

"At least the satellites are working," she muttered sarcastically, focusing in on the map that was now displayed. The device was showing her location to be higher up than she had thought. The summit of the pass did not seem to be very far off—at least not on the colorful screen, with its fields of green and the roadway marked in red, showing a very clear and simple path to the summit and its inn. Sophie had made her decision. She took a spare battery for her flashlight, an energy bar, the pocketknife, gloves, and a pair of protective goggles that she had bought somewhere in order to be more difficult to identify in case she was caught by a speed safety camera. She donned the gloves, stuck the other items into the bag, pulled up the hood of her jacket, got out.

She checked her flashlight, casting its beam to great effect against a reflective marker nearby. She opened the back, removed the container. *All sixty million worth of it!*

She took a few awkward, prancing steps, moving as best she could in the snow. *Giovanni has you beat in that department*, she said to herself, half amused. How glad she was now to have those ridiculous straps! Having shouldered the case and secured the waist strap, she looked into the trunk one more time. She had her personal items, had left nothing behind—or had she? Impulsively, she grabbed the towrope, which she had almost missed, attached it to the shoulder strap, wrapped it around her waist. As she shut the trunk, her foot caught on the uprooted marker.

Why not? She pulled at the wood. After some back and forth, she found herself holding the straight upper part. The bottom had been bent by the impact with her car. She stepped on the bent portion, leveraged her weight until it finally snapped. Better than nothing! She leaned on it, trying it as a walking aid. Unaccountably, it suddenly stopped snowing. She poked about herself with the stick, took a step, then another...

The snow was almost knee deep. Soon she was out of breath. She continued on, focusing only on one marker at a time with dogged determination. Visibility was good enough with the light she had, but she had definitely underestimated the exertion. She started to feel uncomfortably warm. Then she started to sweat. Recalling ski tours of the happier past, she slipped out of the shoulder straps, took off her winter jacket and tied it to the Rothko container with the rope. She shouldered the valuable backpack once more, continued on. *Dear, precious Mark Rothko,* she muttered to herself, *this you surely would never have imagined—what a human being wouldn't do for art, for money.* She stopped to catch her breath. *And for... what? Love perhaps?*

Uli Stark Takes Charge

Uli Stark senses a tingling at the nape of his neck as he turns onto the narrow access road to the Julier Pass. His Hummer's 400 horsepower engine whines.

The alloy wheels, steel snow chains on all four broad tires, grip the snow firmly, hoisting the massive vehicle forward. Uli stretches his head toward his muscular shoulders a few times. Left, then right. Rubs his neck. But the tingling returns after a short while. Not a good sign... not at all. A tingling neck is unnerving, as far as Uli is concerned. A tingling neck is like the silence of the alpine daw before the start of an avalanche—a warning sign. Some kind of signal, a premonition, is being sent to his brain—it is, unsettlingly, up to him to figure out what the warning means, where the danger lies.

In situations like these, he tends to play out the possible events of the upcoming hours in his mind's eye. He is quite convinced that imagined perils have helped to prepare him in the past, have helped him to effectively guard against the worst. He imagines a little homunculus in the back of his head, having been woken by the tingling, and now revealing important images to him. At any rate—Uli was not ungrateful for these signals. He saw them as a proverbial gift horse. It didn't matter how and why they suddenly appeared at the back of his head and in his neck.

He had mounted a battery of powerful searchlights to the roof of his Hummer, which he could move remotely from inside the vehicle. He often preferred, however, to climb onto the roof and adjust the lights manually.

The heavy all-terrain vehicle, weighing close to three tons and with an impressive clearance of almost half a meter, moved at a good pace, splashing mud and snow. Powerful wipers ensured good visibility.

Uli tried to place himself into the mind of the driver who had dared to attempt a crossing of the pass in these insane conditions. Either he was completely clueless, like one of those innumerable sandal hikers who were routinely needing to be rescued, cold and befuddled, from the mountain predicaments they insisted on getting themselves into—or he was stark raving mad.

There was nothing coming through on the radio. No notice of a daredevil ignoring the barriers and closure signs. The navigation system display was dimly lit, sentimental folk music played softly on the radio.

The pass closure had been absolutely necessary. Uli knew the dangerous slope leading up to the summit, where enormous amounts of fresh snow collected. It had stopped snowing now and if a cold snap set in, an avalanche would be a certainty. Leaning over the steering wheel, he peered at the mountain and saw nothing but impenetrable darkness. Not one moonbeam made its way through the thick cloud cover, no hint of glittering stars to signal a cold night.

He felt the passenger seat for the small rucksack, found the side pocket, ensured himself that he had not accidentally left his Garmin GPS behind in the shed.

Looking up, he suddenly saw the back of a car.

Damn it!

He hit the brake hard, swerved with a quick, controlled turn of the wheel. The Hummer came to a stand just next to the obstacle.

It's the idiot! Stuck, of course.

Uli climbed out, jumped into the snow. The Mini Cooper had veered off to the side of the road; it was hopelessly stuck.

Hey! Are you okay?

There was no answer. Uli opened the hatch, looked inside, straightened up, started walking around the vehicle.

Hellooooo. Anyone there?

An ominous rumbling sounded from the mountain, as if in answer. Shielding his eyes from the bright glare of the searchlights, he squinted up to the sky. What he saw alarmed him. The cloud cover had started to tear open over the pass. A few stars shone brilliantly through the small hole. He felt the chill of a cold draft.

Turning back toward the Hummer, he saw the tracks—deep footprints leading up the road.

Shit! He slapped his forehead, appalled, ran with great urgency toward the Hummer, as if he had just seen the abominable snowman. He was behind the steering wheel in a flash, started the vehicle up. If he knew one thing, it was that he had to find this imbecile before the avalanche came tearing down the mountain. Before the crushing snow arrived to bury everything in its path, including the crackpot who had apparently decided to go stomping off down the road...

Mountain Peril

Sophie was seriously considering turning back—waiting for help, getting someone to tow her car. She panted, clutching her broken marker tightly, each step a painful, sinking struggle. She had no idea how far it was to the summit. Looking back, there was nothing but darkness. The flashlight was just enough to find the next reflective marker. She had determined that these were placed about fifty meters apart. If the pass road was fifteen kilometers long, how many markers did that make? It made no difference, of course, except to occupy her mind.

She sank, extracted her other leg, heaved it forward. Sank.

I can't take this much longer!

Her head droned. She saw herself from far above. Ethereal, surreal. Stomping through an endless field of snow, a singular, rust-brown piece of art strapped to her back...a hundred-dollar bill emanated from the painting with each step, landed in the snow and melted away...fragments of mist turned to grimacing faces, the master's spirit mocking her. Alone in nothing but stillness, snow, and ice.

Her foot meets something steady, startling her back to the present. She freezes for a moment, confused, checks her balance on what seems to be firm ground, takes another step, disbelief in a raging battle against hope. She has her footing! She realizes that there is no new snow here. She is standing on the icy road. The recognition floods her with giddy relief. She lengthens her stride, feeling almost weightless. Her weariness has vanished; the dark visions are gone. After a moment she begins to understand that the wind has blown all of the fresh snow off the roadway.

Doesn't matter, she is walking, moving forward. She barely notices the markers now, is also unaware that the flashlight is growing dim. She almost thinks she hears the sound of an engine. It doesn't faze her. Probably imagining things. Rothko messing with her again...She gives an unsettlingly shrill laugh, the ghost of which echoes faintly back at her.

Meanwhile, the tingling at the nape of Uli's neck was growing appreciably stronger. He knew the nature of the imminent danger now. The avalanche was coming. He saw the precise spot he needed to reach—a rocky overhang that would divert the snow from the road directly beneath it. He drove the Hummer on in stony concentration, keeping an eye on the trail of footsteps in the snow. The bumpy ride was tossing the equipment around in the back. Uli always carried the most important tools and provisions including an avalanche transceiver, a powerful emergency radio, rations, a bottle of potent herbal liqueur, and all manner of first aid supplies.

The sound of the wheels suddenly changed to a loud, hard rattle as the snow chains made contact with the road that had been swept clear by the wind. He accelerated, then immediately slowed back down.

The trail—damn it! But maybe not such a bad thing. A lack of prints meant that the mysterious hiker, whom Uli was growing increasingly fascinated with, had been able to get ahead better.

Uli confidently accelerated once more. What he saw as he rounded the next bend toward the protected outcropping, however, did not make him happy at all.

Sophie Disappears

Sophie's first step back into deep snow felt emotionally devastating. She soldiered bravely on because there was no other viable choice, hoping to reach firm ground beneath her feet once more. Seconds seemed like minutes. She pointed her light to where she expected to see a marker. Instead, she experienced a terrible fright—there was no reflection. All she was able to discern was a great, milky patch.

Fog! Oh, God—now she was actually stuck in fog!

Shivering, she fought hard to suppress a rising sense of panic. She stopped, took the container off her back. Breathing heavily, she donned the warm jacket. This small deed somehow calmed her. *Which way to go? Well—straight ahead, I guess! The next marker is bound to turn up at some point.*

But she saw no marker. She laboriously stepped her way away from the road, her haste increasing proportionately to her need of finding the next signpost that must be right ahead...When she finally decided to track back to the clear stretch of road to reorient herself, it was too late. The densest of mountain fogs enveloped her like a shroud. She was barely able to recognize the outline of her own hand by what light her lamp had left to give.

Have to find the road. This is ridiculous. A road can't just disappear.

Indeed, she did suddenly feel something firm beneath her foot.

See. No need to lose it. Get a grip.

She breathed evenly, stretched her back, and loosened her shoulders. She intended to carry on carefully, feeling the direction out by gauging the surface. She was deliberating her next step forward when the snarl of an engine broke the silence. Lights emerged behind the wall of fog, almost blindingly bright as they approached...then turned into a bend.

Sophie screamed, her voice breaking—but the light continued on, unhearing, and was lost. The sound of the engine faded. Within what seemed like a hand's width, fate had taken a different turn. She frantically willed herself to move fast enough not to lose the last of the sound. Chasing the chimera, she threw one foot in front of the other, sobbing. But she was not on the road, as she had thought, but on a naked stone ridge, a good fifty meters from the safe road. A dark thunder replaced the only just vanished noise of salvation. It came from far above. Filled with a sense of terror, staring into nothing, she took a step, then another. Then she fell.

She screamed with all she had in her, even as she fell for what seemed like an eternity. And then she felt the impact on her back...

Uli Stark recognized that he had lost the mysterious person, almost certainly a female, judging by the tracks. She could surely not have made it up this far, particularly since he was unable to see anything at all resembling tracks, even past the bare patch of road, where the snow cover was intact. He drove another hundred meters to the protected area beneath the rocky protrusion, positioned his Hummer in a way that would best allow him to direct his search lights at the surrounding terrain—if the fog ever lifted.

Uli was under no illusion. Mountain rescue basics mandated that he should call for backup. Staring at the radio unit, he was well aware that he really was pushing the limits...if only there hadn't been that issue with his license. He had acted on his own authority once before, in another emergency situation about a year ago. According to the police, he had recklessly endangered the lives of those he rescued.

He had been let off with a warning, and was told in no uncertain terms that his license would be revoked if anything of the sort happened again.

He got out of the car. Even if he did call now, it would be too late as far as they were concerned. He'd be toast...

He took a few steps away from the car and started to call out into the night, again, and again, in all directions. He cupped his hands, yelled with all his might: "Hello...is anyone there...can you hear me...helloooo..."

The echo faded into deathly silence each time. He shivered involuntarily, understanding what this meant. The seconds passed more slowly than the heavy beating of his heart.

The first thing he heard was a sinister rumble. Then came a great ripping sound followed, explosively, by a deafening thunder that filled the valley. The tremendous sound ebbed into the distance, finally becoming nothing more than a backdrop to the howling, whistling wind. Snow billowed, ice rained down. Uli raced to the security of the cab. The violence of the avalanche caused the substantial vehicle to shake like a cheap, plastic toy.

And then, just like that, the elemental force of nature subsided. A profound calm returned as if nothing had ever happened. The fog had vanished as if it, too, had been swept away. A brightly sparkling sky shone over the ravaged, snowy landscape.

Uli held the infrared binoculars up to his eyes, slowly scanned a straight line where he assumed the road to be, over the great mounds of packed snow and ice. A nearly full moon shone brightly, as if to proudly remind the humans that nature was in charge. Uli Stark, for one, was abundantly clear on that without the reminder. Pragmatist that he was, he also knew that there was no time to lose.

The woman had to be somewhere. Of course the woman! If the footsteps had not been enough to convince him, the Mini Cooper—a stereotypical trend among young, successful, professional females—had done the trick. Not that it mattered much at the moment. Whoever it was, she was presumably buried in a deep, white grave, motionless and cold, waiting for the spring thaw.

He directed the binoculars back to the spot where he presumed the Mini to be. As expected, the snow pack there was several meters high. It wouldn't take long for them to find the wreck.

He leaned against the driver's side door, fumbled at the wrapper of a chocolate bar, breathing heavily with frustration. Finally, he just bit through it. Making his way toward the back of the car, he chewed, spitting out occasional pieces of wrapping along the way. He swung himself up, started freeing the roof of snow…

…The ridge from which Sophie had fallen was not central to the devastation of the avalanche, but a little off to the side. It had served as a powerful obstruction and had, in fact, diverted the course of large masses of snow. This topographically fortunate circumstance might have led to Sophie's unlikely survival. The second and less natural circumstance was none other than the very pricey Rothko.

The avalanche had barreled down, spewing powerful fountains forth from every obstacle that withstood its force. With the ridge providing some protection, the alloy container was set in a more reluctant type of motion beneath a lifeless Sophie by secondary kinetic forces from farther uphill, then additionally aided by significant air pressure. Slowly gaining momentum, the container, upon which she remained strapped, was carried away like a sled on the descending body of ice and snow.

Of course, all of this would only be visible from above, by the light of day, when the avalanche's trail of destruction on the land could be clearly assessed. This also revealed the manner in which the sturdy ridge had diverted the snow slide in one particular area, causing a limited portion to continue off to one side, where it had ended in a separate mound of dirty sludge.

It might have been possible to get this woman out alive. The soldiers, who had been sent in to help the mountain rescue teams, searched diligently, finding first a fender, then a wheel—snow chain still attached.

The license plate, spotted by a helicopter pilot, led to the identification of the victim. Sophie Kramer. The disturbing fact that a young woman had been buried spurred the rescue workers on. But hope of finding her alive faded with the passage of time. Resignation had finally set in as the gray afternoon swiftly and ominously turned to night, and the officer in charge had called off the search. The police announced the fatality around midnight: Sophie Kramer from Zurich had perished in the Julier avalanche.

✳

"Ms. Kramer is dead," Schindler noted matter-of-factly as he stepped into Ponter's office that morning.

Ponter paced the room aimlessly, casting a distracted glance at the panoramic view of Zurich. "Dead. Dead, yes." Then, whipping around suddenly: "Where is the Rothko?" he thundered. He stretched his hands up in a gesture of exasperation. "Have they found my Rothko? Do you understand what has happened here, Schindler? My Rothko is gone. Destroyed!"

The lawyer swallowed hard. His dry throat stung.

"I know."

"Sixty million down the toilet. I can't even fathom it. Sixty million just flushed away, Schindler...thanks to you!...You incompetent asshole....Zebrowski will pay for this. You will sue him for all that he is worth—for breach of faith! Now, get out before I actually throw up on you....Sixty million buried in the fucking snow..."

Schindler was close to trying to say something in his defense. But his tongue refused to comply. Instead, he shot from the office and straight to the employee restroom, where he proceeded to frantically shovel water in his face. All the while cursing his father, who had never shut up about the brilliant career his son would have as a business lawyer.

On the Julier

Uli Stark listens intently, as the radio newscaster reports on last night's deadly avalanche. He is driving the Hummer toward Zurich at a steady pace, on a road that is wet but has been cleared of snow. In the pale light of an emerging dawn, Lake Zurich appears like a narrow gray ribbon as the silhouette of the city comes into view.

He clearly must have lost his mind. There is no way on earth he would be making this drive otherwise. Uli's thoughts drift back. He sees himself at the Julier Pass, on his truck bed, holding the infrared binoculars...

...The sudden silence is eerie. It becomes real to him only slowly, as the ghost of the tremendous noise of the avalanche subsides from his ears. In its aftermath, he beholds the mountaintops glistening in the moonlight, towering over the natural devastation. And the utter silence.

He uses the night vision device to systematically search the environment. Right to left, top to bottom. There is a human being down there, somewhere beneath the masses of snow—a woman, of that he is certain. He climbs onto the roof, starts adjusting the searchlights. There has to be at least some sort of trace. He moves the concentrated halogen beam slowly away from the ridge, across the smaller avalanche cone—could she have been caught up in this portion?—and back again. Nothing!

Now there is sound. The aftermath of the avalanche, tons of packed snow and most everything that had stood in its way, sighs and groans as it settles, almost as if regretting what it has done. Then a muffled crack here, a snapping of ice there, a crunching that sounds like giant footsteps.

Uli does not give up. He starts again. Positions the searchlight, emits an occasional, drawn-out, echoing call—like a medieval tower guard calling a stray traveler back to the security of the fort.

The echo resounds mockingly, and that is all. He turns away, exhausted, jumps down, slides into the driver's seat. He holds the bottle of liquor, stares at it indecisively. There! That damn tingling at the back of his neck again!

Was something down there, at the end of the beam—something shiny? Nonsense. You're imagining things now. Just stop. Go home!

But Uli cannot stop. He resists the temptation of taking a warming swig from the bottle. Instead, he climbs onto the roof once more, positions the light on the deadly piles of snow and debris… his subconscious mind—the homunculus—is right. There is something down there! Something with a matte shine that could have been a piece of ice—small, thin, easy to miss. He finds a new angle, focuses the infrared scope on the spot, thinks that he recognizes an object of some sort, but he is unsure what it is.

He climbs down carefully, keeping his eye on the spot, tries to determine a landmark. Difficult.

He gets the Garmin out of his backpack, gets up on the roof for the umpteenth time this night. Having localized the spot once more with the binoculars, he determines the compass coordinates on the GPS, notes them and measures the distance—538 meters. Still occupied with the coordinates on the small display as he climbs back down, *he slips.*

He comes down hard, slamming his knee against the edge of the truck bed. On top of everything else! Searing pain! Swearing loudly he undoes the rescue sled, pushes it down off the truck and onto the road. He follows it down, takes a few tentative steps toward the front of the car to grab the snowshoes, steps into them. His leg seems to be in working order—only the knee hurts like hell. He is furious at himself. *Pull yourself together, man!*

The flat rescue sled is equipped with two long handrails. Uli straps the rucksack and blankets to it, grabs a hand strap and begins his descent.

Needing to get around the ridge, he decides the short gully next to it is his best bet. He lets the sled down on a rope, then follows carefully, slides, digs his heel in to stop himself, uses his compass for reference.

Suddenly, his foot gives way. Waving frantically to catch himself, he screams, grabs his knee. "God damn it…" *Should he go back? This was ridiculous!*

The terrain eventually flattened as he advanced. Uli was now able to pull the sled behind himself, steady himself against the tall masses of snow to his sides. He was finally moving at a better pace.

He did not consult his watch. Time and space had become one, and strangely irrelevant. He, and he alone, determined the course of events. The stars helped, the satellite sent its signals, his brain calculated.

506 meters. He had to be close to the spot he had sighted.

He suddenly sees a dark line—a rope? Is he imagining things? He steps closer, points his flashlight. Yes—a rope, leading to something metallic that he had missed. And there is something else, the sight of which triggers a flood of adrenaline...a woman's boot! And a leg. Hands trembling, he hurriedly unstraps the shovel from the sled, begins to dig, dig...

The realization dawns that the woman is strapped to something...a container on her back...Now he has freed her face with his hands. He acts mechanically undoes the straps holding the motionless figure down, lays her on the sled, sits astride of her...he is moving swiftly, efficiently, yet it feels like everything is taking hours. He performs CP resuscitation, staring, as if in trance, at her face, her soft mouth...time and again, compressions, chin tilt, two breaths...he raises her, shakes her in desperation, screams at her still lifeless form...

"Wake up! Come on, damn it...don't give up you stupid bitch...you can't die..." He stops, sweat pouring down, close to tears.

"Please, lady, please don't die..." He leans over, takes a deep breath, delivers it to her with what seems like his last bit of strength.

In his fervent dedication, he does not notice that she has opened her eyes. He puts his mouth to hers once more, now senses her lips moving, responding to the touch of his, pursing as if in a kiss. He jolts, as if struck by lightning, lets out a victory howl commensurate with all of the weight that has been lifted off his shoulders.

Stark's raucous cry was loud enough to scare the marmots, had these not almost certainly already retreated to the depths of their caves to flee the thundering avalanche. Sophie recalled later that it had sounded to her like the cry of a newborn, announcing its life. It was the second she had realized that she was still on this earth—although the bearded man leaning over her with a distorted grimace certainly looked otherworldly enough. Her initial reaction was one of terror. "What are you doing to me?"

The man wasted no time. He rubbed her arms briskly; the blanket that he threw over her drowned her protest. He put the bottle to her parched lips. "Drink. My name is Uli. I am a mountain guide. You are unbelievably lucky to be alive!"

She was silent. *Hypothermic and confused!* He strapped her roughly to the sled, grabbed the bars. She tried to sit up, fell back.

"Stop, man—my backpack."

"You've got to be kidding!"

She watched as he impatiently pulled the metal container from the snow, looked at it briefly, swung it onto his back…

✳

Another ten kilometers to Zurich. Uli turned around. She was asleep on the back seat, one hand resting on the container. He shook his head.

The ascent back to the Hummer, the drive up the pass, past the inn and down to Bivio—it had taken everything out of him. The pain in his knee, however, had miraculously disappeared. But if he believed that his troubles were over, he was sadly mistaken.

"No. No doctor," she had protested when he had told her, as they entered the village that he would be leaving her here with a doctor and mountaineering friend who had set up shop in this nice little hamlet. And that would be that…

"No doctor, friend," she had almost commanded, as if they had some kind of prior agreement, signed in blood, which had just happened to include saving her life as a minor caveat. "Keep driving."

He was not thrilled with her tone. "Have you completely lost your mind, lady? Tell me right now what the hell is going on here!"

She waved her hand wanly. "Just drive!"

"Fine. I'll be taking you to the hospital in Chur, then," the hero of the Julier Pass said in snippy resignation, and proceeded to roar through the sleepy village and toward the canton capital.

I have a business to run, damn it. Like I need more trouble from the authorities! My license is too precious to risk for this—there was no polite word—*little cu*...he bit his tongue...Uli had been muttering angrily beneath his breath, had no reason to believe that she would hear him. The lower portion of the street was well cleared; they were making good time. The Chur exit was just up ahead.

"Chur has a good hospital. I know a..."

"No. No hospital," she countered firmly.

"*Yes,* the hospital. That is exactly where we are going. Because there are certain rules and protocols that have to be followed! And then I'm going to piss off out of here. I've had just about enough of this, you know..." He started to turn, wanting to skewer her with a look of rage, when he felt something sharp at his neck—*cold metal!*

This was unbelievable! She pressed harder. "Listen to me. Keep. Driving. That's good. You saved my life, but my life is still in danger, understand? So you need to stop acting like an asshole!" She retracted the knife.

He stepped on the brakes, bringing the Hummer to a crunching halt on the shoulder. Uli exploded. "You can kiss my fucking..." There was no end to the stream of gurgling expletives. Sophie was able to catch only a fraction of his obscenities. She waved the knife at him. "Drive over to that parking lot. We need to talk. Seriously."

"Why bother talking," he spewed with angry sarcasm, "when you could just cut my throat with your little toy there?"

"He who acts, has victory already in his pocket," she said, somewhat cryptically, but in a tone of voice, and with earnestness in her eyes, that shut him right up. He put the car in drive. Apparently he had underestimated this woman. He rubbed the scratch on his neck thoughtfully. *No tingling. No alarms.* He twitched his head back and forth a little. *The homunculus was silent. If you say so...*

"I need someone to help me. You were groping me, kissing me..."

"You are insane…My God, you have just had a tremendously traumatic experience. You need rest. Get that into that damn pea-brain of yours!"

"Shut up!" she screamed. "I'm in trouble. We need to get out of here as quickly as possible. I know a safe place in Zurich. That's where you're going to take me—understand?"

He got out of the car without a word. Sophie felt a sense of panic constricting her chest. She threw the door open and slid down from the back seat. "What do you think you are doing? Don't move!" She poked the air with her knife in punctuation.

"Just a moment, girlie." With a swift, continuous motion, he grabbed her fist and twisted her arm onto her back. The knife went flying. "Let me go, you…" she yelped.

He jockeyed her back into the car brusquely. "First things first," he said, kneeling beside the rear tire and starting to loosen the snow chain. "Did your mommy teach you enough manners to say please every once in a while? You're a total mess. And you expect me to help you, and to get myself into shit up to my neck while I'm at it? What the hell is wrong with you? Are the police looking for you?"

She looked at him mutely, color slowly creeping back to her face. A dozen heartbeats, a sigh, and then he heard her whisper "Please." Like a little prayer.

Once he was done with the fourth tire, he tossed the chains into the bed, pulled off his gloves, and sat down beside her on the back seat.

"Alright. I'll drive you to Zurich. And then I want nothing more to do with you."

"Okay, okay."

"You know, what's to tell me that I'm not risking my neck here. Now, why don't you tell me what's in that damn container you're lugging around?"

"A stolen painting," she answered calmly, like she was talking about a picnic basket. "Worth about sixty million dollars, U.S. dollars."

"I have got to be dreaming!" Uli shook his head in shocked exasperation.

"Listen. You saved my life, Uli. Now you're part of the story."

"I should have known it..."

"What? You should have known what?"

"I should have stayed home and watched the damn game."

"Then, my dear knight, you would not have been able to kiss me back to life. Can we go now?"

"I'm regretting this already, *Princess*," he said, climbing in the front and starting the engine...

...An hour later the Zurich West interchange was coming up ahead. Uli checked the navigator, slowed down, looked in the rearview mirror. Sophie was sitting up.

She smiled at him innocently, as if she had never held a reasonably sharp knife to his throat.

"Take the next exit, I'll tell you where to go."

"Yeah. You just keep doing that." He grumbled.

Half an hour later, the Hummer bobbed down the narrow cobblestone lanes of the historic district to a gate, which opened slowly. The host of the manor appeared in the little yard wearing an elegant, navy blue morning robe, suppressing a yawn behind a raised hand. Seeing Sophie's face behind the open window, his face melted into the warm expression that was Shuky Nachman's unmistakable, charming smile.

"Come, my dear," he said. "The doctor is here already. And I'm sure neither of you will say no to a cup of coffee."

Uli Stark suddenly had the unsettling feeling of having arrived in a bigger world. A world that he could learn to like, perhaps—as long as his princess of the avalanche was somewhere nearby.

Nachman Has a Plan

Shuky Nachman would go to any length. He came up with ingenious, often crazy ideas, and his ventures tended to be a happy combination of intuition and hard logic. His modus vivendi was based on lateral thinking. "You have to think laterally," he would advise his friends. "Always stay in motion, if you hit a red light—turn right instead of sitting at it, always remember to weave and bob."

While Shuky's driver carefully went about opening the Zebrowski gallery container with a screwdriver, Shuky had quietly listened to Sophie's account.

The four—Shuky, Sophie, Yorini, and Uli Stark were seated at the breakfast table. Stark looked quite cheerless. A ray of sunshine played on the large piece of art that almost completely covered the wall behind them. "Wonderful, isn't it?" Nachman asked, following Sophie's intrigued gaze. An innumerable assortment of white objects was captured in flight against a blue backdrop, weaving chaotically through the overcrowded sky. "It is a portrayal of the absence of order," the host explained, "but all objects still have their place within the apparent chaos."

She could not stop looking at the painting. The artist had placed a hundred planes in the sky. There was the Concorde with its beak-like nose, a biplane swerving through the muddle, a looping acrobat barely missing a heavy transporter, the queen of the skies, a Hercules, droning along the bottom, then above her a majestic four-engine Constellation... a sea plane; a space ship, a glider.... She kept discovering new machines. "It's incredible, Shuky. Who's the artist?"

"There, look, he also has World War II planes—a Mustang, and the Spitfire over there, see, behind the Messerschmitt," Nachman pointed with his fork. "The artist? An Italian by the name of Boetti. You probably haven't heard of him. I didn't know of him, either, but I had to have this painting. It's a depiction of my world: *Order within Chaos*."

Uli Stark mechanically stirred his coffee, the look on his face unremittingly sour. He had grudgingly accepted the offer to spend the night at the house. Now he felt out of place.

Yorini, who had his father's air of easy confidence, shoveled a forkful of bacon and egg into his mouth, chewed appreciatively, and washed it down with a sip of cappuccino. The things he had fetched from Sophie's loft in the west of town lay in a pile in the entry.

"Your key," Yorini said, mid-chew, pushing it across the table toward Sophie.

Uli pushed his plate away, stood. "Well, I'm going to be on my way."

His attempt at a farewell was interrupted by the driver, who had unpacked the painting and stood it on a chair.

"Mark Rothko," Sophie uttered reverently.

The simplicity, the powerful expression of color captivated her. How the man had suffered, and in his suffering triumphed through his art!

"We have a situation," Nachman addressed the tension. "Sophie, sooner or later it will be discovered that you survived the avalanche. We don't need to wait for the snow to melt on the Julier. This isn't about the painting. I will see to it that Baron Suvorov gets his money. You are what is most important here."

"I want nothing to do with any of this," Uli said defensively. Nachman nonchalantly ignored his objection. "We will fly to Bucharest today, and we will take the painting with us."

Sophie wonders if she has heard right. "Bucharest? Why on earth would you want to go to Rumania?"

"We have to stop for fuel, and I also want to see Paul, our business manager, there. Then we'll continue on to Armenia."

"You can visit Mongolia, for all I care," Uli snapped, "I'm driving back to St. Moritz. Thank you for your hospitality." He took a few steps, turned and looked at the others challengingly. Nachman turned his palms up in a gesture of resignation.

"As you wish. I thought you would be coming with us. After all, you are our hero after what you did last night."

"Armenia?" Sophie asked, recollecting herself. "That's not even funny."

Addressing Stark, Nachman continued unperturbed. "Please, Uli. You showed great bravery. I like you. There is no shortage of mountains in southern Armenia. What do you say?"

Yorini, who had been occupied with his Blackberry, suddenly exclaimed: "What is the name of that Baron from Engadin? The one this painting is supposed to belong to?"

At first they all looked at him blankly, then Sophie answered in a toneless voice. "Suvorov, of Castelberg Castle."

"Yup, that's him. This Suvorov is dead. Murdered." He held his device up for all to see. "It's all over the news." They took turns staring at the display, then Yorini said, "That makes two murders that can be somehow connected to Sophie." Nachman soberly assessed the situation. "Klaus Quadrini at the Dolder, and now Suvorov. Sophie, perhaps you had better stay gone a while longer. I'm afraid that the killers will soon be looking for you. And our dear police will also be able to put two and two together."

Uli had sat back down and was now looking at them, chin resting in his hands. "So, would you care to tell me what you think I need to be doing in Armenia?"

Nachman remained perfectly calm, and what he had to say was disarmingly sensible, man to man: "Uli, look, you just fit in with us, or you wouldn't have stayed, right? You're involved now, and that could lead to trouble. Stay out of the picture for a while. If you go back to Engadin, they'll ask you all kinds of silly questions. You know that. Let a bit of time go by, take a week's vacation with us, maybe two. I will pay for your services as a mountain guide . . . Ten." He held up both hands, all ten fingers outstretched.

Uli turned his head away irritably. "So you think that makes it everything alright then?"

Sophie went to the couch and allowed herself to sink into it, her face pale. The others went to sit with her. With the turbulent aircraft painting as his backdrop, Shuky began to explain how he planned to bring order to this chaos.

Meanwhile, Yorini was downstairs in the office, where he carefully placed the unmarked micro-CD containing the Hornbach brothers' completely vectored warhead construction plans on the back of the Rothko, and covered it with a piece of canvas.

He carried the painting back to the living room, giving Shuky a nod. Mission accomplished.

"The painting is coming with us," Nachman said decisively to Sophie. His voice sounded final. "This ridiculously valuable thing is safest with us, where we can keep an eye on it." And with the secret plans for the construction of a miniaturized warhead stuck to the back of it, its value has probably just more than doubled, he mused silently to himself.

Four hours later, Sophie started the PC-12 turboprop and taxied down the western runway of Zurich-Kloten airport. Taking off, she flew a wide curve, taking course for southeast.

Seated in the copilot seat beside her, Nachman studied the route through his rimless spectacles. In the cabin behind them Uli stared down at the town at the end of the narrow, gray lake. A tingling sensation spread from his head, down his neck, and across his broad shoulders.

Over the Black Sea

The thick envelope made an appearance as they were crossing over the Black Sea. It had been packed under the thin silver Notebook among a heap of bodices and underwear. The rain had been coming down hard in Bucharest when Sophie had taken off in the PC-12 again, bursting through a gray misty wall at full force. Having reached a cruising altitude of 3,700 meters, the nose of the plane glistened metallically in the bright sunshine, and the instrument panel was mirrored in Nachman's broad, dark sunglasses.

Sophie habitually checked the flight data on the autopilot, all the while thinking of the bank, her last encounter with Kleiber, the headlines she had seen on the news during their stopover... *Speaker of the Bundesnachrichtendienst BND justifies data surveillance at Ponter Bank in Zurich... Secret Service suspects Russian Mafia... All lies!... OECD ministers demand that Switzerland implement policy to release financial data of foreign citizens to their respective governments...*

That was really what it was all about! What the hell was Kleiber thinking? Sophie's heart rate quickened as she began to realize how big this thing was, that she seemed to be at the heart of... Uli sticks his head through into the cockpit, squints down at the pale Georgian coastline. He puts his hands on her shoulders, thumbs gently rubbing her neck. It is a welcome feeling, and she purrs like a kitten. "Bring me a Coke, Uli," she mutters.

They had been in the air for a good two hours, the wind at their back, when Sophie took off her headphones and peeled herself out of the tight seat. Nachman took over seamlessly, keeping the machine on course. She made her way to the back, where the luggage had been stowed; found her sleek laptop.

Having been engrossed in a magazine article, Uli now looked with interest at the envelope that Sophie weighed in her hand before sinking into the broad, leather seat across from him. Sophie, herself, was eyeing the object with intense curiosity—*Private, Confidential... Ms. Sophie Kramer... postmarked Vaduz...* She turned the padded envelope this way and that, then flipped it over and began to tear it open.

Where did this come from? *Of course, Yorini had picked it up at her apartment and tossed it in with the rest of the belongings she had requested...*

She pulled out a thin CD casing, placed it on the folding table. And then she looked in astonishment at the documents in her hand—the credit documents! The originals—not copies. A small note fell out onto her lap. She read in amazement. *Dear Ms. Kramer, I thought you may be able to make use of these. Have a look at the CD, too. It's a lot to read... Lots of luck. Yours, Manfred Kleiber.*

"What is it? Bad news?" Uli asked when he saw the confused look on her face. He stroked his beard in concern.

Sophie raised her head. "What? Oh, yes." She composed herself, held the documents aloft importantly. "The original agreements that Suvorov signed with the bank..." Her voice faded. "The proof... original bank documents... now Ponter has nothing on Suvorov anymore."

"Suvorov is dead," Uli said, wrinkling his brow. "Are you okay?" She looked at him absently. "The Rothko is free; they no longer have a claim on it. Look, here!" She waved the papers under his nose.

"I'm still not getting it," he confessed.

"Unbelievable... Okay, listen!" She explained the situation to him. Suvorov had taken out several loans with Ponter SA while alive. He had been in a great deal of debt, which he had secured with his property in

Engadin, the valuable Rothko painting, as well as the contents of his Castelberg Castle estate. "Well, sure," Uli said, "anyone who defaults on their loans has to deal with the consequences."

The original documents proving Ponter's claim were all contained in this envelope: the land charge certificate, credit agreements, authority to realize assets. Sophie laid out all of the details, raised her index finger.

"I find the fine print in here very disturbing." She flipped back two pages. "Listen carefully, it says here:... blah, blah,... here... *the event of death renders the loan due... immediately, the bank is free to demand full repayment or to freely dispose of all listed assets.* It's sickening."

She shuddered. Uli held his head in his hand. The whole thing really was absurd—he had spent pretty much every aspect of his life on the good side of the law and society at large. And now, here he was—stuck with what seemed to him like a bunch of pirates, at an altitude of 3,700 meters, listening to the financial predicaments of a murder victim.

"Freely dispose? The only disposal I know is the kind when you take out the garbage."

A quick smile flashed across her lips: "In this case, it specifically means that the bank has the right to basically confiscate the Rothko—end of story."

Uli turns up his palms. "So Suvorov's murder is really quite convenient, as far as the bank is concerned."

They looked at each other in silence. Sophie momentarily had a difficult time averting her gaze from Uli's clear blue eyes; eventually lowering it to his well-formed lips. For a moment, they share a smile. And now he fully understands that she is the reason why he is up here, flying over the Black Sea—he is here, because this is where she happens to be. "And what happens now? I mean, how are you..."

"Kleiber, the assistant director, has taken off. He...look here, the CD, I wonder what's on it."

Sophie takes it out of its case, holds it daintily between her thumb and forefinger. "It's not labeled." Uli motions his hand loosely to a folded piece of paper in the transparent plastic casing. She opens it, reads wide-eyed, sinks back into the chair. "Account details!"

"That's illegal," Uli says pragmatically.

Sophie's demeanor now turns quite professional. "Did you hear about the BND surveillance attack on the bank? Well, the person who sent this letter"—she raises the empty, brown envelope—"is the same man who leaked the data to the BND, and who is now, no doubt, living abroad under a new identity—in Australia, maybe Namibia, who knows where. We worked together at the bank, I mean, legally, before he did this...maybe he wants to warn me."

"Why? And of what?"

Sophie shrugged her shoulders, stared at the piece of paper. "Of Ponter, I would imagine. This data seems to refer to a hot account."

"Hot?"

"A hot pot. It's what we would call an account registering dubious transactions. It's basically called that, because you are liable to get burned. You have to give it enough time to cool off before the money can be put back into circulation. Get it?"

Uli looks thoughtful. Rarely, if ever, had any opportunity presented itself to him, which would have endangered his fingers in that particular manner. He snorts in amusement. But Sophie is not done. "One has to put the hot pot aside somewhere to cool off. Hot money needs to cool down, and...well, Ponter is the place where hot money is placed to do that. From what it says on the paper, the CD contains details on one of these hot pots."

"All this talk about cooking has made me hungry all of a sudden," Uli says with a grin, digging in the pocket behind his seat for a snack.

The name on the piece of paper was Nedjew. Sophie lifts the Notebook out of her bag, opens it, inserts the CD. "Let's see," she says, looking intently at the screen.

"We're about to land," Nachman calls, turning in his copilot seat. "First pilot, please!" His warm smile puts an end to Sophie's research. She shuts the laptop, puts the documents away, rushes up front where she plops into her seat and fastens her seatbelt.

"Shuky, dear," she smiles broadly at him. "It turns out Ponter no longer has a claim on Suvorov's assets. That includes the Rothko." She puts her headphones on. "We have it all in black and white!"

Zurich

As far as the woman sitting next to Ponter in a gray pantsuit was concerned, her single most important asset was her anonymity. She had never yet shown herself with Ponter in public, had never paid him a visit at home or at the bank, and this despite having known him for over two decades.

She had first met Dragan Nikolic during the Bosnian war, where he had acted as financial advisor for the Serbian Radical Party while Milosevic was in power. His job had mainly consisted of shifting large sums of money into different bank accounts in various countries. It being the war, numerous party loyalists, including commanding generals, had ended up entrusting him with money and valuables, which they had brought home to Belgrade from their marauding expeditions. In 1999 NATO had moved in on Yugoslavia with its high-tech weaponry under the command of General Wesley Clark, in order to curtail the escalation of Milosevic's attacks on Kosovo. As the country was being humiliated and ravaged by devastating air attacks, John Ponter had sent the woman now sitting next to him out to eliminate the turncoats, allowing him to confiscate their monies and redistribute them into his own accounts. The final phase of the war saw generals, who were now being sought as war criminals, disappear underground. Ponter, meanwhile, cold-bloodedly continued to have them clandestinely picked off, then redistributed their assets into secret accounts under the pretext of having a fiduciary duty to protect the funds from the clutches of The Hague Tribunal. He had developed a sophisticated system for laundering money that played out across financial centers as remote as the Marshall Islands, and as close as Switzerland itself.

The woman next to him was tasked with eliminating problems. Her weapon of choice was the knife: a tool that was widely available and which, unlike a gun, did not require a license.

In the 1990s, the Serbian head of government had sent his private banker to Zurich to open a branch. Ponter had acquired the necessary shares of a privately held bank, then gradually replaced management with people of his choosing, until he was able to take over as managing director about ten years later. He had already begun to make a name for himself as being excellent at channeling funds from the East into secure structures.

He had lost touch with the woman during this time. Then Milosevic had been arrested on April 1, 2001, and brought before the International Criminal Court in The Hague.

Among those wanting to avoid a similar fate was Lenka Borsk, who had fled to Greece via Macedonia, later to disappear in Italy as one of countless illegal refugees who never apply for asylum, and thus do not appear on the books. She lived off generous cash contributions, which her former employer supplied her with. The man she was now sitting next to.

Ponter's first encounter with Borsk had been many years ago. He had watched with interest as she had shown a group of grim men at a barracks how to effectively hoist a person up and body slam them.

He had learned that she was one of Arkan's Tigers, and had taken part of massacres and expulsions in Kosovo as part of that dreaded Serbian paramilitary organization.

As Ponter recalled on the training ground, this was not the first time he had seen Lenka. The athletic young woman, a state weight lifting champion, had competed for a spot on the Olympic team. Her face was familiar to Ponter from television reports. The war had buried Lenka's hopes for a gold medal. She had stayed home and, in the post-war chaos, her name was swiftly forgotten.

Looking at her now from the side, Ponter reckoned that the woman may have aged a little, but she had not lost her agility. And no one who had looked into them would soon forget her darkly glinting, deep-set eyes. They reminded him of bullet holes.

His informants had quickly reported back to Ponter that Lenka appeared no less ambitious in her new goals; wanting to be no less than the best by far. She trained diligently with the knife, kept her body in perfect condition, and soon not only gained respect within the president's formidable macho squad, but was feared for the brutality and precision with which she killed. A neatly severed throat, a surgical stab directly to the heart, a broken arm, a shattered knee: she commanded every move in even the most dire of close combat conditions.

None of even the fiercest brutes stood a chance against her.

Ponter recruited her. He paid better than anyone else. Within the last ten years, her pay had risen from two hundred thousand to one million Swiss francs per job. This meant that she was exclusively available to him at any time of the day or night, and to him alone. He pulled an envelope out of his black briefcase. "You did good work."

No names were mentioned. Not Suvorov, not Quadrini: once a job was completed, it was history. And there had been several recently.

Silently, Lenka Borsk opened the envelope, inspected three recent photographs of Sophie Kramer. "Where is she right now?" she asked in a distinctly Eastern European accent.

"We suspect that she is hiding in Zurich." Ponter pulled a color image out of his pocket. She stared at the symmetric lines and profound colors. "What is that?"

"A Rothko painting that she is hiding somewhere. It is very valuable. I want it back."

"Rothko and Sophie. Two jobs, correct?"

"Correct. A million for the Rothko, half in advance, the remainder when you deliver."

"And the girl?"

"The same rate. But keep her alive until she has led us to the painting."

"You are sure she has it?"

He nodded, knocked on the car's divider with pointy knuckles. The driver pulled over to the curb. "Schindler has instructions to transfer the sum to the usual place."

Borsk's lips twitched approvingly, she opened the car door and got out. Within a matter of seconds she had disappeared among the crowd.

PART III

Nedjew in Yerevan

Oleg Borisowich Nedjew owed his meteoric rise to success, at least in part, to his looks. Tall, slender and devoutly orthodox, nobody would have assumed this ascetic figure to be the head of one of Russia's most powerful crime syndicates.

He usually wore thin, gold-rimmed glasses, behind which the Crane's intelligent eyes could coldly evaluate his counterparts, although they could win them over with a warm sparkle. He was not one to hesitate. Anyone who crossed him would soon fall victim to his brutally purposeful resolve. No one had ever needed to teach him to deliberate carefully, then act decisively—he had been born with that inclination.

The news sent by Lord from Munich had reached him barely half an hour before Nedjew's jet took off heading northeast from the Cypriot airport in Limassol, bound for Turkey. At this time, Nachman's PC-12 was still on its stopover in Bucharest. Lord knew that the plane, with the Swiss registration HB-AZP was not due for takeoff to Yerevan until the following morning.

Nedjew rubbed his chin contentedly. Everything was going according to plan. His specialist had been able to extract the secret information from the Jew in Zurich. This came in no way as a surprise, since not even the toughest man had yet been able to withstand Petrova's merciless methods. Nedjew literally shuddered. Was it admiration or disgust that Irina Petrova evoked in him? Either way, he certainly would not want the brutal, shady woman as an enemy.

Oleg, son of a Magnitogorsk steel maker and mechanical engineering student at the Moscow State Technology University, had started his post-graduate career in the army. In the last weeks of the catastrophic Afghanistan campaign he became first a lieutenant, then captain of a supply company for airborne troops. Following the war, the commander of his battalion took the recently appointed captain to a post in Chechnya. Together, the comrades organized a procurement system that eventually reached far beyond troop requirements. It evolved into an efficient underground organization that became known through the Caucasus all the way to the southern reaches of Armenia. Army leadership took a hands-off approach, allowing the Crane (as the greedy vulture would come to be known, owing to his elegant appearance) free flight over broad reaches of the periphery of the crumbling Soviet Union.

The expansion into weapons did not just appeal to his affinity for technology: at heart, Nedjew was a brutal rebel, who only knew law and order when it happened to be useful to him. He had a Machiavellian nose for lucrative deals, left his opponents out in the cold, or had them disappear by means of people like Petrova. He had a further motive. Having witnessed the drudgery of his hard-working parents, he wanted to have them share in his riches and glory—and the opportunity had never been better. This was the vulnerable side of this cold, hard man. The steely commander's rough exterior concealed a soft core. a wounded soul desperate for approval. Those around him were mesmerized by his success. intimidated by his ruthlessness. Nobody recognized that the Crane—the invincible head of the *tolkachi*—was a lonely man, essentially longing for warmth that only his mother could have given him. His marriage had lasted long enough for him to sire two children, but then it had failed.

Fortune had smiled upon Nedjew in at least one respect. His power had found fertile soil in the ruins of the Soviet empire. He seized the opportunity to avail himself of the military arsenals of the debilitated former Soviet republics such as Kazakhstan, Azerbaijan, Georgia and Armenia, snatching what had been left behind and selling it to the highest bidder for exorbitant amounts.

AK 47s, rocket launchers, multiple rocket launch systems, armored personnel carriers, T 72 tanks, surface-to-air missiles in the hundreds of thousands. Finally, he managed to get his paws on a nuclear arsenal in uncontrolled storage. While the empires of lesser Kremlin loyalist billionaires crumbled, hard-hit because they had invested heavily in the types of derivatives and collateralized debt obligations that ultimately caused the global financial crisis, the clever Nedjew remained spared. He did not deal in commodities and avoided the stock market. He believed in the good, old-fashioned hoarding of cold, hard cash. He was also among the fortunate owners of first-rate property on the French Riviera, in Switzerland and London. Weapons were a flourishing market quite independent of the banking fiasco...

...At least that is what he had thought, until he learned that his Zurich bank, too, had fallen prey to the machinations of David Bernoff. Ponter SA had invested a quarter of a billion of Nedjew's monies in the dubious New York hedge fund—and lost all of it.

The Russian made use of a shady network of connections to nest himself within the workings of the Federal Security Service in Moscow. The FSB-agents had tremendous respect for the powerful man; they were happy to provide him with information for which he paid handsomely—in cash. There was nothing demure about their support of him when it came to big business dealings. Those who had not yet been bought off by Nedjew were standing in line to be bribed by him. And so the mob boss had no difficulty exacting revenge for the millions he had lost—and to show the world the price of ripping off Oleg Borisowich Nedjew by leaving the cold, dead body of Shana Bernoff displayed in Central Park.

On this afternoon, Sophie Kramer sat across from Oleg Nedjew in the Zvartnots General Aviation business lounge, ten kilometers west of Yerevan. She had no idea who he was. About as tall as an Abe Lincoln, she thought—but without the unattractively rough features. No. He was attractive, rather like...who? Clark Gable?

The long-legged, elegant man, dressed in an olive-colored military style suit with designer shades had evidently arrived on the white Global Express that was parked outside. Looking at its long, sleek nose, her PC-12 looked like a duckling next to a well-fed swan. No wonder that air traffic control had seemed harried when Nachman had requested clearance to land their dark blue Turboprop in Yerevan. This fat cat had obviously tied up all air traffic—Sophie and her companions had only just made it down ahead of him.

So that was him—the VIP whose bodyguard stood close behind him, glowering at her reproachfully, as if he thought she must be some stewardess who should be in the crew lounge and had no business here. In part entertained, in part annoyed by this, Sophie stood and walked over to the window. In its reflection she could see the pompous ass on the phone, listened intently to the Russian babble.

The Bombardier Global Express was pretty much the latest and greatest in business jets. Her face expressed admiration as she looked at the noble profile of this luxury bird.

Nedjew's arrangement seemed to be going to plan. There was just one, small problem: the resistance his adversaries would be capable of mounting in the upcoming minutes was difficult to predict with any certainty. If Barak was hiding on board, or one of his Mossad people was protecting them, there could be serious trouble. His men had not been able to ascertain the level of threat on the PC-12. His people in Bucharest had not been able to enlighten him either.

Nedjew had therefore opted to play it safe: the ambush was to be conducted with maximum force, and he would be sure to have his adversaries well out-numbered.

"Are you from Switzerland?" she heard a voice beside her say in English. There he stood, looking down at her with what seemed like mild amusement, motioned his chin toward the runway and the racy PC-12 parked there.

"Yes. Zurich. And you?"

He paused, looked at her disapprovingly as if she had committed a faux pas. His derisive expression spoke volumes: *what a tiny heap of a plane.*

It was at this moment that Shuky and Uli Stark returned from the counter holding the formal entry paperwork. "Time to go, we have the authorization..." Uli stopped—Sophie had discreetly placed her index finger to her lips.

So, where do you live? The Swallows Nest in Yalta? Were the Russian words on the tip of Sophie's tongue. This arrogant ass should know that she had command of his language. But she intuitively said nothing.

Judging by the bits of conversation she had been able to catch earlier, when Nedjew had been speaking freely on the phone, the skipper should be leaving Yalta harbor on his yacht. Swallows Nest was the name of a grandiose villa in the city of Yalta, which belonged to an eccentric oil billionaire. The notorious castle-style building was perched atop a cliff in a manner that made it appear to be floating weightlessly, depending on the angle one viewed it from. But then the Russian had issued a few more orders, which Sophie had carefully noted...

The tall, lean man removed his glasses. "I will see you later?"

Certainly not, she wanted to answer, but punished him with a cold shoulder instead. On getting back to the plane, she asked an Armenian in an orange vest lugging a hose who owned the Global Express, employing a discreet nod of her head in the appropriate direction. The driver of the fuel truck lowered his head and whispered, reverently: "Oleg Nedjew, madame." She looked abruptly up toward the lounge windows, swallowed hard, forced a smile. "Ah...*spasiba*...thank you."

Did the big shot somehow know about Zurich? The man from ground personnel rolled up the fuel hose, Sophie hastily made her way up the front stairs, stepped into the elegant cabin. She heaved a deep sigh of relief, leaned into the cockpit. "We should get out of here, Shuky. Oleg Nedjew is the bigwig on the Global Express." She plopped into the pilot's seat.

"Awaiting clearance for takeoff. Destination Baku," Nachman answered, turning the radio frequency dial. Sophie put on her headphones. "Baku? Azerbaijan?"

"A little diversionary tactic." His face had taken on a hard expression. His eyes were fixed on a spot just next to the front door of the Global Express. The round emblem painted there was exactly the same as the one on the naked body of that murdered young woman in New York.

Yerevan, Armenia

The tie-down space for the PC-12 at Zvartnots Airport was in front of a gray hangar, which was bordered by two high earth walls at the edge of the airfield.

"I don't see why I am stuck in this godforsaken hole, Shuky. Really. I mean it. Ponter will no longer be able to document that the Rothko belongs to the bank. I want to fix the situation. I feel I owe that much to the old gentleman. I want to meet up with his daughter, Natalie, and get her approval to put the painting on auction with Sotheby's. I'm sure that it will fetch a premium. People with liquid assets are interested in purchasing art—especially now, when everything seems to be dropping in value. And the timing is quite opportune. Most of the auction houses are filling their programs right about now. Christie's will also be interested…" Sophie Kramer stopped to take a breath, Nachman continued to listen patiently—he currently didn't have much of a choice.

A few minutes ago the tower had delayed permission for HB-AZP's takeoff until further notice. And so he waited.

"He can explain what happened at the Julier," she added, nodding encouragingly for Uli to join them up front. "You can do that, can't you, Uli?"

Stark grinned and called back, "Anything is possible in the mountains! You know the old saying—the Alps know no sin."

"We need your plane, Shuky," Sophie continued resolutely. "I really don't want to take the painting back to Zurich on a commercial flight."

Nachman was barely listening anymore. Why had they relegated him to this deserted tie-down space, anyway? He activated the radio control, looked up in the general direction of the tower. "Hotel Bravo Alpha Zulu Papa—do you have a takeoff time?"

"Hotel Bravo…," the answer came immediately. "Negative. Take off is delayed by approximately one hour."

Something was not right. An hour? Sophie stepped to the open front door and looked outside. She took a deep breath of fresh air. "People, it looks like we are stuck."

Uli rubbed his neck. The ominous tingling had started up again.

He leaned his head out of the cabin window and looked morosely down at the runway.

Shuky muttered something under his breath. Why was the tower not giving a reason for this unusual holdup?

The protective earth wall, which was equipped with a security fence, blocked the view to the green glass front of the ATC tower, which had issued the delay.

Nachman was liking this less and less. Judging by radio traffic, there was not a lot going on; the runways were essentially barren. The skies above Yerevan also showed no sign of congestion. A glance at the weather radar confirmed that flight conditions continued to be favorable. He turned away from Sophie, looked through the side window across the runway, and suddenly emitted a surprised grunt.

Uli Stark shot out of his seat at just the same moment and dove toward the front door.

It was the type of commando-style attack one would expect to see in an anti-terrorist mission. Masked men, dressed in black, were storming the plane. It all went down in what seemed like a flash. The first of the squad, which had appeared seemingly out of nowhere, held his machine gun ready to fire. He pounded up the front stairs, where Uli stood, blocking the entrance with his massive frame. He saw two armed men take position on their knees, their machine gun barrels pointed up toward the entrance and cockpit window.

Uli's reaction would continue to puzzle Sophie. At first she stood behind him, paralyzed. Then she suddenly understood what was threatening to take place.

She saw the tragedy unfold a split second before it happened, reading it in something about Uli's demeanor, a tension like that of a panther about to strike. Horrified, she screamed: "Uli, no!"

Too late.

The mountain guide braced himself in the doorframe with both arms, bent his legs, and delivered a powerful kick straight to the neck of the onrushing figure. The attacker screamed, fell backward and hit the runway below hard. Shots rang.

Stark did not have a whisper of a chance. He was not a member of some task force, trained in close combat—just a headstrong mountaineer who was not going to have this man get past him. Period. Standing tall, he was still looking defiantly at the tangled body of his victim down on the ground, when a hail of bullets tore through his chest and neck. He was deaf to the sound of stray bullets hitting the plane, Sophie's screams, sirens. He was numb to the second salvo of bullets, which hit his legs. He slumped, and rolled head first down the stairs.

Sophie saw the terrorists storm the plane. "Pigs!" she hissed, her whole body quaking. The men knew exactly what they were looking for. They acted with the utmost efficiency, losing no time.

The opening of the container posed no problem. They found what they had expected to find: the microchip with the secret atomic weapon plans was stuck to the back of the canvas. They left the plane with their loot—the precious, multi-million dollar Rothko. None of them had uttered a single syllable.

Uli Stark lay dead on the runway. Sophie sank to her knees, the blood pooling around the blond head of her hero, an image she would never be able to erase.

On the Grounds of the Armenus Corporation

"We have had a lot of traffic over these past weeks," Nico Strom yells into the American's ear as the engines rev.

Cosmo raises his right brow, cups his hand against his ear and turns to face Strom who stretches his arm indicating toward the end of the runway, where the gray roofs of low storage buildings stand out against the dark forest behind them.

"Anatov's have landed. The Russians down there hauled a lot of equipment—really heavy stuff, just like some heavy-duty airborne operation."

They look at each other for a moment. Abramian seems to get the message. He grabs the Swiss man by the arm, pulls him away from the machines. "General Petrov, who knows what the hell he's doing. He's an old, chewed-up war hound. Still acts like he's in the middle of some raging battle."

Strom grins knowingly. "What's his business? Oil? Equipment? Defense?"

They have reached the small cube of an office building, seeing their own wavering images approaching in the glass front, the massive planes filling out the background.

Cosmo stands still, tilts his head toward the high hangars. A tricolor flag hangs listlessly from a mast, next to it the blue corporate flag occasionally reveals the white company logo depending on the whims of the wind. Men wearing white helmets and blue overalls are forklifting heavy equipment from a truck onto the tarmac.

"Competition for the French," Cosmo says. "Project management for oil companies, and everything that goes with the business. Drilling, pipelines, geological studies, software. This is where we marry technology and logistics. The Russians are emulating the French, not to mention the Americans. They're further up. There." Strom's eyes do not follow the direction in which he is pointing, having already viewed the facilities of the Texas-based company shortly after his arrival.

"Armenus Technopark is the engine of the region—no, of the Caucasus. Trade and progress brings nations together that were previously isolated, avoiding all contact with the outside world. My techno-park is the reason that Azerbaijan and Armenia are talking to each other again. Thanks to my mediation, the two presidents are up in my guest lodgings right now, waiting to meet for the first time. Yes. Change is coming to Armenia, thanks to Armenus." He gazes at the ever-icy tip of Mount Ararat, momentarily lost in thought.

Strom was aware of the historic meeting, but had been under the impression that the Russian president had been the one to push for it. As if sensing his skepticism, Jack Abramian continued: "Moscow merely jumped on a train that was already in motion. The Kremlin does not like political maneuvering in its realm. The presidents received an invitation to Moscow after their meeting with me. There was a communiqué.... But the Russians are playing with a stacked deck. They only ever have one goal in mind."

They stopped in front of a palette containing the components of a wastewater treatment plant. Nico Strom looked questioningly into the now concerned face of the Armenian American.

"It is the strategic aim of Russia to bring Georgia, Armenia and Azerbaijan under its control. They will drive the divide all the way down to Iran."

Strom looked doubtful. "A war of aggression?"

"It's as clear as the air over Ararat. They will reclaim the Caspian territory that they held under Stalin. Their advance into South Ossetia last year was just a brilliant dress rehearsal."

"Washington will not let that happen."

"Oh, don't be so sure. All of this here is Russia's backyard. There will be saber rattling, the usual UN nonsense, and then the Russians will back down after a lot of back and forth."

"Maybe."

"It won't be in the way you think. Moscow will drive a hard bargain and finally, after a long show of resistance, they will withdraw from Venezuela, Cuba, Bolivia. When all is said and done, Washington and Russia will merely have renegotiated their respective areas of influence."

"Meaning that we will have to put up with some pretty uncomfortable neighbors," Strom concluded, looking toward the large terrain belonging to the Russian company on the south end of the compound.

"You can say that again. I had to concede a lot of space there. The Armenian government was expecting an equal distribution, you know? I had to negotiate down to a quarter."

Strom lowered his head, impressed.

"This enormous area here, pretty much from the river to the mountain, belongs to me. One hundred percent of it." Abramian's arms waved generously. "For ninety-nine years, and then it goes back to the Republic of Armenia. It was the president's wish that I concede the buildings and facilities down there to the Russians; for good money, of course. Come, let's go grab a bite. I'm hungry enough to eat a horse."

✻

It was the first time since his arrival at the impressive compounds that Nico, the Swiss aircraft engineer, had entered the perfectly shielded housing complex. Its numerous villas, sheds and greenhouses, the general purpose building. All of it was contained by a high, white wall topped with brown bricks. The entire complex was not only elevated, but also a good deal off from the commercial section. After driving through the wrought-iron gate, past night-vision cameras and hidden sensors, there was a surprising, colorful abundance of plantings: low trees, dark green bushes, decorative thistle, a lot of tall wormwood. There were long vegetable beds, and a large, lagoon-style swimming pool. The terrace of the house that Abramian was lodging in had a long, old wooden table, surrounded by a dozen over-sized chairs under vine-covered beams. A slender, long-legged dog ran over to them, nose in the air. It stopped suddenly, growled menacingly.

"Yes, yes, Feedback. Calm down. This is a good friend."

The dog jumped up on Cosmo, who caught her and held her under his arm as he sat down at the table. The sunroof descended over the pergola with a hum. The voices of cheerful children could be heard inside the house.

"My family," Cosmo said with a smile that was almost a bit apologetic. "My daughter has five children. Her husband is in charge of logistics here."

"You have grandchildren?" Strom said in surprise then looking around: "This estate is enormous!"

"Grandchildren and a load of nephews and nieces. Armenians are a whole tribe unto themselves. Blood is thicker than water." His laugh was warm and gravelly. "We stick together, and we like to live in one big heap. Andy!"

The gangly Californian emerged from a utility shed next to the greenhouse holding a large, artfully crafted birdcage. "Sir?"

"Bring us something to drink, please. Mr. Strom will be staying for lunch."

"Of course, sir. Look what I found."
"For your cheeky parrot in Sonoma?" Abramian said teasingly.

✳

Slowly but surely, women and children, girls and boys, began to gather at the table, and the meal was served. Andy poured the wine. Abramian's daughter said grace. The conversation hushed as the family enjoyed their meal, the well-behaved children quietly eyeing the stranger.

"Father is very strict, he has his foibles. The kids do not speak during mealtime," Jana said with a smile. "I am responsible for the gardening, but it's not as if he ever stops telling me what to do."

Abramian pushed his plate away. "I just want her to grow her tomatoes and herbs organically—but let's not get into that." He stood, beckoned the Swiss man to join him.

They walked past the one-story living quarters, through the garden and to the schoolhouse, as Abramian referred to it. Looking through the tall windows Nico saw desks and whiteboards, a gym, a grand piano—probably in a music room. They continued on to the solid gray, windowless block, slightly elevated and built up against a steep slope littered with boulders. Cosmo stepped lightly up the steps to the terrace, turned and stretched his arms like a holy man bestowing blessings upon the land. "There on the left you see the town, it's a little misty right now, and in the front there, where you see the tractors, our farms." He turned on his heels, stepped through an automatically opening door into a bright, futuristically decorated and sparsely furnished hall.

"Our communications center," Jack explained, visibly proud.

"This is where it all comes together. Andy is good for more than opening wine bottles, carving the roast and taking care of our mutt."

"Top of the line and everything you could need," Nico said admiringly as he took in the multitude of equipment and monitors. "It's all the latest and greatest!" He leaned forward, staring mesmerized at a flat screen, which was displaying data from the American Low Earth Orbit satellite system, including positioning, signal strength, trajectory and current altitude. Cosmo pulled him over to another broad screen by the elbow. Feedback had hopped onto a swivel chair, where she sat panting on her hind legs, clearly the center of all that was going on.

"The LEO satellites orbit at an average altitude of two hundred and seventy kilometers over Iran, cycling at approximately two hours," Cosmo lectured enthusiastically. "For a long time, this region was not well monitored. The satellite orbits were to the north and south of here, essentially. For the longest time, the Americans were fixated on hot spots in Iran, while the Russians focused on the Gulf. The Pentagon wasn't bothered with what went on in the region between Eastern Anatolia and the Caspian Sea. I had to give those generals a bit of tutoring." He chuckled to himself.

Strom approached the monitor. "Those are first-rate satellite images."

Cosmo smiled, flattered, and exchanged glances with Andy. "LEO covers Iran for us." He pointed to the large screen, then at the white, empty wall. "We can project the images any time."

Nico stared, visibly impressed by the incredible display of military high tech. *Low Earth Orbit—LEO: the satellite system the Americans used essentially to spy on the whole earth. LEO was used to control reconnaissance drones and cruise missiles.* He addressed the elephant in the room. "Where is the surveillance coming from?"

Cosmo made an expansive gesture. "From everywhere, Nico. These are the same low orbiting satellites that provide our Operation Snowdrop with cell and signal service. But the satellite images are also from the Turkish site on Mount Ararat—you could say sponsored by me. Not without some self-interest, of course."

Strom soberly considered the implications. He could have used a stiff drink right about now. Cosmo continued calmly, "Come, I want to show you the heart of all this. It's behind that glass door. Our ground station. It is the latest in sophisticated technology, Nico. Have a look."

Nico stepped up to the security door that read NO ENTRY, pressed his nose up against the bulletproof glass and beheld a wall of drawer-like white-and-gold installations that stretched as far as his eyes could see.

"It is all quite sterile, yes. There really is not much to see," Cosmo said with an impish grin. "This is no old switchboard. This computer has an enormous capacity. Currently it is set to handle twenty million cell phone connections."

"Twenty million connections," Nico repeated, amazed.

Jack Abramian smiled indulgently. "I could hardly believe it myself, at first. Technology is phenomenal these days. But I retain my deepest respect for my friends at the Pentagon."

Strom raised his eyebrows questioningly. "I thought the CIA was responsible for satellite surveillance such as LEO."

"Not anymore, Strom. Fortunately. Today the military is in charge of LEO. It uses it to steer its cruise missiles, run surveillance, capture images, locate missed targets, and so forth." After an artful pause, he added, "And, most recently, LEO satellites have become the perfect antennas for our air-drop cell phones."

Aid for air-drop cell phones. Strom shook his head in wonder. "It's unparalleled, Jack. How on earth did you pull that off with the Pentagon?"

"I'll save that story for another day, perhaps. I'm from California, remember? Ours is the land where dreams come true, and nothing is impossible." He smiled mysteriously. "Are you surprised that the military is secretly onboard with Snowdrop?"

"No, not really, come to think of it. But won't Iran be able to block the signal?" Strom waved his hand, dismissively, almost as he asked the question. "Stupid question. I'm sure you've thought of that."

Cosmo was in his element. They stepped through to the coffee bar. Several communications specialists raised their heads and watched curiously as they passed. "The frequencies are constantly changed. The Iranians may try to electronically jam the signals, but they don't have the technology. And even if they did, our frequency hopping would make it impossible."

Eventually they strolled back. Feedback raced boisterously through the bushes. Andy had disappeared. They sipped Turkish coffee on the deserted terrace. The host offered to pour some local vermouth. Nico opted instead for vodka on the rocks and lit up a Havana cigar. He gazed thoughtfully at the garden, listening to the tinkling, buzzing sounds of the cool early evening.

"My roots are Armenian, and California is home," Jack Abramian said contentedly. And in the peaceful, relaxed atmosphere he talked of the country, what it meant to him, his people, the Armenians, once celebrated builders of palaces and cities like Isfahan and its incredibly modern infrastructure—in the sixth century, during the Sasanian Empire.

Airfield, Armenus Airport

They heard the characteristic singing of the engine of an airplane approaching, then saw the landing lights. The position lights appeared to flicker as the white elegant fuselage crossed the beam of the lights on runway 03.

Nico's expert eye immediately recognized the model—not one of theirs—a first-class bird, the silhouette of which now disappeared behind the buildings.

Following Oleg Nedjew's command, the pilots steered the plane toward the Gulag—at least, this was what the Europeans at Armenus Park jokingly called the dark, long halls within the tall security fences at the southern end of the runway. The Russians resided there in immense underground facilities and living quarters, well separated from everyone else.

The aircraft stopped in front of the Container—an aluminum cube with windows resembling arrow slits that sat at a distance from the main complex.

Jim, the American air traffic controller in the tower, watching the maneuverings of the newly landed plane attentively, said to his younger German colleague, "You know, Heinz, we used to fly accommodation containers like that up to Thule, on the Northern Cape, when I was in the air force."

Lights came on, men appeared from the Container, ran onto the runway, helped to let down the air stairs. "I would have expected the Russkys to put up a few dachas," the German noted. "Not my problem. Who do you think the big bird belongs to?"

The American peered through a pair of binoculars. "Probably the tall guy. That one there. You see him, Heinz?" He leaned toward the mike, wished the pilots a good night.

"Do you know him?"

Jim looked through binoculars again. "One of those incredibly rich Russian bigwigs, his name is . . . wait . . . it's on the tip of my tongue." He scratched his head, trying to remember.

Heinz checked the flight records, which contained no information about the passengers, only the Russian identification. "Well. That's it for us. Time to close shop," he said. In the greenish light, his young face looked pleased that it was time to call it a day. He stood, stretched and walked across the room.

A dual beam of lights caught his eye behind the tower. A car had turned off the street and was heading toward the gate that secured the entrance to the hotels and apartment buildings.

This was nothing unusual. Armenus Park was vibrant with life around the clock, the bar at the Ararat Hotel was open all night—the two pilots were already headed that way to treat themselves to a well-deserved nightcap. The air traffic controller did not notice the lights of the second vehicle, which had followed the first at this late hour and stopped outside the compound at a safe distance.

The American pocketed his car key, looked for and found the pager that kept him connected to the ATC system at all times. Together, they left the tower, descended in the elevator and stepped out to Jim's car.

Oleg Borisowich Nedjew was curt. Not acknowledging the deferential greeting of the waiting driver, he folded his one meter ninety frame into the luxury car, which took off smoothly and turned into the darkness.

Within a few minutes a series of green lights indicated the secured driveway.

The driver knew the way perfectly, hitting the remote as he steered the Mercedes efficiently down toward the gate. Seconds later they entered a dimly lit hall and turned toward a broad, mirror-like glass wall. The car stopped just in front of a green carpet that covered two steps leading to a bright reception area, in front of which a stocky military man in uniform waited. The red-faced Petrov saluted tautly as the well-known visitor exited and drew himself up to his full stature.

Thrusting his chin forth commandingly, Nedjew addressed the man brusquely: "General! Everything ready?"

"Yes, Excellence, the delegation is waiting in the conference room."

They strode across the soft carpet, the glass doors opening silently to make way into an opulently decorated interior. A short corridor led to an oval room with narrow gold-framed mirrors lining burgundy walls at short intervals. Facing the mirrors were mock curtains of red velour, which hung above a slate gray sideboard at odds with the curvature of the room. From the ceiling, an oversized chandelier with a mass of decorative crystals bestowed a lazy play of light upon the heads of those entering.

Two elegantly uniformed officers arose from chairs upholstered in Soviet red with elaborately carved armrests. The first was short, with a round, slightly tanned face. He did not have a beard, but bore the insignia of an Iranian air force colonel. The white badge above the pocket of his dress uniform read *Rhani* in black letters. He turned to the other with the gold star on his sleeve. Brigadier General Bakhtiar was a slender, wiry officer with jet-black, bushy hair. *Forget the names; remember the faces,* Nedjew thought. He greeted the Iranians politely, carefully scanning their fixed countenances for any hints.

They sat in response to a casual gesture from their host. Petrov had remained standing partway in the room, where he rocked on the heels of his highly polished boots as if he were inspecting a drill, and not standing upon a plush Persian carpet. Two waiters navigated a trolley laden with bottles across the edge of the carpet and toward the sideboard.

"You will understand, Mr. Nedjew," began the brigadier general in fluent English, "there are two conditions that must be met before my government releases the remainder of the funds."

Meeting the stern gaze of the Iranian unblinkingly, the Russian host picked up a glass of vodka and crossed his long legs.

"Our government wants test. We want certainty that product works," the linguistically less proficient colonel spoke up, casually letting the cat out of the bag. He left unmentioned the experience of working with the North Koreans. The Nodong rocket that had been procured under the greatest level of secrecy did, in fact, reach its target when tested. But the so-called nuclear warhead had simply disintegrated into a thousand useless pieces—they were not about to repeat such an embarrassment.

Nedjew silently hid his surprise, but the Russian's assumed composure did not go unnoticed by the Iranian with the gold star. "Are you able to fulfill this condition?"

"A test of an atomic weapon? That is a bit of an unusual request, wouldn't you say? Where are we supposed to aim it? We have no interest in exposing ourselves to radioactive fallout in Armenia for your country's nuclear ambitions."

The brigadier general was unfazed. He motioned the colonel, who produced a map and unfolded it. He pointed to a spot with a slender finger.

"Not to worry. The target is far from Armenia. It is in Balochistan, on the Pakistani border."

"Okay Fine." Nedjew waved to his general. "Petrov, are we able to accept this? Can it be done?" he growled in Russian.

General Petrov turned his vodka-reddened countenance to face the slender captain, who had stepped up quietly. "Can it be done? It must be done!"

The captain, who wore a missile unit insignia on his collar, took another step forward, leaned over the map, and approximated the coordinates of the target area. He then sat wordlessly at a computer, began clicking away with the mouse.

"So, Captain? Yes or no?"

The Russian missile specialist calmly adjusted his glasses and remained silent. After a while, he turned. "It can be done, General—southern Armenia will not be affected by the radioactive fallout."

"Well, then. It's pretty far from here, right?"

The captain remained silent, allowing the Iranian to speak. "This is about whether or not the warhead is functional, gentlemen, not the trajectory," Bakhtiar said pointedly, stroking his thin mustache with two fingers.

"Yes, yes, you have made yourself clear," Nedjew countered with some aggravation. To hell with this annoyance of a man—if the Quran allowed for such a serviceable solution. Not that Nedjew cared. "And just when are we going to blow up Balo...?" he asked, sounding out the syllables with great deliberation.

"*Balochistan*. We wish to see the impact as soon as possible."

"You mean you want the world to see the impact," the Russian shot back. "Fine, what do I care? If there's a party, we're there—right, Petrov?" The general raised his chin and snapped his heels together. Nedjew's voice now had a cold edge to it. "And if you're in a hurry, you'll have to pay, Brigadier General. And I mean: Immediately."

The Iranians lowered their eyes and appeared to be thinking. His forehead furrowed suspiciously, twirling his glass, Nedjew forged on. "And the second condition?"

"The innovation that was promised," the Iranian said. "The Hornbach Papers. We must be given the Swiss plans for the new warheads."

Generally speaking, both conditions were easy to fulfill. The whole thing was about as complicated as a game at a children's birthday party—were it not for the money that was still outstanding. About a billion dollars, to be precise. *Stay calm, Oleg Borisowich!* "A drink?" The Russian offered with an extended hand, raising his glass to his hard mouth with the other and emptying it with one fluid motion. As expected, the Iranians politely, but firmly declined the alcohol.

"Fine. Then let us start the demonstration." Nedjew signaled Petrov. A hidden door next to the sideboard opened as if by magic revealing a railcar with comfortable seats.

"Allow me?" Nedjew went ahead, with a triumphant look at the Iranian's befuddled expressions. "We should not waste time."

The vehicle, drawn by a steel cable, glided noiselessly through the dimly lit tunnel, seemingly forever.

"That was three kilometers," Petrov remarked dryly as they pulled into a brightly lit station, which was filled with a bustle of activity. Men in white overalls sat at monitors, technicians with red hard hats came and went, flashing lights signaled at passages. Nedjew said a few words to a servile egghead wearing rimless glasses, beckoned his visitors to follow him. An electronic watchdog with blinking indicator lights demanded a code. Given its bone, an aluminum partition slid aside with a smooth hum.

The Iranians stood silent and motionless on the other side. Their astonished eyes beheld a small, dome-shaped room. At its center stood a slender rocket, attached to a launcher.

"The Sunburn," the brigadier general murmured to his colonel. "The showpiece of Russian naval rockets and the terror of the U.S. fleet. It can take a two hundred kiloton nuclear warhead. Fantastic!"

Nedjew pointed proudly at the ten-meter-long SS-N-22 Sunburn. "This is the rocket I agreed upon with your negotiator. Nasrallah signed off on everything for Hezbollah. Your troops will be accepting delivery at the border not far from here." He cast a glance at his Rolex. "In precisely four hours, gentlemen, if we can come to an agreement."

The Iranian officers exchanged perturbed glances. "What do you want to demonstrate with this launcher?" the air force colonel said mildly, as if speaking to a recalcitrant child. "We will be dropping the rockets on target with our fighter jets."

"This here is our testing facility," Nedjew explained, somewhat condescendingly. "The rocket is operational, no testing necessary. You may examine it. Its range is large enough to reach Israel, if you use our Sukhoi Su-30." He coughed artfully. "If you manage to get through." He paused for effect, then concluded sarcastically: "Or the decks of U.S. aircraft carriers in the Persian Gulf."

The brigadier general's dark eyes sparkled menacingly. "Don't push your luck, Tovarisch. The Kremlin is also in range, if I am not mistaken. We believe that Moscow will one day want to push forward to the Caspian Sea. We will be prepared for that day."

The Russian made a conciliatory gesture, raising both hands with a disarming grin. "You are right, of course. I am just saying we should not waste time. Do you have any other questions? Shall we go back?"

Outside at the station they took seats on cold, metal chairs facing a large screen on which a technician, following the instructions given by the Iranians, projected a map of the southeastern part of their country. "This here is our testing area," the brigadier general said, highlighting part of the Pakistani border with a laser pointer.

General Petrov, who had remained in the background, cleared his throat. His bulging eyes rolled back and forth between the map and the rocket station. "What load?" he asked in Russian. "A hundred kilotons? The detonation point is high, that means it is calculated to detonate at altitude."

The colonel turned his round face to the brigadier and muttered. "A high detonation point would reduce the radioactive fallout to a tolerable minimum." *Our aim is not to destroy the target area, just to show the world a mushroom cloud. To let it be known that Tehran has the bomb! We can accept a bit of heat and radioactive rays in the backlands, where we have a problem with disloyalty anyhow. Intimidating those people would be an effective and not unpleasant side effect.*

Men in white lab coats carried one of the slender rockets into the station. An expression of something resembling pride flashed across Nedjew's face. "This is it from up close. You will be receiving twelve. It will take thorough preparation to hit Balochistan."

"That is our concern, Mr. Nedjew."

The Iranians were not about to go out on a limb. They did not need the Russians for the test. What they needed was the rocket—just like the one they were currently looking at, and the nuclear warhead.

They finally drove back, settled in the conference room, where an opulent buffet complete with lobster and caviar had been set up.

"What do you target for your testing?" Brigadier General Bakhtiar asked, spooning the black delicacy onto his plate.

"Nagorno Karabach!" Nedjew laughed resoundingly and slapped his thigh, which seemed rather silly. The mood, however, did lighten a bit.

The Iranians ate heartily, enjoyed some tea. They harbored no illusions that the central issue was in any way resolved. The brigadier general was the first to come back to it. He pushed his plate away, took a sip of tea, leaned forward slightly. "Very well. So, where are the Swiss plans?"

Nedjew would not have been the battle worn, tough-as-nails negotiator that he was if this question had taken him by surprise. He shook his head slowly. The Iranians tensed.

"We have them," Nedjew responded, savoring the situation. His swagger showed, but he did not allow himself the indiscretion of giving away the details of how they had been obtained. The microchip containing the coveted plans for the Hornbach engineers' miniaturized nuclear warheads had, indeed, been stuck to the back of the painting in the Jew's airplane—and was now in his pocket. He had been sure to remove the chip from the canvas on the flight south, so as not to have to carry the cumbersome painting around with him.

Nedjew chewed ostentatiously on a lobster claw. "My suggestion, Brigadier General, respectfully, is that we deliver the goods at the agreed-upon time, you pay the outstanding sum into the escrow account, also as agreed upon. As soon as the bank in Zurich confirms receipt, I will hand over the Hornbach plans. At a location of your choosing. But not before the Ponter Bank in Zurich confirms receipt of the money. Are we clear?"

The lean, high-ranking Iranian stood, his expression somber. "We still have a problem."

For a few seconds Nedjew feared that this scarecrow of a man would actually drop the negotiations.

"You cannot charge us for the plans," Bakhtiar said with a dead earnest expression.

Nedjew's eyebrows shot up damn near to his hairline. "Have you completely lost your mind?" he sputtered.

"Hardly. The plans do not exist. They were destroyed in Bern, under pressure of the Americans! The Swiss government is a good shredder, it always does a very thorough cleaning job." A restrained smile crept onto Bakhtiar's face as he gloated over Nedjew's perplexed expression, which was slowly turning to understanding.

"Oh, very funny. Funny man." His smile was forced. The mischievous Iranians had caught him on the wrong foot. Annoyed, he waved at his general who, suppressing a grin, stepped sharply over to a small table and inserted a CD into a black device. The room darkened, a screen lowered from the ceiling.

"How about I double the price?" Nedjew attempted to counter. "After all, I am providing Iran with exclusive nuclear plans that do not even officially exist anymore. I think that's a pretty good deal!"

"Alright. Enough joking," the Iranian countered now looking grim. The verbal exchange remained a harmless intermezzo. Images were projected in quick succession. Plans, drawings, views, details, formulas from the Hornbach papers. Colonel Rhani raised a hand every once in a while, asking for a pause, or to go back. A couple of times he requested an enlargement. After half an hour of in depth presentation the Iranian leaned forward to speak to his general, which they did in whispers. Several times the brigadier general looked questioningly at his technical expert, who ranked among the leading nuclear scientists of the nation. Finally, he turned to the Russian and nodded.

"Fine, Mr. Nedjew. We have an agreement."

"An agreement? Really?"

Brigadier General Bakhtiar smiled for the first time this evening. It was a smug smile. "We accept your conditions. The rockets immediately, the plans later."

Oleg Borisowich Nedjew vaulted out of his chair, extending his hand to the Iranian. "Very good, General. It has been a pleasure doing business with you. I drink to your great country, to Iran! To the new atomic power!"

The Iranians looked on the Russian with bemusement as he knocked back his vodka, grunted in a macho manner, shook himself, put down his glass and looked around, perfectly satisfied. *A country that didn't even have vodka would never have been able to develop the atomic bomb on its own steam!*

✳

When she picked up the keys at the reception desk, Sophie Kramer looked quite drawn and sweaty, with loose strands of hair hanging messily in her face. She took a few steps over to the bar and sank, exhausted, into the cool, black leather of the two-seater.

She had no intention of going to sleep. First she wanted to acquaint herself with this new place, to scope the layout of this Techno Park. She had seen a signpost to the Visitor Center at the entrance and hoped she would be able to obtain a map there.

The news was showing on a screen behind the bar... *the President of Iran condemned the extension of economic sanctions by the President of the United States in unusually harsh words and threatened retaliatory measures, as Member of Parliament Ismail Kowarski told the national news agency...*

The blonde waitress brought Sophie a beer, which she served with a friendly smile just as two men burst into the lobby and headed straight toward the bar. Without hesitation, they sat straight down at her table. Judging by his accent, one of them was American. "Well, hi there, you're up late, too, I see!"

The other raised his hand in a greeting with a smile. As it turned out, they were the two guys from the tower, Jim and Heinz. Before they had even received their beers to be able to raise a toast, Sophie had already found out that the last machine for the night had just landed.

"Some Russian on a Global Express," Heinz revealed importantly. "State of the art, that thing."

Had the pretty woman flinched when he had said that? He definitely thought that he had seen a flicker in her eyes. He went on. "Just get here?"

She nodded.

"Are you here for work? Are you a teacher?"

She raised her eyebrows. "Mmm. Sometimes, maybe. Is that what I look like to you?" Jim, who was gauging her and had already found in favor of the possibility of a little after-hours hanky-panky, said that, yes, there was a school here, and it wasn't unusual to come across a new teacher.

"I am a translator," she informed them. "Russian."

"They're all holed up down there—in the Gulag." Heinz grinned and nodded his head loosely in that direction. "You work for the Russians?"

Sophie saw her chance, gave a general kind of nod. "How do I get down there, to this—what did you call it—Gulag?"

They both grinned broadly. Jim said that wouldn't be a problem at all. One could drive down there. "There's a shuttle."

"Isn't the airfield locked?"

"No. The bus stops at the Visitor Center. Do you want to go there this late?"

She had almost nodded, then deliberately chose to vehemently shake her head instead: "Oh, definitely not. It's time for bed. Nice talking to you." She stood, the guys both jumped up, gallantly said good night in the hope, as they eagerly attested to, of seeing her again the next day.

The voice on the television squawked on in the background... *Moscow's rigid stance on Crimea has raised questions about the Olympic Winter Games in Sochi. And now football. The semi-final...*

"We can give you the VIP tour," Jim offered charmingly in a last-ditch effort. She disappeared into the elevator with a smile. Now she was definitely no longer thinking of going to bed. The plan had already started to evolve, and there was no time to lose. What did Shuky Nachman always say? Was it Goethe? It was good, at any rate: He who acts has already got the victory in his pocket.

✳

Lenka Borsk had backed the stolen Audi between the bushes and shouldered her backpack. She started off in an easy jog. She estimated the distance to the lights at about one kilometer. Her air-cushioned running shoes barely made a sound against the pavement.

She stopped a good hundred meters short of the lit signpost for Hotels and Residences, turning off onto a steppe-like field. She swung herself over the wall behind the little security building, landed on a soft, damp lawn, and crept toward the brightly lit building. Hotel Ararat.

If she wanted to complete Ponter's assignment of finding the Rothko, she had to stay on Sophie's heels. She had no idea where the valuable painting could be, but one thing was certain: Kramer would bring her to it. If patience was a virtue, it was definitely one she could lay claim to. She had until morning—Kramer would have checked into the Ararat. She scoped out the parking lot, discovered the black Golf, covered in dust and mud. She would search the interior in the early morning hours—until then there was nothing to do but wait. She grabbed a folding chair from the terrace and made herself comfortable. From this vantage point at the rear of the hotel, she was able to see through the lobby...

It was past midnight when a figure appeared at the back entrance and vanished into the night. In the dim outdoor lighting, it had only appeared as a dark, slender silhouette, making its way toward the tennis courts, then disappearing behind the shrubs. It briefly reappeared as a shadow against the light blue, shimmering water of the pool before being definitively swallowed by the darkness.

Borsk's vigilant eyes might very nearly have missed the stealth departure, had she not been watching the window to Kramer's room for quite some time. The unclosed curtains had afforded her a good view of Kramer's shadowy movements.

Her victim evidently had no intention of going to sleep. Borsk tensely held her position, shielded by some prickly hedges. Her gut told her that the woman had plans. And so she waited. Then the shadowy movements suddenly stopped, and did not resume. When the figure stepped out of the door downstairs, the patiently lurking Borsk was ready to pounce...

Having reached the Visitor Center, Sophie searched along the bars of the massive fence. She saw the sign for the shuttle bus and easily found the spot. Just as the guy at the bar had said, there was access to the airfield—and, sure enough, it was not locked. The nocturnal visitor turned the brass knob, the latch slid back, and the door opened with the slightest touch. Sophie pushed it open all the way and found herself standing on the airfield. Instinctively, she ducked beneath the shadow of the bus stop awning.

Now what? Just don't start wavering!

She started running toward the large, dark building. There was no one in sight. No lights were on. Coming closer, she saw the forecourt, the outline of a tailfin appeared. She continued toward the corner of the building, pressed her back against the wall, took a few deep breaths.

Then she crept past the locked hangar gates, looking up at the enormous transporter that towered above her in the night with its dark, mammoth form.

Slowly she made her way to the other end, tried to orient herself, always with an eye on the plane where everything seemed to be still.

She had just reached a pavilion when a white moon freed itself from behind the clouds, allowing her to make out the signs on the little building.

Schlumberger, she read, and beneath that Reception and Hours of Operation.

Where were the Russians? The Gulag is all the way at the end, she remembered the men at the bar saying and searched the compound in the assumed direction.

It was then that she felt something on her right leg—a warm something that she felt was creeping up between her thighs.

She spun around, horrified, barely managing to stifle a scream with her own hand. She found herself face to face with a good looking young man with slicked-back, black hair and pale, striking features. He looked surprised. She looked down to see the hands that had just been groping her . . . and discovered a leash, with an odd-looking dog on the other end of it. A dog, who was now sniffing at her from a more respectful distance, raising its nose again and again, trying to capture her smell. She breathed a sigh of relief.

"Feedback, sit . . . good dog . . . she is harmless," the young man whispered hoarsely. "What in the name of God are you doing out here in the middle of the night?"

"What about you? What are you doing here?" She hissed back sharply, taking a step back and looking around. The friendly grin on the gangly young man's face was reassuring. The way he stood there, his whole demeanor, caused her mistrust to melt away almost instantly.

"Taking Feedback for a walk. I love the nighttime, just making my rounds," he said, and pulled her gently by the arm into the shade of the trees.

"Let me go...how dare you!"

"Psst!" He held his finger to his lips.

Then he held her, whispered in her ear. Sophie wanted to tear free. *How could she have been so mistaken about this guy?* But when she made out his urgently whispered words, she relaxed, allowed him to hold her—then jumped back suddenly: "Nonsense. Nobody's following me...Are you sure?"

He nodded. "I first saw her over by the Center. A real snake, believe me. She's somewhere around here. We should act as if we are meeting secretly for some kind of date. That's the best idea...So, what's going on here? My name is Andy, my boss owns everything around here, I mean, really—everything. He can help you...erm..."

"Sophie."

"He can help you, Sophie."

"I have to get to the Russians," she began as they walked away from the pavilion across the lawn, arms tightly wound around each other, Feedback signaling danger with a low growl, Sophie let her ally in on her plan.

She did it all instinctively, her actions entirely driven by her emotions. Her rational mind told her that there were a hundred reasons to not tell this perfect stranger a single word. But Sophie opted instead to trust the feeling that flooded her with a sense of warmth on this still night in the south of Armenia, far from everything she knew. She just let it all go. She felt she could trust Andy. No, she knew that she could.

By the time they reached the aluminum container, Sophie had told him about the events in Yerevan. They crept closer, leaned up against the windowless wall and looked at the slick machine that stood shimmering in the pale moonlight about fifty meters away.

"That's his plane," Sophie whispered.

The airfield was deserted. There was no light in the container office. "It's all dark. We're alone—come, let's go!"

Andy held her back, pointed up toward the roof at the corner of the building. "Cameras."

But Sophie ignored his warning, pulled away from his grip. She sprinted across the airfield, stretched up against the plane, fumbled at the door.

Andy held Feedback on a short leash, peered around, then up at the night sky.

A black wall of clouds was slowly encroaching on the bright crescent moon.

Andy considered feverishly how he might be able to deactivate the cameras... he would have to climb up, turn them off, or... he ran, hunched, to the other side, where he had seen a shadowy pile of stuff. Yes, good! He stood before a barrel, pushed against it. It shifted.

As he looked back at the airplane, the moon vanished behind the cloud and the dark shadows of the machine swallowed Sophie completely. *What the hell was she doing?* Andy felt a sensation of heat in his chest and stomach. The unexpected proximity of this woman had got him all riled up.

At just that moment, a red warning light began to rotate and flash over the container. Its wandering beam gave up just enough illumination for him to catch a glimpse of his new acquaintance as she pulled down the front stairway.

What now? He was just about to run over to the machine when a light went on several hundred meters away at the Russian complex.

Andy stared at the barrel, deep in thought. Feedback sniffed at the thing, almost as if to egg his best friend on to follow the insane idea that had just occurred to him.

A glance over at the plane revealed that a light had just come on there, too. In the cabin. *Was she looking for that painting she had told him about?*

Andy screwed the lid off the spout at the top of the barrel, smelled— *gas!* He shook it. Heard a splashing noise.

He looked deliberatively over the distance toward the Gulag, now hearing the ominous sound of starting engines as he manhandled the barrel toward the airfield on its edges. He hurriedly stripped off his cotton shirt, tore it in two.

The sounds are coming closer. Two, three cars, he guesses. Headlights are coming into view. He sees nothing happening at the plane. *She needs to get out!*

He has drenched the torn shirt in gas, is now stuffing it firmly into the opening—only a corner hanging out. And there come the guards—blinding lights, engines revving threateningly.

Smoking increases life expectancy, Andy quips to himself, ridiculously, as he pats himself down for his lighter. He upends the barrel, pulls the rag from the hole. Gas spurts out. He waits…another hundred meters, fifty…now! Andy pushes the barrel powerfully with both arms. It rolls…and rolls…straight toward the cars, the splashing gas wetly marks its path…he lights his drenched shirt, throws it. The gas lights up, flames race to catch up to the barrel…KABOOM! An explosive flame lights the entire airfield bright as day, the loud thud of an explosion echoes against the nearby hills. The cars come to an abrupt halt. The first has caught fire. Men jump out yelling loudly…

Andy takes off toward the machine, Feedback, yowling, on his heels. She, at least, seems to be enjoying the excitement.

Shots ring out—not meant for him. *Weird! No ricochet!*

"Careful!" Sophie screams from the top of the stairway. He notices—the engine is running. More shots. He ducks, looks up questioningly, can't understand what she is shouting, can't make out what her frantic gestures mean.

She stretches her arm out, pure horror on her face. Andy instinctively spins around as two armed men jump out of a Jeep, machine guns pointed straight at him.

"Get on the ground! Face down!"

He throws himself down, as told, hugs Feedback to his side. He feels a painful kick to his ribs. Out of the corner of his eye, he sees a distorted image of boots pounding up the stairs, two at a time.

It's—over!

He stays perfectly still, clenches his teeth, the man behind him has him covered—or does he?

Two black running shoes appear in his line of sight, come to a stand. A rough voice commands: "Get up, run...Do it!"

He tentatively raises his head, sees the blood-streaked blade, the hand, the arm, the face...He jolts upright, stares at the wiry woman aghast, takes account of the guard, lying in a heap on the ground, the pool of blood...

The stalker! The snake! Andy stumbles to his feet, scrambles for some sort of understanding...The devil is gone...already at the top of the stairs, inside, closes the door.

Feedback tears at his pants leg, howling.

"You're right, Feedback—time to get the fuck out of Dodge." Andy runs for it, dodges under the belly of the plane. The engines rev, heavy wheels begin to move, grudgingly at first. He instinctively grabs a hold of the undercarriage, pulls himself up as he pushes Feedback aside.

She can fly this thing? His thoughts are racing as the Global Express heads toward the start of the runway. He tries to connect the dots, can't. His arms begin to cramp. As the aircraft turns after a good five hundred meters, he lets go, rolls, jumps up. Andy runs out from the plane, waving wildly at the cockpit, screaming in the headlights. The shadowy face of the pilot is staring ahead...he gives up. The powerful bird gives a thrust, the engines howl deafeningly—There! She sees him, a short eye exchange—the Global Express gains traction, momentum, thunders down the runway, takes off...

The moon has disappeared. Andy cowers on the ground. All hell has broken loose over at the Gulag and by the Container. Flashing lights, fire engines, search beams...squawking loudspeakers.

Feedback jumps up on him, licks his cheek encouragingly. They head off into the Armenian night.

Exit West

The Global Express was long range—meaning that it was built for long-distance flights. Sophie had still been checking minor details, such as her fuel situation, as she steered the massive machine down the darkened runway and into the unknown with clammy hands. Her entire body was clammy. *What could possibly go wrong…?*

As she gradually gained sufficient altitude and dared to turn southwest, she was finally able to lighten her grip on the yoke. Her eyes wandered across the multitude of gauges and displays. The fuel tanks appeared to be half full—or half empty. A philosophical question, really. As the pilot, she would have to attend to the fuel-shortage issue with urgency—but she couldn't deal with it right now. This being a long-range aircraft her informed guess was that there was enough to get her to the Mediterranean.

The empty seat next to her reminded her starkly that the copilot would ordinarily be conducting calculations regarding these issues. She was also in mind of the fact that it was generally always deemed necessary to have two pilots on board a plane such as the Global Express—whether it was being flown commercially or privately, let alone when a half-crazed woman decided to take off without a flight plan in the general direction of Turkey in the middle of the night. But Sophie also knew that practically any plane could be flown by a single pilot. *I'm a single pilot flying as a single pilot—get it? It's perfect. Stop worrying.*

Her gut told her that she could probably easily make it to Zurich. She had all the time in the world to acquaint herself with the high-tech cockpit. Levers, switches and the dash were pretty similar in any plane. The deep furrows on her brow had another reason for being there.

She had decided to fly to Israel, to land maybe in Haifa, or Tel Aviv. She would see. The thing was just how to get to the ground without kicking up a lot of attention. That ruthless, thousand-dollar-suit-wearing crook Nedjew would no doubt be pulling every string in his considerable repertoire to put out a global bounty on the hijacker of his aircraft. She had no doubt that her mug and prints would be appearing on every possible law enforcement website in short order.

Shuky had warned her: Nedjew was a gangster, business mogul, and secret service besides. She liked her chances in Israel best, if it came down to striking an arrangement with the authorities. Of course her hopes were partially pinned on Nachman, who she prayed would help take care of things. He had friends in high places—specifically the places that dealt with national security. Should she call him?

She felt a certain sense of relief as she imagined herself landing discreetly on an airfield especially designated by the secret service, further dreaming up a security detail that would escort her to the prepared sanctuary. Where a beaming Shuky would take her in his arms, shaking his head indulgently at her daring escapade.

She quickly found a route that would not stretch her navigation skills too much. The Flight Management System (FMS) was relatively simple to switch to Adana Şakirpaşa. A map of the international airport's runways came up on the display. It was not so much the antique cultural sites that drew her to the Turkish city, but the fact that it was located on the northeastern edge of the Mediterranean. From there, Sophie could turn south ninety degrees and take course for Israel across the water, without having to violate airspace over dicey countries like Iraq or Syria.

The main thing is: I have the painting! She had almost managed to get it out; had already held the container in her hands, ready to leave the plane...and then the sirens had started up... *How quickly plans could change...*

She would soon reach Lake Van. That is where she would have to begin picking up altitude, since the lake bordered on the eastern portion of the Taurus Mountains, which rose up to about four thousand meters. The Swiss Alps had taught her that she would do well to put a generous amount of space between the plane she was flying and a four-thousand-meter peak—treacherous turbulences over chasms and summits had brought down bigger and better birds than the Global Express she was flying today.

On the other side of the range she would come back down into the valley where the proud Tigris River had raged beneath the cliffs since biblical times. She stared with great concentration at the streets depicted on the map. Thin threads meandering from one point to another, towns with tongue-twisting names wove a net across terrains that were as foreign to her as the dark side of the moon. The long, broad pass road began at Van Lake, in the town of Bitlis, and ended in the green looking plain of the distant city of Diarkujew. This was, of course, exactly the area near the Syrian border where the Turks wanted to tame the Tigris with an enormous dam.

Then I should head due west, toward... S-e-r-i-lanu then straight across the Euphrates... another river charged with historic significance... I didn't know that both of them originate high up in Turkey... then a large dam to the right... of course: the Atatürk Dam.

She heaved a sigh of relief. She could now envision her route and had memorized key reference points along the way. She felt quite confident that she would be able to reach the cardinal point of Adana, then head south toward the Israeli coast.

She switched to the navigation system, zoomed in on Van Lake.

The crumpled topography in the satellite depiction looked like she could reach in and touch it. The Tigris Valley, which opened into a large plain, was clearly distinguishable from the craggy eastern Taurus Mountains, which she was going to have to overcome. She hoped that the encroaching clouds that she could make out on the radar would take their time in blocking the light of the moon, because that natural satellite was her good, old friend and secret companion, which could possibly help her navigation efforts. If she was forced to fly low, its light would be invaluable.

She checked the weather radar again then the closest airfields, looked out of the window, winked at the moon. She felt good. Turkey was a developed nation with a secular government. It would abide by the rule of law, of that she was certain. After all, Atatürk had referred to the Swiss constitution when developing a constitution for his own country. He had adopted entire Swiss bodies of law, such as the civil code.

She considered flying under the radar threshold around the Syrian border. At least that would allow her to avoid civilian ATC. She had her doubts when it came to military aerial surveillance. In that respect, she would have to be careful. She sympathized with the Turks and their country. With inborn confidence, she assumed that the feeling would surely be mutual.

European Route E90 went through Sanlıurfa, a strategic intersection that would probably be visible as a reference point at night. The highway meandered along a river and then crossed between mountains before leading to Adana. She would take a closer look at the prominent-looking mountain range later.

She double-checked all of her data on the FMS, adjusted her radio to the frequencies she had determined—and was surprised that there was no attempt to establish communications with her. Nevertheless, she sat back in the ergonomically designed seat, her nerves somewhat assuaged. She adjusted the back a bit and turned on the thigh vibration setting. She was hungry, but was not interested in eating at this point. She would do that once she had thoroughly dealt with the situation on board.

Everything had gone incredibly fast. She had not had a second to fully establish what was going on. This tall woman had appeared like a panther from the darkness outside. What was she up to? Sophie had only seen her silhouette as she jumped through the door. Everything was quiet back there now, as if the cabin were completely deserted. But there had also been an armed man. Where was he? Sophie had turned several times, reflexively, craning her neck back from the pilot's seat—but she had seen and heard nothing. Not a shadow, nor a sound. It was eerie.

And then the woman was suddenly standing beside her. The altimeter was just giving the acoustic signal that the four thousand meter mark had been exceeded, when the slender figure stepped up from behind

187

without a sound and placed her delicate hands, gloved in black leather, on the back of the copilot's seat.

No make-up, not as much as a finger's width of bare skin from the neck down. Her brunette hair was cropped to a few millimeters in length. Her body looked dangerously efficient in its loose, martial attire—a flowing coordination recognizable in even the smallest movement. She was clearly an athlete of some description. Sophie took in what impressions she could greedily, felt immediately uncomfortable. Her body ached.

Her discomfiture had to do with the very hostile aura exuded by this camouflaged villain, who did not blink, whose face was a rigid mask.

She is literally making me sick—her simple presence is sucking the energy right out of me!

Sophie was shaken, her insides in turmoil. She slid forward, stroked her fingers over the controls.

The woman's voice was surprisingly deep and smooth. "There's not much to eat around here. I found some lamb, rice, and vegetables in the galley. Would you like some?" she asked, without the hint of a smile.

Wow. How very un-martial!

"No, thank you, I'm busy." Sophie stretched her chin forward ostentatiously without taking her eyes off the woman. *The bitch is one up. What do I do?*

Sophie squinted at her clothing: long boots with buckles, thick cloth pants, a sack-like jacket that could easily have hidden ten kilos' worth of explosives.

The woman was sizing Sophie up just as intently, if not quite as obviously. She raised her hands, gracefully stripped off the black, leather gloves. Sophie cleared her throat.

"I take it that you're not on board as a stewardess." Her statement dripped with sarcasm.

The woman swung herself elegantly into the copilot's seat. She's taller than me by at least a head, Sophie estimated. "You have no business being here. Get back to where you were."

The women eyed each other like hyenas. The duel lasted for about ten long seconds. Then the taller of the two looked down. "Allow me to explain my little problem to you, Sophie. That's your name, is it not? Sophie?" Again, no hint of a smile.

Sophie jolted as a raspy, Turkish voice suddenly boomed through her headset. She turned down the volume, checked the frequency, waited. There was no second call. But the interruption had really set her off.

"And who the hell are *you*? What is your damn name? What do you think gives you the right…" She was silenced by the unremitting, icy stare of the brush-cut snake.

"Stop the antics, please. You stole this aircraft. Once you land, you will find that this is no laughing matter. By the way, would you care to tell me where we are going?"

"You'll find out soon enough." Sophie leaned forward petulantly, clicked the FMS to activate the communication system. White lettering began to stream slowly across a matte, black display.

"Perhaps you are interested in why I came on board?" She held the gloves in one fist, slapping them rhythmically onto the palm of her other hand.

Evil as a snake, lithe like a feline predator… toned like… she searched for a good comparison. Like a decathlete. Where was her weakness? Did she know Krav Maga? It was the most effective of all self-defense systems. I have to get her on the head, or throat…

"I'm sorry, you were saying? I take it you are one of Nedjew's people. Where is your partner? And what do you want from me?"

"Call me Lenka. I have nothing to do with Oleg Borisowich Nedjew. Nobody except for you knows that I am on board this plane. I have no partner. The soldier with the Kalashnikov who stormed the cabin earlier is dead. Would you like something to drink now?"

Sophie nodded. She could do with a little time to think. Lenka Martialis made her way to the back.

Dead, she had said. There was a dead man on board…just what she needed. This really meant trouble. I have to try and reach Shuky, so that this whole thing doesn't blow up on me when I land in Israel.

Her eyes skimmed the controls, stopped short on the communication display… *Israeli airspace blocked to all air traffic from 0200 hours…*

Sophie frantically scrolled through the message, read more. *Israel fears Iranian airstrike... armed forces deployed... air force on high alert...*

"What is it?" Lenka held a paper cup of orange juice out to her, suspiciously eyeing the display, but Sophie had quickly turned off the ticker.

The woman laughed mockingly. "Not with me, little one!"

Sophie seethed. *Little one? You'll eat those words, bitch!?*

"Let's fly to Belgrade," brush-cut instructed.

"Oh, yeah? Says who?"

Lenka went into a smooth crouch, looked the pilot straight in the eyes. "I want you to listen carefully. I did not get on this fucking plane for some kind of joy ride. This isn't a cocktail party, get it?" She held up a long knife, blood clearly visible on the blade. Sophie tensed. "You will follow my instructions, *darling*." She raised the blade to Sophie's face. Sophie fought down her panic, fought to stay cool. Even her voice obeyed.

"And why all this drama, may I ask? Are you on the run from something, *sweetheart*?" What was so funny?

The snake smiled for the first time—a triumphant smile. "Oh, I think you are the one on the run. You and Rothko." Her eyes narrowed to slits. There was a brief detente while Sophie percolated on the dropped name. She felt her cheeks blaze. She was mentally wide-awake and understood almost immediately. There was only one possible connection between this harpy and the Rothko painting—Ponter.

Did John Ponter sic this killer on me? He wants the painting, of course... Belgrade, it all fits... And once they have me in Belgrade? Sure, Kramer, you're dead, remember? Buried on the Julier. If Ponter has you murdered in Belgrade, he'll only be killing a ghost...

She almost let loose a demented scream... instead she breathed. Acted as if she had to control the instruments, adjust frequencies, whatever... Time passed. Her heart beat loudly in her throat and temples, only very slowly did she get a grip on herself. The snake followed up. "So we agree? Belgrade?"

Sophie had regained composure, if with a great deal of difficulty. "Fine. Whatever you want. Belgrade. We might be short on fuel." The latter was a lie. She had figured out by now that the fuel would easily take them to London. "For now we will maintain our course for Adana, look…"

The woman waved her words aside. "I do not believe one word coming out of your mouth, Sophia. Don't try anything on me. I will know." She tilted the knife, let it glint. "Any funny business and I will let you slowly bleed to death between here and Belgrade."

✳

Sophie looked longingly at the moon, hoping it might send her a flash of inspiration. She looked down into the darkness, random lights here and there, no recognizable landmarks. She flew across the Tigris Valley. There was still no radio communication.

Lenka sat in the copilot's seat, wanted to be informed about every move that was made, monitored their position, let there be no doubt as to who was in charge. The situation, Sophie reckoned, was dire, but not hopeless—as Shuky would no doubt have said, to cheer her up. *What would you do, Shuky, in this shitty situation? Think laterally, darling, if you hit a red light—turn right instead of sitting at it, always stay in motion.*

The engines droned steadily. Was there going to be a war? A catastrophe? Was Iran going to attack Israel? Hamas and Hezbollah armed by Tehran…thousands of modern Katyusha rockets…

Sophie checked the news display:… *a fleet of U.S. aircraft carriers is on course for the Persian Gulf. Air traffic restrictions expected over the Strait of Hormuz and Oman. President of U.S. warns Tehran. USA threatens preemptive nuclear strike.*

For now I have my own, private war to contend with, up here in the clouds, Sophie mused. Then, suddenly, she knew what had to be done. Offense is the best defense—a preemptive strike!

"What was it you were saying about the lamb earlier, stewardess?" Sophie asked casually rubbing her stomach for effect.

Brush-cut wound her way out of her seat with theatrical servitude, walked out without a word. Apparently the order had been taken.

"And a still water to go with that, please!" Sophie shot over her shoulder, tauntingly.

This knife-wielding fiend was an opponent to be reckoned with. Not one that could be simply overwhelmed. She'll be too tough...just look at her...that body!

Minutes later, she was back.

"Will this be alright for you, Captain, or would you rather sit at the table in the back?"

She held the tray in both hands, her tone acerbic.

Sophie looked down her nose at the offering, inspected the pressed bits of lamb, the vegetable morsels. "Fine, that will work. One moment!"

Sophie is ready—and more than fed up. Her body is a single, tightly wound coil. Abruptly, she tears back the yoke, sending the nose of the plane sharply upward.

Then she ruthlessly sends the plane in a three hundred and sixty degree spin around its own axis, flattens it out again. A classic maneuver if you wanted to see someone turn blue and green, then lose their lunch. The Global Express responded exquisitely well—with greater precision, even, than described in the flight manual.

Brush-cut a.k.a. Lenka Borsk screams, waves her arms, does an awkward back flip and comes down hard, colliding with a steel grip with her head, and a boxy pilot's case with her neck. The lamb dinner lands straight in her face. Having braced herself, Sophie is out of her seat before the plane has even righted itself, fire extinguisher in hand. The red metal cylinder makes solid impact with Lenka's skull before the dazed woman is even able to think of clawing herself up from the floor to defend herself. The blow is perfection. Borsk slumps, senses herself falling down, *down toward the dreaded red darkness...*

While the autopilot brings the machine back on course, Sophie drags the unconscious heap to the back, looks up, panting—straight into the glassy eye of a dead man. She is gripped by a primal fear. The corpse is draped across a luxurious, beige leather seat, legs spread wide across the blue carpet. There is a bloody hole where his left eye should have been...blood everywhere. Sophie gags. Breathing heavily, she plucks up some courage and tentatively approaches the murdered man. The executed man, if one wanted to be precise.

She brings herself to remove the handcuffs from the blood-smeared belt of his uniform; uses them on his assassin. She shackles Lenka's arms behind her back, finds several straps in the emergency kit and binds her adversary's legs mercilessly. She joins the leg bonds to the handcuffs, pulls them tight in a perfect hogtie. Then she leaves the captive lying next to the dead soldier on the cabin floor.

She returned to the cockpit, exhausted; fell back into her chair much like a boxer in need of care from a corner man between rounds. And with the engines droning steadily on, her body finally gave in. She nodded off.

But the intensity of what she had experienced had a grip on her subconscious mind. She dreamed of grimacing faces...Uli Stark's calm blue eyes...saw herself chasing through the airport building, the PC-12 was taking off outside with a corpse on board, a woman with freakishly long legs and a brush-cut was following her, a long knife was sticking from her blood covered head...Of course the Israeli had let her go: "Go find this gangster, Sophie! Bring him to justice!"

In her dream, the decision seemed incredibly simple and natural. She found the rental car, sped off...Where to? Of course...she had heard that disgusting miscarriage of an arrogant son-of-a-bitch Nedjew swearing about some shit in Russian in the airport building...Derjmo! Derjmo!...and then...Armenus Technopark, I'm coming down...we're bringing everything with us...Everything...the Rothko...he repeated it to Evgeni his henchman, who had forced his way onto the plane last...the one with the walkie-talkie...who had said, we have the painting, boss, we will bring it on board...Evgeni is dead, boss, we found him lying here in a heap...heap...heap...

The word pounded in her brain, incessantly, she half opened her eyes; the alarm was screaming—BEEP—BEEP—BEEP.

Startled, she shot up, looked outside. Water beneath her, and up front? The ground was flying toward her.

She was too low, corrected frantically, reset the system, rose. Slowly, she gained altitude—an eternity—finally had the bird under control.

Sweating, she entered the flight data: Adana. And then? Israel was no longer an option!

Sophie swallowed, expelled the air in her lungs, her lips a thin, pale line.

Where to? She was sure that the thought had been given to her by the moon. She looked outside. Her secret ally still stood watch in the sky. Of course—she could call now. She was free. It took a few minutes, but she was able to get a connection.

The phone rang, and rang... A new attempt after a short while, again later. No one answered...

Zurich, After Midnight

It was three o'clock in the morning, and there was still light on the fifth floor of the bank in Zurich's financial district. Several minutes ago, security had carefully knocked on John Ponter's massive office door, opened it just a crack. The guard saw two men seated in the visitor's corner, at a low glass table. He recognized the one with the well-groomed coif as Director Ponter. He held a snifter containing a golden liquid, half turned on his multi-functional leather seat, and gazed contemplatively up at the narrow, tall painting with the dollar signs.

"Everything alright, Mr. Ponter?" the man in the black uniform inquired, eyeing the room thoroughly.

"Thank you, we're fine," the host answered succinctly, fished for the cigar box, then turned back to Schindler.

"The Nedjew money is safe and sound in Delaware..."

"The state of Delaware in the U.S., boss?"

"Of course, that Delaware, the second smallest state, and just about an hour's drive from the White House. That tell you anything, Schindler?"

Seeing the lawyer furrow his brow, evidently trying to come up with a quick answer, Ponter loftily continued: "Only an idiot would try to hide his money on the Bahamas, in Liechtenstein, Jersey, or on the Marshall

Islands, or some other exotic tax haven these days. Delaware has developed into the world's best refuge for tax evasion, right under the nose of the U.S. government. The Swiss are a joke by comparison." He paused, took a cigar from the box, clipped the end. "I presume you are aware, Schindler, that I have set up several tax-exempt Delaware businesses for Nedjew. Via the Internet, for... How much would you guess something like that costs?"

Schindler shrugged.

"Eight hundred dollars per shell company, all inclusive. The companies have accounts with banks in New York, in the middle of Manhattan. Nobody is interested in the actual identity of the owner—not in Delaware, for the founding, nor in Manhattan, when we open the accounts. It couldn't be easier. None of the nonsense we go through here in Zurich, where the economic beneficiary has to disclose everything down to his blood type before he can deposit even one, sad Swiss franc. Nedjew's millions are safer in America than anywhere else on the planet. But keep that to yourself. It's our little trade secret."

"I'll have to remember that!" Schindler did his best to appear suitably impressed, even though he was quite aware of the workings. "That would certainly make Delaware one of the most attractive places to avoid paying taxes."

"Bet your bottom dollar. It's the greenest oasis you can imagine. A good five billion dollars—that's five thousand million—of foreign money is stashed away in the glorious Chesapeake Bay. Capital that is sorely missed in the economies of those other countries; say Germany. Ill-gotten gains, the hypocrites in the U.S. Congress call it, when they smear Switzerland as being a haven for tax evaders. It would be laughable, except it really makes one want to weep."

Ponter paused, tired. He toasted the tip of the cigar with a butane lighter until it was smoldering uniformly. He puffed appreciatively, sniffed the pleasant aroma, then blew the smoke toward the ceiling. "In a nutshell, Nedjew's money is as safe in Delaware as in Fort Knox," he concluded. For a while, only the hum of the air conditioner could be heard. Ponter let the smoke from his cigar curl up toward the ceiling, finally leaning forward. "Nedjew's money was doing really well until we fell for that crook, Bernoff." He paused, stared at the tip of his cigar irritably.

"We have to watch ourselves, Schindler. Things are no longer what they were." Ponter cast a quick glance at his watch. "I'm going to be gone for a few days. I am trusting you to take care of things. Are my suitcases ready?" The lawyer pointed his thumb over his shoulder, where two aluminum suitcases were waiting to be collected.

"Good. At least something is going to plan. That bastard Bernoff. There's just no end to how angry it makes me."

Schindler changed the subject. "About the gold. I have prepared a certificate for the gold bars in Limassol. They are valued at about thirty million dollars."

"I will convince the Crane to have them transferred to us in Zurich. We can use them as collateral to raise more liquid assets."

"Have you checked into the weather down there? Limassol is known for its mild climate. It should be pleasant."

Ponter looked at him, nonplussed. "How much did the Crane lose?" he asked gruffly.

"At least fifty million. I have never seen him that angry."

Ponter raised a placatory hand. "The Russian is going to hold us responsible for his losses, Schindler. We have to find a way to avoid that."

"How do you see us doing that, boss? By selling the gold at a profit?"

"The gold?" It seemed that Ponter had not been listening. Thoughts about Garp's plan were circling in his head; a plan in which Nedjew's money played an important role. But Schindler didn't need to know everything.

"Ah, yes. Maybe we will sell the gold bars," he said absently. He sipped listlessly at his Cognac, stood, stuck his cigar between his teeth and started pacing the room.

He finally came to a halt in front of the floor-length window, out of which he stared, cloaked in a dark silence.

Bern, Switzerland

The wind howled, shook the shutters. The rain whipped against Marcel Dulliker's face as he ran, crouching, to the carport. Two in the morning.

"Where are you going? Come to bed," his wife had muttered sleepily as he tiptoed past the bed and to the closet, using the sparse light to find his better pair of pants, which he pulled so awkwardly from the hanger that it fell noisily to the floor.

"I have to go out for a while, darling," he whispered, reaching in his pocket to find the car key. "I'll be back for breakfast."

Squalls tore at the tall SUV in an unpredictable rhythm as it made its way along the deserted A1. The sound of cheerful folk music came from the radio, drowned out in parts by the whistling of the storm. Dulliker navigated the inclement gusts calmly, keeping to his speed. His tires had good traction on the wet, poorly lit tarmac. Thunder rolled, there were flashes of lightning. The news announced that the winds had broken trees, downed power lines...

Dulliker now pores over the state of the world in his mind, his dreary career prospects, recalls the struggles of the past weeks, tries to consider his next moves. He keeps seeing the image that the Brits sent him a few hours ago. A sharp close-up of the suspicious Ponter, leaning casually against the rail of what he has to presume is a luxury yacht. His hand is displayed so obviously on the wooden banister that one has to wonder whom he is showing the opulent ring to; the tall guy in the blue polo shirt? The caption reads succinctly: Limassol, on the *Bastion*, the date, a row of numbers beneath that, then the name *John Ponter*. Those MI6 people were the best. I've always said it. Dulliker applied his brakes. There were emergency vehicles on the shoulder, lights flashing. He drives by slowly, then accelerates again. Then they actually send me a second picture, where this Ponter guy is playing with the ring on his finger, looking off somewhere else. There were close-ups of both images, in which only the ring filled the frame. Perfectly sharp, clear as day.

The images had electrified Dulliker; had prompted him to make the hour-long, nighttime drive to Zurich despite the foul weather.

Baron Suvorov's murder in the Engadin had caused quite the furor. The fact that police had as yet been unable to solve the crime had caused aftershocks in the press that were regurgitated in short intervals. The severed finger with the mysterious missing ring gave rise to the wildest speculations, particularly in the tabloids. No wonder that Dulliker had immediately spotted the connection. Just to be sure, he had researched the relevant police databases, and had landed a bulls-eye just a few minutes in. The summary of the factual report submitted by the cantonal police of Graubünden popped up, giving him a perfect overview. Looking at the attached police photographs, he had come across an earlier image of the stolen ring. He compared this breathlessly to the Limassol shots. Rubbing his red eyes, it was perfectly clear to him just what was going on here.

The ring that John Ponter was so proudly displaying was very likely the famous Suvorov heirloom that the old school gentleman had worn for most of his life with justifiable pride.

Forensics would go on to scientifically analyze the images, but Marcel Dulliker had seen enough to tear Ken Cooper out of a sound sleep of the righteous in the middle of the stormy night.

"Join me for coffee when it's light out," the rudely awoken man had said, in a vain attempt to rescue what was left of his well-earned night's rest.

"I'm afraid this can't wait, Ken. I'll be in Zurich at three."

Cold air blew through the empty hall of Zurich's central railway station as the old friends slapped each other firmly, if somewhat stiffly at this early hour, on the backs. They looked at each other warmly out of tired eyes. The arms of the large clock high above their ruffled heads said that it was a quarter to four. Ken Cooper pulled his head back into the collar of his coat.

"So, where were you thinking of launching your big reveal? The pubs are closed. Should we make ourselves comfortable on the luggage cart over there?"

Marcel Dulliker eyed him with mock suspicion. "You're not going soft on me, are you, Ken?" He turned and led the way resolutely. A few minutes later they had wound their way past parked police vehicles and were standing in front of the brightly lit Zurich Cantonal Police station. "They are waiting for me. Luggage cart!" Dulliker muttered disdainfully. He pushed the door open, clearing his throat as he stepped up to the Formica counter. A young officer unhurriedly got up from behind his computer.

The interrogation room that he opens for them is inhospitably stark, the walls smell freshly painted. They sit on hard chairs. The Swiss secret service man unpacks the contents of his briefcase and silently presents the astonished CIA legend Cooper with his evidence.

One after the other, Ken examines the pictures carefully, asks about the Suvorov case. Marcel Dulliker patiently lays out the facts. Not even fifteen minutes had passed when Ken exclaimed, visibly impressed: "Unbelievable, Marcel. Those are some highly suspicious findings. What's your plan moving forward?"

"We will be arresting Ponter on suspicion of murder. Before the night is over."

"I have to agree, Marcel. How would an arrest work around here?" He motioned his head to indicate the command room.

"I'll be doing it. I'm familiar with local procedure." Dulliker stood, went to press the door handle to open the door. Even as it swung wide, he was already calling for the officer in charge.

Barely a mile from the central station, John Ponter interrupted his nocturnal musings, turned abruptly from the window and walked toward Schindler.

"Quadrini's pot is at about sixty—all of it liquid. If we add his art, and the gold on Cyprus, that brings it to about a hundred million."

Schindler nodded his narrow head in agreement.

"We transfer the cash from Quadrini to Oleg Nedjew—the German to the Russian—make up for the shortfall, decent folk that we are."

"And Quadrini? What do we tell his heirs?"

"We'll fob them off with bonds—if they even ask."

"Ponter Bank bonds?"

"No, shares from our real estate fund. A real pearl. Set to five years. Calculate the interest we can afford, set the price on the high end. Everything will look just fine on paper. There won't be a franc missing from the Quadrini portfolio, get it? Pretty on paper, good value, and everything will be right as rain."

Schindler leaned over his notebook. As he jotted down a few key words, he realized something. One of these days, when some grass had grown over the whole affair, the bonds would be made to disappear from the portfolio. He kept his eyes fixed on his notes, racked his brain, sparking his synapses to perform true fireworks. Following the unanticipated disappearance of Kleiber, he had been made responsible for the cooking of numbers.

"We are rather long on Nedjew," the lawyer ventured, with discernible concern in his voice.

"What we are doing is not legal, Schindler. That is the point. I can't tell you just how illegal, you're the lawyer here. But from all I hear, Nedjew has crossed a line that we cannot really afford to be indifferent to. Mind you, it is likely that nothing will be pinned on him. Even the fact that he is running a nuclear weapons bazaar."

"Are you sure about that, boss?"

"I'm not blind, Schindler. But you appear to be, and deaf to boot. Where do you think the hundreds of millions are coming from? Who, dear Mr. Schindler, pays in cash these days? Who lugs around sums of that scale in suitcases?"

Schindler's forehead took on the appearance of a freshly plowed field as he tried to determine how to best answer this particular pop-quiz. Smiling smugly, Ponter answered his own question.

"The pirates. They do their business in cash, understandably. Not to mention arms dealers."

Schindler's only response was to look silently up at the ceiling. Risk would always be an irresistible temptation for Ponter.

He was, quite simply, a gambler; a cunning, all-or-nothing kind of player who exploited his clients' every weakness. Enormous amounts would flow into the transitory accounts of Oleg Nedjew from Israel or Cyprus, from Beirut or Kazakhstan—and Ponter would not be able to resist. He would leave the money in the temporary account for days, perhaps even weeks, and cultivate it there, like so many little seedlings in a nursery. He would take the money and engage in day or swing trading. All very short term, of course, while he carefully prepared to safely transfer the sums to their offshore destinations. He would often make a killing thanks to his delay tactics. Thousands of dollars for every day that he was able to put off moving things along, including weekends and holidays. It was a regular gig, since Nedjew easily channeled a hundred million or more through the Ponter Clean-O-Rama money-laundering machine. But now a scandal was brewing, one which could bring down the entire bank. Only John Ponter himself knew the details of how dubious monies ended up back in regular circulation—by purchasing villas, or entire swaths of land, by stocking up an airplane fleet, commissioning a larger yacht; by making a serviceable contribution to some minister or other, chief official, commander, or cultural attaché. The mullahs' dollars wandered from one dirty paw to the next; by the time they reached him, things were already a done deal.

Ponter saw Quadrini's assets as the life raft that could be used to restore the losses that he had incurred at the expense of his number one client, Nedjew—by hiding it fastidiously in an assortment of investments, and by walling it off in a Liechtenstein trust. The scheme was very much in line with the plan that Garp had coerced him to abide by exactly two days ago.

"Garp..." the callous banker sighed. The man was a mysterious U.S. agent who held a knife to his throat. Ponter was loath to replay the encounters with this essentially quite charming young man in his mind. Clearing his throat, he turned to the patiently waiting lawyer.

"I want you to electronically transfer as much as possible onto Ned-jew's account. Do it immediately."

Even if there may have appeared to be a conspiratorial relationship between Schindler and himself, the boss remained cloaked. He was not willing to risk further familiarity. Buying time to think, he circled the room a few more times before planting himself directly in front of the lawyer, his hands firmly on his hips.

"I will take care of it, boss," Schindler bleated, raising his notebook as if to intimate that everything was as good as done. Ponter found his tone annoying. "And now to Suvorov, Schindler," he said. "I am awaiting word from my, eh…" He avoided the word agent. "Confirmation that the Rothko is back in the hands of the bank." He looked contemplatively up at the high, windowless wall for a moment. "That would be an excellent spot for it, don't you think? Oh, never mind…" Schindler was clueless when it came to art. "Meanwhile, just you focus on handling our securities. No reason why that shouldn't make us a few million, if you do your job right."

Without waiting for an answer, Ponter walked behind his desk, his posture slightly slouched. He fell into his chair. Lips pinched, he reached mechanically for a file.

His expression said *I'm busy*. Schindler stood. Ever the loyal subordinate. He knew well the rebuffing facial expression, despised the contemptuous arrogance from which it derived. Nevertheless, he nodded obsequiously several times, then scuttled out.

The financier to all Russian mobsters, go-to man to shady oligarchs, reached for the telephone receiver and dialed the number of his best, utterly dependable, most brutal of enforcers: his very own Borsk. Savoring the thought of the conversation to come, a malicious smile spread across his face.

He listened expectantly, impatiently drumming his fingers on the desk, looked at the receiver reproachfully, then finally hung up. Well, she would surely make contact. For now, he would just revel in the text that had surprised him the night before: I HAVE S&M, it had said. John Ponter had boisterously slammed his right fist into his left palm—*Sophie Kramer and Mark Rothko*. So, she had found them…good girl!

The next call that Ponter placed was to order his driver up to take his luggage to the car. Petar Ivanovic had been apprised of his night shift, and appeared fresh and composed when he appeared. He followed the instructions of his boss to the letter, scrupulously and politely as always, never leaving the slightest doubt as to his loyalty. He disappeared with the suitcases, went to sit patiently behind the wheel of the car.

✳

"We have enough proof to electrocute you twice, for good measure," said the American, who had introduced himself as Garp.

The words hammered in John Ponter's mind when Ivanovic ably pulled the Maybach to the curb a short while later, stopping next to a figure dressed in a raincoat and a black baseball cap.

Garp had specified the meeting place by phone just a few minutes earlier: in front of the National Museum, opposite the central railway station. Typical of this secret service asshole, Ponter thought resentfully. He checked his gold watch. Five past four.

Garp got in lithely, sat next to Ponter in the back. He nodded at him silently, his chiseled features expressionless and mask-like. "We'll drive over to my car, then take the highway to Bern."

Ponter slid the partition aside, gave Ivanovic the instructions. When he leaned back and looked over at Garp, he saw that he held a black pistol casually balanced on his thigh. "I'm left-handed," he warned him.

Ivanovic started the Maybach up, glided smoothly back onto the roadway as he reached down inconspicuously with his left hand. He pressed the hidden button on the recording device. All the while, in the back, Garp was studying the face of his new recruit. "My plane is at Payerne military air base, John. It is set to take off in two hours."

Ponter drew his own conclusions about this announcement. If Garp had a special plane waiting for him at a military air base, he had to be quite the hot shot in his cursed organization.

"How much is in those cases?" Garp asked, closing his fingers around the grip of his nine-millimeter Glock.

"A million in thousand franc notes in each case, as agreed," Ponter responded listlessly.

They changed vehicles at the Marché, a popular restaurant that bridged the entire freeway. Ivanovic drove the Maybach back to Zurich, but not without first noting the license plate of the sleek Mercedes, in which his boss was going to be continuing his journey to western Switzerland.

The drive would take about an hour and a half, Ponter reckoned, trying to precisely place Payerne in his mind. The town was part of the canton of Vaud, not far from Neuenburger Lake. It was located on a plain, and home to one of the largest military air bases of the Swiss air force. Ponter leaned back and closed his eyes; insides churning...

...It had been a few days ago. He had met the American at the Brasserie bar. They had entered the elevator together and taken it to the top of the small tower. Upstairs, they ascended a short, metal staircase to a room with a large telescope, which was aimed at the overcast night sky.

"Welcome to the observatory," the American had said, then flashed his ID. "Call me Garp."

"CIA?" a visibly confused Ponter took a step back, eyed the brash young man from top to bottom. "What do you want from me? This is not the Bronx. I could probably have you arrested, you know. Your outfit is not very popular around here."

Garp shook his head with evident disgust. "You can cut the bullshit, Mr. Ponter. I'm in no mood to listen to it. Either you play along, or your police will be receiving information on some of your business dealings—with a certain Mr. Quadrini, for instance, or the sadly deceased Mr. Suvorov."

Ponter's face crumbled, his hands practically clawed the rail in front of the telescope. "What do you want?"

Garp's left hand did not move from the pocket of his leather jacket. "You will authorize a few transactions, which I will lay out for you. Then you will join me on a short trip."

"Where to?" Ponter asked breathlessly, his eyes fixed on the bulge in the pocket.

"Limassol. We are going to visit Oleg Nedjew on his yacht. A good friend of yours, I believe. I guarantee you safe passage." Garp stepped up to the telescope, leaned over to look through the eyepiece.

The moon appeared as a white disc, just peeking out behind a break in the clouds, startlingly close, its craters clearly defined. "Only as long as you prove to be cooperative, of course."

The color had returned to Ponter's face. Something briefly sparked behind his cold, lifeless eyes as his old resolve took hold.

"Perhaps you will be so kind as to explain just what it is that you think you have against me. This happens to be a place of astronomic research in the free country of Switzerland, not Guantanamo."

"Come now. Don't try and play coy with me, Ponter. You know the skeletons in your closet. Are you really that keen on being dragged through the media, to be made famous for being Nedjew's sock-puppet, financial lackey and money launderer? Or for your war crimes, Dragan Nikolic?"

Pallor had definitely reclaimed the territory of Ponter's face. He remained silent for a long time. He first nodded hesitantly, then shook his head, chewed absently on a hangnail on his index finger.

"What happens now? What are you going to do?"

"We will grant you immunity."

Ponter looked at him, perplexed. "Immunity against what? The measles?"

"We will agree not to prosecute you for your crimes if you collaborate."

"You don't have proof of anything," Ponter hazarded stoically.

"Money laundering is just the beginning, Ponter."

"I think I should call my lawyer. I have definitely had quite enough of this."

Garp shrugged his shoulders, a disdainful look on his face. "Your lawyers will stonewall, try and lecture us about what does and doesn't constitute money laundering, demand evidence. Fine…When all is said and done, and after you have spent a million on lawyers' fees, you will still be finished, Ponter. Destroyed."

"What the hell do you know, Garp? You're just another arrogant

American blowhard who thinks that you're in charge of the entire world, and you have a real hard-on for Old Europe. It's not going to work on me."

"We can make our facts publicly known within a matter of hours," Garp bluffed. "Starting with Quadrini, the boss of the German shipping company. An old European—as you would say. You helped him turn his dirty money into art. Then there was the weapons dealer who drowned in Lausanne harbor. A bigwig, whose demise wasn't entirely unwelcome, correct? And how about the legendary Fortunato Gritti?" Garp acted as if he were consulting a very long mental list. "I had already mentioned Suvorov, investigations into that are under way, not to mention the Crane, that hard-boiled criminal..."

Ponter was completely expressionless.

"Leave Oleg Nedjew alone, you dwarf. Or he'll hang you by the balls with his own, bare hands."

"Maybe, if he doesn't hang first. Nedjew stands for arms trading, murder and drugs. We extracted quite a bit of information on him from your very own bank."

Garp heard him hiss "data theft," then Ponter thundered with only partially feigned outrage: "All of that is highly criminal, you...you...arrogant bastard!"

"That may well be, but that doesn't make it any less useful. We have your signature on certain, incriminating documents. You know how that goes. Guilt by association. So, do you still want to call that lawyer of yours? How about we talk about my proposal?"

Ponter's head sank to his chest.

"There you go," Garp smiled. "I knew you'd be reasonable."

But the crafty banker wasn't about to give in that quickly. He had been momentarily fazed, but now recovered.

"You want to destroy me, Garp, me and my bank, so that your little MADOF-outfit can skim all of the cash. What did you say MADOF stands for, again?"

"Monetary Agency for Detecting Offshore Fraud. We track tax evaders, and bring in their money."

"Right. The money goes to America—home of the free and brave, where Wall Street runs the government, and Wall Street has never been a great fan of Swiss competition."

"That's about right," Garp confirmed, unimpressed. "You will agree to transfer the Nedjew monies to us, and you will testify against him in front of a Senate panel."

"Why Limassol, of all places?"

"You seriously have to ask? Have you forgotten the hoard of gold that your bank stores on the island? And the Russian is practically a permanent fixture there. You will have him place his money with our New York investment firm." Garp did not reveal any more details of his plan; instead he produced a list with a theatric gesture and read names and key words that stood for further transgressions. Just to drive the point home. Who knows how long he could have spent on this gloating display, had a bunch of teenagers not come banging and giggling up the stairs...

... The driver hit the brakes, starting Ponter from his reverie. The lights of Bern shone to their left as their car passed a tow truck, then sped off over the long, high bridge toward western Switzerland. The way that Ponter's head sank between his shoulders, they might have been driving along in a convertible with the top down in the rain. As if to accentuate the illusion, he closed his eyes—the weather was—indeed—growing increasingly unfriendly, that much was clear.

PART IV

Night Over Isfahan

At about the same time that Ken Cooper was being raised from a sound sleep in Zurich, Cliff Matoyan was checking the altimeter.

"We're low. Seven hundred feet."

His copilot, who sported an Irish four-leafed clover on his bomber jacket, grunted acknowledgment. He looked out the front, then turned around.

"Alright. Get ready! Three minutes to the drop!"

The loadmaster confirmed with two thumbs up, slapped the drop officer on the shoulder. It was the second flight to Isfahan that night.

The pilot accelerated, climbed to the calculated altitude. The sea of lights that was the city swam toward them.

"I'm going to go down there one of these days, I swear," the Irishman said, pointing outward. "They'll be celebrating us as liberators. Women will be falling at our feet."

"Nah. They only ever show up in little clusters, modestly veiled. Trust me, it's not our thing."

"I don't know. I heard that there's a beautiful bridge, where they sit on the stairs by the water at night and..." He threw his head back and yelled, "Drop altitude, one minute!"

There was a bustle of activity. The hatches unlatched.

"Drop!" The Irishman shouted, and was barely able to hear his own voice. A cold burst of air rushed in, the hatches opened completely, the noise of the engines multiplied and droned loudly, even through the headsets.

The drop system contributed with its own set of noises, interspersed with hoarse yelling.

The men complied. Nico Strom had practiced the drop with them and the other crews day and night. There had been dry runs, without the loads, but they had been drilled in every move and sequence. It had paid off. The load master was relieved to see that the timing was on point, the adjustments worked, the containers were opened, and the monitor on the cabin wall showed what had gone, registered the blasts, kept an ongoing count of units dropped.

After half an hour, it was all over.

Matoyan took a deep breath, exhaled.

"One hundred sixty thousand and three hundred," the loadmaster called through the cabin once the hatches were closed, and the noise had subsided.

"Insane," the Irishman commented.

The mood had lightened significantly on the flight back. Not that they were any less attentive—quite to the contrary. The crew knew that insidious dangers often lurked around the apex of any given operation. Something could still go wrong. And so each of the men remained focused in his own way, on his own job. But the nervous tension that had been pervasive at the beginning of the mission had now given way to something like self-congratulatory admiration.

Matoyan laughed out loud. He was looking at one of the LEO cell phones. "This is too cool."

"What is?" The loadmaster looked over at him, his curiosity roused.

"This text. It says: *Being gay is not a crime—or is Ahmadi a criminal?*"

"Is the president gay?"

"A couple of New York journalists have said he is."

"He wants to annihilate Israel."

"Since when do you speak Farsi?"

Matoyan, who was of Armenian heritage, ignored the question. Another of the crew jabbed an elbow into the questioner's ribs.

"He's descended straight from Farah Diba...no joke, man. His mother is Iranian."

Isfahan Bazaar

The powerfully built Ali Nalbandian stepped abruptly in and let the carpet drop. His eyes wide in terror, he stared up at the ceiling, from which he could hear a sinister crackling noise. *The bazaar is being shot at,* was his first thought. *The Revolutionary Guard Corps is attacking!*

Ali ran back to the storeroom, tore carpets from the pile until he was down to the bare floor. The board beneath which the weapons were hidden was marked with a simple notch. Another hail of bullets rained on the roofs of the bazaar, closer this time. Ali ducked reflexively, expected the bullets to be followed by explosions. Finally he lifted the board, revealing the hiding place. A loud bang shook him to the core. Glass broke, windows shattered. Ali threw himself to the floor, swore heartily. Almost immediately, he clambered back to his feet, tore the Kalashnikov from its hole. He raced to the front of the store, emitting a scream that seemed to come from the very core of his soul.

A young man stared at him. He was holding his delicate head up with great effort, his face contorted with pain. He lay on his stomach, one leg oddly angled. The young woman at his side looked at the furious merchant with a distraught, pleading gaze. He stopped dead in his tracks. Her unveiled face was of a captivating beauty, her thick, black hair cascaded on her bare shoulders. She held an object clutched tightly in her right hand, like a trophy.

"By the beard of the prophet!" Ali ranted.

The young man made efforts to sit up, wiping blood from his cheek. The angry stallholder shoved the barrel, dripping with gun oil, in his face.

"Stay nice and still, young man. Don't move. What do you want?"

Instead of an answer, further crackling could be heard through the partially caved in dome. A silver-gray package slapped onto the pile of carpets, a little white parachute collapsed next to it. A second hit the glass table like a stone. Ali instinctively ducked, while the faces of the couple who had fallen from the roof lit up: "More! More of them are coming!"

"What is this nonsense?"

Ali lowered his weapon, heard the happy cries from the roof, the excited cacophony of voices. No war!

Only now did the young woman seem to realize her bareness. Blushing, she looked up, searching for her headscarf, adjusted her dress.

"We are so sorry," the young man stammered. "We ran onto the roof when these things started coming down. We were looking up, and not paying attention to where we stepped. Suddenly the roof gave way beneath us." He raised his arms appeasingly. Ali was far from appeased. "What things? Stop talking rubbish!"

"These. Cell phones." The young man angled for one with his fingers. The merchant, not inclined to believe a word, vigorously shook his head. The sound of voices was heard from the street, approaching footsteps, the intermittent sound of motorcycles. Young women cast shy glances into the store. "We also got one!" Ali caught fragments of what was being called out, again, and again... "Telephones...cell phones..."

The girl had gotten up, was looking at him through large, dark eyes. She showed him her prize.

The merchant had seen the few types of cell phone available in the country. But he had never yet laid eyes on this sturdy silver model. "May I?"

The girl hesitantly placed it in his outstretched hand.

"It is fully charged," Ali determined. He read the Farsi text. "You can begin using this telephone immediately, and for free. *Allahu Akbar!* Your voice is there to be heard. You will receive messages every day. Share them. From this day forward, there will be freedom of thought."

The shopkeeper, who had seen much in his lifetime, shook his head skeptically. Using his index finger, he carefully keyed in his own number. It took a few seconds, then the old-fashioned, black device on the small, oval tea table began to ring. He placed Allah's gift back into the hand of the girl, went to the table, picked up the receiver...listened.

"Can you hear me?" The girl asked, her back turned to him. Ali muttered something inaudible. She turned, eyes blazing, nodded in confirmation. "It works. Isn't it wonderful? Thousands fell from the sky."

The carpet dealer numbly put down the receiver. The boy held his gift from the heavens out to him. "Take mine, too. And we will repay you for the damage." He shoved shards of glass aside with his foot. "Here, my address." The man pocketed the boy's business card. He was already grinning benevolently again. Such was his nature. "Come, my angelic messengers. Let's go look."

They stepped out into the night. The bazaar was at the south end of an enormous square. Numerous alleys circulated through a mess of stalls, shops, storage sheds, small mosques. It was all covered by roofs, interrupted by rooftop windows, picturesque domes, rooftop exits with protruding ladders.

The large road, at which Nalbandian sold his precious carpets, was full of loaded handcarts; motorcycles stood in niches and alcoves. The first cell phones had started falling from the sky about half an hour before. The market was now almost completely deserted.

The crowds had run, practically falling over each other, across the rooftops, streamed out to the central square, Naqsh'e Jahan, to Ali Qapu—the Imperial Gate Palace. It may as well have been raining gold.

Such was the commotion in front of the big mosque, that the guards were forced to close the gates and alarm the security forces. In the general commotion, nobody was initially able to explain what had happened. Like Ali at the bazaar, the mullahs had suspected a dangerous uprising of some sort. Not an attack, necessarily, but the scenes were reminiscent of nasty popular revolts. Still, people of every description were cheering, embracing one another, collecting on the large lawns, streets and pedestrian zones. They ran about excitedly, climbed into the round basin of the fountain. Some were holding their heads, or proudly showing off their bumps. Illuminated by the headlights of the cars and motorcycles coming in from all around, the excited masses appeared to be growing rowdy. Shadowy figures intermingled, grappled with each other; chairs and the occasional table toppled in the marquee-covered coffee houses in front of the arcades, glass shattered.

From where he stood behind a tall window in the ancient royal palace, young Mullah Akbar Javanfakr had an excellent overview of the commotion on the square. "They are also on the rooftops." Farhad Pajooh, the older, shortsighted cleric retrieved his glasses from his flowing robes. He climbed on a chair, put the glasses on and peered intensely over to the other side of the square, where the bazaar entrance was located. He saw men climbing up trees in order to gather bits of white cloth that were hanging from the branches. "Indeed. Do we know what is going on?"

"The bazaar people, if you ask me. They are the root of all evil. I am sure that they are protesting the tax increase again." At this moment a group of armed men burst into the large hall. The young men in their olive uniforms stood respectfully as their leader stepped forward and bowed down low. "We have it, Mullah Akbar, the thing that the people are looking for all over."

"Show me!"

The leader motioned to his group. Two men brought a basket to the fore.

"Mobile telephones?" The mullah pulled one from the basket, carefully eyed the little parachute. "Bring me the commander."

"He is dining at the Hotel Abassi with the mayor and the French ambassador.

"Bring him to me!" Mullah Akbar repeated.

Farhad the cleric descended in a dignified manner from the chair, holding his lower back. He inspected the device that the leader handed him.

The leader stepped closer in response to a friendly, conspiratorial nod. He felt honored by the warm demeanor of the highly regarded man. Together they leaned over the device, both immediately and equally fascinated by the little technological wonder.

"It works. They all do," the uniformed man said, hesitantly—not quite sure whether to inject enthusiasm or indignation into his tone.

The cleric took off his glasses. "And what is written there?"

"Propaganda... outrageous!"

"Well, my son, if I understand correctly, the little machines fell from heaven, and it says here... a gift from Allah. Keep it."

"Thank you, thank you... but there are thousands out there, there is not much we can do about it."

Mullah Akbar Javanfakr stood very erect at the head of the table, his chin stretched upward, a telephone receiver held to his ear. He was connected to the Abassi International Hotel. He listened, nodded, walked about, gesturing. Finally, he hung up. "Unbelievable," he stammered. "The whole of Isfahan is in a turmoil. I have just spoken to the commander. There is talk of an incredible number of telephones that have fallen upon us—as on other cities throughout the country."

"What are we to make of all of this?" the cleric asked as the soldiers exited the hall. Mullah Akbar shrugged his shoulders. "I do not know. May Allah show us the way!"

"A few words from Tehran may be more helpful at this point," his mentor said with a smile.

"A few words from the Great Ayatollah?" the younger man breathed reverently.

"No. The minister." Farhad was thinking of the president's favorite, who headed the Ministry of Intelligence and Security. "This matter is a worldly concern, not one over which the keepers of the faith have much influence."

The mullah stared at him, aghast. Only the utmost respect for this teacher and scholar kept him from accusing the man of blasphemy. But his mind was racing.

"Have you noticed something, my son?"

Mullah Akbar shook his bearded head. There was a petulant look on his face. Farhad smiled benevolently. "The people are happy. Look. Listen!"

They stepped to the open window. The racket had calmed down. The people sat peacefully on the lawns, at the coffee houses, around the fountain, at the water's edge; typical groups of blackly clad figures with light faces practically glowing in contrast. Veiled women moved in little groups from place to place, while men stood casually about. Time and again, elated calls echoed up to the palace windows.

"They all have the telephone at their ear, or are looking at it with enchanted eyes...The dam will burst."

"A scandal! Foreign rogues and crooks are responsible for this," the mullah ranted. "The phones must be forbidden immediately."

He already had a plan. An underground tunnel led from the palace to the bazaar. The troops could be sent out beneath the square, unnoticed. They would arrest the bazaar keepers and collect all the phones. Dole out harsh punishments to chastise the people.

A few executions would put a stop to the foolishness. Disbelievers and deviants had to be weeded out. He looked furtively at Farhad, who laid a fatherly hand upon his shoulder. "Well, dear Akbar, what does our Prophet tell us about found items?"

The young mullah's eyes widened. "Hadith verse thirty-two...Al Luqatah?"

Farhad Pajooh nodded, quoted with deep veneration: "A man came to the Prophet, peace and blessings be upon him, and asked him about anything found on the way. The Prophet answered 'Remember the description of its container and the string with which it is tied. Make a public announcement of it for one year. If nobody comes and claims it, then utilize it, but keep it as a trust with you. And if its owner comes back one day seeking it, then return it to him...' You see, Akbar—there is providence for everything! The disturbances merely herald the hour!" He nodded solemnly, bowed almost imperceptivity, and left the dumbfounded mullah standing there.

The pool of forty columns has twenty tall, graceful pylons supporting a pavilion on one side, which are languidly mirrored in its lovely light green waters.

Following his meeting with Mullah Akbar, Farhad Pajooh had descended onto the large square and mingled among the crowd. He enjoyed the young faces, the casual talk, the simple happiness—an impromptu festival was taking place. He stopped before a group of young students, who were laughingly typing on their new phones, and apparently sharing their discoveries. The generation of the future, the learned one thought. Progress cannot be stopped! Mobile telephones had been a highly sought-after rarity, always in fierce demand, and now—unbelievable!

And now tons of them had simply fallen into our laps.

Our? A mischievous expression crossed his face as he strolled on, the prized cell phone clasped firmly in his hand.

It brought to mind the stock market. He intended on risking the comparison at tomorrow morning's lecture. The phones would be traded, they would have a going rate. Anyone who didn't have one would want to move heaven and earth...

He continued through the arch, deep in thought, turned toward the pool. The remaining light shone delicately through the colorful stained-glass windows in the recess behind the columns. Farhad went toward them. The water of the beautiful, old grounds shimmered in the fading day. Farhad loved walking along the pool. The place was usually marvelously peaceful—and tonight was no different, even with the revelry on the large square.

Farhad had fought for intellectual freedom, but he was well aware that he lived dangerously. He was of the opinion that the experiment of Islamic rule had failed in his country. But to express such views openly would be akin to bringing a death sentence upon himself. He cultivated discreet discourse with a few critical students, who communicated with other similar-minded people under assumed names on the Internet. The Net held an important role for the small, close-knit community of bloggers in Iran. The people were not blind, nor stupid. Perhaps twenty thousand or so exchanged ideas with America and the rest of the world, but the government kept a close eye on the virtual traffic, and periodically halted the entire platform entirely. "They'll have no chance with the mobile telephones," the learned man muttered to himself, his high spirits adding a little skip to his step.

He feels a draft of air.

Spinning around, he is horrified to find himself faced with the grimacing features of Mullah Akbar. He is holding an object in his raised hand. Not a phone...

"Akbar, what...?"

The iron bar makes hard contact with his high forehead. Farhad stumbles, loses consciousness.

Mullah Akbar glares around intently. Not a soul in sight. He stoops over the fallen man. His patron and mentor is still breathing, his tough heart beating. A trembling hand reaches out. Is he trying to say something?

"It is a shame that you have strayed from the path of righteousness, Farhad. This is the end of your wickedness," the mullah hissed, raises his arms toward the darkening sky. "*Insha'Allah*—if it be Allah's will!"

He drags the lifeless figure through the flowerbed, a few meters down to the edge of the pool, presses his head under water, holds him down until the body stops jerking.

He searches the dead man's pockets, finds the phone, a wallet, tears the gold necklace from his neck. He hastily stows everything in his wide robe.

Standing back up, he hears happy voices sounding from the colonnades. A group of women is approaching, veiled in black, chattering cheerfully. Mullah Akbar jumps back onto the stone path, disappears in the shadows of a mighty tree, whose lime green foliage lends the pool's water its color by the light of day.

In the water, silver spectacle frames glint next to the head of the beaten and drowned man. One less traitor! *It will look like a robbery. Allahu Akbar!*

Armenus Park, Control Center

"Insane," Andy giggled ecstatically at the Armenus Park Control Center, "they are reporting successful drops on all targets." The data of the planes' computers were gathered and calculated on his end, giving him an ongoing tally—Tabriz, Hamedan, Isfahan, Bandar Abbas, Shiraz...

Abramian leaned forward. "How many in total?"

"A good two and a half million. We are still waiting on Tehran and the second drops on the southernmost towns," Andy explained.

"We haven't heard from the Hercules. They should have reached Tehran by now."

He turned the dials of the radio receiver. A voice swelled.

...Iran. Radio Basra reports that Farhad Pajooh, a cleric who has been critical of religious leadership in his country and had called for free elections, was murdered in Isfahan...

"This is us," Andy turned the broadcast to speaker.... *The unrests being reported in Isfahan, which police are not acting on at this time, appear to have a different reason. The city has allegedly seen a mass drop of activated mobile phones. The general population is clamoring to obtain these new devices, which are already said to be circulating regime-critical messages...*

Cosmo reached over Andy's shoulder, turned the speaker off. "Keep your mind on Strom's C-130, damn it."

"Of course, sir. Checking on it now."

The radio operator across from them took off his headset. "Radio silence, sir. That would be expected on a covert mission."

Cosmo turned, placed a hand on a slender shoulder cloaked in a black scarf. "How are things going, Trita?"

The Farsi translator looked up, puzzled. "It's strange, sir. As of yet, there has been not a word mentioned on Operation Snowdrop in the Iranian media.

"I'm sure they're just speechless, Trita. The snow that our boys have dropped is like lightning out of a clear blue sky to those mullahs. What they don't know is that this is just the start. Nothing on PressTV either?"

Trita gently shook her head. She banished an unruly strand of her golden brown hair back beneath her scarf. "It's not the kind of propaganda they like to report on. They'll be giving us their own version tomorrow. The only predictable aspect is that the evil Americans will be to blame..."

"It won't do them a bit of good. Our phones will drown out their media propaganda. I'm heading over to analysis. We're receiving thousands of text messages..." He went on his way smiling broadly.

A rotund Iranian woman with a mischievous face was in charge of the messages that were broadcast to the AiD phones, as they had now taken to calling them. Cosmo had input on subject matter and how it was to be expressed. The team of people engaged in formulating, editing, and finally coming up with succinct, catchy messages was an eclectic mix—authors, students, historians, journalists, Middle East experts, economic geographers, psychologists, housewives—and Trita Parsi, of course, who was responsible for translating the final messages into Farsi.

Cosmo took a seat at the small coffee bar in the analysis sector and looked down at the bustle. A waiter brought him his vermouth on the rocks with a twist of orange. He sipped at it thoughtfully while a sports show played on the television, half paying attention to the news ticker at the bottom of the screen:

... militant mullahs threaten to conduct nuclear testing. U.S. President issues warnings to Tehran, sends Secretary of State to Tel Aviv to assure allies of U.S. support in case of Iranian attack...

The interview with the Yankees coach was cut off abruptly. "We interrupt this broadcast for breaking news," a Korean-American newscaster announced earnestly. "Joining us is our Iran correspondent..." she continued.

Trita had stepped up to the bar. "That's us." Abramian smiled at her warmly. "Coffee, or something else?" he offered. Instead of answering, she pointed to the television. The screen now showed a reporter with a long, flushed face, unruly hair and wakeful eyes. He was standing in front of a long bridge composed of a multitude of stacked ogival arches, which rose out of the shimmering water. Young women dressed in jeans, black coats and colorful headscarves stood along the riverbank in the light of the bridge and news crew lamps.

The camera zoomed from the ancient, broad bridge, with its great arcades, back to the disheveled correspondent. "Thank you, Nancy. We are here in Isfahan, standing in front of the lovely Si-o-se Pol Bridge... There was a mysterious occurrence in the city today—a large number of mobile telephones, first estimates are around one hundred thousand, were dropped onto the city by plane. Just imagine! The amazing thing is that these robust, modern devices, which floated down like snowflakes on miniature parachutes, were already charged and in service. They are fully functional. Look here!" He raised one of the cell phones up to show the camera, then held it to his cheek—counted one, two, three. "Can you hear me?... Okay... There is a text message on the display. It says: *You will receive messages every day. From today forward, there will be freedom of thought.* Isn't that incredible? Freedom of thought. Well, the French ambassador, who had just met with Iranian representatives of commerce, shared with me that the regime decision makers are quite confounded. It quickly became known that the same thing has occurred in a multitude of other Iranian towns. Telephones have literally been falling from the sky. People are calling anywhere they wish. There was great commotion on the large square earlier. I have discovered that it has been locked down by the military, but things have remained peaceful. Rumors that militant mullahs have ordered executions are...have not been confirmed. The police do not appear to be intervening against this unanticipated tide of new technology..."

"Are there any ideas about where these cell phones are from, Chuck?"

The correspondent waited, nodded. "That is, indeed, the question that seems to be on everyone's mind, Nancy. We do know that they were dropped by airplanes in great number...one moment please." The reporter turned, pointed excitedly at the night sky. "Unbelievable! It looks like another load is coming down! Dropped from a great height—there are no planes visible. There seem to be a whole bunch of little, white parachutes, just floating down. There! On the other side of the bridge." The camera shakily captured a cloud of descending parachutes.

Abramian turned excitedly from the screen. "Any news from Tehran?" he asked, his loud voice seeming almost electric. Music from the commercial break sounded surreal in the silence. Trita muted the television. A communications specialist raised a hand. "Sir! Banda Abbas is reporting problems."

Heads turned as Cosmo slid from the stool and hurried to the communications desk. Someone held the printout up for him to see.

"It's not looking good, sir."

"Who's the pilot?"

"Probably Richie Forrester, sir."

Forrester's head felt ready to burst. Blood rushed mercilessly to his brain, which screamed against the constraints of his skull as he allowed the plane to nose-dive toward the coastline of the Persian Gulf. The altimeter blurred before his eyes. The Iranian fighter jet had appeared out of nowhere. Joel, the Frenchmen, had been closely monitoring their radar, but had seen nothing. They had just completed their second drop, and were preparing to head back. Richie had just entered the data and started an eighty-five-degree turn when the jet spat past them at a terrific speed, very nearly missing them. The slim, black silhouette shot past the nose of their plane at eye level, two red spots disappeared in the darkness.

"Merde!" Joel slapped a hand on his heart, breathing hard.

"Where is he?" Richie screamed.

They saw nothing at first.

"Keep an eye out," Richie commanded over the intercom. "We have company. It's a Russian Sukhoi Su-24 by the looks of things."

They suddenly saw a bunch of tracer projectiles shooting toward them. Richie instinctively ducked, bringing the Falcon down. The bright yellow and orange sheaves fired by the Iranian cannons whizzed over their heads.

"A hit!" Joel bellowed. "We've taken a hit! What do we do now?"

Richie kept the Falcon in the dive.

"Those were warning shots, Joel! Do you see the idiot?"

A warning light blinked over the engine 3 display. Then Richie's headset slipped; a radio call. A stammered staccato that he could not decipher. He hit the control to answer, then thought better of it, kept searching for the jet. He saw nothing but darkness.

"Engine three is on fire!" Joel screamed.

They stared out, searched the night sky. The radio crackled once more. This time Richie heard a high-pitched, strident voice in broken English. "Islamic Republic of Iran Air Force…land plane…follow me, or I shoot…"

Where was this madman?

Richie's thoughts raced. Following the demand to land the plane certainly seemed preferable to going down in a ball of flames. On the other hand, what were those crazy mullahs capable of doing to them down there? Would they be tortured and publicly executed after they had reached the ground safely?

"The fire is out, we've lost the engine," Joel announced, now somewhat calmer. He looked at Richie's furrowed face. The third engine was the rear engine, he contemplated. What would this loss mean in terms of efficiency?

"We're going down," Richie decided, hitting the talk button. "Air force...this..." he began. The remainder stuck in his throat.

They all saw the deadliest of threats at the same time.

"The bastard!"

"Rocket!" Joel screams. The fiery tail is coming from diagonally below them, heading for starboard.

It is weaving, as if the heat-seeking device is actively looking for the target's weakest spot. The Falcon is marked...but Forrester is a battle-hardened Royal Air Force pilot—the Balkans, two tours in Iraq.

A split second's hesitation, then the veteran squadron leader tears the Falcon downward, gives it full throttle as if he is sitting at the controls of his Tornado fighter jet. Joel's eyes are wide with terror, his legs braced against the nearest solid object. Was Richie simply going to ram them face first into Persian soil?

The pilot's bottom lip is bleeding. He cannot feel himself biting it. *Is this heap going to hold up? Hopefully the Dassault engineers had incorporated the latest air force technology into their structural design.*

Joel tries in vain to sight the missile. He feels sick to his stomach, close to passing out. His hands clench at his thighs, then at the upholstery. Soon it will all be dark. It will be over. That is his last thought.

Richie pulls brusquely upward, the fuselage vibrates, gives a tortured sound as if giving its all not to burst apart. Richie turns, heads back down...he repeats the hair-raising maneuver two more times. It is an air combat tactic that he has practiced with his squadron to the point of passing out. And he feels as if he is about to do just that. The smell of fresh vomit fills the air.

"There, there!" Joel gurgles, holding his stomach. The fiery tail shoots past them portside, into the distance, into nothing, spinning down. Richie rights the plane, slowly, deliberately. The glow of the explosion lights up far below them, somewhere among the crazy mullahs. There are cries of relief and elation in the cabin.

"Where are we?" Joel coughs.

"No clue," Richie pants. "But we're getting the hell out of here. Do you see the coast?"

They took a few moments to breathe, checked the gauges and displays. In the back, the crew had regained their bearings, started clearing up, peered out of the windows, searched the skies. There was no sign of the IRIAF fighter. The radar showed the skies to be completely empty. They may as well have been flying over the North Pole.

A half an hour later the Falcon was six hundred feet above sea level and making good time westward. Richie radioed the control center at Armenus Technopark.

"Exit toward Emirates. Emergency. Engine trouble. We need to talk to Nico Strom."

Nico was the man who would almost certainly be able to use his connections in Qatar and Abu Dhabi to ensure a safe and expedient landing without a bureaucratic nightmare.

"Negative. Nico is on a mission. No contact. What's going on?"

"We were intercepted by the Iranian Air Force. Missile attack. Barely made it out. Probable hit to one of our engines. We are heading toward Doha."

The radio remained silent for a while. Richie fidgeted with his headset. Then the familiar, hoarse voice. "Jack here. I'll take care of it, Richie. Keep your chin up. Do you have enough fuel? Just a moment."

The Falcon 900LX really did have the stuff of a fighter jet, Richie contemplated with an admiring nod.

"Fire in three again!" Joel called out, frantically trying to activate the built-in extinguisher.

Minutes passed.

"Richie, this is Jack again. Doha negative. Permission to land in

Abu Dhabi, armed forces base, an escort has been arranged. Here is the frequency…"

Richie adjusts the knobs, takes a deep breath. He turns in his chair.

"Joel… guys, everything okay? We will be touching down in Abu Dhabi, and then, I swear…" he made the three-fingered gesture of an oath. "I will be sending those Falcon engineers a crate of whiskey."

His words were met by raucous cheers.

"Bravooo, Richie!"

"And I… I'll be eating bananas before our next flight," Joel said with a pained grin.

"Why? For the potassium?" one of the drop team asked.

"No. They just taste better the second-time around."

Loud laughter.

An hour later, a UAE armed forces helicopter escorted the Falcon 900 onto the emergency runway behind the sickle-shaped building of the officer's club. The machine was smoking profusely from the third, rear engine. The ground crew quickly extinguished the fire. Then the plane was towed into a hangar, and the doors closed behind it.

Richie's knees shook like brittle leaves in a late fall wind as he descended the short flight of stairs—he tried to mask the embarrassing fact with a broad grin and firmly squared shoulders. All the while knowing that he had been very close to displaying something far more humiliating than a little trembling…

Tabriz, Northern Iran

Omar stepped outside the house, took a deep breath of cold air. The small log cabin he was approaching almost appeared to be crouching beneath the mighty cedars towering over it with their wide branches, perhaps ashamed that, in this Islamic state, it had once housed a frivolous sauna. Omar's father had been able to purchase the idyllically situated house decades ago from a Finnish pilot who had found himself forced to return to his homeland when Khomeini had seized power.

Omar had attempted to use the Nordic sauna a few times, but had never been able to figure out why subjecting oneself to heat of a hundred degrees Celsius would be at all appealing, as the yellowed poster that the prior owner had left hanging along with a faded picture seemed to suggest.

The yellowed directions were illustrated. The photograph showed men laughing in the snow—probably the man's British work colleagues, who had flown helicopters for the wood works back then. Someone had written something on the poster in Farsi. The Finn's Iranian wife, who was born to a family close to the Shah that had later fallen from grace, had spoken Farsi.

Omar had studied the gushing testimony to the virtuous effects of sweating on both body and soul, but he had soon given up trying to get to the bottom of this strange, Scandinavian ritual. Today, he used the little building as storage for, among other things, a box of vodka that the Finn had evidently forgotten in his hasty departure.

"No wonder they left, and probably for the best," his father had said. The mullahs would have had little appreciation for the fact that the Iranian woman had been an intellectual teacher. Let alone one who frolicked about with a foreigner in a little hut some nights, occasionally rolled around naked in the snow with him, it was said.

Omar had not been able to sleep, and had awoken just past midnight. After some tossing and turning, he decided to get some fresh air. He put his fur jacket on and opened the door to the backyard. It was dark, and cold. There was only very little light from a pale half-moon, which shone in glimpses through the passing clouds onto a thin blanket of snow that had turned the garden into a frosted wonderland. There was going to be bad weather—the wind that blew past his cheeks smelled of more snow.

Breathing deeply, he strode slowly on. He had awoken with a tangle of unquiet thoughts on his mind. Now he tried to calm himself. He had reached the door to the sauna. It opened with a creek. Nearby, a black bird laboriously loosed itself from the thicket. A sharp gust of wind hit his face. Something seemed to be brewing.

He looked up at the sky, listened. Nothing. Then, suddenly, he heard it for the first time—the distant sound of a motor.

A deep, dull rumbling from far up north. A sound similar to those he sometimes heard from the heavy Iran Timber trucks. But this sound was more powerful, like...like...

Omar felt for the switch, flipped it several times, but the light didn't come on. He decided to go back to his warm house. The Finn had left a large hunting knife on the wall, like the ones they apparently wore up in Finland when they went prowling through their woods. Another ritual object left behind, it still hung in exactly the same spot.

As he was about to close the door behind him the noise suddenly swelled, as if carried by a strong gust of wind. Omar hesitated, took a step outside. As Allah was his witness, those were no trucks. He listened intently. Tanks, with their rattling chains and that typical, loud revving. That was what this sounded like. There was no doubt. The noise did not subside, but seemed to be coming closer.

Omar rushes into the bedroom, quickly gets dressed. He feels that something very strange is going on. He ties his boots tightly, puts on the bomber jacket lined with sheepskin, takes the helmet from its hook. On an impulse, he grabs the belt with the hunting knife and pulls it around his waist, checking to see if the blade is seated in its sheath. Outside, he pushes open the door to the shed, heaves the heavy motorcycle off its stand.

He knew his way around engines. The purchase of the Finn's house many years ago had been no coincidence. Omar's father had been a mechanic at the British helicopter company during the Shah's rule. By the time Omar turned a military age, the once successful firm had long been taken over by the new regime. Most of the pilots were Iranian now. The mechanic's son was recruited as a rookie helicopter pilot for the army.

It is not snowing. The skies seem to be clearing. Omar pulls the protective shield on his helmet down further, steadily speeds up. He had returned to Tabriz after two years in the army. Like the Finn, he now flew for Iran Timber.

His job afforded him a great deal of freedom. He found plenty of opportunity to discover villages and towns, to gather information on building sites and in forests. He was able to form an opinion about the mood of the people, the decrees of the mullahs, new streets, buildings, and many other things. Above all, he knew the area like the back of his hand. Omar was no son of the desert. He loved the mountains, knew the vast forests, didn't mind the cold.

As he stops the Honda a few minutes later, turns off the engine, he has a good idea where the noise is coming from—to the north of the village. Abu-Mard was a half an hour away from Tabriz. It was well known to the loggers who harvested the forests of that area.

A few stars glint between heavy clouds, there is very little light upon the grayish-white appearing landscape. Looking down at the broad front wheel of his bike, he sees that the street is dry.

Omar takes off his helmet, listens. Silence. In his mind, he has determined the area where he presumes the noise had been coming from. The large through road ran through the mountains to the Armenian and Azerbaijani borders about a kilometer north. To the southeast, it meandered across mountainous terrain all the way to Tehran: six hundred kilometers away.

Omar rides slowly through the night, into the deserted village. Were people listening behind their windows? He continues past the village exit, rambling slowly, his eyes searching the countryside. Everything looks peaceful. Had he been wrong? At the fork he sees fresh crawler tracks, deep furrows across the sod and leading into the field. The heavy vehicles had turned into the forest. Omar stops, looks across the dim field to the forest rising gloomily against the sky. He slaps his forehead. "Of course!" The tracks lead to the old lumber stores, then on to the barracks, airstrips and landing pads. The military compounds deep in the forest had not been used in years.

But that is clearly where the tracks lead. He takes a closer look, recognizes the dark outline of a vehicle; behind it, the ominous darkness of the woods.

Without further thought, he accelerates, his boot held just above the ground as he carefully takes the turn. Coming closer, he sees figures apparently stretching their legs next to the armored personnel carrier.

Suddenly blinded by a light, he stops.

The four soldiers are probably the crew. The one with the powerful flashlight walks up, sees Omar's bomber jacket. "Pilot?"

Omar nods. "Have you broken down? Do you need help?"

The other three come closer, curiously eyeing the motorbike. Heat rises like a mist from the Honda's light, aluminum cylinder head. The smallest of the four sticks his head out. "Can you get us something to eat?"

"Sure. What happened? Is someone coming to tow you?"

The leader turns off the flashlight and puts in his jacket. "It may take some time. They're all back there. Do you know your way around here?"

"I do. I'm a helicopter pilot. I know the old barracks. Is this a maneuver?"

They look at each other. The leader shakes his head. "Top secret mission. You know how it goes. They don't tell us much—but if something goes wrong..."

Omar starts the bike back up, "I can get you provisions. What do you need?"

"Women," the diminutive one says with a grin.

"You know. Anything—just no military grub," the one smoking a cigarette calls.

In his headlight, Omar recognizes the military pennant on the hauler's antenna. "You're Air Force, wow!"

The soldier with the cigarette takes a drag. "Don't get all emotional. We're ground crew. We just keep things tidy for the guys up there."

The little one evidently feels a need to share their plight. "We're in a mess. Our steering is out," he bleats.

"What are you going to do? Where are the aircraft?"

"Who knows? It's not like they tell us anything," the smoker gripes.

Now the fourth man pipes up. His broad goggles identify him as the driver. "We have rockets. Live warheads, man. Just waiting for the go ahead."

"Warheads?" Omar repeats incredulously.

"Yep. What do you think we'll be sticking under their wings? It's the really new ones, too."

"Shut it," the leader says gruffly.

Omar skids off through the field. *I'd best head to Tabriz; there may still be a stall open at the bazaar.*

Mentally repeating what the crew of the armored personnel vehicle had revealed to him, he approaches the first, peripheral houses of Tabriz, crosses the railway track that is part of the Istanbul to Tehran route. The capital of the East Azerbaijan province is 1,400 meters above sea level. Victim of a turbulent, often tragic, history, it had been captured and occupied by foreign forces time and again—the Mongols, the Russians, Stalin's troops in 1941. It is bitterly cold. Omar pulls the scarf over his face, tightens it beneath his helmet. Fortunately there is no snow on the ground. He weaves a little to test the road, his tires grip and hold.

He rides down the long street to the park. There was a lake, a small regal building in its midst, the water frozen—Omar could easily have taken the Honda across the solid ice. But the structure was only a summer retreat. Even the river that coursed through the city and continued down through the vast valley had frozen over. The Tabriz region was known for its harsh winters.

Omar has no interest in the Blue Mosque. He takes a turn, instead, toward the bazaar, putters through its towering entrance and parks his Honda.

The market stalls in the vaulted halls—which were decorated with a splendor of intricate mosaics and tiles—boasted leather boots, carpets, woolen caps and colorful fabrics. The wares were piled high, and displayed from the ceilings. Kurds, Turkomans, Armenians, Iranians, even Indians and Chinese had offered their goods here in peace and harmony, side by side since antiquity.

Omar hurried past the closed stalls, turned into a little alley where he hoped to find Hassan in his grocery store. The alcove lay in the shadows, the gate closed and locked.

He returned to his Honda, left the town center and returned to the park, from where he could see the lights of the El-Goli Pars.

The five-star hotel was situated by the lake. Omar trundled to the rear courtyard, where green, neon light spilled out from the kitchen. He rode his bike to the threshold, revved a few times by way of a greeting.

Salim came out of the office, a huge grin on his face, wiped his hands on his white apron.

The man on the Honda made a feeding gesture with his hand to his open mouth. "You wouldn't happen to have some food for a few hungry souls?" His friend allowed him to explain the situation, then headed to the cold storage. Omar turned his machine around, waited until Salim reappeared with a pack of provisions. "I'll be back later," he said, but now with a drinking gesture. He revved the engine and took off back toward the main road.

He had traveled about a kilometer and a half when snowflakes as large as handkerchiefs began to fall.

Snowflakes? Huge, white shreds were coming down, clouds of them. In showers! Omar stopped abruptly. He stared into the dark sky, where his astonished eyes were met by a dramatic spectacle.

This wasn't snow—these were little parachutes! An airdrop. The Russians? The sky was filled with them as far as his eyes could see.

The little traffic there was came to a halt. Car doors opened, lights began coming on in the houses. Within minutes, the deserted street was teeming. Omar slowly began to understand. *They are dropping flyers! How strange!*

He parked the Honda, grabbed at a parachute. Something hard hit the bike's tank. People were running back and forth now, grabbing up what had fallen from the sky. Omar had two. They weren't pamphlets.

Cell phones! Utterly dumbfounded, he stretched his head back, searched the sky for a plane. His mind flashed on the men from the ground crew.

Sirens howl. Omar decides that it is time to depart from this surreal and wondrous scene. He stuffs the phones into his saddlebag, drives off in a curve, avoiding the objects on the tarmac.

If he had imagined that he would be able to quietly contemplate the situation at the hotel, he was sorely mistaken. Lights were on in every floor. Guests stood on their balconies, little flocks had gathered practically everywhere. Cooks, wait staff—they all bustled about, their excitement palpable.

Omar rode over to the kitchen in search of Salim. He finally found him nearby, on the ice. A girl had taken a nasty fall and broken her leg. A few drivers had parked their cars in a way that would allow their headlights to illuminate the pond, giving a ghostly appearance to the scene of individuals straggling around, bending down, slipping on the ice and barely catching themselves. Or not. Cell phones everywhere, bedded and draped in little white parachutes.

Omar helped to bring the injured girl to the lobby. Only then did he have time to examine one of the phones more closely. He was astonished that he was actually able to use it instantly, just as he had heard some people stubbornly proclaim. He tried to call the emergency number for an ambulance—*nothing*—he stood up—there! The answering dispatcher could be heard with perfect clarity.

"Pars Hotel, we have an injured girl with a broken leg. We need an ambulance."

"You're not the only one. We are swamped with calls. It could take hours. Do you have a vehicle?"

Omar pressed the red icon, ending the call. *How was this technically even possible?* Then he thought of something.

He grabbed Salim's sleeve; pulled him away from the whimpering girl. "Salim," he whispered, "I have a feeling that this could be our chance."

"Look, there's already a message on my cell phone. What if I just try to answer it?"

Salim looked very much unconvinced. "You have to be careful! They'll find out."

Omar shook his head. "How? I have a number, but nobody knows that I am connected to it." His eyes sparkled conspiratorially. Salim understood. "You mean you think you can text him?"

He was referring to their secret contact at Camp Ashraf in Iraq, where the Iranian resistance was organizing.

"Yes and no. I was not thinking of Bob." Robert Armstrong was a very down-to-earth American, whom Omar would never have suspected of being a CIA agent.

"Look. I'll just reply to the message I received." He showed him what he had typed: AIR FORCE TROOPS SOUTHEAST OF TABRIZ ARMED WITH ROCKETS.

He hit *send*. They stared at the display, mesmerized.

"It really worked! Message sent!"

"You see, Salim. Whoever did this is on our side."

They returned to the lobby. A woman with a broken arm sat, shaking, next to the girl with the broken leg. A mother was talking to her son in soothing tones while carefully tending to a nasty contusion on his forehead.

"Your anonymous friend is leading the mullahs onto very thin, very slippery ice," Salim said, ominously. Omar looked at him, startled. "You know, you could be right, Salim."

Of course. Salim had seen the big picture. Somebody had devised a truly brilliant strategy. "If only I knew exactly what is behind all of this…" Omar looked down at the phone in his hand, hastily pockets it as he sees a patrol car round the corner.

The three policemen got out and turned their flashlights on, then set off onto the frozen pool shoulder to shoulder.

Omar took the food that his friend had packed earlier out of his saddlebag. "Alright, man. It's not as if anything has gone according to plan tonight. At this point we may as well eat the food ourselves. This is about survival."

Tel Aviv

Far below ground, at a commando center of the Israeli Air Force north of Tel Aviv, Nir Barak was also contemplatively weighing one of the silver cell phones in his hand.

"Like snowflakes from the sky. Unbelievable! He actually pulled it off. What do the text messages say?" He tried to calm himself down, to no avail.

The young captain wrote something on a notepad in English, tore off the page and handed it to Barak. The older man finally found his glasses on his head, put them on.

"Rockets positioned east of Tabriz," he muttered. "Is that really what it says? Can I rely on your translation?"

"Absolutely, sir," the translator said, clearing his throat as he removed his rimless spectacles. A thickset air force colonel with a wide, forbidding face and a cigarette dangling out of the corner of his mouth sat half of his behind down on the edge of the desk. An aide silently stood guard over a battery of technical devices in the next table.

"Do you know anything about this, Colonel?" Barak asked, regarding him questioningly over the top of his reading glasses.

Colonel Levit wore the Air Force Intelligence insignia on his sleeve beneath the epaulet. There was, famously, no love lost between this proud, independent service branch and the Mossad. Members of each avoided one another like the plague.

"About what?" the colonel barked.

"About the fact that Iran may have positioned cruise missiles with nuclear warheads."

Colonel Levit found that the moment had arrived to stand and pull himself up to his full, proud posture. "If such positions existed, we would have known about it long ago. We rely on precise aerial reconnaissance for our information, you understand? Not on..." he searched for the appropriate term, gestured condescendingly with his right hand "...on Internet chat rooms or things of that sort."

Barak came a few steps closer, holding the silver airdrop cell phone in his outstretched hand. "Millions of these were dropped over Iranian towns. The people there are sending messages like crazy, Colonel. We have received a few on this phone, intercepted others, others again have been brought to our attention. I am inclined to take this very seriously."

The colonel stiffened.

"I am not authorized to take action in this matter."

"Fine, but can we at least evaluate the aerial surveillance? That is your job. You don't need direct orders to perform it."

The aide raised a hand to gain their attention.

"What is it?" the colonel growled, deeply annoyed.

"The Turks are reporting a hijacking, Colonel. The machine is in route to the Syrian coast."

The news hardly excited the colonel, but it was definitely opportune. He'd show that damned arrogant Mossad donkey with his ridiculous cell phones who did the real work around here, protecting the country day and night. He stepped up to the small command console, gave the aide a few curt instructions in a low voice.

The room darkened. The border territory between Turkey and Syria appeared on the oversized projection screen.

Two uniformed individuals came in from the room next door, hastened to take their seats behind vacant monitors, flipped open their notebooks and readied their pens.

"Position?" the woman asked.

"Monitor two," the aide called out.

It took a few seconds then the plane came into view. Barak stepped behind the woman, noted her rank.

"Are we able to zoom in on the ID, Lieutenant?"

He noticed her soft, herbaceous scent as she cast a quick glance at him over her shoulder. She clicked on the mouse a few times.

"This is the best resolution we can get. Elegant machine. Okay, they're heading for fog."

"Record it," Barak commanded. He felt a claw-like hand on his shoulder. Colonel Levit pulled him away from the station politely, but firmly.

"This is Air Force business, Barak. I give the orders here."

In the meantime, the young captain had translated all of the Farsi messages into English, typed them out and printed them. He handed the paper to Barak with an almost pleading look, evidently in regret for the colonel's rudeness. "Evaluating these text messages, I have to say that the existence of these rocket positions appears likely. If you look here, for

235

instance, it says: *The sound of tanks tonight. Are we at war?* And this even seems to be a set of coordinates, do these make sense?"

"We will check them, thank you."

"This one sounds authentic: AIR FORCE TROOPS SOUTHEAST OF TABRIZ ARMED WITH ROCKETS," he added.

Barak patted him on the shoulder in acknowledgment. "No need to convince me, Captain. I will be needing you."

He went over to the lieutenant, who had absented herself from the monitor with a note containing what she had been able to make out of the plane's identification. "It is incomplete, I'm afraid. I could not make out one of the four letters."

She suddenly blushed profusely as his eyes admiringly took in her face, resting for a moment too long on her pale lips.

"RA-OB...probably a Russian ID," Barak murmured. "Are you able to determine the holder?"

She squinted over at Colonel Levit, who had taken up her vacant seat. He sat slouched, debating heatedly with the officer at the next desk.

"No. We have no access. I can tell you that the machine is a Global Express."

"Thank you, Lieutenant, excellent."

Barak sat, groped for his cell phone. Shielding it from view with one hand, he propped his pointy leather shoes on the table and spoke quietly.

He flipped it closed and looked up. The colonel had positioned himself in front of him, chest puffed like a pigeon. He held a lit, gold lighter in one hand, cigarette in the other, and smiled a superior smile. "Satisfied?"

"I am quite impressed, Colonel. Really. What happens now?"

"With the aircraft?"

Barak nodded. "The north sector command has been informed, interceptor fighters are on alert."

"Good. And why, if I may ask, does this missile site not appear to bother you? All of Israel is terrified of an attack, and you seem to not give a shit about this possible acute threat. Why?"

"Very simple, Mr. Mossad. Because Iran does not possess cruise missiles. None." He drew an oval shape in the air with his finger. "And most certainly no nukes. We are focused on the Shihab-4, as you are aware. That is where the real threat lies. Command will hardly wish to split the forces and go chasing after rumored sites in the middle of nowhere. Tabriz!" He lit his cigarette, took a deep drag. You know what's up in Tabriz, Barak? Not a damn thing. Just a bunch of pretty rivers and the wind whispering through the trees."

"So you wouldn't mind me taking a look with the lieutenant?"

The colonel expelled an exasperated puff of smoke ceiling-ward, turned away without another word. Barak almost missed his dismissive wave. He jumped up and followed the Air Force man.

The lieutenant's colleague, a communications specialist of equal rank, was responsible for the LEO system. He located the northern Iran, zoomed in on Tabriz, searched the surrounding area.

"The target further southeast."

"We're out of luck, then, I'm afraid," said the officer regretfully. "Your target seems to be in the blind spot."

"You don't say!" Barak exclaimed, smiling at the colonel.

"Sorry," the man barked. "That area is of absolutely no strategic importance."

"Let's say you wanted to get a satellite image of this blind spot from the southeast, what would you have to do to make that happen?"

Barak was on his cell phone before the officer had a chance to answer.

"Just a moment," he gestured, turning his back. He was on the phone for barely ten seconds. By the time he turned back to face him, the officer had the answer.

"The Low Earth Orbit System, LEO, is a global system operated by the Pentagon. The Americans are the deciding factor for what type of surveillance takes place where. We would have to put in a request with Washington."

"I understand," Barak said. Although he really didn't. It was probably better that he kept the objection that was on the tip of his tongue to himself. That, along with the information he had just obtained on the hijacked aircraft. His razor-sharp, analytical mind—a gift that had seen him rise to the top of the world's most effective secret service—suddenly told him that two events, both of which had been discussed in this room within the past half hour, might just be connected. However, his golden rule was Keep your thoughts to yourself. And so he politely said his farewells, leaving the colonel in the happy belief that he had just scored a point.

The hijacked plane, as Barak's analysts had established in record time, belonged to Oleg Nedjew, the Russian mobster who played only in the very highest of criminal leagues. A little emergency meeting was definitely called for. Furthermore, Barak was now certain that the missile scare was not just a scare. The missiles existed. Ironically, he considered the fact that there was nothing to be seen absolutely anywhere to be particularly damning. The Iranians had deliberately positioned them in a blind spot, where they knew that they could not be seen by omnipresent U.S. eyes.

Situation Room, Tehran

The IRIAF grounds were now in full view. The shimmering runway, the sharp contours of the command center were rising decisively from the plain. The General relaxed, placing the worn briefcase on his knees. He dug a page out, skimmed the illustrious participant list. He mentally rehearsed his speech, going through key phrases, with which he intended to open the briefing. All the while the old fox was well aware that everything could go counter to plan. Like war. Even as the first shot sounds, the loveliest battle plan may no longer be worth the paper it is written on...

Having successfully mastered its obstacle course, the Soviet take on a Jeep came to a standstill in front of the massive entry gate. The smart, lightly armed air force soldiers guarding the gate recognized their commanding officer. A flurry of activity ensued, the gate was set in motion, an officer appeared on the scene, snapped to attention, saluted, shouted orders.

They waved the Big Brass through reverently; Ali hitched forward, after a few meters the nose of the all-terrain vehicle dipped, rolled down a ramp toward a second steel gate, which opened on time with a grudging squeak.

The General arrived at the reception bay, alighted with dignity, reciprocated the greeting of the hastily advancing troops with a sharp raising of his hand. He crossed the spacious loading dock with an energetic stride, gracing the rigid, fiery-eyed private who set the revolving door in motion for his passing with one of his charismatic smiles. He stepped into the elevator, exiting two stories below ground seconds later and stepping into the Air Force Command Center of the Islamic Republic of Iran.

※

General Nassiri bowed slightly before the bearded man.

"Mr. Vice President, it is an honor to have you with us for this briefing." *He probably only bothered to come so he could make sure I am toeing the party line.*

"Proceed, General," came the gravelly reply.

"Certainly," said the general, forcing himself to adopt a slightly subservient tone, and began introducing the attendees, as he had so many times. As he was doing so, his thoughts strayed involuntarily to his deceased wife's nephew.

Vice President Seyed Shapasandi, with his beady, deep-set eyes, headed a key ministry, where he was not known for being temperate. His power was based on fear. The Ministry of Intelligence consisted chiefly of a well-masked, all-powerful secret service that spread terror throughout the land. The Vevak obscurantists watched every move, listened to every word spoken among the Iranian people; they were worse than the East German Stasi in their heyday. Students, bazaar merchants, young women, scientists were hauled off with no legal defense, interrogated, tortured, convicted, hanged—as Ahmed, the Tehran student had tragically experienced firsthand. The image of him on the university campus, holding a bloody shirt above his head, had been released into the world and gone viral.

"By Allah, get back, they will shoot you," Ahmed had yelled at his demonstrating peers, waving the bloody shirt for emphasis. "This shirt belongs to Hassan, they are shooting into the crowd." The journalist's perfect shot landed on the desk of Shapasandi's intelligence agents. They beheld the young man's terrified face, everything from his dark, wide eyes, black hair held back by a headband to his well-groomed, preppy beard. The way he held up the shirt of his shot fellow student. All of it was a slap in the minister's face, an intolerable insult, a provocation to the regime. The moral guardians were outraged. Days later, Vevak agents appeared on the campus... and a terrible nightmare began for Ahmed. Arrest, interrogation, torture... twice they led him to the gallows... Later, miraculously, he was able to flee from the sickbay... General Nassiri would carefully make contact with him in Paris, one day, in better times...

...Hassan Nassiri felt the eyes of the civilian chief of staff of the Ministry of Defense on him. He did not look. Where had he left off? He looked around and suddenly realized what was bothering him. The good ones had not come.

The absentees spoke volumes: the minister of defense and chief of staff, for instance. He saw their non-attendance was as a sign. *Watch yourself, Hassan Nassiri. Shapasandi is not one to joke around with, you have to keep him happy. Forget your introduction, save the motivational speech for later.*

He broke the uncomfortable silence by clearing his throat.

"We have recently been able to acquire twelve new Sunburn rockets of the latest model, equipped with nuclear warheads."

He let the announcement sink in for a while. Some heads turned, glances were exchanged. The mullah and vice president had a whispered exchange. "The weapons are ready for operation. Brigadier General Bakhtiar, proceed, please."

The wiry officer with the black, bushy mop of hair stood up.

"We have inspected the material. It is in perfect condition. Our Russian partner has been true to his word."

"So, we can attack?" The voice of the Vice President of the Islamic Republic and Minister of Intelligence was laced with impatience.

General Nassiri's eyes focused on the brigadier general, who was smoothing his thin mustache with one finger. "Yes. Generally speaking, we are prepared to deliver an offensive strike, if necessary." He directed a veiled glance at his superior to reassure himself before continuing. "The Air Force is of the opinion, however, that the risk would be unjustifiably high at this time."

"You are out of line, General!" a mullah of short stature flared angrily from the back row, pulling at the lapel of his gray gown, which appeared to be color-coordinated with his unkempt beard. "That decision is ours to make! Whether or not to attack a target once we have the capability to do so is a decision reserved for the high religious leadership in accord with the strategic counsel. What is the status of your plans, General Nassiri?"

The air force general lowered his gaze. There was no strategic counsel. The mullah regime was by and large rational in its actions. While this did not go for Shapasandi and his cabal, which this nasty dwarf apparently belonged to, it was true for most other leaders of the regime. *We aren't some barbaric state that would see another country burn in a nuclear hell, or may the devil take me there personally!*

"General, you heard the question," the vice president spat angrily.

"I am not deaf, Minister." Nassiri was obliged to display the brassy countenance of a commanding officer for his people. "If I may: the Air Force restricts itself to operative planning, which has yielded several options. Currently first and foremost would be a surprise attack with the new Sukhoi fighter aircraft, which is compatible with the Russian Sunburns. Our intelligence tells us that Israel is focused on the Shihab-4, which they fear as a long-range missile. If we attack with fighters, the element of surprise will be to our advantage. Their missile defense systems are on high alert, since it has evidently been leaked that our government is preparing to test atomic weapons. We will have to find a hole in their defense. In any case, we should not act in haste."

Nassiri had broken a taboo with his casual allusion to a possible turncoat. Officially, a traitor existing within the high ranks of the Islamic republic was unthinkable. And yet, officers had been muttering behind closed doors for days about the mysterious disappearance of the leader of the officially non-existent Iranian nuclear program. *In all likelihood,*

Nassiri thought, eyeing the vice president, *one of the factions within the regime was opting for the flight forward and...*

"So what is the earliest point at which we can proceed?" the vice president demanded, interrupting Nassiri's train of thought. "You speak of the valuable element of surprise, General. We should not squander that with unnecessary wavering."

Nassiri furrowed his brow. *That is most definitely not what I said.*

"When we eradicate the Zionists, that root of all evil, the infidel lackeys of the American Satan, once and for all from the face of this earth—and we will—then, by Allah, I want to be prepared; be it right now or tomorrow. And I am not interested in you merely giving your best, General. This is a matter of the utmost importance. I will tolerate nothing less than superhuman effort." He took a breath, looked at his audience, doing his best to suffocate any perceived budding of doubt or protest with a ruthlessly penetrating stare.

"Pardon me, Minister, if I must temper your plans," General Nassiri interrupted, to the horror of all those present. "Should our government decide to attack Israel, and should the air force be chosen to fulfill this mission, we will not be able to do so without significant preparation. A nuclear attack cannot simply be launched on the spur of the moment. We will require a certain amount of advance notice. For both material and organizational reasons, I am unable to say exactly how much notice—at least not now, not today, not here."

"When will you be able to launch the attack?" the minister asked, seemingly relenting.

The air force general spread his arms. "Well, even with the help of Allah, not before the rockets are physically on the base. Currently they are in the region of Tabriz. The transport is underway. This rather complex operation calls for extraordinary precautionary measures."

Brigadier General Bakhtiar noted his superior's nod in his direction and went on to clarify: "It has been determined, for obvious reasons, that the Sukhois are the carrier system of choice. They are stationed in Shiraz. It will take time to load them with the Sunburns; to prime the warheads. We are doing more than our best, Minister." It was a small dig.

It was also less than true. The air force had been having problems with its Sukhoi pilots for some time.

Many of the young men, who were qualified strictly in terms of being able to fly the aircraft, were lacking in combat experience, not to mention experience in implementing air-to-surface missiles, such as the Sunburn. It would be pure insanity to send these boys into the hell that was the airspace over Israel without thorough training. At best, Bakhtiar could scrape together four complete crews—and that was if the major designated to become squadron leader came back from his training in Moscow promptly!

The general needed to buy time. As far as he knew, neither of the government representatives currently staring him down was authorized to independently reach decisions on matters as critical as the launching of nuclear weapons. *So, if they order me to attack Israel in spite of this, then it is possible that there is something rotten in Iran, very, very rotten. And it would be wise to follow an alternate route.*

The vice president shook his head in disgust. "That is not good enough, gentlemen. Not even close." He was not going to tolerate discussion on this issue. The military existed for one reason: to follow orders. *If Nassiri stalls this operation, or tries to interfere in any way, we will hang him from his feet and chop his balls off. Literally.*

"You will be ready in forty-eight hours, General," Shapasandi ordered callously. And, having spoken, he waved to the helicopter pilot, who was at the ready and had been watching through a glass window in the soundproof door. Turning his back on the gathered officers, the powerful and unpredictably dangerous Minister of Intelligence and second in command of the regime strode to the door without one further word or gesture.

All eyes turned to the Air Force General. *Arrogant piece of shit,* his thoughts appeared to read rather clearly. General Nassiri did not need to take notes. The order had been unequivocal. He glanced at his watch, looked back at the mullah, who had remained to keep watch—in the manner not unlike a good, Stalin-era Soviet political officer. The general decided that the next best course of action would be to look busy. "Get to work, people!"

He signaled his closest confidants to join him, wishing all the while that he could just be allowed to wake up from this very bad dream.

Seven Five, Got a Knife

The aerial perspective was comfortingly familiar to Sophie. Her father had always insisted that she should get to know the world from above. Even as a little girl, she had often sat next to him on his flights through the mountains. Since she had learned to fly herself, she was forced to think of him constantly, which always lent her excursions a melancholy mood. She had left the Tigris Valley behind. Later, she would be able to remember exactly where the saving idea had occurred to her—she had been crossing Sanliurfa, in southeastern Turkey.

Quite exhausted from her heroic act, which would later amaze her every time she thought back upon it, she had found a nice piece of vacuum-sealed cured ham in the galley—probably the Russian's favorite treat. She chewed the lean smoky meat appreciatively; glad to be taking in some much-needed protein after the extreme stress her body had been through. As if her neurons were responding gratefully to the valuable nutrients, a thought flashed through her mind. Of course! She leaned forward, turned the transponder dial. The setting showed the desired ID on the display: 7500.

"Seven five—got a knife," she mumbled cheerfully, sensing a second wind. She tore off another hearty bite of meat with her teeth. *Still alive*...it was almost miraculous. There was something sensual about the act of eating after what she had just survived. It unleashed a lust in her. She had been sleeping alone for the past year; she could suddenly have killed for a hard, live body. How wicked, that this horniness would assail her now, and here of all places, high above the clouds where such notions could only accentuate the misery of her non-existent love life.

Seven five zero zero was the international signal for hijacking. She brushed across her mouth with the back of her hand, hit *send*, leaned back and waited for whatever was going to happen next. But she was unable to relax. A brown speck of lamb on the window caused her to get out of her seat and go back to the cabin to check on the knife-wielding witch who had assailed her. Lenka Martialis stared with wide, rage-filled eyes, her contorted features pale. Sophie fetched a plastic bottle, supported her back, held the water to her dry, puckered lips like a good Samaritan. The frail woman raised her head, hesitated—and butted her with brutal force. Sophie screamed. The killer's forehead had made solid contact with her face, knocking her backward. It hurt. She got up, furious. "Bitch!" She kicked reflectively between the assassin's open thighs, enjoyed her gurgling moan, the sound of which somehow allowed her own pain and anger to dissipate as she plopped onto a cabin seat.

The Turkish air traffic controller in Adana tower was apparently the first to catch the call. A short while later, it must also have been picked up by the command of the Northern Air Defense Regiment of the Israeli Air Force. At any rate, it quickly unleashed a hive of activity on the ground. A hijacked aircraft in the midst of a crisis situation spelled acute danger. This could mean anything—above all, air defense had to consider a terrorist attack. Four Sufas started from the twenty-first air base in Haifa to patrol over the Mediterranean as an immediate preventative measure. *Sufa*, the Hebrew word for storm, was the name of the Israeli version of the F-16, which was armed with Python 5 air-to-air missiles.

"Romeo Alpha Oscar Bravo November. This is Adana…"

Sophie started, ran in the cockpit, pulled herself together, replied professionally: "Here Romeo Alpha…November. Adana, request clearance to land."

"Negative, Adana is closed to traffic for technical reasons. New destination Limassol, switch to the following frequency…"

Listening carefully, the pilot mechanically adjusted the frequency, checked the new route. Then she announced in a breathless voice, feigning stress: "Romeo Alpha Oscar Bravo November, understood, Limassol." Then she dutifully repeated the instructions she had received as she proceeded to turn the Global Express RA-OBN slightly southwest.

"And just like that, I'm an international incident," she giggled, gingerly rubbing her cheekbone as she curiously searched the night sky to see if she was being discreetly escorted by a few handsome men in fighter jets. Speaking of handsome men . . . *no! Not that again.* She squeezed her thighs together tightly, scooted in her seat, banishing the demon that was trying to lead her to the land of fruitless fantasy.

OBN—Oleg Borisowich Nedjew. What might he be doing? He has to be furious, but I haven't heard a word from him. Whatever. Sophie pulled out the map she was sitting on, studied the island upon which she was initially going to land. Smoothly, she hoped. She entered the data to check the airport and weather information for Limassol: Sunshine, twenty degrees Celsius. If that wasn't a good omen!

Hours Earlier, Over the Caspian Sea

Humming reliably, the Hercules circled about 300 meters above the Caspian Sea. The darkness of night enveloped the round-bellied plane; the cabin lights were low. The green glow of the controls lent Nico Strom's features a mysterious gleam as he looked back and forth between the radar and the flight management system.

Maintaining close surveillance of the air space was paramount at present, and both pilot and copilot were, likewise, fully concentrated on this task.

While the machine patiently maintained its holding pattern, three crewmembers had grouped around Nico Strom in the cockpit.

"We actually practiced Snowdrop for several months over Angola, Zimbabwe and Ruanda," Nico said, focusing on the monitor. "We dropped tons of combo-packs for a humanitarian aid program sponsored by the UN to combat hunger. We used the exact Hercules we are on today. Snowdrop truly is the best drop system for aid missions—even from great heights. And that's important, because we have to be out of reach of shoulder-type rocket launchers and flak."

"How much did you drop there?" asked the man crouching behind Nico.

"A lot. We were able to load up to sixteen tons. That equaled about ninety thousand food rations. We covered entire cities, whole stretches of countryside. If you looked down during the day, it really did look like snow in the drop zone."

"The cell phones are a lot lighter than a food combo-pack," the same man considered.

"Sure. Basically we're talking about exactly the same principle with a far smaller and lighter individual load. Of course that allows us to load a far greater number of individual units into the containers and sub-containers."

"You've certainly been around the block a few times, Nico. And you've probably dropped a lot more than food rations for the hungry masses," the copilot said, half-turning toward him.

Strom ignored the comment. "I've pretty much always dealt with this type of plane—in the air and on the ground."

"What goes up in the air must come down, as we all know," the pilot quipped.

"They called on me as an expert, because the operators in many countries had no clue how to maintain these aircraft. I was quite popular. Mostly for condition analyses and crash investigations."

"I've never heard of a Hercules crashing," a voice said from behind him.

"Sure. The list of accidents and planes that were shot down is actually pretty long. Apart from the Vietnam War, most of the crashes happened in Iran. Too many crashes, if you ask me; mostly on training flights and under bad weather conditions. Of course the Americans stopped all support and pilot training after the revolution. The same goes for fighter jets—the F-4 Phantom and the F-15 Eagle that were around during the Shah era. The inventory of what was once a proud air force slowly turned to junk. The Iranian C-130s probably crashed as often as they did because of poor maintenance and insufficiently experienced pilots."

Strom's gaze stopped on one of the instruments. What he saw caused him to smile a little. He checked his watch, consulted with the pilot in a whisper, then leaned back in his seat.

"Iranian air force officers told me about the worst crash. A C130H went down south of Tehran in 1981. There were eighty fatalities, the minister of defense and other high-ranking officers among them. I find this particular crash noteworthy, because I later found that machine's registration number on another Iranian aircraft. Clearly some doctoring had gone on. It seems that the mullahs don't like gaps in their serial numbers—probably because crashes and other mishaps simply cannot be seen to exist...I remembered that."

Ever the experienced entertainer, he allowed the general amusement to die down of its own accord.

"I first came into contact with members of the Iranian air force in 1994. I met them at a Hercules crash site in Nagorno-Karabakh, that's in..."

"In Azerbaijan."

"Correct. An Armenian-backed breakaway region. They were shot down by Armenian rebels on their way to Moscow on the 17th of March. Bam, bulls-eye! We found almost no debris on the rough terrain—nothing that was of any use, anyhow. We had better luck with the next crash, which was caused by the Iranians."

Strom held the crew's undivided attention. They crowded around him.

"This time—this was on December 6th, 2005—it was a C-130E military transporter. It crashed into a densely populated area in Tehran, hitting an apartment building that was inhabited by air force personnel, of all people. Terrible. One hundred and twenty fatalities. Over sixty journalists died on board. They had been on their way to witness a troop maneuver on the south coast."

The men posed a confusion of questions: "Did you go to the crash site? Were you the technical expert?"

Strom checked the radar and their position. The engines hummed evenly.

"The Hercules isn't called Queen of the Skies for nothing. It is incredibly dependable—just like the one we're sitting in. If something goes wrong, it's usually down to pilot error."

"Is that what happened in Tehran?"

Strom nodded, remembering. The brigadier general in charge of the investigation had been very closely shadowed by a cleric. He had been determined to find a material flaw, a technical fault. Strom found nothing of the sort. The black box and snatches of crew conversation pointed in another direction—blatant operating error.

He had comported himself diplomatically, had obliged the brigadier general to some degree. They had managed to agree that a broken weigh shaft, or something of that nature, had probably caused the aircraft to go down. Strom had helped himself to an intact piece of equipment that he had found within the severely damaged cockpit. *A little thank-you for the fudged report, he told himself. If the Iranians recycled registration numbers of downed aircraft, then why shouldn't I recycle this little part for something useful at some point?*

He tapped his watch.

"Just one more question, boss," the radar specialist interjected. "Why did the Iranians call for you, of all people?"

Because, when it comes to the Hercules, I am the uncontested best, he almost wanted to say. "Well, they couldn't very well call the Americans," he answered shortly. "And the Swiss have always enjoyed a good reputation in Iran."

He raised his hand in a clear sign that conversation time was over. H-hour was drawing close. The crew's faces were now earnest; everything was strictly business. As he searched his backpack for the written instructions, Strom kept a sharp eye on the displays and data. Then he crouched next to the copilot's seat, checked the functioning of the loot from that downed C-130E on the instrument panel one last time. He stood.

"Ready." It wasn't a question or appraisal. It was an order. Things were dead serious now.

"Three minutes," his voice thundered over the intercom.

"Transponder off?"

"Correct. Transponder off," the pilot confirmed.

As briefed, they would not be sending an identification signal.

"Incognito, people. We're so anonymous, we barely know ourselves!" Strom said with a grin.

✳

A different discussion had kicked up in the back, in the crammed cargo hold where the ten-man crew huddled next to the drop-ready containers in small groups.

One of them checked his watch. "Any moment now."

Others were talking shop about the cell phone that was the star of tonight's feature presentation. "About two hundred and fifty grams," the loadmaster said knowingly, weighing one in his hand. "Heavier than most. That's because of its strong transmission power."

"It's also more durable than most," his neighbor added, examining the silver casing. "It calls, it texts—that's really all you need."

"This thing will survive anything," the loadmaster grinned.

"It has a hard rubber sheath, it's well padded," the board mechanic grabbed it from his colleague. "Look, the display is scratch resistant, anti-glare, waterproof. It'll work even if someone drops it in a tub, or decides to stow it in a freezer. Amazing."

"What is really amazing, people, is that it receives its signals from LEO," said the loadmaster, hanging onto an overhead bar and stretching his muscular torso. He pointed upward. "It sends and receives via satellite. The mullahs down there have no chance of interfering with the signal, let alone disabling it."

"Cosmo told me his people used it under water," another man burst forth, as if he had been the one to invent the thing. "Then one of the testers literally threw one off a dam, onto a heap of rocks. You think that's cool? Here's the best part: then they drove over it with a crawler while the time announcement was on...and it just kept going!"

His neighbor, who was sitting cross-legged on the floor, held the device up to the dim light. "The sound on these things is loud. You'd still hear it ringing in the middle of a night club, with the bass pounding."

"Do night clubs even exist in Tehran?"

"Sure. Private clubs," a Swiss mechanic interjected.

"Yeah. They smoke weed and everything else that Allah frowns upon. Iranians are human beings, just like us. They eat, shit, fuck. What their holy clerics forbid, they do behind closed doors. The craftier young women smoke behind their veils and push the clothing regulations to their limits. I've seen it myself. They even use Botox."

"It's a pity these don't have cameras," one of the crew muttered.

The droning of the engines grew louder. The men looked toward the cockpit.

"They're still calculating," the loadmaster said, yanking at the straps on a container that was loaded with seven thousand of the miraculous units, to check if they were secure. A green light blinked. The explosive charge had been activated by the altimeter, but it would not be armed until the drop height was reached. A question came from the darkness. "How do you charge them?"

"Take a closer look, Smarty. The cable is right there."

"Why not make it more obvious—like a bright yellow, so that it's easier to see?"

"Hell, they want to make the whole thing as inconspicuous as possible. That's the point! People could get into serious trouble for having one of these—or get into fights over them."

"The best thing is," said the voice from the darkness, "that free speech will be possible again. There's really nothing they can do about that now. It has to make Allah happy that people will be talking to each other again, right?"

"Now," Strom called out. "GO!"

The pilot pulled the yoke back smoothly, simultaneously giving the calculated amount of thrust. The trusty engines gave the Hercules lift. Strom tersely checked the displays. The copilot counted down the seconds. "Thirty...twenty-five...twenty..."

The engines were fully engaged. Everyone who could tried to catch a glimpse out of the cockpit window.

"Fifteen...ten..."

Azerbaijan Airline J 25 had taken off from Baku GYD at its

scheduled time of 22:00 hours. It had headed 158 degrees southeast to Bamak then turned toward Tehran over Armud. The landing at Imam Khomeini International (IKA) was scheduled for twenty-three ten. The pilots had checked all of their data, the weather report indicated mild headwinds over the Iranian mainland. As on almost every other night, the scheduled flight to the Iranian capital went without a hitch. The time-tested, somewhat worn Boeing 727 traveled through the clear night sky at a steady, energy efficient six hundred kilometers per hour.

When the J25 approached Iranian airspace and became visible on radar about an hour in, the copilot followed his usual protocol and contacted ATC in Tehran to announce their scheduled landing.

Aboard the Hercules, Strom yelled: "Five seconds . . . Go! Go!"

The bow righted itself horizontally, and at this moment the crew saw the Boeing. Strom watched the approach with laser concentration. Before he had fully registered, he heard fragments of sentences being called out by his crew. "Incredible timing." "Good job." "Awesome, guys!"

The black hull of the passenger plane cruised smoothly along, about fifty meters above the cockpit of the cargo transporter. The 727s position lights blinked a welcome signal. Everything had gone perfectly.

The Hercules had approached from the black of night, had positioned itself beneath Azerbaijan J25—precisely according to Strom's plan. They had followed the mother ship like a shadow, penetrating Tehran's airspace undetected beneath its wings.

The beginning of the mission could not have transpired more smoothly. But this thing was far from over. Nobody knew better than Nico that the massive Hercules was bound to cast a far greater shadow on the radar than a slender Boeing 727. The unusual image would stand out to an experienced air traffic controller.

It was always going to be an all-or-nothing gamble. They would just have to see how it went. But that was not to say that Nico had not prepared for all possibilities. Only two men knew of his backup plan: Cosmo and the Hercules' pilot. Said man, Shelly Askenasi, was carefully adjusting their position, pushing the plane's snub nose beneath the center of the Azerbaijan J25's fuselage. A mere thirty-five meters now separated the two aircraft—an aeronautical feat that Askenasi mastered without appearing to break a sweat. He kept a perfectly constant altitude and speed, putting both the crew and the turboprop engines through their paces.

Strom was not surprised. He knew Shelly exceptionally well. Starting with his missions south of the equator. Caucasian aircrews in Africa called him The Phantom. It was said that one could never know where he was, nor how he got there. Strom would never have signed on for Operation Snowdrop over Tehran without him.

Night Over Tehran

The two air traffic controllers on duty at Imam Khomeini International saw nothing but the usual suspects on their monitors just before 2300—a machine from Bandar Abbas on B441, the J25 from Baku on G667.

The KLM 433 from Amsterdam would be landing on time at 23:10. A military transporter requested permission to land at Mehrabad. The ATCs read the identifications directly from their screens. The IDs, which were transmitted by the cockpit transponders, automatically displayed next to the radar point, signifying the respective aircraft.

J25 from Baku was on time to the minute. It was a night like any other. Reza Naimi leaned back. He saw nothing amiss with the luminous dot that was slowly moving across the marginally sharp radar screen, nor had he been trained to conduct more than routine readings. He stretched his legs onto the table and cursed his job. All day long he had to watch planes come and go—from faraway places like Frankfurt, Moscow, London and Paris, watch them take off to alluring destinations like Hong Kong, Calcutta, Zurich, Buenos Aires. It was enough to make a man want to despair. What about him? Why did he have to be trapped on this side of things?

He was essentially a glorified prisoner. They had even revoked his passport, the bastards! And for what? All because he had joined a group of bloggers who had been officially allowed to travel to the United States in October of 2008 to report on the presidential elections. It had either been a small sensation, or a mishap within the censorship bureau—at any rate, the participants had gathered down here in the airport hall, brimming with excitement. It had been too good to be true. Of course officers from the culture ministry had shown up at the last minute and collected everyone's passports, much to their collective dismay. Most—air traffic controller Naimi among them—faced hours of interrogation by the secret service. The minister in charge made a succinct announcement, stating that blogs were new to him, and he had simply changed his mind—taking the opportunity to add that the USA was responsible for alleged mistreatment of Iranian journalists. It was nothing but a bunch of horseshit.

Reza Naimi distractedly checked his radar, checked in with KLM 433, and announced a frequency change to the J25. He wished fervently that his country would one day allow all its people to speak their minds and to travel wherever they wanted. Time ticked by. He performed his job mechanically, strictly according to protocol. As far as he was concerned, they could kiss his...

The lovely Saba had been sitting next to him at the airport back then. They had struck up a conversation. Even her name, gentle western wind, had excited him; fired his imagination. He could see himself walking with her on a Miami beach, in Manhattan maybe, or even on the Golden Gate Bridge over in California. Reza started, rubbed his eyes. "Hey, the J25!"

The machine was separating. It was falling apart. The dot on the radar screen was turning into two. "As Allah is my witness—that thing is calving!"

His agitated voice alarmed his superior. The chief air traffic controller stepped up, leaned over, rubbed his short beard. "What's going on?"

"J25 from Baku just split in two. There, that dot is continuing its flight."

"Are you sure, Naimi?"

"Am I blind? This second object just appeared—it has no ID."

"No ID," his superior repeated, perplexed. "What the devil is going on here? Just a moment—could that be a second aircraft? Is that possible?"

Naimi shrugged his shoulders. It was no great surprise to him that the man in charge was clueless. He would just continue doing his job by the book.

"There, it's rising. Do you see that, Naimi? That is clearly a second aircraft. Do we have an ID? No? Damn it. Get your lazy asses moving! I'm alerting the air force."

Reza watched the theatrics in fascination, heard his boss calling air defense behind him.

Nico had calculated the drop point precisely. The Hercules emerged from the shadow of the Boeing, pulled off to one side, started its climb to the correct altitude. The maneuver went as planned. The crew in the back began its preparations for the drop. Conveyor belts moved the one thousand containers through the enormous hold toward the drop hatches.

The execution was hectic, but as precise as a Swiss clockwork. Not an extraneous word was spoken, only a few short commands. Nico's attention was focused on the position coordinates. He began the countdown exactly twenty minutes after their separation from Azerbaijan J25. "Sixty seconds left, men," his familiar voice echoed through the speakers.

The plane's four engines droned reliably; the crew was as tense as they would have been before an assault. It was the kind of situation in which anything could happen.

The young, hot-shot fighter pilot peered intensely through the night vision device of his fire control system onto the massive, dark aircraft below just as its voluminous fuselage started to stand in relief against the sea of lights from the capital below. He lowered the pointy nose of his F-5 to position himself. "Ready to fire, Mohamed."

His captain in the jet next to his looked over to the side. "Wait. Do you see an ID?"

"Negative. No position lights, either. We have the all-clear to shoot, Mohamed."

The air defense radar had alarmed the surveillance squadron in Mehrabad. The operation controllers had decided that drastic measures were in order.

The mysterious invasion of several unidentified aircraft, which had managed to drop material over Iranian cities unhindered, had deeply shaken the leadership in Tehran. The items dropped could easily have been bombs! It was insanity! Their air space surveillance had utterly failed. Who was responsible for this mess? The Russian engineers? A nervous minister of defense had consequently issued the order that aerial police, who were on high alert, were to shoot down any aircraft that remained unidentified after inquiry.

Strom stood upright in the passage to the hold, stretched his arm up: "Five seconds...Attention! Drop! Drop! Yes! That's right, boys, let it snow on Tehran..."

Only seconds later, the cockpit issued a warning. "Nico, we have visitors. Nico!"

Strom's flight of euphoria trundled to a sudden halt. He raced back to the cockpit. The three hundred and sixty degree detection radar had informed the copilot of the Iranians' position.

"Two IRIAF fighter jets. What do we do?"

Strom's face dropped. "Nothing. Stay on course!" he blurted, his mouth grim. Then, to the pilot: "Give them the signal."

"Okay."

Shelly Askenasi activated the flight transponder with a quick motion. He wore the expression reserved for dead-serious combat situations. Playtime was over. What was happening now was nothing to smile about.

The transponder that Nico had secretly rescued from the wreckage of the C-130E immediately started transmitting its military Islamic Iranian Air Force identification code.

"It's heading southwest toward the airport," the captain of the F-5 formation assessed.

"Our altitude is too great for it to be going in for landing there, Mohamed. We have to bring it down."

"We're over the capital. It will be catastrophic if we bring it down over a densely populated area."

"And if they drop bombs, then we'll be the ones to blame. Forget it...I request permission to attack with air-to-air missile. Immediately!"

Aboard the doomed Hercules, Strom's apparent composure was well played. His nerves lay bare. Would the trick work? "What are they doing up there?"

"No change. Shadowing us," the copilot called out with a noticeable edge to his voice.

"Fine," the older fighter pilot growled several hundred meters above them in his F-5. "But not until I cover my ass. Calling control center, this is Delta One, we have a situation..."

His wingman chewed impatiently on his lower lip as he listened to the radio exchange. The red safety cap over the rocket launcher had been released, his thumb hovered a centimeter over the fire button, at the ready. The tail of the hostile plane shifted perfectly into the crosshairs of the target radar.

"Come on, Mohamed, let's get the bastards!" The F-5 hotshot was unable to see the containers. The night swallowed the black boxes as they dropped, then sprung open.

"Request permission to shoot," he heard Mohamed's voice on the headset.

Only when the parachutes opened to sail like a sea of flowers toward the city with its ten million inhabitants, did the Iranian pilot's heart drop to his stomach.

Those had to be small bombs floating down. Bombs on Tehran. Thousands...He hit the radio button, aghast: "Do you see what I see, Mohamed?"

"I have radioed control. They say to stand-by. The minister has to decide. Over."

"Gutless wonder," the young fighter hissed into the cockpit. Then he saw the signal, activated the display. The amazement on the faces of the bearded ones being rained on by cell phones suspended on little parachutes had nothing on the look that spread across the pilot's features.

The machine in the crosshairs was signaling 2088!

"Shit! I can't believe it, Mohamed. We have a signal. ID two zero eight eight. Those are our people! What does the eight eight at the end stand for?"

It took a few seconds, then the calm voice of his superior came back in response: "The code is used by military craft in nighttime, low altitude flights. It is a special code for special missions. It also means we need to get out of here. Let the people on the ground deal with this shit. It's above our pay grade, Delta Two."

"No detonations," Delta Two determined. "Let's go see what's going on down there."

With that, the F-5's dipped down toward the city below.

Freedom Prevails

Weeks later, Nico would tell the story of how millions of cell phones had sent the Iranian capital into a frenzy of joy and excitement. There had been traffic accidents, unrestrained reactions by the police, the deployment of several service branches. The telecommunications system had been totally overloaded. Everyone—young and old—had called friends at home, overseas, sent millions of text messages by the grace of the gifts from the above.

A completely blindsided government had gathered to hold marathon meetings.

In the capital, everyone had been wild to get their hands on the new devices. The Ministry of Information and Communications Technology in Tehran issued denials, as usual. It did its best to convince the masses via its favorite outlet, PressTV, that this was a blasphemous, subversive attack by the American infidels who wanted to tear the people from the righteous path of the Prophet's teachings, may peace be upon him.

But the masses knew better. They felt the coming of a new age. They were receiving uncensored messages from all over—from like-minded individuals, friends, relatives; nearby and overseas. Even government officials were caught up in the intoxicating rush. Nothing remained as it had been. Wherever freedom reared its head, the mullah regime learned the meaning of fear. Free speech swept the land like a storm. Anyone who did not possess an AiD phone was suddenly socially irrelevant, and was willing to move heaven and earth to get their hands on one.

Many people called Iran their home. Aside from the Persians, there were Azeris, Kurds, Arabs, Balochistanis, Turkmans, Syro-Arameans, and other ethnic and religious minorities. The non-Persian nationalities constituted over half of the more than eighty million citizens of Iran. Despite being independent, with their own languages, cultures and histories, they were not recognized by the regime. Millions of proud Iranians had grown sick of such discrimination. They were the first to call for the government to step down, and for the creation of a new, modern constitution. It was a call that spread like wildfire across the AiD network.

Meanwhile, at the Ministry of Information and Communications Technology, one could practically see the smoke rising from ears in tendrils. There was a desperate scramble to come up with ideas of how to stop the subversive texts that were circulating widely and uncontrollably. But none appeared workable. Freedom of thought was, it seemed, unstoppable. The regime swaying under the pressure exerted by the cell-phone wielding masses and approaching elections, the ousting of the mullahs—it all appeared inevitable in hindsight. Although it might have taken a while longer, had it not been for the nuclear explosion.

The secret service, led by Minister and Vice President Shapasandi, was responsible for the decisive error that pushed the historic overthrow in Iran into overdrive. Shapasandi had planned to turn the fates to favor the mullah regime with a nuclear test explosion, but an ironic twist saw him succumb to his own calculations.

The Iranian bomb that was detonated that night in the southeast, in Balochistan, evoked a psychological tsunami within the country and the entire world. It proved to be the death-knell to those in power. Not because Iranians were opposed to nuclear armament per se, but because they now saw clearly that the mullahs, in their religious fanaticism, saw fit to lie to the people. The atomic bomb was not the achievement of Iranian scientists, as they had claimed, but the result of a dirty weapons deal with the despised Russians.

On the surface, it may have appeared that the Islamic experiment had fallen victim to the atomic megalomania of power-hungry, religious zealots, who had dragged the country to the brink of a nuclear apocalypse. However, the historic turn, as journalists, political experts and historians for once appeared to unanimously agree, was triggered and driven by the cell phones, which had been dropped from the sky, and which had forever burst the dams of censorship and suppression of free opinion. Freedom brought fear to its foes, wiped them out. The entire world added words to its vocabularies, such as *AiD,* or *airdrop* or *snowdrop phones,* or *les mobiles parachutés.*

Farhad Pajooh, whose life had been brutally cut short in the beautiful pool of forty columns, had not been allowed to see this historic turn of events. He would likely have felt sorry for his murderer, Mullah Akbar, who was driven in shame from the palace and beaten to within an inch of his life by enraged bazaar keepers.

Two Days Earlier

There was much activity on the Armenus Park grounds. Cosmo's people were as busy as an overwrought colony of ants.

Andy stripped off his parka and protective eyewear, put his phone down. It was not one of the legendary silver ones, but an RAD, used to detect and measure radiation.

"The convoy left the grounds just after the Global Express incident. It was heading toward the border. I was well situated, near the bunker exit. Six vehicles passed me, including three large, modern trucks. Russian make, probably three tons a piece."

"And? Come on, get to the point," Cosmo urged.

"The measurements were almost off the chart."

"Enough with the drama. Radiation?"

"Yes. Extremely high—in the dark yellow zone. So I followed the trucks on the Kawasaki…"

…He felt the cuttingly cold wind on his face. Andy adjusted his protective glasses, closed the collar of his mountaineering jacket. The light trucks ahead of him had a modern appearance, with slanted noses. They took the corners easily. They were heading south, toward the Iranian border. The convoy was making good time as it followed the river into the plain. They crossed a flat landscape of nothing but streets, trees and a few sheds; then the forest appeared, the street rose, curved its way along a dark wooded area. Andy had no plan but to stay on their tails and see what happened.

Nothing did. Andy steered his heavy bike absently, his thoughts on Sophie. The unexpected, initially pleasant encounter had taken a shockingly dramatic turn that haunted him—the other woman who had boarded the plane. *Why? Where could they be now? Instead of chasing after a bunch of stupid Russians on a dark road with my lights out, I should be figuring out how to help her. She trusted me. She needed my help—I'm such an idiot!* He was about to turn around when he realized with fright that the obstacle that suddenly appeared out of the pitch dark was the back of a truck. He hit the brakes instinctively, veered off to the side. The convoy had evidently stopped for a break.

Andy killed the engine, rolled for cover—a low shed with lights on its other side. He checked his watch, realized that he had been following them for two hours.

He felt his way along the dilapidated boards of the wall, took in the scene that was partially illuminated by the parking lights of one of the trucks. The drivers blew into their hands to warm them, drank from cups, walked about, pissed in the bushes. Andy caught a few snatches of what sounded to be Russian. These guys hadn't bothered to keep guard. Why would they, in the middle of nowhere?

Andy finally had a plan. He turned around, crept to the back of the last truck, checked the lock to the flap that covered the back.

He opened the strap, gripped the edge and hoisted himself inside. What now? It was dark as pitch. His trusty lighter helped him once more. By its flickering light he examined the boxes. They were hermetically sealed—tight as safes. Resigned, he was about to get out of there, when he saw a sign.

The writing was Russian. Cyrillic. A few numbers. *"A model number."* Andy pulled his multi-tool from his pocket, opened the knife. He removed the sign with a few decisive motions, pocketed it.

He heard voices, what sounded like orders. Boots crunching in the snow. They were on the move.

He crept cat-like across the truck bed, jumped lithely out, ran, hunched over, to his bike. Just in time. The rested men began climbing behind the wheels of their trucks.

One, presumably the leader, walked around the perimeter of the convoy shouting orders. The men started their engines...

"Here's the sign, Jack. Maybe someone can..."

"Igor, come here," Cosmo commanded. "What does this say?"

"Alright, alright..." the summoned man rushed over. "Let me see, here. It says..." He noted a translation in capitals: P-80 MOSKIT, 3M80, MKB RADUGA. "No idea what it means."

"I know what that is," a gangly dude with a shaved head and earrings said importantly. "That's a missile identification. NATO Code: SS-N-22 Sunburn, range: approximately two hundred kilometers. Radar equipped, can be armed with nuclear warheads. Manufactured by Raduga. Anything else?"

Veins began to swell on Abramian's gray-haired temples. "That dirty son of a bitch," he huffed angrily. "I should have known that bastard was up to no good. And on my Armenus Park, no less."

"No wonder he didn't raise a stink about the stolen plane," Andy remarked. "He needs attention like a hole in the head right now."

Cosmo gestured impatiently. "Alright people. We need to get on this right now. We're about to piss in this man's Corn Flakes like he wouldn't believe."

They followed their boss, who strode purposefully toward the analysis sector, where a huddle of three quickly vacated the conference table upon seeing the boss's crew banging their way between the chairs and desks.

Cosmo started bellowing names to all sides halfway through the passageway. The editorial team had gathered, pens and notepads at the ready, before he had dropped into a chair at the round table.

"This is urgent. Take down what I say. This is my suggestion for a text that should be sent immediately and repeatedly. Ready?"

His words were met by eager nods, red cheeks and affirmatives all around.

"Message to the population of Tabriz. No, Alert. Alert, okay? *Russian nuclear warheads have been smuggled across the northern border to Iran. The mullahs are planning a nuclear attack on Israel.*"

"Isn't that a bit much, boss?" the slender, bespectacled Turkish woman asked.

"This isn't the time for polite understatements, Aiça! Okay, continue... *nuclear attack on Israel. Stop the convoy of Russian-made vehicles.* Right, Andy? We're talking Russian jalopies here?"

"Right. Three of them were particularly distinct minivans with slanted front ends."

"*...Stop the convoy...* where was I?"

Aiça read the last sentence back to him with a devoted gaze.

"*The transport is headed for the area of Tabriz. Notify us of your observations. This dangerous missile transport must be stopped. Call our number...* Andy! Give them the hotline number. Right. That's it. Edit it. Where is Trita?"

"Here, Mr. Abramian, I'm on it."

He turned his head to see the translator, who had gently placed a hand on his elbow, as the chief editor read back the content of the message. Cosmo stood. "Come with me, Andy!"

He continued to speak to his protégé as they walked, motioning animatedly. They stopped in front of a map in the communication room. "I don't mean soldiers, Andy. We want to keep the Armenian army out of this. The men we need are hiding out around here." He pointed to a spot in the eastern mountainous terrain. "These are rebels operating in

Nagorno-Karabakh from this base. We need about a dozen of them. They are well trained. Bring them back here. Take the helicopter."

"I want to see you in the air at the first crack of dawn. Are we clear?"

"We're clear, sir. Just... it may be good to bring a bag of cash."

"Sure. Whatever. Ranko can take care of it. I'll get that bean-counter out of bed right now."

Cosmo Fights Back

A violent glare filled the cabin of the Hercules, lighting it up more brightly than the brightest day. Being that the round nose of the machine was pointed upward in its ascending flight, the crew was not able to visualize the explosion on the eastern horizon. But they knew, instantly, that they had just witnessed the detonation of an atomic bomb. No one spoke. They stared at each other, transfixed. They could read one another's thoughts by looking into each other's eyes. Had the USA attacked? Was Israel behind this? Was this the beginning of a global war?

Shelly Askenasi coolly turned west, pressed the plane's nose down to descend. He knew only one thing: he was there to do a job—and his job was to bring everyone home in one piece. "And if the world goes to hell, then so be it," he said through clenched teeth.

The Hercules had the wonderful ability to fly both slow and low. Shelly corrected the course to southwest in order to bypass the mountains. He would later turn north, heading over Tabriz toward home base in southern Armenia. The machine droned across the land at low altitude, constantly emitting its ID: 2088, *military craft in nighttime, low altitude flight*. Shelly allowed himself a grim smile. A bit of adventure, a hint of excitement, a solid machine in his capable hands—what more could a man want?

Back at the communication center, Cosmo was in his element. He held the sheet of coordinates for Tabriz International Airport in his hand—38 degrees 8 minutes east, 46 degrees 14 minutes north. He watched tensely as the screen filled up with light brown terrain, shot through diagonally with light gray roadways; there were bits of dark green forest to the back, interspersed with small, whitewashed buildings with red roofs.

"Down there at the bottom right, the hangars. Bring them in closer."

The operator zoomed in on three semicircular runways with hangars at their sides."

"Good. Now a full map view."

The names of towns scattered across the screen, yellow lines signifying streets divided the green land, dark-blue bodies of water, brown, rocky terrain completed the view, with a segment of the Caspian Sea showing on the right border.

"The airfield is to the north of town, on the A01 that goes from the city of Marand to the Armenian border. That's the stretch the trucks are on. Can we see it?"

The operator shook his head. "Not yet, sir. There's still dense fog up there right now."

At the map table, others were studying the airfield, with its approximately two and a half kilometer long strips, which the IRIAF used as a combat base.

"The infrastructure is here, next to these semicircles, sir."

Cosmo briefly glanced at what he was pointing to. "Do you see any activity?"

"I can't detect any, sir."

"Good. What's the latest from Omar?"

Titra's high voice filled the room. "Yes, sir. This just came in: 'Am in position on the airfield with my people. All ready.'"

"Any news on the transport?"

"We're on it. The connection is poor. We have one unconfirmed report that the convoy has passed Marand."

"How far is that from the airport?"

"About one hundred kilometers."

Cosmo tersely eyed the satellite image, his lips a thin line.

"The Hercules is in a holding pattern, sir," someone whispered behind him. "Should we call it off?"

Cosmo waved this aside, shaking his white mane. At this moment, the faces of the analysts turned toward him, among them a young, smart-looking man who now raised his finger. "Listen, sir," he said.

"The convoy has passed us," a clear voice sounded over the speaker.

"Where are the vehicles, Nassim? Can you give us their position?"

"Yes. From where we stand it's about an hour or so to the airfield."

Cosmo quickly strode over to the analysts. "Hand me that...Thank you...Hello, this is Jack...Okay, Nassim...Are you absolutely sure?"

"Yes. My device got a hit."

It took a moment for them to understand.

"He has an RAD," the smart one whispered. "A radiation-detecting phone. The resistance is equipped with them, they work like Geiger counters."

"You have an RAD? And it reacted?"

"When the vans drove by."

"Where were they headed?"

"To the main road, toward Tabriz."

"Do you know the airfield?"

"The air force has a base there, on the southern end. Omar knows it. I have to go."

The connection was lost. Cosmo was suddenly very clear on one thing—this was it. It was going to be now or never. "Get me Nico Strom!"

0535. The Hercules patiently stuck to its holding pattern over the great lake west of Tabriz. Strom had conferred with Shelly and they had agreed on an altitude of three thousand feet. The flight transponder continued to emit a constant: 2088, the ID for military craft in nighttime, low altitude flight—just in case anyone on the ground happened to take an interest in the lonely bird circling the night sky up above.

Strom covered his face with his hands, tapping his fingertips against each other. They had tried to find out more about the atomic explosion in the southeast. There had been many agitated voices, but even Cliff Matoyan, whose native tongue was Farsi, had not been able to make out much actual information in what they said. He summarized the conversations, which they had listened in on. "It's mostly emotional nonsense. People are afraid. One of them says that it was a Pakistani attack."

"Why does Cosmo want to keep us in this holding pattern?" the copilot asked. "It's not like we can do anything up here."

Seconds later, as if to answer his query, Cosmo's gravelly voice sounded over the cockpit speaker. "Nico, it's Jack here. Are you good? Listen. You are to land in Tabriz. Repeat: Tabriz Airport. Do it immediately, do not wait. Do you copy?"

Strom dutifully repeated the order back. Thoughts shot through his head. It would be absolute suicide to land right in the middle of those bearded fanatics. Their air force base was down there. They would be paying close attention. What was Jack thinking?

"Does this have something to do with the nuclear blast?" Nico ventured carefully.

"Negative. Here's the deal…"

As Shelly Askenasi pulled the Hercules from its pattern, preparing for an approach on Tabriz, Cosmo laid out the entire plan. He described clearly and in detail the anticipated sequence of events, the actions arranged with the resistance, the contact with Omar and his people, how they could be recognized…A lot of it was still up in the air, but it sounded feasible. Strom took notes, as he was accustomed to doing when taking military orders for all those years. "As long as it seems feasible," he muttered. *Feasibility is ninety percent of the deal. The rest is thinking on your feet. And that's what we're trained to do.*

He really didn't owe Cosmo anything—certainly not blind obedience. Strom alone carried the responsibility for his crew. He could defy Cosmo's crazy request and choose a safe landing at Armenus over this madcap commando maneuver. It would definitely be a grand coup. But what came next would require improvisation. Strom wet his lips. That was what fascinated him. *Who knew, perhaps the nuclear blast over southern Iran really had changed everything!*

If I go in for this pact with the devil, it had better be for something world-changing, he swore to himself. Adrenaline shot through his chest, arms, and thighs. Fit for the fight, he thought. Let's do this!

The runway lights came into view. Strom noted that the copilot was speaking on the radio. He had almost missed the fact that Matoyan had taken the seat. Of course, Cliff spoke Farsi like—what had they said when they were teasing him?—like Farah Diba's own son . . .

Strom called his people.

Limassol, Cyprus

Sophie Kramer fixed the runway lights from afar as she curved in for landing over the Mediterranean before Limassol. The town lay to her left, beneath the yielding shadows of dawn. To the east, the fluctuating skies promised a sunny day over Cyprus—not a day like any other, however.

Sophie knew what lay ahead—and it wouldn't be easy. She looked out toward the airfield, searching for the signs of movement that a hijacked plane might be expected to elicit. Nothing.

The autopilot brought the Global Express in smoothly. Sophie put it into reverse thrust, felt the slowing, let it taxi down. Now she noticed the activity—armored personnel vehicles, fire trucks, flashing blue lights. She followed directions from the tower, came to a final parked position. She shut down the engines, took a deep breath, and waited. She sat in the pilot's seat for almost a minute, maybe longer, mentally preparing for the interrogation that was sure to come.

Emerging from her thoughts, she looked out of the window. The plane was surrounded by sharpshooters, air stairs were being rolled in her direction. She got up with a sigh.

The television crew in the broadcast vehicle behind the high-security fencing was not the only one to capture her face. Marios's camera clicked and buzzed as the door opened and a woman stepped out onto the platform, much to his surprise. She slowly descended the stairs, arms raised above her head.

"Quite a hot number, that one," he grunted, holding the record button down in continuous mode. "Hey, what's she carrying?"

Having reached the ground, Sophie continued toward the police officers with a steady gait. She could see that they were wearing body armor over their white shirts, which lent their bodies an almost inflated look. They had emerged from behind the armored vehicle that secured the area with a cannon from about twenty meters away.

George Constantinou had been allowed to drive his indestructible, boxy, open-topped Land Rover all the way to the mobile command post thanks to a special British ID, where he had parked, protected by the armored vehicle.

He climbed onto the driver's seat, peered across the top of the armored vehicle while Marios stood on the hood, buckling the metal with his boots. George followed the drama on the runway with great interest. He looked up to the cabin windows. No sign of movement.

"Enough!" He plucked at the cuff of Marios's pant leg. "Do you see anything in the cockpit?"

Marios shook his head. "That thing she's carrying on her back. Any ideas?" They watched, entranced, as the young woman gestured energetically.

"Give me that!" George wrested the camera from Marios's hand, looked through the zoom lens. "It's some kind of flat container, maybe an easel," he guessed.

The woman appeared delicate next to the bulky police officers, despite the large object she was carrying. She gestured up at the plane repeatedly. Evidently she had managed to make herself understood. One of the officers—really, they looked like Michelin mascots, Sophie decided—spoke into his walkie-talkie, causing a huddle of half a dozen men to come forward from the row of sharp-shooters within seconds. They seamlessly gathered into a formation, ran to the plane, and stormed up the stairs.

It seemed to George, looking at the faces of the special unit members, that they seemed somehow disappointed that the RA-OBN hijacking was apparently not going to entail much action.

Later, during the debriefing in the airport security offices, an apparently calm Sophie Kramer reported succinctly what had happened.

The five people in attendance were all men with serious miens. They monitored the woman closely as she spoke. Every once in a while, one of them would interrupt to pose a question. One of them laboriously typed everything that was said into a computer, which—here as at police stations across the globe—drew things out rather annoyingly. Sophie occasionally looked up at a blond civilian, who appeared a little out of place.

He wore a stretched-out V-neck sweater and black jeans. The expression on his rakishly mustached face was concentrated, but not unpleasant. As if he had sensed the attention, he suddenly asked a question. "Where can you be reached, miss. What is your address on the island?"

He doesn't look like a police officer. A journalist, maybe? He scribbled on his notepad. No. He looks more like a hobby pilot, or maybe, let's see . . . she suppressed a smile . . . a friendly lifeguard?

"Miss?"

"Yes. Excuse me. Well, I'll probably be heading back. I have to return the plane to my boss," she lied without batting an eye. "If possible, we'll take off this afternoon, once all of this is cleared up."

She gestured expansively with her arm, looking quite endearing in her theatric awkwardness. The men smiled sympathetically. Hats off to this woman—she had been through quite an ordeal.

There was paperwork to get through. Sophie signed the interrogation protocol. A doctor checked in, a speaker for the airport suggested a media conference, which she agreed to quite deliberately, at eight—about an hour after she planned to be gone. They could all just kiss her rear end goodbye.

Finally she made it back to the general aviation pilot's lounge, where she could consider her next steps—check on weather, wind and other possible restrictions. Israel was still blocking its air space.

A U.S. aircraft carrier fleet was crossing the Strait of Hormuz—chaos in the streets of Iran... Tehran announces new elections... thus were the news flashes on the ticker next to the current weather report for Limassol. Sophie's plan was clear—she thought.

A half an hour later, she stood outside at the taxi bay, the warm sun on her face.

She suddenly felt the full force of everything she had been through. It was as if someone had pulled the plug on her energy. She was a wreck. Haggard, achy joints, tired, hungry... her face was the picture of misery. A demon of negativity had settled in her bones. *I stink like a pile of dung and look even worse.* Disgusted with herself, she shook herself, took a step back, hoisted the Rothko container from her back—and promptly upended the small bag containing her few belongings.

"Can I help you?" It was the man with the rakish mustache. "I'm going into town," he said with an irresistible smile. "Come. Get in." He picked the container up by its straps, took her by the arm as if she was in need of being comforted, led her the few meters to his Land Rover. Once there, he helped her gallantly into the surprisingly comfortable passenger seat, carefully lifted the container onto the back seat. Sophie half-turned and wrapped one of its straps around her wrist.

"Not to worry," said George, laughing roguishly. "Your treasure won't fly away, I promise." He put the car into first, scrunched up his features, then took off at a good clip.

He looked over at her a few times. Her distant, confident demeanor kept him from trying to strike up further conversation. It was only as they were on the new autoroute, along the bank of the Salk Lake, that she broke her silence. "You're the... lifeguard. The one who sat in on my interrogation."

He turned his chiseled features to face her, brows furrowed. "I'm George. I think you need a bit of rest—and a shower. I'll take you to my place."

Limassol

George's place turned out to be a tastefully decorated penthouse with a large, open-plan living area and two bedrooms. Sophie came out of the bathroom with wet hair and wearing a silk, scarlet red dressing gown. She tied the belt tightly around her waist and stepped onto the terrace, sighing deeply as she turned her face up to the sun. She felt the tense knot in her stomach dissolve, felt the evil spirit leave her bones and disappear across the water. The house was situated on the shore, halfway between the airport and town. The sea glistened in the sunlight, gentle waves lapped on the sandy shore. George smiled broadly at her across the two mugs that he was holding. "Coffee?"

"I'd love some," she returned his smile. Putting the cup to her lips, she blinked up at him, took a sip. "I like your place, George." She stood next to him, looked out across the water. Their hips touched briefly. "This is wonderful."

He sensed her eyes on him, tried hard to look straight ahead. He rubbed his forehead, noticed her bare feet. "You know what, dear Sophie? You really need some new clothes." He placed his free arm around her waist, gently swung her around and led her back into the apartment. Three seagulls sitting on the gutter and searching for crumbs heard the man murmur at the terrace door, "A woman to laugh and cry with." One of them took flight with a screech, almost as if in response.

A little later the motorboat took off, turning west toward town, with its elegant seaside boutiques. Freighters lined the horizon, further west a container ship made its way toward the harbor. George gave an exaggerated shiver. "It's nippy today. Too cold to swim, unfortunately." Sophie nodded dreamily. She was swaddled in a thick jacket, which she wore over one of George's old, stretched-out pullovers and oversized shorts that were held in by a belt.

She was wearing her own moccasins.

"So, you're flying back tonight?"

She nodded. "I'd love to stay a while, believe me." She leaned against him. "You live here full time?"

George steered with one hand, keeping his other arm and chest free—for her. The woman was lovely, intelligent... He looked longingly across the water, seeing images of her body, her laugh, her deep, dark eyes... *Just keep your eyes open, George, the heavens will take care of you,* he heard his mother's voice say, soothingly. Was this his dream come true? He shook the fantasies off, his face earnest then stole a glance of her face. She opened her eyes. "What is it? Oh, Lord, my hair!" She tried to tame her mane, which was blowing every which way in the breeze.

"Do you really have to leave? I'd love to have you stay a while..."

"I know—it's just not possible right now."

"You don't fly for Oleg Nedjew—that was a cover story, wasn't it?"

She turned, startled. How well he had pronounced the name, this lifeguard—and God knows what else he was. George was an honest soul. She could sense that. *Why don't you stop this stupid cat-and-mouse game, Sophie. You need a strong shoulder to lean on.*

"You're right, I don't," she admitted meekly. "How did you know?"

George expertly navigated several waves that had been caused by the wake of a freighter. "You know, *lifeguards* tend to hear a lot. The fisher's wife heard from her lover, the harbor master, that the Russian's paramour had dinner with a British agent, and that...umm..."

Sophie laughed breezily. "And that the lovely lifeguard, who happens to be a British agent, started a fling with the Russian's concubine...Right?"

Her expression suddenly turned solemn. He was unflappable. "It's all true—except for the messy last bit, Sophie. Seriously. We are very interested in Nedjew, also known as the Crane. To be honest, I can hardly believe that you came in on his plane, that you overpowered your kidnapper, that her accomplice is dead." He shook his head, backed off the gas. The bow sank deeper into the water, revealing a view upon the small marina and beachside promenade.

"I hijacked the plane, George. The other woman, she called herself Lenka something, followed me...she wanted to force me to fly to Belgrade. She killed the soldier, not me." Again that look from her deep, dark eyes. He remained calm. "I couldn't tell the aviation officers that," she said, adding with a searching gaze, "otherwise I wouldn't be in this boat with you."

He seemed not to want to react to her allusion, instead he answered, "And what do you plan to do now?"

She turned away a little. "I can't talk about that."

Even her cold shoulder is attractive, George found himself thinking with a smile.

"And here I was, thinking we were in the same boat."

She looked at him in surprise. Beneath the banter and bravado, her spirit was troubled. Sophie had not been able to stop thinking about Shuky Nachman. She had lost touch with the Israeli ever since the tragic event at the airfield in Yerevan. She was gripped by sadness when she thought of the mountain guide who had rescued her. Uli had been such a decent, upstanding human being. *Where was Shuky? What was he up to? He had to know by now that the Crane had stolen the Hornbachs' plans for atomic warheads from the back of the Rothko. Was Shuky going to try and get the plans back?* In that case, he would likely have gone back to where it had all started—Armenia. She felt that she had no choice. She would have to go all the way back across Turkey and straight into the lion's den.

The thought was horrifying, but there was no other option if she did not want to abandon him.

She said nothing for quite a while. George landed the boat, tied it up and helped Sophie onto dry land. Nothing further was said of the matter during their shopping trip, but George's interest had been piqued. He had been given a task, he felt, a task that held meaning and importance, finally. He allowed himself to brush his right shoulder against her left in an intimate gesture. She smiled and did not evade the touch. *Yes, perhaps this task would give meaning and importance to his life…*

A narrow, cobbled path wound its way past the mighty hotels with their lounge-chair-strewn lawns and the sandy beaches, where various merchants advertised their tourist installations. Large sun umbrellas, a beach-side bar, bistro tables, volleyball nets and boat slips played in an array of shades and colors that seemed ever-changing to George Constantinou's alert gaze. His thoughts, however, wandered to Sophie, who had burst into his world and appeared to be the dear, intelligent, longed-for woman of his dreams. He felt drawn back to his apartment, where she had made herself comfortable and shown herself considerate of the fact that he had some business to attend to. Business...

... The rotund man who slid from the stool of the hotel's garden bar and appeared as if by accident next to the starry-eyed George on the beach path rudely interrupted his reverie with a friendly slap on the shoulder. "Hey, great timing, George." He held his watch up with a smile.

"It's about the Russian. I need your help, Marios," George began, casting an amused sidelong glance at his buddy's waddling gait.

Massive piers, reinforced by large boulders, stretched into the sea between the beaches, where they enclosed small harbors or acted as breakwaters. Each of the small, bay-like beaches had its own fanciful name, its own colors, and cloth pattern. Muscle-bound lifeguards moved between attractive establishments and lounge chairs, extended broad canopies, carried air mattresses for the ladies and otherwise courted the many bathing guests.

Armonia Beach was a few hundred meters further down. People strolled along the coastal path in both directions as the afternoon sun beat down. An older couple came along at a vigorous pace—she, white-haired and wearing stylish shorts with a white linen jacket, swinging two walking sticks in a powerful staccato; he in well-worn jeans and red loafers, with a scruffy, gray mane. A jogger came up behind them, ran in place, huffing, waiting for a space to pass.

A panting, black Labrador retriever tugged at his leash, his owner trying with all her might not to break into a trot to accommodate him. She gave George a pained smile.

"Hi, Susan," he greeted her. The Labrador lady gave a stressed little wave and was gone. "Susan's husband manages the Four Seasons," George noted as Marios turned to gaze after the pair, his camera swinging off of his no longer flat stomach.

Cyclists and skateboarders were not allowed on the popular promenade, but wind-surfers occasionally crossed the path, carrying their boards above their heads to make their way down to the beach for a ride. By night lovers wrapped their arms around each other on the piers, or sought out the cozy shadows of the palm trees that dotted the little harbors.

Dear Johnny had his hands full as George entered the shack with the sign that read ARMONIA BEACH.

Two Danes were renting a surfboard, a father with three small kids was negotiating the hourly rate of the boat with the 90 HP outboard motor.

"Check his boating license," George whispered to his hustling assistant as he helped him guide the vessel into the water. "I'll be gone for a couple of hours. You can reach me on my cell."

"Sure, boss. I'll be fine."

"Sounds good." George's smile was catching. One would have been hard-put to pick the better feature: his deep, blue eyes, or his blindingly white smile. A wide-brimmed straw hat with a blue band advertising Gin kept his ample hair in check—only his thin, well-groomed mustache and a few strands pulled back behind his ears showed that he was blond.

George was very fond of his mustache, a fact that Marios enjoyed giving him a hard time about. He had aptly noted the vanity behind the carefully manicured facial hair. "What do you aim to achieve with the pornstache?" he would tease him.

"What's that supposed to mean?"

"It means that your mustache makes you look like a porn star. It's kind of the facial equivalent to what we would refer to as a landing strip on a woman's privates. Sends a clear message, you know."

"Don't give me ideas." George grinned.

George Constantinou's people had been watching Nedjew for quite a while. The Russian was a regular in Limassol, where he moved about quite freely. The fact that he harbored his *Bastion* on the southern coast of Cyprus, often conducting his business meetings on the luxury yacht, made the job of surveillance interesting and not unattractive. George

275

counted on the talents of young Marios for this. The freelance camera-man from Delphi had done work for the British foreign secret service in Athens even before George's time.

Armed with his resourcefulness and high-tech camera equipment, his legendary snapshots had delivered striking proof that a British embassy employee had been spying for the Russians. The attractive assistant to the British military attaché had leaked strictly classified information to her Russian lover about an allied mission between the Sixth U.S. Fleet and the British Navy in the Mediterranean. In time, Marios's clandestine pursuits had given him a sense for the way women reacted to certain Russian types. And these empirical findings had proven rather useful for George's mission on Cyprus.

Marios had rented a studio above a mini market in a little white building not far from Armonia Beach. The two friends had walked over from the boat shack, crossed the busy main road. While George shopped the market for razor blades and shaving cream, deciding to add a couple of cans of beer while he was at it, Marios had opened the blinds upstairs to let fresh air into his apartment.

The photographer had woken his monitors. The colorful images now displayed on the big screens, with soft Blues playing in the background, brought a bit of life to what was otherwise a rather bleak abode. Marios deposited his beer on the printer, sat, searched through his photo archive with a practiced hand, clicking on icons of images in order to zoom in on them.

It took a while. He rolled the images back and forth, zoomed in and out while deciding on a selection.

Meanwhile, George looked around. There were some portraits on the long wall, and spotlights highlighted some excellent shots of kite surfers next to the hallway. George saw himself whirling ten meters up in the air, a dynamic black silhouette in the glaring backlight. Above, one could see the silver parachute lines. This had been at Kourion, on the coast where the rock of Aphrodite defied wind and sea, and also held surfers at a respectful distance—those unbidden defilers of the goddess's birthplace.

Marios downed the rest of his beer, rolled his chair over to another screen, where he had readied the images for viewing.

"I've got them. Come here."

Together, they analyzed the pictures, which showed Nedjew in various poses—on his yacht, at the Four Seasons Vista Bar with a buxom blonde, gesturing toward an elegantly dressed man, who was leaning casually against the rail...

"Who's the swank-looking guy?"

"No idea. But he looks like a proper cutthroat, probably a financial consultant or something. Keep going."

But Marios zoomed in on the image. The man wore a white shirt and tie. He held his arms outstretched, his eyes closed. What interested him about this managerial-looking individual were his hands, which rested daintily upon the precious wood rail—particularly one of them. "Look at that thing. What an exhibitionist!" Marios stood back, allowing George to look. He enlarged the image even more.

"You mean the ring?"

"Sure I do. What a clunker. Set in the finest gold. Who wears something like that?"

"Someone who wants to impress." George took a step back. "Just look at how obviously he's holding his fingers. Nedjew has to have noticed—the guy certainly wanted him to. It's probably worth a fortune. You know what? Make a print. I'll send it to my guys—I want them to identify this airbag." His friend muttered approvingly.

"Put it on my tab." His guys, of course, were the British MI6.

Next, they saw Nedjew getting out of a limousine, walking up the stairs to his private jet, waving—George could practically hear the shutter of the Nikon single lens reflex camera as he viewed the razor sharp images.

"Marios—the Cranes of Ibycus!" He suddenly exclaimed.

"What's gotten into you, George?"

"Nedjew goes by 'The Crane.' Cranes were the only witnesses to the murder of the Greek poet Ibycus. On this very coast, if I'm not mistaken. I associate cranes with crime because of that. It's just so fitting, you know?"

Instead of answering, Marios waved his flat hand back and forth in front of his forehead a few times. "He left Natasha behind this time," he said, getting back to business, as he opened the digital images of the airfield.

"I know," George muttered. "He left her all by herself. Wait. I think I have an idea…"

Marios threw him an amused look, sipped his beer, smiled contemplatively as he considered the role that he had been assigned. "We can get this thing rolling right now." He turned to the screen. "This one seems like a good pick, the Lebanese chick, look! She really is overwhelming. That body is enough to make a man weak."

"You're right. She'd make a perfect rival. Can you make it happen?"

Marios merely nodded and set about working on the imaging program for about fifteen minutes. Once he was done, he leaned back and waved his hand proudly to present the result.

"Leila is a successful model. She recently landed a pretty great *Vogue* feature spread. That should be enough to drive the other one nuts."

George appraised Marios's work. He nodded. "Print it, and then let's get going."

Two hours later, at Limassol harbor, the woman wearing a sporty blazer left the deck of the *Bastion*. She strolled down the blindingly white walkway, got into the waiting taxi and drove off.

"Natasha," Marios confirmed. George hit the gas. They followed the taxi in his white Cinquecento after it drove past them at the end of the pier and later turned onto Franklin Roosevelt Avenue.

The drive did not take long. They turned into a side street off the promenade. Natasha got out.

"Jewelry," George said knowingly, pulling in next to a building site. The district consisted of a long row of elegant boutiques with brightly lit displays, in which necklaces, bracelets, earrings and other adornments of gold and precious stones shimmered. Natasha disappeared in the oval entranceway of St. Andrew Gold Market. George's eyebrows rose on his forehead. "Well, she certainly has an eye for the best." They crossed the street, slipped into a passage off the sidewalk. Marios raised his camera, snapped as he panned back and forth. A leather boutique provided good cover, but also obstructed a clear view of the street in its entire length.

"They're wrapping something for her," Marios reported, lowered his zoom lens. "What's the plan?"

"When dealing with women, you have to be decisive. Every second counts. If they're interested, you have to go straight for the kill, or you're done. Never count on there being a second chance."

Marios looked appraisingly at George's shabby jeans. "You don't look too impressive, if you ask me."

George yanked his waistband up, pushed his hips forward. "This is the bait, my boy. Move! She's coming out."

Natasha strolled slowly toward Makarios Avenue, her large leather bag slung casually over her shoulder. The men caught up to her in front of the Italian Ristorante La Piazza.

"May I invite you for a cup of coffee, beautiful lady?" George asked, stepping next to her and flashing his irresistible smile.

Marios appeared on her other side. "This is George, my name is Marios."

The woman paused, took off her sunglasses, looked at one man, then the other with raised brows. A quick smile crossed her lips, but she sounded snippy. "Coffee is boring."

"I agree," George said with a ready laugh, promptly calling an order out in Greek to the waiter who was leaning in the doorway. The man grinned conspiratorially and dodged inside.

She followed George's gesture and took a seat at the nearest outside table. "The Champagne should be here shortly."

They gallantly sat to either side of their conquest, George stretching his legs out in a way that caused his tight jeans to show off his thighs. The lovely lady looked him up and down from behind her sunglasses, which she had since put back on. Marios could have sworn that she had checked out George's expertly presented anatomy for a little longer than could be deemed decent. She chatted easily. "Are you from around here? Don't you have anything responsible to keep you busy in the middle of the day?"

"This is where I was born and where I lost my virginity. And where I fought the Turks...I rent boats. There's not much going on today. Marios is a photographer for *Vogue*. He's always on the job."

Marios playfully aimed his camera.

She raised her eyebrows in surprise. "*Vogue?*"

The shutter clicked, he checked the image, showed it to her on the display. "Lovely, don't you think? It would be perfect for *Vogue*."

She smiled, obviously flattered, turned to George. "I like your style."

"And I like your perfume."

She took his hand, rubbed his wrist against hers. George raised his wrist to his nose. "Hmmm. What a lovely scent!"

Marios reached in his jacket, pulled out a postcard-sized photograph and laid it on the round table. When the waiter arrived with the bottle and ice bucket he raised it once more. "I took this. Do you know Leila Snow?" He held it up for her to see.

Her red lips pursed disparagingly, followed by a negating twitch of her face.

The waiter filled the glasses carefully, placed the bottle back on ice.

"Cheers, to your vacation!" George exclaimed. "Are you here alone?"

Again the twitch. "No. Our yacht is in the harbor...my...umm...my husband is gone for a few days. On his jet." She sipped at her flute, allowed the message to sink in.

"We can't compete with that, of course," George confessed. "My boats are..." he stopped as Marios brought forth a second picture. "Your husband doesn't happen to be Oleg Nedjew?" He turned the image of the Russian striding across the runway for her to see. She leaned forward abruptly. "Are you insane? What do you want to do with that—publish it? If he finds out, it will be the end of you...you don't know who you're dealing with, man!" She raised the glass to her lips.

"Don't worry. Marios has no intention of feeding the fish in the harbor. But we should tell you that Oleg is cheating on you."

Straight for the kill. Marios pulled out the third photograph. "With this woman," he whispered. "The Lebanese. See for yourself—that's Leila."

Marios's perfect montage was dreadfully incriminating. The breath-taking beauty was pressing her flawless tan skin against Nedjew, his thin lips touching her high cheekbone as his eyes rested on her voluptuous breasts; her skirt barely covered what was between her provocatively splayed legs.

Her perfectly manicured, red nails rested on his white shirt, just above his silver belt buckle.

The glass shattered. Natasha screamed, horrified, blood shot from her hand. George leaped forward, tore the napkin from the ice bucket, quickly fashioned an emergency bandage. "It's not so bad, here, hold on to this."

Her face had turned bitter. She had taken in all of the unsavory details. The business jet, with his logo next to the door, Nedjew's expensive, tailor-made suit, the bitch who had been all over him. Natasha's lips quivered—there was no doubt. The bastard was seeing another woman.

George helped her up. "I'll take you to the doctor."

Marios hailed a taxi.

Tears stood in her eyes. "I...can't...believe this..."

Hours later, in the cozy atmosphere of Andreas's little seafood restaurant, the young Russian woman began to talk. George had not expected any details. It seemed, at any rate, that he had been correct in his assessment of Nedjew's character—cunning and devoid of scruples. The Russian didn't involve women in his business dealings. But Natasha spoke of a trip to Latakia on the Syrian coast, of a visit by armed-to-the-teeth mujahideen; suitcases full of money...of visitors to the yacht of whom she knew no more than their first names...of missiles, even. The harvest was plentiful.

George suddenly appeared no longer interested. After the main course he reckoned all of that was really not that important. And, in regards to his infidelities—she should just be patient, the Crane would never give up a woman of her caliber. Natasha had gotten the weight off her chest.

The good food, the kindness of the two boys, the soft music playing in the background had all done their bit in alleviating her distress. The trauma of the little cut and subsequent, brief visit to the doctor had all but been forgotten. She sighed deeply. "I think I need a bit of rest." She swung her bag over her shoulder, started getting up. "If you would like to accompany me?"

They drove the little Fiat down to the pier. There, she said goodbye with a tantalizing smile, suddenly turning specifically toward George—seemingly on a whim. "Would you like to come on board for a nightcap?" Her suggestive look did not fail to have its intended effect on George. Coupled with her captivating scent, it almost caused him to give in. But in the end he waved his hand regretfully. "I'm sorry, but I really can't."

"That is a shame. But if you change your mind…maybe I will still be awake. Alone, in my bed."

She waved her bandaged hand and swayed up the ramp to the discreetly lit, luxurious deck of the *Bastion*.

"What a dud!" Marios sneered as they got in the car. "Why didn't you go after her?"

"You obviously don't know women, buddy. How do I know that everything she told us was true? Nope. I'll stay off that thin ice, thank you very much. Better to stick to my own turf." He pulled up his knees, as if to suppress something.

A short while later, in Marios's Armonia Beach studio, the two men got to work. The close evaluation of what they had learned from Natasha added a few pieces to the mosaic which, when added to the information from the MI6 analysts, appeared interesting indeed.

Their job was done. At about one in the morning, Marios took the bottle off the kitchen shelf, stepped to the open window. With the dark surf breaking beneath them, and by the shine of a dim moon, he filled their glasses with an old Scotch. He raised his, grinning at George.

"The only thing left to do now, is the transmission tomorrow—I mean, this morning," George said with a satisfying burp. "And now I must hurry home to my wonderful guest."

"What was that again?" Marios grinned. "Go for the kill!" He genially tapped his fist against his friend's chest. "Working with you never gets boring, George."

Tabriz Airport and Air Base

The gray delivery van, conspicuously labeled on both sides and the back, pulled up to the gate of the dimly lit military base. Omar read the green lettering, adorned with red ornamental patterns in Farsi and English: SECOND AIR BASE. A tall man came out of the low building, paused for a moment beneath the national flag, which hung limply, undisturbed by any wind. He carried a machine gun in front of his abdomen, his right hand on the grip. He approached the vehicle slowly. Salim looked out of his open window, holding a sandwich wrapped in plastic in his hand. A spotlight came on, bathing the visitors in bright light.

"What do you want?" The air force soldier wanted to know. Omar leaned across to the driver's side in order to get a better look at the guard. He noticed that the soldier bore the same insignia on his sleeve, just beneath the shoulder, as the stranded armored vehicle crew he had encountered the night before. He felt a twinge of guilt at having left the comrades in the lurch, not bringing them the food he had promised. But the face that now looked into their vehicle, checking the interior and Omar's white chef's coat, belonged to none of the four he had spoken to.

"Provisions," Salim said, succinctly, motioning to the lettering on the side of the truck with his thumb. El-Goli Restaurant and Catering it read there in red, ornate script, in Farsi and English. The guard stared at the sandwich that Salim was now holding out to him quite casually.

"Who are you here for?"

Salim turned his head to his passenger. "Who called in the order?"

Omar pulled out what looked to be an order book, leaned forward, looked to be searching for the pertinent information. "Hessami ordered."

The guards tone grew a little friendlier. "Saeed Hessami is the commanding officer."

"General?"

"Colonel. I have to call him. Protocol." He took a step back. "It won't take long, okay?"

Salim shrugged his shoulders nonchalantly. "We have time. We aren't the ones who are hungry."

The guard disappeared into his office, emerged only a short while later. The barrier was raised. "You're clear." He motioned for them to proceed.

"Here." Salim handed him the sandwich. "The bosses shouldn't be the only ones who eat well."

The guard grinned, watched the back of the receding van as he tore the plastic sandwich wrapper open with his teeth.

"And what is your uncle's opinion on our cause?" Omar asked, banging the arranged signal on the back of the cabin with his fist. Three knocks.

"Why do you keep asking? Nothing has changed since we left. We can trust Uncle Saeed. He needs the job. We only ever spoke about the resistance one time."

"And?"

Salim turned in front of the air base command office, stopped the engine. "What he wants is the separation of religion and politics. My uncle is cool, okay? I'm going to bring this stuff in now. You keep your eyes open."

As Salim opened the door, he was met by engine noise. Hot air blew against his face. Seconds later the great outline of a transporter majestically touched down on the runway barely a stone's throw away.

It was the Queen of the Skies. Salim cracked the back door open. "That's it! The Hercules!" He took the food basket from an outstretched hand. "Are you ready?" The question was directed at his comrades, who were busy exchanging their white kitchen uniforms for army issue camouflage jackets, which they had hidden in food containers.

Salim walked along the balustrade to the entrance, balancing the basket on one hand like a waiter, looking straight ahead to the green corridor behind the glass door. He tripped. "Damn it!" He had almost fallen. Cursing, he looked back and discovered the small step.

The aide's office was at the end of the corridor to the right. Salim poked his head through the door. He said hello, holding the basket up. The factotum, his uncle had once teasingly called the pudgy office manager, with his friendly, perpetually flushed face and shiny bald spot. Salim reckoned this meant that the aide, who was smiling warmly and motioning to his boss's door with his thumb, had simply been doing this job forever.

Air Base Commander Colonel Hessami sat behind the desk in his uniform shirt. He was on the phone. Salim waited respectfully at the door. The office was sparse. Aside from the desk, it was furnished only with a metal cabinet and two chairs. There was a picture of the religious leader on the wall. An old grenade, painted black with a red lever, was displayed next to an Air Force pennant. The colonel hung up. "Come in, Salim!"

"Hello, Uncle Saeed." Salim stepped up to the desk.

"It seems busy out there. Is all the commotion because of the nuclear explosion?"

Colonel Hessami made a dismissive gesture. "Pasdaran—the Revolutionary Guards. They were moved here yesterday to guard the airfield."

Salim put the basket down, accidentally dropping the white napkin with its plastic knife and fork on the linoleum floor. As he quickly stooped to retrieve it, his cell phone fell out of his open breast pocket. He snatched it up, coughed, pointed sheepishly at the brass plaque that was affixed to the grenade. "It has your name on it, Uncle Saeed."

"An aircraft bomb. Disarmed, of course. It was presented to me for my service anniversary." The colonel made an inviting gesture, Salim sat.

"I didn't order anything, Salim."

"What?! Sure, you did!" He dug around in his pocket, found a piece of paper. "There! It's all on here."

"I still didn't order anything, Salim. Well, it doesn't matter. You're here now. Will you eat something with me?"

Salim stared at the piece of paper, slapped his forehead. "I don't believe it, Uncle. This is yesterday's order. I'm really sorry."

Colonel Hessami waved, ignored the basket. "Where did you get the cell phone? Let me see."

Salim had little choice but to put the heavy black thing on the desk.

"It's not one of the new ones," the colonel remarked with a raised brow. As proof, he pulled his own silver one out of his breast pocket and smilingly held it up for comparison. Then he took Salim's in his other hand. "Interesting! Where did you get this?"

"Black market," Salim whispered, rolling his eyes conspiratorially. "It's not one of the ones that were dropped."

Uncle Saeed eyed the RAD device for a long time. His mind appeared to be working. Did he know that it was a detector for radioactivity? Salim sat on the edge of his chair as if on hot coals.

The office phone rang. Colonel Hessami picked up, straightened up almost imperceptibly, listened attentively. Salim made use of the opportunity. He stood, very conspicuously put his phone away, grinned apologetically, pointing to his watch as he started a crab-like, sideways walk to the door. Saeed was still reporting—"The machine is two hours early, General." Salim was out in the hall, turned around, rushed outside, his collar wet with sweat. He jumped over the step on his way out. The van was gone.

Cliff Matoyan was the beacon of calm in the cockpit, which was practically exploding with tension. He was the one conducting the radio communications with the tower as they touched down on the principle runway of Tabriz Airport, calmly translating instructions for the pilot. "You see the red lights, Shelly?"

"Positive. The man waving in front of the truck there."

"Correct. That is where we need to park."

"That's what I thought."

In the tower the military air traffic controller, a low-ranking officer, had been told to expect the arrival of a transportation carrier. No further details. He didn't need details. It was his job to make sure the planes landed safely, and to direct them to the appropriate freight depot once they had. He really didn't give a damn about whatever else went on around the airfield. Special troops were responsible for the security and loading of the freight carriers. Two companies of a battalion were on standby in a nearby forest—at least that is what he had heard in the canteen. The ground crew is probably counting on me to worry about everything. I'm sure they don't give a damn that the machine landed much earlier than scheduled.

The higher-ups make the decisions—not for us to understand.

The vast contours of the Hercules taxied down the semicircular runway past the two hangars with a low grumble. It came to a halt in front of the third, where two uniformed men with protective earmuffs waved their red lights. In front of the plane's nose, the runway continued in a moderate curve to where it met up with the main runway further along. Shelly killed two of the four engines, the other two continued to idle.

"Shelly, open the cargo hatch!" On Strom's command, the hydraulics were activated. The rear opened slowly, the broad steel ramp lowered with a hiss, hit the asphalt hard. Spot lights came on, lighting up the hull.

The Coup

Salim heard the whistle. Now he recognized the van standing in the shadow of the shed, which he had not seen driving up. He sprinted toward it, disappeared in the darkness.

Omar and his men stood ready. They had removed the magnetic restaurant decals, replaced them with smaller ones with Farsi inscriptions.

"Ready?" Salim looked each of the hardened men in the eyes. "Use your weapons only if absolutely necessary. You all have military training. You know what to do. Who are you?"

The question was directed at young Mohamed, who was looking at him earnestly, his face blackened with shoe polish. He was wearing combat gear with a corporal's badge.

"Air transport division. Secret commando. Code two zero eight eight."

"Good. Stay together! Watch each other's backs! Let's go! Get in!"

The six men got into the van. Salim started up and drove from the protective shadows onto the lit runway. They approached the Hercules slowly, from the front, drove around the wing, stopped beneath the center of the fuselage.

Meanwhile, in the airfield command office, Colonel Hessami had finished one of the excellent tuna fish sandwiches and lit up a cigarette. The call had come from Shiraz Air Base. He did not know the people in the south personally. He had traveled all over the country on duty, of course, but knew only that they seemed to be a bit full of themselves down there in the southern provinces. Like they had invented the wheel, or something. They were very proud of all their oil, and the fact that they held a strategic position on the Gulf meant that they were always well treated. Recently they had received the new Sukhoi SU-30. Of course those presumptuous asses thought of the farmers' sons up north, in the icy hinterlands of Tabriz, as vastly inferior, if they bothered to think of them at all. As far as they were concerned, all they knew how to do was fly the Shah's old scrap heaps, Phantom F-15s, and nothing else . . . When Hessami had informed the brigadier that the transporter had landed far too early, he had been soundly snapped at. "We'll get there when we get there, Colonel. You just take care of your own business." The end. Evidently they had known of the early arrival and not bothered to inform anyone. Being the old soldier that he was, he should have known that it was better not to bother superiors up the chain of command unless one was spoken to first.

Hessami grabbed his binoculars, stepped to the barred window, focused in on the imposing Hercules. He always enjoyed seeing these machines. There were several of them in operation. The van came into view. The colonel adjusted the focus until he could make out the lettering. Mobile Provision Squad, he read out loud. The thus inscribed van came to a halt, men got out. For just a second one of them looked like his nephew, Salim—he blinked a few times, looked again. The men had disappeared in the shadows of the fuselage. The similarity of the figure, the hair—surely a coincidence. At any rate, there was something that stopped him from wanting to think too deeply, or know too much, about Salim and his doings. With a deep sigh and heavy gait he went to his aide's office and ordered him to send a telex. CONFIRM TELEPHONE

CONVERSATION WITH COMMANDER OF AIR TRANSPORT BRIGADE. TRANSPORT MACHINE ID TWO-ZERO-EIGHT-EIGHT (2088) LANDED IN TABRIZ TWO HOURS PRIOR TO ARRANGED TIME. AB CMD COLONEL HESSAMI.

"If there's a problem, at least we're covered."

Why would there be a problem...? the silently raised eyebrows of the experienced aide queried.

The captain of the Revolutionary Guard, who was standing next to the first of the Kamaz trucks, saw the men appear beneath the ramp of the Hercules. They wore the usual fighter jackets. One climbed up the ramp and disappeared inside. The other five strode toward him, circling their right arms energetically—circling arms meant start the engine, prepare to move.

The captain hesitated to pass the command on to his drivers. He did not know the men who had now stopped their approach, but were still circling their arms.

Salim stepped from the group, trotted over, stopped in front of the grim captain, saluted. "Captain, you can start." He held a modern device to his ear, the likes of which the officer had never seen before. "We are ready. Our window is very limited. We would appreciate it if you could initiate loading immediately."

"Forward, march!" Omar yelled, standing broad-legged in the loading hatch. Without waiting for a response, Salim ran around the three trucks, bending down to the axles as if checking to see it they were in good order. What he was really interested in were the RAD readings. The red of the three-color fields lit up brightly—there was clearly radioactive material inside these trucks. *These were the nuclear missiles!*

The captain finally gave the first driver the sign. The Kamaz slowly followed the officer toward the ramp.

"Loading documents?" Omar called down from the platform, where he stood next to a pile of chocks.

The captain shook his head, annoyed. "Not necessary. Your boss knows. Call him."

"One moment." It took a while, then Cliff Matoyan's dark, slender face appeared. He combed his fingers through his long, slicked-back hair, adjusted his goggles, then jogged down the ramp, greeted the captain jovially. "You are right, we're not interested in the contents. But the weight list—do you have that?"

The captain of the Revolutionary Guard grinned disparagingly, produced the document from his uniform, and handed it to Matoyan.

Cliff hesitated. "Twelve tons? Is that all?" He eyed the vehicles skeptically.

"Each of these trucks weighs about three tons, the remainder is the load. We're moving technology, comrade. Not scrap metal." Thus he spoke, then turned to his people and commenced issuing orders.

Omar directed the first truck onto the ramp. The driver was not performing this maneuver for the first time. He held the tracks precisely, disappeared into the hold where the crew immediately applied chocks and steel cables to secure the vehicle.

The second now had its front wheels on the ramp, while the third switched to a low beam and followed behind.

Nico Strom danced around the cargo hold as on hot coals. He checked the time, exchanged looks with the pilot. A good hour had passed since their landing. Up until now everything had gone according to plan, but time was running against them.

A uniformed man is standing in the shadow of the fuselage, a few meters below Strom. He is hidden from view by the van, pissing on the runway in a wide arc, a cigarette dangling from his mouth. He is amused by how the air set in motion by the slowly moving propellers is scattering his urine. In no hurry, he takes his time to thoroughly shake himself dry, steps up to the driver side window as he is zipping up his pants. Seeing nothing in the darkness, he goes to the back and shakes the door. It opens. What he dimly makes out looks like white aprons, provisions and the signs. He pulls one of them half out, is taken aback. *Catering… Restaurant.* He examines the logo on the side of the van:

MOBILE PROVISIONS SQUAD. *By the honor of my grandmother, it looks like someone has swapped the signs! Strange.* He grinds his cigarette out with the tip of his boot, steps back toward the bright light of the loading ramp where he sees his captain gesturing.

✳

"We have identified an aircraft approaching Tabriz from the south." Cosmo's voice electrifies the crew. Nico runs to the back, tries to get an overview. Truck number three is still on the ramp. "Get the vehicle loaded, get a move on!" he hollers.

Two man stand gesturing beside the driver's cabin. Both are wearing reflective leg bands over their uniforms, on their right calves—the identifying mark. These are helpers of the resistance, who now appear to be waving their arms helplessly, calling something that is lost in the engine noise. Omar runs up the ramp, breathing hard. "The commanding officer has stopped the truck. He is inspecting our van back there."

"Damn it to hell," Strom cursed.

Shelly's voice sounds urgently through the speakers. "Six minutes, Nico!"

Omar assesses the situation coolly. "If they find us out, we're done. That truck has to be loaded. I'll take care of it."

Below, the captain steps into view, turns his face up and hollers: "The van back there. Something is not right. Stop loading immediately."

"Why, what's the matter?" Omar yells back, a chock in both hands.

The captain waves his hand gruffly. "Doesn't matter. This stops now!" He fiddles with the walkie-talkie that he has strapped to his chest.

Omar raises the chock with both hands. The officer takes a step forward, has now freed the walkie-talkie. Omar drops the chock. The mass of metal heavily skims his head, then lands squarely and heavily on the captain's shoulder. He crumbles to the ground noiselessly.

Nico looks up over the runway, sees landing lights. The second machine is heading in—no doubt the one belonging to the IRIAF.

Alerted by the thundering of the engines, the airfield commander runs through the corridor and out to the balustrade. The tower was right—the transporter is landing on his airfield! And it's the one from Shiraz, punctual almost to the minute. *Who in the name of my dear mother's soul are the people in the Hercules that is already on the ground? The colonel rushes back to his desk, looks for the list of command posts. His aide had to know the telephone numbers! Where the hell was he now that he needed him? Gone for the day?* He finds the list under an aviation journal. Command…command…there!…Airport security. He fumbles frantically with the phone, manages to dial the number.

The two soldiers wearing the reflective bands do not hesitate for one second. They see the captain crumble to the ground and nod to each other. Everything will continue according to plan. They tear the truck doors open at the same time. The blindsided driver is unceremoniously thrown to the asphalt. Mohamed is at the wheel. The engine sputters to life, revs, the gear takes hold and the Karmaz jerks forward. Mohamed steers it up the ramp with the engine whining. Now the voice of the loading master, in a sharp tone: "Ready to close the ramp!"

His crew busies itself, every move practiced and coordinated. The loading master is on hand to anticipate and avert any possible hitch. This load has different physical properties to cube-shaped containers. The trucks have springs, their bodies have some tilt, their mass must be stabilized to withstand the enormous forces in effect during takeoff. It is harrowing work.

"Where is Omar?" someone yells as the hydraulics begin to whimper.

The van comes into sight, skidding around the bend, the unsecured rear door slamming open and shut. For the first time this night shots are heard. Nico hears them, at any rate, as the thundering of the Antonov transporter dies back. The mighty fuselage with the red, white and green flag taxies to a halt. "They're nuts."

Matoyan is unclear whether Strom is referring to the shooting soldiers, or the men in the van who are swerving toward the ramp at a breakneck speed under a hail of bullets from the Revolutionary Guards.

"Ramp low," Matoyan yells. He dives to the command box, pushes the lever down. When he looks up, Nico Strom and the other Swiss man are standing in the hatch, broad-legged, side by side, firing their assault rifles from the hip for all they are worth.

"Hold down the left," Strom yells, releasing a salvo toward the group that has taken cover behind a command vehicle.

The rising ramp stops at a height of about one and a half meters. Way too far to allow the fleeing vehicle to enter! The van is speeding straight for a collision with its edge. The ramp starts descending again; moving at an incredibly slow pace to all who are watching, appalled, from above.

No one says a word. The Hercules' engines roar. The plane begins to move.

"We're rolling," Strom screams, and at that moment sees the outline of armored vehicles appear on the access road behind the command building. "Go, go!" He fired the next salvo at the hostile position.

The van decelerates only minimally. Sparks fly as bullets hit the body. A decal flies off in a high arc.

The brutal bang with which the ramp hits the asphalt is as music to Nico's ears. But the front wheels of the van have rammed its edge just a split second before it is down. The van hurls upward, crashes down as Matoyan rips at the lever to raise the ramp back up. Transfixed, they stare at the tilted vehicle—a wheel hangs over the edge, turning against nothing, the axle is stuck.

"Fire extinguishers, activate the hoist!" Matoyan barks in a mixture of English and Farsi. The Hercules gains ground, swings onto the runway.

Standing at the balustrade of his command building, Colonel Hessami was treated to the most grotesque scene that he was ever forced to witness during the entire length of his military career. A kind of forklift gone terribly awry...A giant maw unable to swallow its prey...A calving whale? Hessami flipped open his little notepad in order to commit these thoughts for later, as good material for one of his poems or short stories.

The men aboard the Hercules succeeded at the last possible moment. The steel cable on the powerful hoist tore the van from its unfortunate mooring. It rolled, fell down into the hold—just in time for the ramp to slam shut, the bolting device to grip. The Hercules thundered down the runway, then rose in heavy majesty.

Nagorno-Karabakh

The two Super Puma helicopters approached the town of Shushi, a good two hundred kilometers east of the Armenus Technopark, and one thousand five hundred meters above sea level, in tactical low flight under VFR conditions.

Andy saw forests, ditches and hilltops go by from a window seat in the main cabin. The pilot had informed them a few minutes ago that they had crossed the border to Azerbaijan. Andy irreverently put his boots up on the thick leather satchel containing the cash and looked for some point of reference in the desolate, wild terrain. That was Nagorno-Karabakh down there—officially part of Azerbaijan, but Armenian-controlled, close to the Caspian Sea. There was not even a village to be seen.

"The Caspian basin harbors enormous energy reserves," he remembered Cosmo saying. "There are estimates of over two hundred billion barrels of crude oil and over seven billion cubic meters of natural gas. At any rate, it is a tremendous store for the global economy of this century. Russia, Turkey and Iran are in a struggle to control this strategically critical region between Europe and the Middle East. Armenia, which lies at the western border of the Eurasian transport corridor, holds the trump card. If natural gas and oil from the Caspian Sea is to reach Europe, then Armenia cannot be avoided."

"We are preparing to land," the pilot announced. "Shushi is just ahead." Andy started to make out reddish buildings and a large church." The province of Shushi borders on our country," Cosmo had taught him. "Resistance fighters have set their base in town. You will meet their leader at the Cathedral of our Holy Savior."

The Super Puma leaned into a turn, prepared for landing. They passed an old Russian tank on the ground below—rusting away on a memorial pedestal. "Shushi has survived several massacres, but Na-gorno-Karabakh has stabilized since the cease fire of 1994. Azerbaijan seems to have accepted Armenian control over the region."

About two dozen armed men in camouflage stood in groups around the landing pad as the great, dark machines with their towering profiles circled and touched down like ill-omened vultures. Andy had barely set foot on the once bloodily contested soil when three men took him into custody, rushed him to a light Toyota truck, hustled him into the passenger seat. Within minutes the escort was crunching to a halt on the wide square before the mighty place of worship.

Getting out, Andy looked up at the two reddish towers of unequal height with conical domes, but barely had time for sightseeing as the men were already herding him toward the main entrance. They strode through the tall, rounded arches to an oasis of Sunday stillness and asylum.

"Our Savior's Cathedral," one of the men whispered solemnly as he tiptoed through the high-ceilinged central nave toward the cloister where a gray-haired figure sat on a low bench, his back toward them. Cosmo's words were on Andy's mind. *Their faith is everything to them,* he had said. *If you want to have any chance at success, you must show the chief of the province your reverence. Pull yourself together, Andy. You can't afford to be messing around...*

"Safar Natadschjan," his attendant said gravely, bowing as he retreated. This was not a holy man. His eyes sparkled roguishly as he turned, stood, pulled himself up to his full, impressive height. He assessed Andy with a look of amusement, evidently seeing him as a bit of a half-pint. Still, a not unfriendly smile played around the corners of his bearded mouth.

"Welcome to Shushi. I have been told of the reason for your visit. So we should get to business, young man. But before we do, do you have any idea what you are standing on?"

Andy returned the greeting, looked down at the stone slab, perplexed. Was he sacrilegiously standing on some kind of gravestone with his dirty shoes?

The man closed his eyes in deep thought. "Almost one hundred years ago, the Turks and Azeris created a bloodbath in our town. They assassinated my people. Tens of thousands dead—no one knows exactly how many. A flock of women and children hid down here in the crypt for days...My grandmother was one of those brave souls. If she had not done what she did, I would not be standing here today." Natadschjan slapped his great paw on Andy's shoulder, bringing the meager Californian almost to his knees. His laughter echoed loudly through the magnificent neo-Romanesque structure.

"Andy. My name is Andy...I am very honored, Commander..." He had wanted to add that he appreciated the reason for their meeting at this place so rich in historic meaning and spiritual importance. Natadschjan grabbed his sleeve with a grin. "No need to go pale with awe, Andy. We know your boss, Jack Abramian. A good Armenian. What he is doing for our country is appreciated. We will help where we can."

They made their way toward the exit. Andy held the bag of money tightly. Outside on the square covered in fine, reddish gravel, a well-polished, older-model Mercedes stood waiting.

Andy looked twice—a young woman was standing next to it. She wore a well-tailored, quilted uniform jacket and elegant, high boots. Earrings accentuated her polished appearance. She looked at him with an earnest face.

Natadschjan playfully wagged a finger under Andy's nose. "Better watch it, Sara is my daughter." Andy muttered *hello* a big grin on his face, adding somewhat hoarsely, after an almost embarrassingly long pause...*Sara*. The beauty rewarded him with a gracious smile. They drove off. It was nine in the morning. Natadschjan's people stood by the helicopters in formation. The commander strode down the rank, plucking at a uniform here, checking a gun and ammunition there. Andy trotted behind him. The men stood at attention, their grim faces as if hewn in granite. A fierce squad!

Natadschjan appeared content. He dismissed the men with a bellowed order. They dispersed and ran up a knoll, apparently to take a break. Natadschjan led Andy back to the Mercedes by the arm. "We take off in half an hour."

The residence, an old, beautifully restored house, lay elevated in a well-tended park setting. Getting out of the car, Andy had a good view of the Super Pumas below. Cosmo's messenger placed the bag of money on the rough wooden table of the eat-in kitchen, next to several bottles. "The down payment, Commander."

Natadschjan filled three glasses with vodka, while Sara checked the contents of the bag at her father's behest. An old, wizened woman wearing a white headscarf and an ankle-length apron carried in a platter and placed it on the table next to the breadbasket.

Natadschjan helped himself generously, chewed on the dried meat, raised his glass.

"Twenty thousand dollars," Sara noted casually.

Although straight vodka was not his drink of choice, Andy bravely kept up, stuffing his mouth with meat and bread, then demonstratively chasing it with the stuff. All the while, he discreetly sought Sara's proximity. She had rid herself of her jacket and was now sitting in her pleasingly tight shirt, occasionally looking down at the stacks of money with a smile. After a fourth glass in celebration of their friendship, Natadschjan mercifully called it quits and announced their departure. They drove off, buoyed by alcohol and good will.

"A beautiful town, and a wonderful region," Andy rhapsodized, and found that he really did mean it.

"You should come and stay for a few days," Sara suggested charmingly. "Our lives up here are all about long winters and seclusion. But we also have wonderful hot thermal springs—very healthy for the body and the spirit." Looking at her, Andy believed that entirely.

The squad of mercenaries stood waiting by the helicopters. The material was securely loaded.

"We will discuss details on our flight back," the commander decided, climbing into the cabin behind Andy. The rotors started up, sped to the characteristic, loud whopping noise.

The Super Pumas took off easily, banked into the bend to the west. Fascinated Andy looked at the landmark cathedral and the tank monument then over the town draped across the gently undulating hills.

Turning away from the view and sitting back in his seat, he looked at Sara, as if seeing her fully for the first time. The young woman sat diagonally across from his seat, her slender limbs appearing to be displayed just for him. Her large, dark eyes looked steadfastly into his, on her lips a warm, yet distant smile.

Andy felt the blood rush to his chest, his heart, down to his loins. He hoped fervently that she wouldn't notice what was happening to him! Blushing, he tried to evade her glance. But he couldn't. Not until Sara Natadschjan slowly turned her face away, as if nothing, absolutely nothing, had just happened...

Zurich

In Zurich, retired Federal Chief Inspector Marcel Dulliker had no reason to see the world through rose-tinted glasses. He stood, chilled, in the bustling courtyard of the Ponter Bank, observing the activity of the Cantonal police, who were packing box loads of seized documents into gray vans. He was waiting impatiently for Ken Cooper, who had nothing better to do than stock up on cigars at Vollenweider's new store over on the Bahnhofstrasse. Now, of all times! He shook his head, was stomping around indignantly as he sensed something to his rear.

"Sorry to bother you, Inspector," a man said respectfully. He wore what looked to be a chauffeur's uniform; the only thing missing was the cap you always saw in old movies.

"Ivanovic, I am Mr. Ponter's driver," the man introduced himself. He held a flat parcel pinned beneath one arm. Dulliker looked at him absently.

"Well—no need to be concerned. There won't be any dismissals today. Just continue your work."

Ivanovic held the parcel out to him. "I thought you might be able to use my recordings."

The detective furrowed his brows, eyed the package skeptically. "Recordings, you say—where did you get them?"

Ivanovic explained briefly, yet thoroughly.

Turning into the yard, Ken Cooper saw Dulliker standing next to the shiny Maybach limo. The front door stood open, the driver appeared to be talking to Marcel. Cooper gave the kind of jovial mock salute that only battle-scarred veterans can really pull off. "You may be jumping the gun there, Marcel. The jalopy isn't on the liquidation list yet." Ken grinned, lit up a short thin cigar, kicked a tire like an experienced used-car salesman.

"We're going in to the station," Dulliker said shortly.

A surprised Cooper decided that it might be better to get in the back and keep any further commentary to himself for the moment. He eyed his friend expectantly.

"You and I have done things, Ken, that no other agent in our country could have pulled off."

"I'm very touched, Marcel. Now would you care to tell me what's going on?"

Marcel motioned his bearded chin forward, toward the chauffeur. "He has evidence that can help us nail Ponter. We're going to take a look at it. You know my theory."

"Which one?"

"The one that Nedjew, the Crane, could also be a bigwig in Russian intelligence."

"You couldn't perhaps go with something a little less complicated?"

"And how do you reckon the smuggling of atomic weapons, or the acquisition of the Hornbach plans, would be possible without the support of the KGB?"

"What does all of this have to do with Ponter?"

"Let's just listen to the tapes."

They sat in silence, each pursuing their own thoughts, until the limousine pulled up in front of the Cantonal police precinct minutes later. Cooper took a long drag of his cigarillo, imagined the trim, female CEO in the buff.

Shaking off the attractive image, he grudgingly got out of the car. That was what life had become—the only excitement these days were things like illicit tapes, not racy women in their mid-forties.

＊

Fine. But what is Ivanovic's motive for hanging Ponter out to dry?"

"Traumatic experiences. Revenge. He saw the Special Forces drown his father in a cesspit in the Bosnian War. Ponter, who then went by the name of…" the secret service agent flipped through his notes, "…the name of Dragan Nikolic, a lieutenant colonel, headed the commando unit. He gave the orders."

"Do we have proof of that?"

Marcel shook his head. "Hardly. But that's not our issue. The main thing is that we have the tapes. Ivanovic took the position with the bank so that he could avenge his father's death."

"And he's been taping conversations for God knows how long so he can blackmail him?"

"Get him put behind bars, more like it."

Cooper nodded his head toward the chaos of documents and tapes, yawned openly.

"How much longer is this going to take?"

"We're almost done. Ponter's escape yesterday was well prepared, if you ask me. Someone flew him out of the country on a private jet. From Payerne Military Air Base."

"That's something only the Services would do. And only for big fish."

"You're the one who said it."

Cooper grinned at him broadly. "Aren't we getting a bit long in the tooth to be messing with your colleagues?"

"Maybe you are, Kenny," Dulliker shot back impertinently.

PART V

Limassol

Do things ever turn out the way you expect? This was the question on Sophie's mind as she woke late that morning. She blinked, having come to terms with what had happened as she slowly surfaced from her sleep. She was forced to admit that things had not gone at all the way she had sensibly planned them.

George sat at the breakfast table. On a small television screen a bearded cleric with dated glasses spoke into a long row of microphones: . . . *The new government has our full confidence . . . spiritual matters should remain separate from earthly matters, this is the will of Allah, Iran remains a strong country, in which politics and religion will focus on their own concerns. We support the new constitution, which allows religious freedom, but non-believers will be felled like rotten trees by the next storm . . .*

George turned the ayatollah off, took a sip of coffee, smoothed his white shirt. He rolled up his sleeves, peered into the reflection of the screen to check his appearance. He stood, impatiently, started pacing the room, finally heard the sound of the door. Sophie walked, smiling, from her bedroom—*floated*, it seemed to him.

"Morning, George. Hmm, that coffee smells wonderful." She leaned up, kissed him on the cheek.

This was his moment. He put his hands on her hips. "Sophie. Will you allow me to be part of your adventurous life? Will you marry me?"

He was so utterly disarming that she rested her head against his cheek.

Never had a man proclaimed such intentions toward her—not in jest, and certainly not in such an enigmatic manner. She was speechless. He was the first to profess a willingness to make an actual commitment toward her. Unlike those who just wanted to play around, who were in it for the thrill of the chase, or just wanted a little something on the side.

George was different. She sensed this quite clearly. He looked at her, unblinkingly. "Do you want to marry me, Sophie?"

She remained silent, gently caressing the nape of his neck. Finally, she whispered very softly into his ear, as if to break it to him gently, "I don't know you well enough, dearest."

He stepped back, his voice sounding hollow. "I understand. I'm not interesting enough for you. Just the simple lifeguard, that's all."

She looked at him. "No. That's not it at all. I'm just...this is so unexpected. I mean, I'm not some sort of instant prize...do you gamble? Then you would know what I mean."

"I asked you because I have feelings for you, Sophie."

"Have you done this before?"

"What?"

"Proposed."

"I've tried a few times."

She sat down abruptly. *This was getting better all the time!* "And who, may I ask, were the lucky ladies? Chance acquaintances from the beach? The handsome lifeguard and lady's man. Of course. And who would I be to resist the Adonis of Armonia Beach?"

She bit into a croissant, poured herself a cup of coffee from the silver pot.

George stood in the middle of the room, looking distinctly downcast.

"No, no. Listen to me. It was always destined to be you...it has to be what you hear people call love at first sight. Even at the airport I found myself rehearsing what I wanted to say. I said it to myself a hundred times. I know now that there was only ever you, Sophie...and when I said what I did just now, it just came out. I was as surprised as you. It's almost as if something just spoke through me."

Her warm eyes rested on his face for a long time. When she persisted in her inscrutable silence he turned, stepped out onto the terrace and unsuccessfully searched his pocket for his cigarillos.

"I like your maturity," she called after him. "I sense your courageous soul, George. I can see the spark in your eyes." She had stood, now joining him on the terrace. "You are pent-up; a restless adventurer—I like that. An untamed spirit who controls his desires. You should study philosophy and discover yourself."

He turned, a look of surprise on his face. "I've never heard anyone sound so wise. What are you, a psychologist?"

She dismissed the question with a lighthearted laugh. "In my profession—that is, when I still had one—I learned to understand human psychology. Just like a doctor, or lawyer, who always has to consider her client's deeper being."

"You're a lawyer?" He held the small cigarillo box in his hand, indecisively.

"Far from it. I studied physics. The soul only enters into that field when the smallest of small particles accelerate to the brink of the big bang and one has to ask oneself where the dividing line is between God and matter."

"And so you're a pilot? Are you looking for the divide up there?" George sat down on a teak armchair, drumming his fingers on the armrest.

"Unfortunately not." She spread out sideways on the recliner. "I decided not to become a professional pilot. That might have been a mistake."

"Do you have any idea," he interrupted her with a charming smile, "how breathtakingly beautiful you are?"

Sophie playfully stretched her legs into the air. "Why, thank you. That's partly owing to your help, of course. She jumped up, spun around elegantly.

"You picked well." George assessed the elegant, white pants that tapered above her shapely ankles, the colorful, soft wool sweater that accentuated her lovely form.

"In the end I ended up at a Swiss bank, of all uninspiring places." She perched on his knees, put her arm around his shoulder. "A good paycheck, a secure job, I thought. Ha! Well, that went up in smoke, that's for sure...What a life." She stood, restless, walked to the railing.

"You are an exceptionally talented woman, I knew that from the instant I met you," she heard George say, and felt his proximity at the same time. "The embodiment of drive and energy, capable of so much, Sophie." His hands rested on her shoulders. "And your beauty is mesmerizing, as if you were not a single woman, but ten, twenty..."

Sophie turned to face him. George looked at her with eyes that were almost misty. "You will always have a hold on me. Your life is so full, the world is open to you, everything is possible. And you know it. I'm too ordinary for you. A nobody!"

She pressed her finger to his lips, but he drew back.

"My father was shot by the Turks. I had to take care of myself from an early age. To you I'm just a good-looking islander, a useful companion. I understand. It was an illusion—a dream to want to go through life with you by my side. A lovely illusion...a wonderful, short dream that was over too soon."

George went over to the table, took a cigarillo from the box. "Will you be flying out today?"

She watched in silence as he broke the first match, struck the next against the striking surface, held it to the cigar and puffed. He seemed demoralized. She had somehow pulled the ground out from under him.

Again, the helpless silence. How could she walk away from everything to throw herself at this man, wonderful as he was? Just let everything run its course? It wasn't possible. There were open ends, loose threads that needed to be taken care of. Her situation was complicated enough as it was. Every fiber of her being yearned for this amazing man. But her mind warned her. *Don't pull him into this mess that you have created for yourself!*

The events of the past days echoed like a casualty report from a faltering terrain: Quadrini, Suvorov—dead. Uli Stark lying in a pool of his own blood—your fault! Lenka Martialis—neutralized. Not to mention the adversaries who would be gathering to mount a counterattack: John Ponter, who would like nothing more than to tear her to pieces. And, as if that weren't enough, she had managed to antagonize that Russian gangster. George, I want to keep you safe, and when the time is right...

He was calm now, blew a puff of smoke into the air. "When will you be heading out?"

Sophie looked contemplatively at his sensuous mouth. She had to do something! "We could go dancing," she gushed. "I want to be close to you, George. Do you dance? Aside from what you do on the waves, of course."

"Dance? That's a bit nostalgic, don't you think? Did you want me to take you to a disco?"

"I want to *dance* with you, George. Here—on the beach, on the ocean, in town." She spun around. "I feel so shut down, drained. My body is yearning to move. I need some oxygen to the brain. You inspire me." She shimmied her legs again. "Enough talk. Come now! Let's do something!"

"Alright, but you can't expect me to be totally thrilled about it, Sophie." Suddenly he grabbed her, kissed her firmly on her red lips.

He held her close for a long moment, felt the warmth rushing through his body. This was what he yearned for.

"Not now," she whispered.

"Whatever you say, baby, whatever, and whenever. You just say the word."

They drove to the British base, mostly in silence. The waves of lust had subsided. There was a gentle breeze. He knew the way to Akrotiri in his sleep. He stopped at the gate to the air base, looked over to the guard booth. The sergeant, recognizing his tan face and thin mustache, raised the gate. The British had a Tornado fighter squadron and several infantry helicopters stationed at Akrotiri. No one looking at the barracks-style buildings would have reckoned that the sand-colored facades hid components of one of the largest espionage compounds in the world, even if the actual secret service headquarters were situated at the rambling Episkopi camp. The news agency in front of which George now parked the dark brown Land Rover was in a forlorn spot behind the small canteen. He went to the door, keyed in the entry code and pushed open the glass door to the communication room. There, he went through the most recent reports, which were almost exclusively about Iran and Israel. He grabbed the summary report, almost missing the light brown envelope poking out from beneath the latest issue of *The Economist*, which bore a striking image of an atomic cloud on its cover. George pocketed the report and envelope, grabbed the magazine on his way out, skimming its pages. On returning to the Land Rover, he handed it to Sophie. He plopped behind the wheel, started the car and turned onto the road that led off the base and toward town.

"I am taking you to the most beautiful place on the island. There, we will dance," George hollered over the noise of a starting helicopter.

Something in her eyes told him that she would be willing to do anything he wanted if he took her to that ancient site.

"We're just going pop in to see Marios." He patted his jacket. "Drop off some paperwork. Then we'll be on our way!"

A gorgeous, blue sky stretched over the undulating coastal land-scape, which was covered in large part by facilities, streets, sports grounds, shooting ranges, transmission towers, and entire villages belonging to the British army.

After about an hour, George parked the Land Rover in front of an ochre colored building that turned out to be the visitor's center. Together, they strolled past it and to the scaffolding of the archeological site at the lookout point.

He gently places his arm around her slender waist. "Do you see that large, pointy boulder?" They are standing at the top of the hill. He stretches his arm out, pointing across the steps of the amphitheater and toward the ocean behind it. "That is where Aphrodite rose from the sea. Come. Our dance floor is down there."

They skip down the stairs of the ancient cultural site, down to the stage. The ocean is glinting in the sunshine. A gentle breeze strokes through Sophie's thick, dark blonde hair.

"The ancient Greeks were a terrible people," George tells her with a smile. "Uranus, father of the Titans, was castrated by his son with a sickle. Cronus then took his member and cast it into the waves—right there, where that boulder is."

"Why did he do that?"

"No idea. Legend has it that his seed and the ocean mixed to create a foam, out of which Aphrodite was born. The boulder is named after her for that reason."

"I thought Aphrodite was the daughter of Zeus."

George put the portable radio and CD player down on the bottom step.

"Don't go messing with our mythology, now," he said with a grin and hit the play button.

A cheerful, rhythmic melody magically filled the ancient auditorium, which opened out to the sea.

"Come. Sirtaki!" George bows dramatically, then sweeps the startled Sophie off across the ancient stones that make up the stage of Kourion's theater.

Sophie suddenly frees herself from his gentle grasp. She sways and twirls in a little circle as George stands watching, swaying his hips in time to the music, stepping rhythmically in place. She appears to lose herself entirely in the dance, her face enchanted, eyes half closed, body and music becoming one.

Up above a group of tourists slowly begins to trickle into the arena. Individuals look down, take photographs. A Japanese couple, both of small stature, comes to the edge of the stage. The man directs the woman toward the position he has chosen for a good snap shot.

The music escalates toward an intoxicating crescendo. Sophie is twisting, turning, twirling faster and faster. The tourists begin clapping to the rhythm.

Suddenly she grabs him, draws him firmly to her body, transitions to a slow, almost dragging rhythm. The Japanese bride has now also dared to venture out onto the stage, dances smilingly for the clicking camera.

"When I am dancing, I feel that everything is right with the world," Sophie says, catching her breath.

"Isn't this place wonderful?" George says in answer. "We go paragliding on the beach down there sometimes."

As the music fades, she puts her face on his shoulder, stands still.

"Are you afraid of being alone?" he whispers. His full lips brush against her hot cheek. She nods, slightly.

"And you? Is your mother still alive, George?"

He nods. "It would be wonderful to be alone with you right now."

"But it's not time for that," she laughs, playfully pushing him back. She walks over to the now silent CD player, hits repeat. "We're not done here yet! Come, my island man," she calls out, swaying her hips in a snake-like fashion, acting out the music with her body. "Come!" She takes an encouraging step toward him, pushing up her tight top to reveal her bronze, lean stomach.

George pushed his hips forward, bending his knees. He brushes his loins against her thighs almost casually, spins around, twitches his ass cheeks comically, his arms stretched straight up in the air.

She laughs, grabs him from behind, kisses the nape of his neck.

"We should go," he whispers, looking up the tiers where the tourist group has spread along the stairs.

Sophie sighs. "Oh, that was wonderful!" She wipes the sweat off her brow. "I've never done it outside before."

George looks at her quizzically.

"Dance, I mean!" She playfully slaps his rear. "In the sunshine, before the birthplace of Aphrodite. What were you thinking?"

"I'm going to get us something to drink," George said with a smile, grabs the CD player and leads the way up the stairs. Having reached the top, Sophie takes a seat in the Land Rover while George visits the small souvenir shop. To pass time, she pages through *The Economist*, pushes her sunglasses up to hold back her hair.

George half-danced back to the car, humming a tune. He tossed the small ghetto blaster and the bag with soft drinks in, heaved himself behind the steering wheel. He looked over at her, was taken aback. "What have you got there?"

Sophie was staring at the images with large eyes. "Look at that! That's where I was, George. That's Armenia. That hotel, the big plane...look!"

"It's a Hercules transporter," George recognized expertly.

"That's where I met Andy…at the Armenus Technopark…the Global Express was right outside that building…"

"They reported on that story on TV."

"What story?"

George tapped the page with his finger. "The story about this high-tech compound in southern Armenia. There was a big media uproar. The global press was all over it. Politicians flew there to meet with the guy."

"Who are you talking about? What guy?"

"An obscenely rich American. Some eccentric. He managed to get armed, nuclear missiles out of Iran; some commando mission, like Entebbe. I have no idea how he did it. Russian missiles. Anyway, it was a huge sensation. Didn't you hear about it?"

Sophie had slept obliviously through most of it. She had been momentarily disconnected from the insanities of the world. "You know, I totally missed that."

She soaked the story in like a sponge as George backed up the Land Rover, then coasted easily down the broad asphalt road to the bottom of the hill. As they passed the gate, she rested the magazine on her knees, let out a deep breath. "This is insane," she muttered. She had no idea how to process the dramatic events.

She barely heard George mutter into his three-day stubble, wondering who this Andy was.

✳

Black clouds had gathered over the mountains and advanced down to the coast, darkening the sky with their rapid arrival. As George pulled off the four-lane street to the mini market and parked the Land Rover on a reserved spot, the first heavy drops of rain started to fall.

They rushed past the store to the building entrance and up the stairs. They were practically propelled into the studio by a powerful clap of thunder.

Perhaps it was Zeus, Sophie thought, wanting to make it known that he, and he alone, was father to Aphrodite—just as Homer had said—and that nobody should forget it.

"This is Marios," George said, motioning at the figure who was frantically closing windows and adjusting blinds. The rain was coming down in torrents now, sweeping dust and debris from the square below.

The thunder continued to roll. Marios, having completed his hurried task, dried his hands on his floral shorts. He looked up, surprised. "I just got in myself. Where did you come from?"

George gallantly introduced Sophie. Marios stood barefoot on the hardwood floor, looking a bit bashful. He combed his hand through his unkempt hair, shifting his weight back and forth. "Would you like some coffee or tea, maybe?"

They all went to the small kitchen to make coffee. Marios conjured a few chocolate biscuits on a plate, immediately taking the first one himself. Chewing hungrily, he leaned over to the desk. "There's mail for you, George. There. The light brown envelope."

"Did you look to see what it was?"

He shook his head disapprovingly.

"Someone called from the base. It seems to be urgent."

George took a sip of coffee, walked over to the desk. He ripped the envelope open with his thumb, took out the contents.

"This weather doesn't seem safe to fly in," Marios noted meanwhile in the kitchen. "Weren't you planning on flying out of here today?"

The casual question reminded Sophie uncomfortably of her dilemma. She shrugged circumspectly. "We'll see. You take great pictures!" She walked along the wall, balancing her cup of espresso. "I see mainly portraits."

"There are more in the gallery. I can show you." He began to lead the way, motioning for her to follow him, but did not get far.

"Marios, you have to take a look at this!" George called out over the weather. The thunder was now no longer quite as imminent, the storm moving further away. "Do you remember these shots?"

Marios briefly glanced over George's shoulder. "Of course, the guy on the yacht. The one with the ring."

"Exactly. And do you know what?"

"I have a feeling you're about to tell me."

Sophie stared, entranced, at the beautiful, serene eyes looking back at her from the image on the wall. *Eyes* was the name of an exhibition of Marios's work that the poster was advertising. George lowered his voice. "The Brits sent the pictures to the Federal Office of Criminal Investigation in Bern. They helped to expose a murderer. They are congratulating you—me too, of course. Look, this ring, they say it belonged to the victim. It was cut from his hand along with the finger he wore it on. Strange…"

"What's strange?"

George raised his voice. "The name of the victim—Suvorov! Wasn't there a famous Russian general…"

A sharp voice caused the men to turn abruptly.

"Did you just say Suvorov? And something about murder?"

Sophie stood before them, tense, pale, practically shaking. The world seemed to focus on the sheer force of her intensity. George involuntarily took a step back. She snatched the photographs from his hand, stared at them as if looking at her own corpse. "Ponter! That's John Ponter!"

She sank into the nearest chair, her legs splayed before her. Her arms hung limply at her sides. It had stopped raining.

"I saw that ring on the old Suvorov's finger with my own eyes. That's the one. There's no doubt!" She held up the image of Ponter's enlarged hand showing the object in question.

It was the men's turn to look confused. Marios grimaced. George forced himself to regain composure. "Alright. You need to tell us everything from the start, Sophie. You know Ponter?"

"You can say that again. I worked for him. He's the cause of the whole odyssey that led me all the way to fucking Armenia, and then here, to Cyprus."

Thank God for that, George wanted to say. *In that case, if it hadn't been for him I would never have crossed paths with this incredible woman!*

Sophie had pulled herself up in her seat, was now looking back and forth between the pictures and the men's eyes, gathering her thoughts.

How was this possible? How on earth had Cyprus come into this? She finally asked a question of obvious interest. "Where did you take these?"

"On the Russian's yacht," George informed her, openly. "Oleg Nedjew. The Crane. I told you about him."

It made sense. Nedjew was one of Ponter's best customers. It was entirely unsurprising that he would invite the banker to visit him on his yacht. Even the tabloids had reported on that. "Do you know if the police in Switzerland have done anything?"

George fetched the letter from the table and scanned it. "It says John Ponter, also known as Dragan Nikolic—did you know that about him?" She shook her head. "That there is an international manhunt on for him."

Marios had discreetly withdrawn to the bedroom in the back, where he had turned the radio up and was noisily bustling about. George motioned his head in the direction the sounds were coming from. "We should talk about this in private."

Sophie jumped up. "Yes. Not here, George. Do you feel like going for a walk?"

George went to the window and peered out between the blinds. "It's getting lighter again. Let's go." He reached for his car keys and cell phone. "Marios! We'll be out for an hour or so. Hold down the fort. You can reach me on my cell."

Marios waved consent through the open door as a pompous voice reported on the radio that the USA and Iran would just have to see past the hostile aspects of their relationship and focus on the geopolitical issues. The question was not whether the world wanted to deal with Iran, but rather with *which* Iran…

Captive

There was only one correctional facility within the Republic of Cyprus—in Nicosia—where condemned and accused women, men, all people of all ages over sixteen, were sent.

The special task force that had retrieved Lenka Borsk from the plane had initially followed standard procedure and booked her into a single cell at the airport detention center, which was primarily conceived to manage illegal immigrants. The mysterious prisoner had shown herself to be exceptionally intractable from the start.

The officers had had their hands full with the stroppy woman. She resisted having her prints taken, pushed the food she was given away untouched, had to be forcibly held by fistfuls of hair in order to allow her picture to be taken. When she was brought to face investigating officers in the interrogation room in cuffs she was apathetic, as if she had suffered some terrible trauma and was incapable of communicating. She refused to utter a single word. The custodial judge—not unaccustomed to dealing with hardened criminals—was moved neither to sympathy nor patience. He rid himself of the nameless woman by remanding her to the central jail's high security block. May she rot there. The mug shots, front and profile, were sent to central headquarters, again, according to standard procedure. From there they would eventually make their way through the channels of the police information system, such as it was, and finally to Interpol.

The A2, which later merged with the A1, led from Larnaca Airport inland to Nicosia. The green Bedford van may have been a little the worse for wear but was making good time.

Lenka Borsk sat apathetically on a hard bench in the back facing a robust, broad-shouldered female officer whose hands were playing with a club in her lap. Next to her, a likewise broad-shouldered and generally muscle-bound man wearing a tight black T-shirt and blue jeans smoked a cigarette and listened to music on his ear buds. His face was expressionless beneath his closely shaven, thick-looking skull.

The corpulent sergeant leading the transport had taken the passenger seat up front. This latest prisoner was not particularly noteworthy as far as he was concerned. The thin file on the seat next to him contained nothing of great interest. She was a case for the mental ward, is what he had heard. The drive into town, on the other hand, was a welcome diversion in and of itself. According to the schedule, it would allow him to enjoy a dinner at Lukas' place. Following his retirement, the deputy commander had made a second calling of his passion for the culinary arts and had created a popular gathering spot for his former colleagues.

The partition to the back opened with a squeak. A pair of thick lips nearly filled the small rectangular window.

"The lady has to use the facilities. Where are we?"

When the boss uttered a few curses in protest, the lips added: "They didn't let her go at the detention center before we left."

The boss ducked down in order to be able to see her eyes. "God damn it, Alexia. Fine. Pera Chorio is coming up. But you had better make sure that she doesn't harm herself."

The driver slowed as they approached Exit 8. After a few hundred meters he turned toward the rest stop, which was situated—as all rest stops and gas stations are in Cyprus—off the freeway. And so the Bedford took the rural B1 to the nearest roadhouse.

The prisoner transport came to a crunching halt on the gravel in front of the low building. A sign showed the way to the toilets in the rear, where a thin wall separated the entrances for men and women.

Alexis directed her charge to the ladies toilet, waving and poking her with the club to make herself clear. A mother and her young daughter were washing their hands at a sink in the brightly lit restroom, but quickly started gathering their belongings when they saw the strange couple arrive—the disheveled figure with a disturbingly shifty expression in handcuffs, the woman in a police uniform waving a club.

"Okay," said Alexia, once they were alone and her prisoner held her wrists out. Borsk motioned with her now freed hand to her open mouth, stepped to the sink. Alexia watched as she bent down to the running water and started slurping.

It was one of the last things that the police officer would see clearly in her relatively short life.

Armenus Technopark

The dairy farm had two long stall buildings that met in an L shape. Behind them stood a two-story house with a fiber cement roof. A little off to the side an ochre-colored dwelling stood surrounded by lush, green lawn. Near-by a large shed housed tractors, forklifts, mowers, and other bulky—mostly red—equipment. The two Super Pumas were parked in front of the wide open doors, shielded from curious eyes by the dwelling. The Swiss expat farmer and his Armenian wife had prepared a hearty brunch consisting of eggs, bacon, hash brown potatoes and coffee for Natadschjan's men.

The kitchen window afforded a view of the stalls and the black and white Holstein cows herded by two young men wearing blue vests.

Jack Abramian cut a piece of cheese, popped it into his mouth. "Delicious. How many head do you have there?"

"A hundred milk cows, about thirty calves."

"Two were born just last night," the farmer's wife added proudly.

"Ah, a good day for the herd! Congratulations," Jack said, beaming. "And thank you for accommodating the men."

The farmer made a magnanimous gesture. "There was a lot going on last night down in the Park. We saw it on the news."

Andy, bundled up in a bulky army jacket, knocked discreetly on the open door.

"That's why I need the squad out there." Jack stood. "Thank you, again, for your hospitality." He shook the farmer's hand. "I must go now."

Following Andy out he heard the farmer ask, "Do you really have nuclear weapons down there?"

Not bothering to turn, Jack responded in a gruff, monotone voice. "Look after your business, I'll look after mine!"

In the shed, the men cowered over a model that they had fashioned using sand, wood and bricks. Sara leaned over a number of aerial images of the Gulag that were spread on a long table, comparing them to what the men had created.

"There's nothing like playing in a good old sandbox," Natadschjan said as the two entered. He motioned toward another group further back. "They are trying to recreate a model of the interiors." One of his men leaned across the table with Sara, checking the construction drawings of the compound, Jack understood as he addressed the rooms of the entrance area. He stepped closer.

"These are the Russians' power distribution and communication centers." He tapped his finger on the map, motioned for the commander to join him off to one side. "Come, Safar. Let's go through this one more time."

They stepped over to Cosmo's black Grand Cherokee. When Jack looked around to find Andy, he saw him walking into the ochre house—with Sara by side.

Escape

Lenka Borsk drank the water, every fiber of her body tensed, searching for a good center. Her body assumed the position of a tiger prepared to pounce.

Alexia's eyes took in the wiry woman's waist, grazed, somewhat enviously, her firm behind and strong legs. Her assessment gave her the fleeting, ominous sense that she may have underestimated this woman...her hand grasped the club more firmly. She mentally located her pistol, the grip, the lever she would have to push to release it from its holster.

Borsk spins around so suddenly that the police officer, much as she may have sensed the danger in this situation, has no chance to respond. The side of Borsk's hand hits her neck with iron strength. She sways, stunned. Borsk grabs her by the hair, spins her, drives her knee into the officer's back. From behind, she grabs onto the Alexia's chin with both hands, yanks her head back with lethal force. The cracking of the spine as her neck snaps is the only sound that is made—the lethal attack has taken mere seconds.

Borsk drags the lifeless body into a stall, locks it from inside. She releases the holster, takes off the uniform jacket...seconds later she is outside, propelled by an ongoing, enormous rush of adrenaline. Moving smoothly, and with great precision, she makes her way to the parking lot next to the restaurant, keeping an eye on the Bedford over on the other side.

The mother and girl come out of the shop carrying a few bags. They walk, chatting, toward the white BMW. Its lights flash as the woman unlocks it with her remote.

Borsk waits for them to get in, steps up to the driver's-side door and knocks on the window. "Police. Exit the vehicle!"

The woman gets out, a worried look on her pale face; eyes taking in the barrel of the pistol that is pointing at her, the uniform, the face...*that face*!

"Get in the back. Not a sound or I shoot. Your little brat will be first."

The uniformed woman abruptly jerks her weapon toward the little girl in the passenger seat. Her mother barely stifles a horrified scream. "Well then...you get the picture." Borsk gets behind the wheel, drives slowly from the parking lot and onto the street that will lead to the freeway onramp in a few hundred meters. In the rearview mirror she sees the doors to the Bedford open. The men get out and start jogging toward the toilets.

"Your cell phone!" Borsk commands as she merges onto the A1 toward Limassol. A shaking hand extends it to her. "Please, please..." the voice stammers from the back.

"Shut up! If you talk, now or later, I will come back for you and I will finish you. And I mean kill you!" She aims the pistol at the roof of the car and fires. The girl is stunned into a terrified silence. The mother shrieks in fright, then just sobs quietly.

Limassol

"So all of this for a painting?" George stopped, his face pensive.

"Not just any painting. This Rothko is worth a fortune."

They had driven down to Armonia Beach in the Land Rover. From there, they had walked along the beach path, avoiding puddles and rivulets as Sophie told her story beginning with her job for John Ponter, Manfred Kleiber's data theft; she left nothing out—not the dramatic adventure on Julier Pass, her affection for Uli Stark and his tragic demise, her close relationship to Shuky Nachman. She recounted in detail the trip to Yerevan, her encounter with Andy, who had helped her get to the plane.

"And this Lenka Martialis, as you call her, you had never come across her before?"

Sophie shook her head.

"I am certain that Ponter sent her to get me. She wanted to abduct me to Belgrade. Me and the Rothko, that is."

George thought of that call from the air base. Perhaps the Brits had managed to find out more about the kidnapper by now.

"Come. Let's go back." He looked up at the black clouds that had once again gathered. "Quickly, it's starting to rain again."

"I really don't care that much about Ponter," Sophie said as they passed by the Four Seasons parking lot. "But I do have a score to settle with Nedjew. Do you think he'll show up here?"

"You mean because of his plane?" George shrugged doubtfully. "The local police are done securing evidence, you know. They have released the plane. You could fly if you need to."

She stopped abruptly. Drops of rain ran down her astonished face, making it look as though she were crying. "You want to get rid of me? You want me to go back?"

"I'm just saying. Come on." He started running. The rain was coming down harder, and the thunder was once again starting to roll. Having reached his building he stopped, winked at her, kissed her quickly on her half-open mouth, then pounded up the stairs to the door.

Up in the penthouse, Sophie pulled her beau toward the bedroom by his belt. "Come with me. I want to show you something."

What man would not have followed such an invitation with a sense of hope and mounting excitement? She stood before the large bed.

"There. That's the Rothko!" The aluminum case stood open in the corner of the room, revealing the painting and its wondrous composition of color. "It really comes alive when you look at it, don't you think?"

"Henri Matisse was his role model," George said knowledgeably, noting the astonished look on her face. "Yes. He was an abstract expressionist. He is known for his abstract blocks of color. I somehow feel..."

She blinked her eyes up at him, sweet innocence personified. "You feel what? You secret art aficionado."

"That this Rothko is my competition all of a sudden. Here he is, right next to your bed, enjoying the best possible views of the woman I want…"

Laughing, she pulled him by the belt again. This time toward the bed. She sat down, while he remained standing before her in a wide stance. Much to his disappointment, she evaded this suggestive position by playfully rolling off to the side and nimbly jumping back to her feet.

"We should cover this voyeur up. No spectators allowed. Come—help me."

They closed the container. Sophie lifted it up by its straps and carried it out. George followed, but not without casting a disappointed, longing look at the bed as he went. In the office, Sophie propped the container against the wall next to the bookshelf, noted a few volumes with interest.

"Careful now," he warned in a teasing tone, "there's a secret lever right behind Balzac."

"A secret lever for what?"

"A fold-down guest bed." His pager buzzed. Sophie turned away from Balzac, saw George's furrowed brow. "I have to make a call." He leaned over the phone on the desk.

It had been the Air Base paging in regards to the special flight that had landed at Akrotiri airfield a few hours ago.

"Damn it," George grumbled. "I have to go down to the base. I'll be back soon." He looked grim as he left. From the hall he called out that she should put the Champagne on ice so that it would be ready for them when he returned.

Running toward the Land Rover, he failed to notice the slender figure that was standing in the shadows of the entrance to the apartment block across the road…

As George drove along the fence toward the Air Base entrance he noticed a sleek aircraft with a pointy nose—a Gulfstream G250—standing in front of the barracks. It seemed light, almost ethereal. There was no identifying insignia to be seen on its tail fin above the two rear engines, or else it was not plainly visible on the dark gray paint job that lent the machine a military look.

"We have a problem," Major Hanbury, the intelligence officer, said by way of a greeting. He sported a gray brush-cut that framed a round, weathered-looking face. His uniform jacket struggled to contain his corpulent midriff. Hanbury rested his pipe on the ashtray, stepped from behind his desk. He motioned his head stiffly toward the adjacent room.

"American Secret Service, a certain Agent Garp, pretty full of himself. Just arrived in the fancy bird outside, along with two pilots and a civilian who immediately left in a taxi. Ponter was his name."

George started back. "What? Ponter? John Ponter, the banker?"

"That's the one. Agent Garp wants to quarantine him until some issues have been clarified."

"And what issues would those be? Why Cyprus, of all places?"

"Feel free to guess. The guy isn't giving anything away—silent as the grave. It's some top-secret American operation." He grinned almost mischievously. "You might want to try YouTube. You'll have a better chance of getting lucky finding information there."

"What's this quarantine nonsense?"

"Good question, George. Apparently Ponter is to be interrogated on some ship. And this Ponter guy, hang on…" He went back to his desk, daintily fished a piece of paper from under a pile of files. "Ponter is also a police matter. There's an international warrant out for his arrest. What do we do in a case like this?"

According to a bilateral agreement, the British routinely exchanged intelligence with the police.

"Surely the CIA can't just ignore the warrant."

"Are you really certain that this Garp is CIA?" George asked.

The Major gently patted the door to the adjacent room. "Nope. But you're free to ask him yourself. Are you ready?"

Garp stood at the window gazing out at the G250. When he turned, George found himself looking at a chiseled face with almond-shaped eyes. He estimated the man, who now walked toward him, hand outstretched, to be in his late thirties. In typical Yankee fashion, he greeted him with almost uncomfortable joviality and got straight to business. "I asked to speak to the commanding officer, George. Are you his aide?" As he spoke, the impeccably dressed American appeared to be eyeing George's get-up with mild amusement. "I am here on an urgent mission. I do not want to be kept waiting!"

George remained unfazed. "Are you Californian?"

"Yeah. Good guess, man. Now, can we get on with this show?"

George gave him a meaningful wink and motioned for Garp to follow. Together they exited through the major's office, out onto the wet tarmac. To the west the clouds had broken, revealing glimpses of a stunningly pink sky behind the forbidding gray. They walked over to the plane. Major Hanbury stood at his office window and carefully stuffed his pipe. He watched as the men paced and gestured. He puffed, holding a lit match above the bowl, waved at the smoke with his hand. Outside, the two men stopped and faced each other. One threw up his hands, and then they commenced their pacing—round and round the G250, as if it was the object of their heated negotiations. About twenty minutes later, George was back.

And? the major's features asked, brows raised high on his forehead. George cleared his throat. "Ponter is at the Four Seasons. Garp insists that this is necessary. Although it could be argued that putting him up in such luxury is a good example of pearls before swine. He insists that we treat the matter with the utmost secrecy.

"Police authorities are not to be notified. He intends to give us further details tomorrow."

"Fine. I guess I can live with that," the major grumbled.

"To be honest, I don't trust this whole setup. Garp...Do we have any intel on this guy?"

"He's CIA alright," Hanbury said, nodding. *"Appellation d'origine contrôlée,"* he added jokingly, with a bad French accent. He lowered his voice as Garp came back in, wanting to inquire about getting into town.

"Before I forget, George, these are the data I just received on the woman who tried to hijack the Russian's plane." Hanbury handed him an envelope. "A real she-devil of a woman. You wouldn't believe the crimes she has committed."

George was wide awake. "Really? Tell me about her."

"She escaped this afternoon. Those dumb-ass cops..."

He stopped as George jumped up and tore out of the office, swearing under his breath. Outside, he ran across the strip and to his Land Rover at a breakneck pace.

Lenka Borsk saw the well-built man with a full head of blond hair hurry out of the building. She felt the urge to leave the protective apartment entrance as soon as she saw him get behind the wheel of the Land Rover, but she forced herself to remain patient. She had to be sure that Kramer was actually in the apartment upstairs before she went off half-cocked.

Good fortune had not abandoned her. In fact it had smiled broadly upon her just a short while ago. Having been momentarily undecided on what her next move should be, she had taken a seat on a vacant beach recliner and bided her time. She had heard the name Four Seasons mentioned during the interrogations and assumed that Sophie Kramer would be staying there. A bamboo umbrella provided her passable protection from the rain. She was able to keep a sharp eye on the outside of the hotel with its four stories.

She had tossed the stolen cell phone into the back of a truck that was stopped at a red light and about to turn onto the freeway. There was enough change in the woman's purse to use a pay phone. She decided that she would start by asking for Kramer at the hotel reception. If this did not prove successful, she would call the neighboring hotels. Eventually she had stood, pulled up the collar of the windbreaker that she had purchased in a cheap shop. That is when she had seen a couple approaching at a jog. It had been as if a bolt of lightning had surged through her veins—Sophie Kramer! Carefully, she had ducked back beneath the umbrella until they passed, then taken up pursuit. This was how she had arrived at the entrance where she now stood.

She heard the sound of a police siren that swelled, then receded into the distance. She needed to hurry. Borsk had changed her appearance as well as she had been able to. She had purchased a blonde wig in a discount variety store. The sales assistant had feigned admiration for how well it suited her. But she didn't harbor any illusions about the sophistication of her disguise.

A throwing knife had caught her eye toward the rear of the crammed shop. "Made in Brazil," the sales assistant had informed her. The steel blade and handle measured about thirty centimeters. It had a good feel in her hand. Better to have and not want…she thought to herself with a wry smile and paid with the Euros from the purse she had taken from the woman with the little girl. Next, the blonde woman wearing a new outfit had crossed the walkway to the other side of the street. She had strolled into the Telecom shop and purchased a pre-paid cell phone on sale. She pocketed the remainder of the cash and tossed the purse into a garbage can.

Still in the half-dark of the apartment entranceway, she dialed the emergency number that she had only ever used one other time—when she had texted her boss to signal her success in capturing Sophie and Mark. Somewhat prematurely, as she had been forced to recognize, much to her chagrin. But this time she was calling in a critical situation. She hoped that Ponter, wherever he was on this earth, had his phone turned on. The repeated, unanswered buzzing on the other end was getting on her nerves.

There was a sudden crackling in the line, a short "Hello"—then nothing. The connection was lost. She hit redial and was rewarded with a busy signal. Should she send an urgent text? She was in the process of entering a message when the phone began to vibrate.

"Hello," she said hesitantly. "Who is this?"

"Where the hell are you?" the familiar voice thundered. She explained. The line was silent for several seconds.

"Hello? Are you still there?"

"I am close to where you are. Come to the Four Seasons Hotel."

"I can't. I am about to complete my mission. I need a vehicle."

Ponter wanted details. As soon as he had grasped the situation, he had a plan. Luck had caught up with him again. Borsk had turned up at exactly the right moment. It was ingenious—he would be able to deal with two issues all at once!

A short while later Borsk rang the bell that she supposed belonged to the penthouse apartment. No answer. She rang again, her lips half forming the words she wanted to say when someone answered the intercom. Nothing. Was Kramer sleeping? Was there some other exit? Borsk crept around the building, tried to see if she could get a view of the terrace. As she was about to return to her starting point, she saw a large, blue and white dinghy next to a garage entrance. She flitted past the trailer and down the ramp, disappearing into the dark entrance. She found the door behind some bicycles. It opened easily when she tried the handle. She was in the stairwell.

George felt guilty for having left Sophie alone. He floored the gas pedal, only to immediately hit the brakes. A construction truck was taking all the time in the world to back out onto the street. George leaned on his horn, which earned him a few shaking heads and the attention of two traffic cops who were parked across the road in front of the pizzeria.

He waited with mounting annoyance, then proceeded in a patient manner until he was out of the traffic cops' line of sight. Why had he not inquired about the hijacker after she had been booked?

He slid around on his seat, rocked impatiently. It didn't really make him feel any better. Traffic remained a tedious stop-and-go. He pounded his fists against the steering wheel in frustration. It was infuriating! The driver in front of him dawdled along at a snail's pace until the light turned yellow, then stopped obediently. He was hit by a flash of foreboding. He hadn't locked the door in his rush to leave...

Sophie Kramer stood under the shower, raised her face to the warm water, ran her fingers through her hair, rubbed her scalp vigorously. She felt a rush of well-being. Everything finally seemed to be working out fine. She was sure that she would be able to get through the next and hopefully last stage of this ordeal with George by her side. The man radiated such confidence and love of life. He was down to earth and reliable despite the pleasant, easy way he had about him. She rinsed off the soap and shampoo, fished the towel from its rack and stepped in front of the mirror. She eyed herself critically from her head to her firm thighs, rubbed herself down energetically, donned the white bathrobe and started looking for the hairdryer. There was a sound in the hallway.

"George? Are you back already?"

Perhaps she should see to the Champagne. She towel-dried her hair, stepped into the slippers and walked out of the bathroom. She caught her breath. The woman was standing about an arm's length from her.

"Hello!" she hissed. An evil grin, a taunting snicker, a bare blade in her hand. "And so we meet again."

Sophie froze. Taking advantage of her shock, Borsk deftly flicked the robe open with the tip of her blade, then rested the edge of the knife on Sophie's stomach, just below the navel.

"Well, well, well. Would you look at that! Naked and ready for action... Has he fucked you yet, your little friend? Does he even have anything in his pants?"

She pokes at her, piercing the skin, and blood starts to trickle down. Sophie backs away with a suppressed moan.

"What do you want?"

"What do you think I want, sweetheart? Have you already forgotten how you kicked me in the cunt? Because I haven't." She casually slices at her again, this time right above her still wet bush of pubic hair. "Maybe I should make your pussy a little bigger." She jumps back, slashing the air in front of Sophie's face. "But first I want the painting. Take me to it— move!" With lightning speed she slices the blade in one smooth, precise motion thinly across the skin of Sophie's neck. Drops of blood start to form along the long scratch. "Your tits are next! Get moving—where is the fucking thing?"

Sophie slowly backs into the bedroom, to where her clothes are, covering her wounds with the robe. She takes the T-shirt from the bed, puts it on, slips into a pair of shorts. She points toward the office. "There. It's... in the room next door."

The container is resting against the smooth wood veneer of the wall next to the bookshelf. Sophie steps aside.

"Open it!"

She does as she is told. Once the painting is revealed Borsk motions her aside by jabbing the knife menacingly through the air. "No funny business now, little girl."

She kneels down, cuts the protective plastic. Sophie's hand moves down the shelf behind her back. *There is a lever behind the Balzac.* The woman starts to cut the painting from its frame, never taking her eyes off Sophie.

"Get your hands where I can see them! Now!"

Sophie finds the lever, obediently jerks her arms up over her head. At the same time a spring releases with a loud click. A part of the wall is released and falls forward, the bed frame unfolds, comes crashing down. Borsk dives to the side before it hits the ground, burying a mess of painting, wrapping material and container beneath it.

Sophie is ready. It has been some time since she last practiced her martial art—Krav Maga, the self-defense technique practiced by the Israeli army. But she feels her muscles move with ease and precision. Her powerful kick, delivered with an outstretched leg, hits the knife-wielding woman in the throat. She falls back with a gurgling sound, then screams angrily.

Sophie senses a mounting rage. She kicks again, a kidney this time, positions herself for the decisive blow when she is hit hard in the back. She stumbles, falls face first into the bookshelf, pulls herself up painfully, preparing to ward off the next attack.

John Ponter is standing in front of her, holding a car jack in both fists, his face beet-colored, at a loss for words.

Lenka Borsk rises slowly, menacingly drawing back the hand holding the knife. Her flushed, angry face says it all. *You have embarrassed me. Nobody makes a fool of me. Now I will finish you.* She hauls off.

"Stop!" Ponter bellows, jumps between the two holding up the car jack to stop the blow. "Nobody move!" For a second they all stand as if transformed to stone. Ponter eyes the two opponents sharply, raises his head commandingly. "The painting. Move! Get it." Borsk kneels obediently. He follows his order with a hissed "Bitch." He spins around, grinning, scoffs: "Well look what we have here. The corpse from Julier Pass has come to life! But look at you, all covered in blood, Sophie. Go to the bathroom and get yourself cleaned up. We're out of here in two minutes!" He swings his jack through the air like a caveman swinging a club.

Sophie opens the bathroom cabinet, rummages through a box of cotton swabs, compresses, creams. She rinses the blood off, sprays her wounds with disinfectant, sticks a few adhesive bandages across the cut on her neck, sneaks to the door. Where was Ponter? She listens carefully, hears a few unclear snatches of conversation. "Bring her to the harbor...yacht..." is all she manages to make out. She goes back to the sink, takes the bar of soap, uses it to write on the mirror. She rushes to the bedroom, past Ponter, who follows her and watches appreciatively as she slips on a pair of jeans and a jacket.

"Very good, Sophie. You be sure to behave yourself." She wanted to scratch his eyes out.

Just seconds later the strange trio left the apartment. An outside observer might have experienced a mixture of admiration and envy seeing the well-dressed gentleman accompanied by two young ladies. The same observer probably would not have paid much attention to the heavy object that the man was holding, nor to the fact that one woman was oddly close on the other woman's heels. In the end, the general demeanor of the group may have been the thing to give him pause—no smiles, no conversational gesturing. The woman with the dark blonde hair looked particularly downcast, as if she were heading to a funeral. But the only observer was a sleek grayhound, which turned on a dime at his master's distant whistling and took elegant flight to heed his call.

The car into which they jostled Sophie was a bronze Japanese make with a red car-rental license plate. Ponter got behind the wheel, while Borsk sat in the back with a sadistic grin on her half-averted face. She kept her weapon directed at Sophie, more than ready to inflict permanent damage on her pretty prey should the slightest opportunity arise. Ponter gave a jarring start und pulled onto the coastal road.

Air Force Base Near Tehran

Air Force General Hassan Nassiri banged his fist down on the desk, the veins on his forehead and temples bulging. His loyal chief of staff of many years had rarely seen him this enraged.

"And those sons-of-bitches just let it happen. What does that make us? The laughingstock of the entire world…I can't fathom it. Some gang of criminals comes along and snatches our atomic missiles from us on our own turf. Who are these people?"

For a brief moment he was tempted to acknowledge what was almost a hint of admiration for the incredibly daring commando mission that had been pulled off in Tabriz. It was an unthinkable indignity that he could under no circumstances tolerate. His head was on the chopping block. As the highest commanding officer of the air force, he would be the one to bear the final and full responsibility for this incomparable humiliation. His chief of staff gingerly pushed the multi-page report across the desk.

"They had the element of surprise going for them, Hassan…And the Hercules was transmitting our own identifying code, it…"

Nassiri swiped the papers from the desk with a violent motion. "Screw all of that. Call the lieutenant colonel in here at once. We're getting those damned things back." He stood, stepped in front of the projected map of southern Armenia. A slender officer wearing combat gear and paratrooper boots entered briskly, stopped and saluted, eyes bright.

Nassiri got straight to the point. "The target is this industrial park in southern Armenia." He indicated the area that had been zoomed in on with a laser pointer. "What are you equipped with, Lieutenant Colonel?"

"MI-8 helicopters, General. Armed as customary."

"Number?"

"Thirty-six men, special forces."

"Good, Lieutenant Colonel. My staff will apprise you of the situation." Nassiri cast a hawkish glance at his watch. "I expect your plan of attack to be on my desk in precisely one hour."

The lieutenant colonel gathered the papers from the floor and waved the Special Forces officer to the map table while Nassiri stomped back into his office and hit the intercom button. "Sergeant? Bring me the brigadier general."

Brigadier General Bakhtiar had negotiated for the Sunburn missiles with the Russians at Armenus Technopark. He had picked up the test missile and would be able to relay information about the location to the commander of the Special Forces. It was crucial that the preparations be as thorough as possible.

Meanwhile, Intelligence had not been idle. The threat assessment describing the resistance to be expected was on his desk. They had not discovered any on-site combat troops. The nearest possible allied Armenian army resources lay far to the north. There was a fire department and approximately two dozen armed security guards. Security included the surveillance of the massive compound by means of sensors and cameras. The southern border was protected from possible infiltration by means of a sophisticated system of cameras and intermittent patrols, supplemented by drones as needed. Nassiri anticipated that security would have been heightened following the successful return of the Hercules commando.

He sank into his office chair, opened the drawer and retrieved a carton of Marlboros. He smacked it open against the edge of the desk, opened a pack, lit up a cigarette and inhaled deeply. He needed the nicotine right now. The landline buzzed. General Nassiri picked up the gray receiver and listened. The communication was short and one-sided. He answered several affirmatives and hung up. The chief of staff stood in the doorway, fixing the general as he sat, slack-jawed, cigarette dangling from the corner of his mouth. He raised his hollow eyes. "I have been ordered to report to Tehran," Nassiri said.

"When?"

"First thing tomorrow."

"That determines our timeline," the chief of staff concluded. His statement was met with a silent nod.

Southern Armenia

As events were unfolding precipitously at Armenus Technopark in southern Armenia, a helicopter touched down practically unnoticed in one of the more remote areas beyond the terminals.

Its two professional pilots landed the large, modern aircraft on the flat roof of the Russian complex.

Nico Strom was standing on the wing of the Hercules, overseeing engine maintenance. He noted the cheerful, almost elated mood of his crew only peripherally. He was concerned with the security not only of his people, but also of the deadly cargo that they had just brought home with them. He had assessed the missiles that they had plundered from the Iranians on the flight back. They were impressive: almost elegant in their sleek design, armed with nuclear warheads. The thought sent shivers down his spine. Sunburns were the Russian-made surface to air missiles that the Americans feared the most. It was said that U.S. aircraft carrier fleets would be powerless against them.

The thought of what could have happened had they crashed or been shot at by hostile fire defied imagination. Well, at least the things were safely not just on but under the ground now. But that was no reason to get overly comfortable. Nico sensed that there was something in the air. When he identified a Sikorsky helicopter coming down, he raised his binoculars for a better look.

What was Abramian thinking? What would happen with these highly sought-after weapons of mass destruction, now that he had them? There was no doubt that the Americans would love to get their paws on them. The Israelis would want to know if Iran had access to any more of them. The Russian reaction would be interesting, to say the least—after all, the revelation of these weapons opened them up to the accusation of having engaged in a covert arms deal with Iran.

A tall, haggard figure hastened to the helicopter, bending forward to brace against the rotor wind—men pushed several rectangular boxes into the hold. Nico's view was partially blocked. When the helicopter took off again, the man was nowhere to be seen. He had obviously remained on board. *A quick, stealthy pick-up,* Nico concluded. *Who was this guy?*

The question served to remind him that he had neglected his contacts over the past several days. Unsurprising, given all that had happened, but maybe it was time to make a few calls. Nico continued to follow the departing Sikorsky with his binoculars. It had a G-identifier. England. Not that this revealed anything about the identity of the lean man. Neither the crew nor its passengers were necessarily linked to Great Britain. Still, Nico noted the letters as a matter of course, typing them into his electronic notebook. He sat down on the wing and consulted his address book.

"Nico! Jack wants us at headquarters." It was Cliff Matoyan's bushy head of hair that appeared beneath the wing. Wearing a broad grin he tapped his watch, raised both hands with outstretched fingers to show the hour.

"Okay, Cliff. Hang on." Strom slid across the wing, let his legs dangle, then jumped down, landing lithely.

"We should be on the lookout, Cliff."

Matoyan looked up at the sky. "You're not talking about the weather, I take it." Together they made their way to the hangar, where the Range Rover was parked next to the gate. Nico scrolled through the addresses on his iPhone with his finger, occasionally looking over at his buddy. "Is someone monitoring the airspace over the border? I wouldn't put a damn thing past the Iranians!"

"They are well and truly occupied with their own internal mess right now, Nico. There is a revolution going on. Did you ever imagine that things would go down like this?"

"Don't get too happy too soon. Their military is all about their pride and prestige. We just humiliated them down to the bone. That's dangerous."

Matoyan was silent as he took a seat behind the wheel of the 4x4. He started to roll before Nico, lost in his gadget, had gotten all the way in.

"Cooper. Good old Cooper!" he called out, holding on to the grab handle.

Matoyan turned his head. "Cooper? Gary Cooper?"

Strom chuckled as he dialed. "No. *Ken* Cooper. The man is a secret service legend—CIA, FBI, Homeland Security, even. He always seems to pop up in the hot spots, wherever something needs to be taken care of." He held the phone to his ear. "Damn it!"

"What?"

"Stupid recording. *Your party is unavailable, please call again later.*"

"Maybe he's getting his groove on somewhere," Matoyan quipped with a grin.

"Could be. I've known Ken for almost twenty years. We exchange season's greetings, sometimes he shares a bit of intelligence with me. Classified aeronautical stuff." Strom hit send, dispatching the text into cyberspace. "My old mate will call me back, trust me."

"I'm sure you have your own stories to tell about some of those... what did you call them? *Hot spots*."

Matoyan zipped around the bend and on to the forecourt of the ComCenter, stopping in front of the entrance.

As they got out the pale sun was shining across vast fields. The roofs of farm houses shimmered here and there. A peaceful stillness lay across the land. Haze suggested the town in the distance.

They took their sunglasses off in the shaded control room, stared at the quote on the screen. NO ARMY CAN STOP AN IDEA WHOSE TIME HAS COME. *VICTOR HUGO*

"What would your reaction be, gentlemen? That is my question. Put yourself in the shoes of the Russians, in the shoes of the Revolutionary Guard."

They were a small, select group, Strom noted as he took a seat between Matoyan and two other pilots. The men were silent. They looked intently at the words, then back at Cosmo, who motioned encouragingly for them to express themselves.

"Do nothing, lay low, deny everything," Matoyan ventured. One of the pilots countered: "I would get the goods back. Either by military or by diplomatic means—by exerting pressure on Armenia."

"That's if they even know where the missiles are," another considered.

"The news spread like wildfire," Cosmo interjected. "People in Tabriz were using our phones like crazy. There's no way any of this can be hidden or denied—especially after the news crews showed up here. Fortunately they've taken off again."

"The Russian has been duped, Mossad is lurking in the wings, Iran is ready to engage in desperate measures—the ultimate nightmare scenario, as far as I'm concerned," Strom said. "Anything could happen at any time. Do we have any news on the air space? Is anything going on? Why did you call for us, Jack?"

His cell phone vibrated. Strom stood. "Ken! You old buzzard! Hang on a second…"

He rushed outside the room. The others saw him speaking with great animation, a broad grin on his face, before he turned and strode to the window.

"You should see the setup down here, Ken. It's insane. Jack Abramian—you know, Cosmo? He's behind it all. He has greater clout than the president. Have you ever been to Armenia? Where are you at right now? Aha—so you like Switzerland, huh? Listen, we're sitting on a dozen nuclear armed Sunburns…"

"I know, Nico. I saw the reports. I have to say, that was quite a coup. Congratulations. Your compound is in Syunik Province, not far from Sisian. I studied the terrain. It's pretty susceptible to a counterattack from the south. I see your problem, Nico. You're concerned about retaliation— am I right, or am I right?"

"You're on the nose, Ken, as I would expect from you. What would you do in my place?"

"Position the anti-aircraft guns, get everything on high alert and take cover."

"Are you serious?"

"Hey, you're sitting on a bunch of Sunburns down there—not me. And you told the world about it—Look here! We have these nuclear missiles! You're thinking the same thing I am. Armenus Park has become a hot spot. Those missiles are dangerous enough to pull the Americans in because they will deem it necessary to keep them out of the wrong hands. You can't seriously think that this is a done deal now. Iran just detonated an atomic bomb. Israel is in a state of shock. The States are on the spot. The Russians are trying to figure out how the mullahs got their grubby hands on the goods… And you honestly think you can pilfer these Sunburns and simply shelve them…"

"Are you in touch with the Israelis? Of course you are!"

"Why do you ask? The Israelis aren't going to get involved and risk anything blowing up—if that happens it'll make Chernobyl look like peanuts. They know that. And so do the Turks. You have to negotiate."

"Sure. Easy as pie," Nico responded listlessly.

"No need to hang your head yet, Nico. I'll put a call through to Israel for you."

"Who's your contact there? The chief of staff?"

Cooper's voice was suddenly cold. "My contact is my business. Are we clear?"

"Of course. That was a dumb question. Sorry. We'll stay in touch. Keep your spirits up, Ken."

"Just my spirits?" He laughed and the line went dead. As Nico returned to the control room he heard Cosmo say: "I have spoken to the president of Armenia. He assures us that we have his full support. After all, as of yesterday Armenia has just become a nuclear power."

Cosmo let the sentence hang for effect; a proud smile creased his face. "The president is sending troops to protect the compound. And not just a couple of guys with muskets, gentlemen. This is what we are getting!" An image of a sophisticated-looking twin gun system and two men working at a control unit now appeared on the screen.

"For a while it looked as though ground-based anti-aircraft cannons had become obsolete. But in light of threats that have recently been seen in Afghanistan, for instance, or the struggles between Israel and Hamas in the Gaza Strip, they are experiencing a renaissance. The type of system you see here provides the best protection against asymmetric missile attacks on troop concentrations or military infrastructure. Who recognizes what this is?"

Nico had barely taken a seat. "The Oerlikon Skyshield by Rheinmetall Air Defense. The very best out there," he said.

"Thank you, Nico." Cosmo smiled. He continued: "The Armenian army is equipped with several of these units. Of course Armenus actively supported their acquisition."

That might have been the understatement of the week, Strom smirked to himself. Cosmo had personally financed the high-grade

Swiss armaments for the Armenians and had bartered an attractive rate of interest for himself while he was at it. *That's why he was so well informed, the sly dog!*

"The system's modular design allows it to protect very defined areas from critical objects at close range by means of a sensor unit. Two cross-linked, fully automatic thirty-five millimeter revolver cannons fire as a unit at a combined rate of 2.000 rounds per minute. The munitions used are based on air burst technology.

"They have self-programming capability, which allows them to release a cloud of sub-projectiles at an optimal distance before the target, maximizing their efficiency. They can be used to defend against even artillery grenades or mortar attacks."

Strom appeared impassive. "When can we expect them to arrive?"

"Three units are on their way. We can expect them to arrive to-morrow. The question is what do we do until then? Any suggestions, Nico?"

"Well, I guess we should just hang tight and wait…" His colleagues stared at him, dumbfounded. "After we mount the guard, of course," he added, dryly. This drew a few chuckles. The mood lightened further when the bearded rebel was called to join them.

"Commander Natadschjan will now tell us how he and his men are going to protect the compound," a voice announced from the semi-dark-ness. Andy walked forward, a happily tail-wagging Feedback at his heels. He casually saluted the commander, who had posted himself next to Cosmo and was eyeing the men sternly. He grumbled, rather than spoke: "We will go outside. This is not a matter for the lecture hall!" And with that he briskly strode through the rows.

Cosmo waved his hand toward the exit, causing the group to stand abruptly and follow the commander outdoors.

Outside, Nico Strom heard a soft voice behind his back. "Will you come with me?" The young woman who had spoken was standing next to the Jeep. She was dressed in a tailored fighter jacket and tight black jeans, leaning casually—seductively, Nico thought—against the hood. He was immediately interested.

"I'm headed out to the farm, to our troops. Would you like to join me?"

Nico nodded, a smile formed on his lips. "Sure. Absolutely. I wouldn't mind a bite to eat. As long as it's not army grub."

A short while later the Jeep stopped in front of the residence on the dairy farm. "We prepare the men's meals here. Follow me. It's Nico, right?"

Sara strode into the kitchen, proceeded to check the counter surfaces, brought out a piece of meat, put a pot of water on the stove. "I will make you some braised beef. How spicy do you like it?"

"Oh, I like my meat as spicy as possible," Nico smiled, moving the curtain aside with one hand. He saw several men hoisting a box onto a truck. When he turned around, she stood before him with a ladle in her hand—looking utterly captivating. "What are your plans for the future, once this is all over, Nico?"

"Well, perhaps…" he stared at her full, half-parted lips. "Well…" He got no further. Sara slid her arms around him gently and kissed him. "I want to get away from everything," she said. She looked outside, into the distance, with a sad longing in her eyes. "Will you take me with you?"

Sara was beautiful. Young. Her deep blue eyes captivated him. He was unable to say the words she wanted to hear from him right then. Instead, he started telling her about his travels to the Emirates, to Africa, about glaciers and snow-tipped mountains in Switzerland. "Like Ararat?" she asked, checking the pot.

"We have a hundred Ararats in the Alps—there is no end to the breathtaking summits, peaks and valleys with their pristine, white caps, but your Ararat is the loveliest."

She spun around. "Do you really mean that?"

"Of course I do. You are so beautiful, Sara, and a little untamed…"

She embraced him, leaned her head against his chest.

"Hi there. Am I interrupting?" Andy stood in the door. There was a look of distaste on his face. "She promised you the beef, too, Nico?"

Strom jumped back, Sara turned away, flushed, her eyes filled with tears. She turned suddenly and ran out without saying another word.

Nico felt a stab of concern. Had he hurt her? He went to the door, brusquely shouldered Andy aside and ran after her. Feedback gave chase for a few meters, barking loudly, then stood her ground, growling. "Easy there, Feedback. Let him live!" Andy said with a grin. "He's on our side."

Drôle de Guerre

The Revolutionary Guard had been created as Khomeini's loyal counterforce to the military in 1979. Initially, it served to enforce the new system. In time it developed into a powerful force with three classic service branches and a traditional military command structure. Brigadier General Bakhtiar, who had brilliantly negotiated and orchestrated the acquisition of the Sunburn missiles from Oleg Nedjew, had risen quickly through the ranks of the air force before being entrusted with the establishment and leadership of covert task force units. The general climate of secrecy meant that barely anything was known of their composition, armament or tactics, and members' identities were strictly guarded. One of these units was Kyros, named after the great Persian leader. The Americans compared the cloak-and-dagger units with their own Special Forces, but Bakhtiar had really used European special services as a model. He had been particularly inspired by the French and the Swiss AAD 10.

The three MI-8 Kyros helicopters had flown out over the Caspian Sea in a triangle formation as evening approached. The water's vast expanse lurked darkly in the dusk. A town's lights glittered on the shore; behind that lay the dark-green contours of the cloud-covered coastal range that needed be overcome in order to reach Ardabil Province in the west.

The route led across the high valleys of northern Iran to the border-defining river Aras and the southern tip of Azerbaijan. The rural E002 and the pipeline that ran parallel to the river would provide the commander orientation in order to follow a nap-of-the-earth flight course into the tributary valley, and up to the Armenian border. The commander planned to circumnavigate Kapan, the first larger Armenian town in the south, and head directly north to the easily visible Armenus Technopark compound.

His orders were simple—advance through southern Armenia, take possession of the Armenus Technopark runway and create favorable conditions for the landing of up to a battalion of airborne forces. It was crucial that this offensive be carried out swiftly. Security forces, which were presumed to be weak at this point, were to be overcome and the nuclear weapons were to be located. Bakhtiar had made use of information gleaned from the abundant cellular traffic. His people had been able to filter practically every detail of the enemy's maneuver, including the Hercules' flight path, from euphoric text messages and conversations. The brigadier general, having visited the Russian facilities, had been able to provide the Kyros commander with precise intel on the compound—in addition to aerial reconnaissance images.

North of Tel Aviv, at the command center of the Israeli Air Force, a bleary-eyed colonel was also studying a flight route. His top-secret endeavor had much to do with the extremely tenacious comportment of a likewise bleary-eyed Nir Barak. The Mossad agent had, in the wake of his recent command center performance, been led to a conclusion bordering on certainty by the ever-increasing intercepted text messages coming from the area of Tabriz: a handover of missiles in northern Iran was clearly imminent, and these were likely armed with nuclear warheads.

The Air Force was commanded by Colonel Levit, who made no secret of his animosity toward the Mossad. In accordance with the Intelligence assessment, the colonel found the situation to be too inconclusive to warrant any more than the placing of an F-16 unit of the 4th Hatzor Squadron on critical alert and assigning his staff with the preemptive planning of a possible route of attack.

A call placed in the late afternoon by a certain Ken Cooper to the high command of the Secret Services headquarters had led, precipitously, to a new and urgent assessment of the situation in those quarters. This was almost immediately followed by a call from the chief of staff to the air force command center, resulting in a significant change of pace. About an hour before, one of Nir Barak's Mossad men had caught wind of the critical worsening of the situation and passed the information on. Barak had made Colonel Levit's planning staff well aware of the concerns. They had subsequently proceeded to work on determining the fastest and stealthiest route through northern Iran and to the Armenian border for the F-16 Sufa squadron.

The pointed briefing that the air force officers were given by Nir Barak in advance of the official channels did not fail to have its intended effect. They were thankful, really, to be able to make use of the heads-up. The age-old rivalry between the two security branches suddenly lost a significant amount of its bitterness.

"Twelve operational Sunburns, presumed to be armed with 200 kiloton nuclear warheads, are located at the so-called Armenus Techno-park in southern Armenia," Nir Barak had commenced. "They were appropriated from the Iranians in a daring coup comparable to our legendary Operation Yonatan." He had paused for a moment. Looking at the faces of the younger officers he wondered if they remembered that the reason for the naming owed to Lieutenant Colonel Yonatan Netanyahu having lost his life when his commando successfully carried out the counter-terrorist rescue of hostages held on an Air France machine at the Entebbe airport in Uganda.

"They simply *took* them!" Barak went on to explain how the situation had grown increasingly acute following the operation in Tabriz, and that Intelligence was warning of an imminent threat of escalations.

"We must assume that the Iranians will not tolerate this embarrassment without retaliation," he had drummed into his audience. "It is likely that special units of the Revolutionary Guard will use force in an attempt to fetch the missiles back. I don't need to tell you the dangers our country faces if Iranian militants get their hands on these deadly weapons. At this time, the Sunburns represent the only means by which the Iranians could deploy a nuclear payload against us. We assume that a Sunburn was the source of the nuclear detonation in Baluchistan, and that the warhead was not developed by the mullahs. And so it is in our strongest possible interest that these air-to-surface missiles, which they can use their Sukhoi fighter jets to carry and fire at us, stay exactly where they are—in Armenia!"

✳

Hours later four Sufas—the Hebrew for *storm*, as the modernized F-16s of the Israeli Air Force were called—flew undetected over Jordan, then over a part of Saudi Arabia toward Iraq, before turning north.

They expected to reach the Armenian border within the calculated time frame. The experienced squad commander heading the formation looked over at his wingman to the right. The father of the young pilot had led the 1981 air strike on the Iraqi Osirak nuclear reactor near Baghdad, a thousand kilometers from Israel. High command had given them the same route back then, which simplified the planning of this mission. Past Baghdad the route would take them north through a little-known region, toward the Iranian border. All four pilots knew each other well. They had shared intense aerial combat training and were confident that they were among the best in the world at what they did. Their mission was to secure the border and to prevent enemy invasion of Armenian airspace.

"Nobody has any idea that we are on our way down there. How does that feel?" the commander asked. The answers were enthusiastic. This did not stop him from keeping a close eye on the flight management system for the current air situation in particular, and the operation control news feed for other information in general.

Several thousand kilometers to the north an Armenian army convoy consisting of six tank-tread vehicles rolled across Republic Square in Yerevan around midnight. The heavy, dark noise of the engines echoed off the old facades. The rubberized tracks made a particular, swooshing sound that coaxed a number of curious individuals from the few bars still open across from the Ministry of Foreign Affairs, out into the cold night air. They wondered about the heavy double axel trailers with their heavy, misshapen tarps that appeared to be covering ordnance. The noise dissipated quickly as the convoy moved swiftly on, taking Beirut Street and heading toward the E117, which would take them to the area of operations in the south.

Having taken his usual nightcap from the carafe at his bedside, the president of the republic had already retired when the engine noise, which was loud enough to rattle the windows, reminded him that he had promised Jack Abramian the support of his army's new anti-aircraft weaponry. So the boys were on their way! He contemplated drinking to their health, found the occasion fitting, and poured himself a swig of the eighteen-year-old Macallan Highland single malt scotch, of which Jack had sent two boxes to his presidential office. He grunted happily as the liquor warmed his chest, laid his head on the soft pillow in the comforting knowledge that his orders would be carried out punctually and precisely. Still, he was troubled by one small matter. What to tell Russia? Armenia had forged a close, if not entirely comfortable, allegiance with the Russians. The general feeling being that one did not have to love them, but that it would certainly be unwise to start any trouble with them. But Jack superseded all of that. He was a true Armenian, a patriot who did everything for his country. It wouldn't be easy to convey this newfound loyalty to the powers-that-be in the Kremlin... having turned a few times, the president eventually did manage to get to sleep with a relatively clear conscience.

The aircraft carrier fleet that was configured according to operational requirements in the Persian Gulf currently consisted of the USS *Dwight D. Eisenhower*, two missile cruisers, a submarine defense frigate, two attack submarines, and a supply ship containing munitions, diesel oil, materials and provisions.

The digital clock read 17:53 in the *Dwight D. Eisenhower's* dimly lit combat information center when the captain received the message from fleet command.

"Aerial activity over Iran and Iraq," he called into the room.

"We see them, sir." The intelligence officer manning the Low Earth Orbit monitors answered, zooming in on the images.

"Three aircraft, probably helicopters, in the northeast. Heading toward Azerbaijan. And four planes moving north rapidly through northern Iraq."

"Do we have ID?"

"Negative in the northeast, sir, presumably IRIAF. We do have an ID code for the planes over Iraq...one moment..." The officer clicked on a link. "IDF, sir, Israeli Air Force. Four F-16's."

"Israelis? What the hell are they up to?" The captain now stood behind his intelligence officer, leaned over his shoulder. "They're heading toward Armenia and...there, look, the Iranians are heading in from the east. It looks like they're on a collision course. I'm not liking this, if you ask me."

They watched in silence as the flight paths slowly approached each other on the screen.

"What do we do, sir? There's still time, but if they keep going they'll meet up in about two hours."

"The question is, what does CENTCOM do? Our mission remains unchanged until further notice. We keep an eye on what's going on up there. If those Iranians really put those Sunburns to use, it's going to get mighty uncomfortable mighty fast."

The captain who looked young in his khaki shirt and blue cap left the operations room and headed to his cabin to change for inspection. The missile defense system worried him. He put on his combat gear, took a swig of water and took the lift down to the flight deck, where the helicopter stood waiting. The Aegis was their magic bullet. The Aegis Ballistic Missile Defense System was meant to protect their otherwise possibly vulnerable fleet from enemy attack. But recently rumors had emerged saying that the Aegis was powerless to defend against the Russian Sunburns.

"Let's see if the radar specialists are up to snuff. Won't do any harm to test them a bit," he muttered as the rough wind on deck hit his face. His aid saluted respectfully, trotted to the helicopter next to him.

Back at the Armenus Technopark, Natadschjan had stationed a dozen of his soldiers around the terminal and tower. He had armed them with two shoulder-operated Stinger surface-to-air missiles and a dozen rocket launchers. He would personally lead the other half of his men to storm the Russian compound. Abramian had given him the mission of taking possession of the facilities and searching them for weapons. "Take care, Safar," he had warned. "General Petrov is in command down there. He's a nasty piece of work. Likes to shoot first and ask questions later."

As it turned out, the Russians were surprisingly docile. It seemed that, their great leader Nedjew having taken off, they were not too eager to go to any great lengths on behalf of the obscenely rich oligarch. Of course, Natadschjan had also gone in with a good plan. He had a group of men rappel down an airshaft into a deserted gym. The few blind-sided Russians that were found in their beds quickly and quietly surrendered to the fearsome looking rebels and showed them the way to their headquarters.

It was here that a critical situation had arisen just a short while before. The general and a few of his loyal followers had entrenched themselves behind some vehicles in the large garage, next to the loading bays. A gun battle had ensued. It soon became clear to the raiding party that the Russians had merely engaged in delay tactics in order to abscond. But where to? Where was their secret escape route? The question was answered when the rebels searched the abandoned position and the group leader found the neatly stacked, pale yellow brick-sized blocks. He had been in the process of turning his back on the building materials when he saw a blinking red light attached to a ticking black box… "Explosives!" he bellowed.

The CIA listening post in Tiflis was situated on a hilltop outside of the capital, in an old restored monastery surrounded by fields. It gave every impression of being the harmless domain of a long-gone monastic order.

Within the modern interior, accessible to agents via an underground garage, a message had just been decoded. The 18th Russian motorized rifle division had been put on alert on the Georgian border. As had a division of paratroopers, whose position intelligence was still trying to determine. This message was sent to the chief of staff's desktop, laptop and cell phone—only, the holder of all of these technological marvels had descended into the throes of a sparkling reception held by the young and dynamic Georgian president in honor of an anniversary marking the beginnings of cooperation with the West. And so the important message was ignored. No analyst was forced to put in a night-shift at headquarters, the U.S. president continued rehearsing, undisturbed, his next admonishments of the United Nations. The Germans slept soundly, so that they might rise refreshed to set their tax investigators upon their harried populace at the crack of dawn, and no other political power found it necessary to point out the seriousness of the situation.

Armenus Technopark

The man they called Cosmo placed two glasses and the bottle on the kitchen table and sat. Things can only get better, Nico." He filled the glasses to the brim.

Strom, who had one hand on the radio unit, raised his glass with the other. "What do we do with the Sunburns, Jack?" Abramian looked at him for a long while. "What would you do with them?"

Abramian noted Nico's shrug and continued: "The Turks and Armenians have grown less hostile toward each other since our conference in Yerevan. Azerbaijan has commenced diplomatic relations. Borders that were closed between nations are opening. So far, so good. There is a lot going on in terms of trade and economy. But the only universal language that is really understood by numbskulls everywhere is the language of power. Power has always been the queen on the chessboard that is the Caucasus and Anatolia. What do you say, Feedback?"

To Nico's amusement, he scratched behind the dog's ears and pretended to answer for her in a squawking voice: "They have always believed in pawn sacrifice. They spill blood like water."

"Right, you little wolverine." He bent his head down to his terrier, then let her jump off his lap and to her food bowl. He took a sip of his drink, brought the glass down hard. "The nuclear weapons belong to the Armenian people. I gave the damn things to the president. His troops will come to claim them." Cosmo absentmindedly looked at his watch, as if their arrival was imminent.

"That should mix things up nicely," Strom said with a laugh.

"It sure will. It already has. Delegations from the neighboring countries are already en route to Yerevan. They wish to negotiate their positions with the new nuclear power, Nico. Unbelievable, the effect that a couple of warheads can have on people."

They grinned at each other jovially.

"I wouldn't be surprised if the pipelines to the west went through Armenia next year, and…" He smiled impishly. "And the holy Ararat became officially part of Armenia once more."

Nico Strom raised his brows. "Noah would be very pleased, I'm sure." A fierce explosion shook the house to its foundations. The glasses danced on the table, the bottle toppled, windows broke and shattered on the terra-cotta floor. Feedback tucked her tail and ran, yowling, under the sideboard.

The men had jumped up. They ran outside, instinctively holding their hands protectively over their heads. An enormous, black cloud was rising, sirens howled, they heard screams.

"The Russian compound," Cosmo determined. "They've blown it up!"

They rushed over the gravel to the 4x4. Halfway toward the airstrips they were met by the open Jeep, which was coming toward them in a cloud of dust. Natadschjan stood at full height on the passenger side, holding on to the front window. The vehicles ground to a halt next to each other.

"What happened?" Cosmo yelled out the side window.

"It got two of my best men. They were trying to defuse the bomb," the rebel leader spat grimly. "I'll pay those bastards back."

They got out.

"One thing at a time, Safar," Cosmo tried to placate the angrily pacing commander, who now stepped up, put a silver hip flask to his thick lips and tossed his head back. "It could be worse," he panted, offering Cosmo the vodka. "The rest of my people were barely able to get to safety. And the missile station is intact."

Abramian respectfully declined. "Any missiles left at the station?"

Natadschjan shook his shaggy head. "As far as we could tell, the son of a bitch took them. According to the technicians, he left with the last three. Sunburns, they said."

It suddenly dawned on Strom. "He fled on a Sikorsky. I saw them load the material."

"The boss?" Cosmo asked. "Did the men mention a name?"

"Sure. The Crane!" Natadschjan hoisted himself back into the passenger seat. "I have to get back to my people!"

The Jeep spun around, cloaking Abramian and Strom in dust. They got back into their vehicle, coughing, and drove slowly down to the runway. Jack turned his head. "Nico, what would you think of me signing the command of this whole place over to you?"

Strom placed a hand on his chest. *"Me?"*

"Sure. Who else? You are like a son to me. Feedback prefers the weather in California, you know that. Not to mention Andy."

"Do you really want to leave?"

"Oh, you know, I like to get around. There's plenty going on elsewhere, too. There is a bank I'm interested in over in Zurich."

The explosion had thrown debris all the way onto the runways. Power shovels were already clearing them. As they got out, they were met with drifts of acrid smoke.

"Ah, well. Perhaps it's for the best," Abramian said, always happy to see the bright side of things. "I've been wanting to get rid of the damn Russians for quite a while now. So has the president, by the way."

Bloody Mary

The majestic yacht sailed straight along the coastline where Aphrodite's mighty boulder protruded darkly from the sea.

The struggle on board was short and fierce.

This time Sophie was not going to give her rivals a second chance. Ponter stood in the spacious lounge: the surround-sound stereo was playing some singer bawling to a hard techno beat, the glass sliding door to the sundeck was wide open. His back turned to her as Ponter rolled up the Rothko canvas, laid it on the glass table and began to wrap it, cumbersomely, in plastic. Sophie sat tensely on a lounge chair, where her pinched eyes had long been trained on the piece of sports equipment next to the long fishing rods. Seeing her former boss occupied, she rose quietly and lithely.

She tore the harpoon from its hook, raised it to her shoulder and fired. The sharp, barbed arrow zipped away and bored into Ponter's shoulder. The booming bass swallowed his scream. Sophie braced her legs against the wooden threshold, started the electric winch. The thin steel cable pulled the prey mercilessly closer, despite his desperate attempts to free himself. Sophie wrapped the line around his neck several times and tightened the noose. She took a heavy carafe from the decorative bar cart. A golden whiskey shimmered enticingly inside of it. She shattered the crystal against Ponter's skull.

Then she ran through the salon and to the bridge. The door to the galley stood open. The cook stood at the stove with a rag, was just putting down a freshly polished pan.

"Where is the steward?"

"I don't know. In his bunk, maybe," the cook muttered churlishly and turned his back to her. Sophie whacked him over the head with the copper pan, found a long knife, walked out and closed the door behind her. *I need a proper weapon!*

She crept along the corridor, peered around the corner—there! Lenka Borsk stood on the bridge next to the captain, whose arm was out-stretched. They both looked in the direction he was pointing to. Sophie flitted past the stairs leading up and took the short stairs down to the lower deck. *So far, so good!*

The guard lay on a sofa in the crew's common room, smoking a cigarette and staring at the television. He had taken his holster off and laid it on the little table. Sophie noticed that his pants were unbuttoned. The man turned his head sharply when he heard the soft whistle. What he saw left him completely speechless. There was this hot chick making titillating gestures with her hands, and with her tongue— Oh, Lord. The blood rushed down to his groin. The top of her pants was undone. She pushed her flat hand down her stomach and then down further...

"This is nuts...I'll be damned...You want to do it right now, don't you?" He got up, walked toward her with a very large grin on his face.

"You're a guard, aren't you? I love strong, armed men. You've got a nice, big piece for me, haven't you?"

As he stood looking at her, mouth agape, she used a classic tai chi combat move, attacking his head and legs. Succumbing to the deft and precisely landed blows, the brawny strongman dropped noiselessly to the floor. Like a weasel, Sophie swiftly grabbed the heavy automatic pistol, checked the magazine, carefully loaded the chamber. "Good to go," she muttered. She stealthily began to make her way back up to the bridge. If she was not mistaken, that only left the captain, the steward and Borsk. She didn't waste a thought on the young, amiable waiter.

"Cut the engines! Nobody move."

Borsk spun around reflexively. The barrel of the nine-millimeter made her reconsider. The captain's calm demeanor seemed put on. He did as instructed, the engine noise subsided, the yacht settled in the water. He turned slowly.

"Get the dinghy into the water. Now!" Sophie swung the barrel to face the captain. "Good. Keep moving." She hurried the group aft, past the galley, over Ponter's lifeless body. Sophie did not react to Lenka Borsk's hissed curses. She kept a distance until they all came to a halt at the back rail. The two obediently climbed down onto the loading bay, let the dingy into the water, got in, undid the line and pushed off. Before the captain climbed down the ladder, he handed Sophie the remote. "Just be sure you don't run her aground, you crazy bitch!"

Sophie tried the controls, pressed the stick forward. The hull shivered to life as the engines started back up, ocean spray shot up as the two propellers elevated the yacht in the restless waters and moved it forward, away from the dingy, in which the captain was trying to get the outboard motor started. Sophie rushed back to where Ponter was stirring. "You are making a big mistake, Sophie. We could be happy together..." She looked for the bar cart, took the next carafe—filled with dark, twenty-year-old port—and crashed it over Ponter's skull. This time the banker made a noise that sounded eerily like a death rattle.

On the bridge she took the wheel and turned. She aimed the bow toward the coast; there, where the big boulder rose from the water. She pushed both throttle controls all the way forward. The yacht reared, its powerful engines making the instrument panel shake. The bow reared from the water as the vessel sped up.

She searched for the radio, for flares, couldn't find anything in her agitation. The bow continued to race toward the boulder—hang on. She blinked. That's...of course. She was seized by a sense of relief. She sensed that she was back in familiar waters. *I wonder where you are right now, George.*

She slowed the yacht down, blocked the rudder, took the few steps to the main deck, rushed to the salon. Not a soul on board? No one in sight.

The roll lay carelessly on the table—wrapped in a scant piece of plastic. Not very nicely done, Ponter, but whatever...Sophie took the painting, raced back, turned the corner with her head lowered, running at full speed. She collided with the woman turning the corner in the other direction...

Irena Petrova, Nedjew's executor, had been in the luxurious sleeping cabin downstairs, stretching out languidly on the large cozy bed, when the harpoon fired by Sophie had hit John Ponter in the shoulder.

Irena's intoxicated senses were miles from what was going on just above her. Her legs were splayed wide apart; between them lay the blond head of the young, strongly built steward, who was following her precise instructions. Upon completion of the intense session of cunnilingus, he roughly tossed her onto her stomach, grabbed the black whip and, sitting next to her head, began whipping her bare behind with the hard leather in time to the balalaika music. Moaning lustily she reached for her captor's hard instrument and kneaded it ecstatically until she suddenly uttered a sharp scream, then lay motionless. After a short pause, she elbowed the young man aside rudely. She heard him hurriedly grab his things and make off for his bunk. Irena, meanwhile, had lit a cigarette and slipped into a pair of jeans, a T-shirt, and black leather loafers. Then she strode up the stairs to the deck, freshly energized.

When a stunned Sophie opened her eyes after the collision, she saw herself angrily rubbing her head in the mirror. *Hang on! That's not a mirror.* What she had first taken to be a blurry image of herself was, in fact, another woman. Both females remained confounded for a second or two, both trying hard to regain their composure. Sophie was the first to stand and start running, to the left, up the stairs, the valuable roll in hand. She had left the gun upstairs on the table next to the rudder. The knife? No idea.

The battle-hardened Petrova was not let down by her reflexes, either. She had chosen the stairs leading aft, mounted them with greater speed and had the gun firmly in her had when Sophie arrived, panting, in the wheelhouse. Later, she would not be able to explain exactly why she had acted the way that she did in the next few seconds. Was it Petrova's treacherous face? Her threatening stance? A foreboding that this woman would fight to the death? Whatever the case may have been, Sophie instinctively whacked her in the face with the rolled up painting. Petrova pulled the trigger at the precise moment when the plastic-covered roll hit her head and put off her aim. The bullet tore through the mahogany ceiling. When she was able to see clearly again, Kramer was gone. Petrova had chased her aft, racing along the rail, then had stopped abruptly. At first she saw only the roll bobbing in the backwash. Then a head popped up, arms parting the water with powerful strokes. "Piece of shit!"

Sophie Kramer had jumped ship and was swimming for shore. Irina Petrova slowly lowered her weapon and relaxed. Ah, well, one less pleasure to look forward to in life. She would have liked to torture the bitch—differently, longer, more brutally than the poor devil in Zurich, the one they had called Tabah, who had finally given up the secret to the plans she had been after.

But despite her perverse leanings, Nedjew's executor kept a cool head. She had gotten a grip on herself. Why chase after Kramer, cut her to pieces? She had more pressing things to attend to. She had to get to the rendezvous point agreed upon with Nedjew days ago. And so she stepped onto the bridge, turned the yacht away from the approaching shore. She knew enough of nautical matters. As a member of the Soviet Spetznas special forces, she had learned to manage all manner of boats, cutters, ships—how to capture, steer, sink them. She didn't need a captain. One man less on the payroll. After heading out into the open sea for another half an hour, she radioed Oleg Nedjew, and got a prompt response.

"Do we have the gold?" he asked. She confirmed. She had had enough time to fetch the bars from the bank and to stow them securely on the lower deck.

She would make the rendezvous. Of course she would. When she heard the shuffling noise, she spun around, alarmed. The steward walked onto the bridge, rubbing his eyes with a yawn. He started at her barked order.

"Clean up the mess in the back, Igor. And bring me a Bloody Mary, damn it."

Race Against Time

George Constantinou knew that he was too late even before he crashed into the hallway of his apartment.

He called for Sophie, ran through all of the rooms. He took in the mess with mounting anguish—signs of struggle, drops of blood that led him to the bathroom. He stopped in front of the mirror, took a deep breath.

Harbor...yacht... smeared onto the mirror with soap. Of course! The *Bastion*! Oleg Nedjew's luxury yacht. Ponter...On his way back into the office, he dialed Marios's number on his cell. He sat down behind the desk, opened the bottom drawer. The nine-millimeter Beretta was wrapped in an oily cloth next to a box of bullets. George pinned the phone to his ear with his shoulder, released the magazine, loaded it. He ended the call when the voice mail picked up and dialed the harbor.

The ringing seemed to go on forever. He slid the magazine back in place, pocketed the gun and strode through the living room. He needed air. Where were these people? There, finally, a voice. "Limassol Harbor."

"Listen. Is the *Bastion* still anchored?"

"One moment," came the calm reply.

George paced the terrace, looked out across the sea into the blinding light. "Hello?" How long was this going to take, damn it. Finally he heard footsteps, muttering voices. "Sir? The *Bastion* is just leaving port right now, it…"

George hung up. The official at the harbormaster's office shook his head disapprovingly, his tanned face marred by a frown. "What ever happened to manners?"

He wasn't able to reach Marios. No hope for backup. Considering how long it would take to reach the harbor, get his hands on a boat to give chase, he knew that too much time would have passed. George also knew there was only one way to do this. He called the air base.

The gray and black Royal Navy Merlin helicopter thundered along, keeping low to the beach at first, then pulling up and out across the open sea with all of the might of its three Rolls-Royce gas turbine engines. The crew consisted of two pilots wearing green overalls and a lifeguard in a red jacket who was responsible for manning the winch. George crouched behind the pilots, indicating the direction with his hand.

Back at the air base, intelligence officer Major Hanbury scratched the back of his head as he skeptically checked the journal entry, finally deciding to officially sign off on it with a bit of a grunt. "It'll be fine," he muttered to himself.

He had immediately approved the urgent request for a helicopter mission, fully trusting George, who had never yet let him down. The on-call crew had taken off within minutes of being alerted and had picked George Constantinou up from the beach. Hanbury found his team on the control monitor, where it was represented as a blinking dot heading southwest across the sea. He had promptly classified the mission as a rescue operation.

Stuffing his pipe as he stared at the screen, he hoped fervently that something was going to be rescued—anything that could be taken to justify his frankly unwarranted decision.

As the intelligence officer stepped over to the window, holding the flame of his lighter over the bowl of his pipe, he saw the racy Gulfstream 250 taxiing toward the runway.

"Lo and behold, Agent Superman is sodding off," the Englishman grumbled mockingly, yawned, and went to the phone to have his observation confirmed by the tower. "Yessir. Destination London. Mr. Garp is on board."

The pilot was the first to see the vessel. He corrected his course and flew toward it. Evidently the elegant luxury yacht had circumnavigated Akrotiri peninsula, crossed Episkopi Bay and was now heading southwest.

"It's almost in line with Kourion," George noted. The light walls of the ancient site, where he had danced with Sophie only yesterday, were clearly visible against the green hills that rose off the shore.

The pilot nodded, turned his helmeted head. "What do you want us to do, sir?"

"Get closer." George searched eagerly with the binoculars, trying hard to find a point of reference; anything that would help him realize the plan that was slowly forming in his mind. It seemed that the *Bastion* was moving ahead at full steam.

"I'm going down," he yelled into the microphone. "Get closer!" He turned to the soldier in the red jacket. "Can you put me down on that yacht?"

The men eyed each other earnestly. They were silent types, who tended to face their often perilous missions without much fanfare, and they had overcome many a challenging situation together; from dangerous rescues on stormy seas, to recovery missions in the high mountains, to abseiling onto disabled cutters. Such experiences had bonded them. But putting an agent down on a fast-moving yacht was an altogether different cup of tea in two regards—for one, there were the technical difficulties entailed in a maneuver requiring such precision. The other issue was that this was not a distress-at-sea call. Rather, it was an invasion of private property, where they might encounter resistance. The pilot summed up his concerns. "You had better be damned sure that you are doing the right thing, sir. I hope that this is not a mistake." He nosed the helicopter down toward the yacht, starting their approach. George felt for his weapon, tightened the belt. He went to the winch man, who handed him the abseiling vest.

In the end, it was the watchful eye of the copilot that led to the decisive turn of the nature of this mission. George stood at the door, his line firmly anchored in the snap-hook, prepared to abseil, the noise and wind whipping his face. At first, he did not notice the crew's shouting and gesturing.

Training and long years of experience led the copilot to think laterally—the pilot's full attention on the yacht was sufficient for the job at hand. He knew that it was always important to remain attentive, and to keep an eye on the big picture, even if the mission appeared clear and complete. And so he trained his binoculars on the sea, systematically scanning to the shore and back until he suddenly saw a small dinghy. Adjusting the focus, he was rewarded with a clear view of a man in naval uniform handling the outboard motor and the woman at his side.

"There's a dingy at three o'clock, two passengers on board," he announced over the intercom. He waved to the back. The winch man had heard his announcement and understood the wave. He patted George on the shoulder, released the line from the hook and led him to the cockpit, where he handed him a headset. George looked through the binoculars for a good, long time.

"There's no doubt—it's her, the escaped convict. Get closer, Captain!" He ordered, without lowering the binoculars.

In no way displeased with the turn of events, the pilot turned and dropped lower. George was anything but clear on what was going on. Why was Borsk, whose mugshot was known to every village policeman at this point, heading back to land? Where was Sophie? What had happened? He looked over at the copilot, who had resumed his scanning in an attempt to see what point of the shoreline the dinghy might be heading for.

He heard the copilot's authoritative voice at the very moment that he detected movement in the water: "*Body in the water!* Ten o'clock! It appears to be a woman. She's swimming."

✳

The person down there was swimming energetically toward shore. When George trained the binoculars he saw the ancient amphitheater against the hillside right above where she appeared to be heading. Was it really a woman? "Get closer, Captain."

The pilot took a sharp turn, George clung to the back of the seat. When he was once again able to focus his binoculars, he found that the swimmer had stood and was wading to the beach through shallow waters. Not Aphrodite, but definitely a woman—his woman, he caught himself thinking.

"I'll be damned if that isn't Sophie," he gasped. "My God, that's Sophie—and the dingy has turned and is heading toward her."

At this moment they all saw clearly what was going on. The dinghy had turned and was dashing diagonally to the point at which the swimmer had risen from the water, was now running, fell, picked herself up once more. The pilot turned his head. "What do you want to do? Go down?"

"I'm going to jump," George yelled, ripping his headset off. He swayed back to the door. "Okay," he heard as he stood in the opening, at the same moment he saw the dinghy roughly run ashore. The *Bastion*'s dinghy. And Lenka Borsk, who was jumping out, had only one goal in mind: Sophie! That much was as clear as the day over Kourion. The winch man slapped George on the shoulder, gave him a thumbs up. George jumped, stretched in order to avoid coasting, hoped a split second before hitting water that the captain had steered clear of the shallow, rocky area.

Splash. Water rushed powerfully up his nose, his lungs ached as he dove down. It had been a smooth entry. He emerged swimming fiercely, gasping for air. After a few meters he was able to see the sand through the water and touch ground. The unbelievable pilot had positioned him perfectly! *Hats off, Royal Air Force!*

Having panted up the pebble beach George comes to a halt on the beach path. His heart is pounding in his throat. Which way had Sophie gone? He screams her name into the thicket of bushes and low olive trees, looks up to the semicircle of the amphitheater, then left to where the beach path and coastal road meet. He starts to run again, following the direction of his hunch.

There were no reliable reports on the aerial incident in the no-man's land over the border between Armenia and Iran. The Israeli Defense Force (IDF) applied the gag order that was a matter of course for missions conducted over territory deemed out of bounds. The Iranian news reported the unfortunate collision of two MI-8 helicopters during a training flight over the northern mountains, which had resulted in the death of all soldiers and crewmembers on board. Not one word was mentioned about aerial combat.

The Israeli F-16, which had been shot down by a missile fired from a MiG-29, was not listed in the official statistics.

The pilot who was killed in the incident was considered missing in action. What could not happen *did* not happen. According to official records, the IDF had never engaged in a combat mission over northern Iran.

The three men drinking tea at the *INS Herev* officer's mess late that afternoon were somber. A modern corvette first deployed by the

Israeli Navy in 2002 was positioned off the southern coast of Cyprus on a secret mission. Good visibility and low winds afforded ideal conditions to deliver a decisive blow against Oleg Nedjew's criminal empire, which threatened world peace—so Nir Barak had dramatically put it to his friends Shuky Nachman and Mendi Meron at the gathering he had called shortly after the nuclear explosion over Baluchistan.

Ever since then the lines had been running hot in the analysis center of the Israeli Mossad. Following the F-16 mission in Iran, Barak had focused his attention on Oleg Nedjew's flight from south Armenia. The Mossad had long been gathering a wealth of intelligence on the Crane—his profile, his contacts, his banker and precise details on monetary transactions. Barak's bet was on the *Bastion*. He reckoned that the oligarch's yacht was not merely a love-nest for a changing array of scantily clad companions. Nedjew used it to receive business partners—usually in international waters, where secret doings could hardly be detected, let alone eavesdropped on.

"His yacht carries cash, gold, drugs and weapons, Shuky," he had said, summarizing his plan as the three friends sat in a helicopter on their way to the corvette.

"And we will probably find documents, lists, addresses, account numbers. As devious as the Russians are, you know they are also pedantic bureaucrats," Nachman had added.

Now, in the mess of the *INS Herev*, Meron stared dumbly at the sharp images obtained from the Combat Information Center. His gloomy countenance was deeply furrowed, as if he had suddenly aged by many years. His only son had very nearly been hit in his F-16.

"Uri saved his life," he said in a grave tone. His friends did not badger him for details of the secret mission. Barak took a sip of tea, Nachman lit a cigarette, allowed the bluish tendrils of smoke to drift across his face.

"Our pilots discovered three combat helicopters. MI-8—very deadly when firing missiles at ground targets," Mendi reported in a steady voice. "Our boys attacked as the Iranians violated the Armenian border. It was short and decisive. Two of the helicopters were directly hit, the third hailed all the bullets it could from its machine guns and turned off. We let it go once it was back in Iranian airspace."

"And then? What happened then?"

"Our squadron regrouped to return to base when the MiGs appeared. Six of them. MiG-29s."

"NATO code Fulcrum," Nachman noted. "Comparable to the F-16, if not superior."

"That's right. The fight against the Iranians, who outnumbered us, was fierce. We shot down four MiGs. But they got Uri. He selflessly saved two of his comrades from a certain hit. Including my son. He put himself in the line of fire." Mendi pulled a picture of the fallen pilot from his pocket. His name was legible next to the emblem of the squadron. All three of them had known his father, the hero who had led the Osirak reactor airstrike near Baghdad. They looked silently at the image of the beaming young man in the cockpit. Mendi pressed his lips together, Nachman wiped at his eyes. Barak, ill at ease, stepped over to the porthole.

Just then, the siren started to wail.

The Shoot at Kourion

Kourion's amphitheater was being used as the location for a film shoot. The area surrounding the arena was beleaguered by the seemingly random bustling and scrambling of the crew, its catering tent, trailers, trucks, technical equipment, cables, costumes hanging from things. Barrier tape and a gaggle of skinny girls channeled curious tourists past the ancient stage.

The technicians concentrated their lights onto a burly actor with blond, curly hair, who had taken his position a few steps above the stage. He cast a wild look out at the beach, where the ships waited for those fleeing the island. *Action!* came the cry. The camera assistant snapped the clapperboard.

"Redouble your efforts! Hold them back! Just a few moments! Do not yield to the mob and protect the path to the vessels. Come, we have been betrayed. We must hasten to escape!"

"Cut!" the director yelled. "That's not right." The powerfully built old master got up from his folding chair, combed his fingers through his white mane. He stepped next to Orestes, laid a great paw on his shoulder. "One more time, my boy. You are fleeing from the temple grounds, you come down the steps of the arena over there, your sword drawn, ready for battle. Like this!" He took the sword from his hand. "This is a real weapon, made of pure, gleaming steel—you have to make it feel authentic." He brought the blade down against a lamp base with a clanging noise. "I want to literally feel the sharply honed blade, the fierce determination to fight, in your demeanor...your eyes should have the power of lightning—they should electrify us. Understood?"

Orestes strode back to his position, nodding. The make-up artist dabbed his brow, artfully arranged a strand of hair onto his face. The lighting technicians arranged their spots and boards. The cameraman raised his thumbs.

"And you turn to Iphigenia only when you say, *'Come, we have been betrayed'*...and then."

The director ducked away. "Then you suddenly see the king, and you hesitate. Got it? Okay, get ready."

The background actors waiting for their appearance on the arena's stairs fell silent. There was a sudden rush of activity on set, everyone knew their moves—be it the cable boy, sound technician, or best boy, then a sudden silence.

"Lights...sound...camera...action!"

The scene was now more dramatic going in the can and Orestes had played the hothead with gusto.

"Cut. Good. We'll do one more take, what do you think?"

The assistant with whom he had spoken nodded in agreement, pressed the clipboard against her stomach and took her notes under her perky breasts.

"We should follow with the beheading scene." She looked up at the sky. "The light, the ocean, it's all perfectly right now."

"What does the script say?"

She consulted the script on her clipboard, turned back a few pages.

" 'They throw the corpse off a steep cliff and impale his head on a stick'...before that they beat the victim's head with a club. Were the Greeks always this barbaric?"

The director laughed. "The son of Uranus cut something else off his father and tossed it in the ocean down there..."

"I know that myth," the assistant grinned, adding "but you're the one who should be concerned in that department, not me."

"This film takes place on Tauris, my dear. The men who are sacrificing shipwrecked sailors to the goddess Diane are Taurians. First we're going to do the scene with Iphigenia...we'll start where she is pleading to the king: 'Oh, unhand your sword, consider me and my plight.'"

He grabbed the head electrician by the arm as the man loped by and briefed him. His assistant pursed her ruby-red lips and jotting down notes, sought out the production manager, who was staring out to sea from under the broad rim of his straw hat, one foot on the retaining wall. To his right a narrow set of stairs led out to a platform. The walled outlook point was reminiscent of an eagle's eyrie as it sat on the steep, stone outcropping high above the frothing waves. On the stairs below two costumed Greeks were practicing a sword duel. The crisp sound of the blades as they met, glinting in the bright sun, was carried up to the stage by the breeze. Off to the other side, the street wound its way up from Venus beach, past rubbish dumps and scraggy bushes, to the parked cars. The production manager pointed down, sandwich in hand. "Look at that woman running up here like she's seen a ghost. Only thing missing is an Olympic torch." He took a bite, sipped from the can of iced tea.

The assistant leaned across the rail. "No kidding! Is she one of us? By the way, some of us are heading into Paphos tonight. Would you like to join us?"

He turned toward her with a warm smile, wiped some mayonnaise from the corner of his mouth, treating himself to a good look at her generous cleavage as he did so. "Shall I declare to you the secret exultation of my heart," he quoted roguishly.

"Very cute, funny man," she said, amused, as the shouts and screams grew louder.

❊

The piercing sound of the ship's siren put an end to the men's torpor in the officer's mess. They gathered their things under the relentless noise, rushed out doing up their quilted vests. Seconds later they reached the navigation station. The corvette captain stood at the windows in the middle of the broad room, peering through a set of binoculars. Three officers were focused on the screens and measurement displays at the gray control console behind him. A guard stood, alert, at the engine telegraph next to the shiny brass speaking tube, the mouthpiece of which protruded from the wall in an elegant arch.

The Chief Petty Officer handed the visitors olive-colored field glasses as a pleasant-looking Lieutenant with a weathered face appeared from the map room and beckoned the group to the tinted panoramic windows. Nachman estimated that the *INS Herev* would have made it to within three nautical miles of the *Bastion* by now.

"We have contact, sir," the radar specialist called from behind the console. As if on command, the men raised their binoculars.

The helicopter came from where the sun stood in the sky. It was hardly visible in the glaring backlight at first. Barak only clearly recognized its contours once its elegant fuselage was hovering over the yacht.

"They're touching down behind the bridge," Nachman commented. "What's the plan?"

When he looked up, the captain was standing next to him with a sharp crew cut, angular chin in a turned up collar, the characteristic hard look of a man prepared to head into battle.

"We're going to board," he said, shortly, unaccustomed to having to contend with civilians on his bridge. "Or have you changed your mind?"

The question was directed at Barak, who moved over to the console, where he sat staring at the radar. "No. That's good," he called over, then said to the radar specialist: "Do we have an ID on the helicopter?"

"Not yet, it's likely to be a civilian machine."

"Full speed ahead," the captain ordered.

The guard at the engine telegraph repeated the order smartly, turned the dial to the red field. The push of the high-powered engines was felt instantly. The Sa'ar-5 class corvette headed toward the *Bastion* at full bore. Mendi Meron plucked at Nachman's sleeve and motioned toward the television screens. "That's aft." The black and white images showed men in black combat gear sorting their equipment on their rear deck and gathering in a half circle around their leader. "Our storm troops," Barak noted dryly.

✳

The *Bastion* numbered among the vessels known as luxury mega-yachts. Its elegant fifty-meter hull was painted deep blue. Above it towered the white structures containing the cabins, lounge, sun decks, the gigantic dining room, and numerous, highly stylized rooms designed for business conferences, fitness and wellness. The helicopter-landing pad lay aft, up on the open part of the bridge.

The panoramic windows on the bridge, which could be seen from afar as a broad black stripe on the upper deck, provided the marksmen of the *INS Herev* a good landmark for target tracking and fire control.

"The captain probably wants to cut the yacht off in her track," Nachman, who was watching the approach intently, whispered. Being the owner of a midsized motorized yacht, which he harbored in Cannes, he understood enough about large boats to realize that the *Bastion* should have discovered the corvette quite a while ago. But the yacht appeared to be speeding up instead of heaving to, as the practices of maritime law would have dictated.

"The helicopter has a RA registration, if I am not mistaken," he commented in a low voice, lowering his field glasses. "It looks like a lead duck going on an expensive cruise."

"What do you think it can do in terms of speed?" Barak asked in his customary booming tone, which promptly earned him a disapproving look from the captain.

"Twenty five knots at most," Shuky whispered and added, anticipating the next question: "This corvette will do at least twice that with its combustion turbines."

The officers focused on the maneuver that was now underway. The tension was palpable. The monotonous drone of the powerful engines was occasionally interrupted by sharp orders and their prompt acknowledgments. Meron nudged Nachman with his elbow. "Your duck has taken flight."

Indeed, the helicopter was taking off. In the air it appeared anything but leaden as it hovered lightly over the bridge for a moment, then dipped its nose and proceeded across the bow, quickly gaining height. The machine was easily within reach of the 20 millimeter Oerlikon, not to mention the surface to air missiles that the corvette was armed with. The officer at the target radar looked tensely to the captain, who was just turning in his direction.

"Civilian aircraft, English identification. It's an absolute no-go, Lieutenant."

"Do not fire at the helicopter," Barak translated, sotto voce this time.

The Sikorsky headed into the distance, rapidly growing smaller until it was barely a dark speck against the sky.

On board, Oleg Borisowich Nedjew looked wistfully back at his *Bastion*. Two duffel bags bulging with cash lay in the hold, next to three crates containing the Sunburns he had taken from Armenus Park. Sadly, there had not been time to pick up more from the *Bastion* on this short stopover that had been so rudely interrupted by the navy. Ponter? The poor devil... The Crane patted the breast pocket of his jacket, which resembled a Russian officer's uniform, with satisfaction. His long, manicured fingers felt two gems—the disc containing the Hornbach plans for nuclear warheads that he had plucked from the back of the Rothko painting, and the document that John Ponter had signed—with some mild convincing from Petrova—before they had left the harbor. It was a faxed copy, stating that the banker had transferred all of Nedjew's holdings with Ponter Bank to the safety of a new tax haven... Ponter's last words, the Crane thought, grinning maliciously.

*

On the bridge of the *Bastion*, Irina Petrova forcefully pushed the cruising range lever to its hilt. The ship had reached its speed limit of twenty-six knots, its hull positively groaning under the pressure.

The war vessel was heading diagonally toward her port side, sending a wide arc of spray as it cut through the water. Next to the bridge a light was flashing long and short sequences. Petrova didn't bother trying to decipher the Morse alphabet code. She likewise wasn't bothered with the sailors whom she saw waving flags through her binoculars. Why would she waste her time trying to figure out codes and signals that clearly meant only one thing: *a demand to cut the engines and heave to!* "They can kiss my ass," she hissed, abruptly putting the yacht in a steep turn port side.

"Attention, collision course!" the Israeli Navy mate cried out.

The *Bastion* was now heading more or less straight toward the *INS Herev*. The captain anticipated the maneuver. "She is going to try to scrape past. Prepare to shoot across the bow. Course fifteen degrees south."

The course adjustment meant that the corvette would end up parallel to the yacht. Petrova cast a triumphant glance at the frothing, slowly turning stern.

"Bastards. Come on, then!" She raced through the door and out to the exterior steering position where the bodyguard was cowering on the large, bright yellow H, nervously fingering a long pipe, which he extended, and to which he attached a pear-shaped grenade. "Get it ready to fire, Igor!" she hollered. "They won't dare shoot at us."

She was mistaken. She had hardly yelled out the words when a bundled sheaf of tracer bullets whizzed silently across the bow. The crackle of their detonations followed a few split seconds later.

Petrova ran back to the rudder, issuing expletives as she went. She reduced the thrust, slowing the *Bastion*, and allowed the war vessel to approach broad side.

The captain of the *INS Herev* was dubious of the yacht's maneuver. "What is that guy up to on the helicopter deck?"

The corvette had quickly minimized its distance from the pursued yacht. It now employed its speakers to order the crew of the *Bastion* to stop in no uncertain terms... "This is the Israeli Navy. Cut your engines. We are coming aboard..."

"That's what *you* think!" Petrova screeched, giving Igor the sign.

All men on the bridge of the *INS Herev* beheld the sight at the same time. It was frankly breathtaking to those who were not yet battle hardened—a bright, orange ball of fire, the dark outline of the missile.

"Rocket launcher," Nachman said flatly. Barely a second later it hit the corvette somewhere further back. The explosion rattled the bridge. At the same time the ship's monitor began flashing a red alarm light, precisely showing the point of impact.

"We've been hit mid-ship. Captain's cabin."

"Sons of bitches," the captain grunted and gave the order to open fire.

The automatic sprinklers quickly extinguished the blaze in the captain's cabin behind the officer's mess. The same could not be said of the *Bastion*'s emergency system a few minutes later. Sheafs of twenty-millimeter explosive ammunition tore the bridge to pieces in seconds. They also tore Petrova's head from her shoulders before she knew what was happening. As he tried to reload, the bodyguard was blown overboard backwards by the massive hail of bullets.

A fire started and spread rapidly. Black, acrid smoke rose from the ship, the engines died. The once proud vessel drifted to its end, its bridge deck utterly demolished. Before she had grown completely still in the water, the masked, black-clad storm troops had reached her stern. They successfully extinguished the flames, gathering the befuddled cook and the rest of the crew, and recovering an injured individual, whom they found in a grotesque position—a middle-aged man, who had been speared by a harpoon and was bleeding from a head wound.

The sun was a deep red circle on the horizon when the *INS Herev* came to anchor at Limassol harbor hours later. A tug with a great, blunt bow approached, accompanied by a speedboat with flashing blue lights belonging to the harbor police. The crew released the towline and attached a steel cable to the damaged *Bastion*.

The corvette's military sickbay was equipped for emergencies.

"We have an X-ray machine, a reanimation room, an anesthesiologist and all necessary lab components," the slender, dark-skinned medical officer informed the civilians as he took them back into the operating room that smelled strongly of disinfectant. A halogen lamp lit John Ponter's body, which was draped from the waist down. He was prone on a modular operating table, almost obscenely, his legs strapped down. A rectangular plaster covered the wound that had been torn open by the harpoon, and was once again closed. Strands of hair lay on the floor.

A pressure bandage had been applied to his skull, which had been partially shaved.

Ponter was awake. Nachman stepped over to him, bending to meet the banker's wandering gaze. The wounded man finally looked at him, his eyes resting on his furrowed features for a long time. Even in the glaring light and under these circumstances, Nachman's charisma commanded attention.

"Where am I?"

"On your way to prison." Nachman turned away without another word.

"He's stable enough to be transported," the medical officer pronounced.

Nachman felt his left shoulder and grimaced.

"Is something the matter? Are you hurt?"

Nachman shook his great head, smiling grimly. "Will you join me in the mess, Major? A hard day's work deserves a drink—that's the way things have always been in the Service, am I right?"

The Struggle

Sophie breathed in short rhythmic bursts in an attempt to conserve her strength as her legs reliably conquered one lunging stride after another in her ascent. She drew confidence from her regular skating practice and runs and was grateful for her tight moccasins, which had fortunately remained on her feet through her swim. She was in excellent physical shape, her body ready and able to meet any demand she put on it without protest. She noted not the least sign of fatigue or weakening. She was even able to quicken her pace as the sandy path led through a short, green hollow on the way to the next incline. Her decision to reach the summit was firm. She could see the Visitor's Center in her mind's eye, up on the hill overlooking the arena, where she had waited for George in the Land Rover. The image was crystal clear. She remembered the dark yellow sign with its black inscription that showed the way to the park ranger's office.

I just want to get to that office. Please, let there be someone there. I need to get to a phone and...what? George would have figured out by now that she had been abducted on the yacht.

Doesn't matter. You have to get up there. Run, Sophie, run...It's just a race. You've run hundreds. You're making good time.

Bullishly motivating herself, she tried to push creeping doubts and demoralizing fears aside. Her head was a mess of churning, fragmented thoughts. The only thing helping to ground her agitated spirit was a tenacious, inexorable focus on reaching her goal. As she panted up the ever-steepening hill, an image began to take shape. It was as if she had floated upward, leaving her body. She saw herself from a great height, running over the rocky ground with the last of her strength and onto a ruby red, shimmering path... *Where would it take her?* She felt that she needed to find something buried deep within herself—an incredible, magical wonder, and it just had to be waiting for her at the end of the path; like a treasure after a long ordeal.

But she felt that she had come to the end. No—the red path was not going to lead to the promised land, but down to the inner circles of hell itself...Where had she lost her way? It was as if fate was calling to her, trying to warn her, she just needed to listen... *Run, Sophie,* the voice pounded in her head...

Only when she reached the paved road, gasping, did she dare to look back. There was no one behind her. Had Lenka Martialis a.k.a. Borsk thrown in the towel? That was clearly wishful thinking—she almost had to laugh at how delusional that hope was. Borsk would never give up. *Expect the unexpected, Sophie.* Who was speaking to her? The ruby red path had disappeared, making way for black tarmac. Her feet sensing the new surface, she looked up.

The sight of dark forms in the distance, seemingly a bunch of vehicles, gave her hope. But they were so endlessly far away. Nevertheless, she gathered herself, lifted her feet, pushed ahead, arms swinging widely.

The ominous sound seemed to her like the rising then immediately abating sound of an angered hornet. The grumbling noise rose up the hill, turned to a sudden yowl, then back to a grumble. Sophie was filled with a sense of doom. The car park that she was able to see more clearly now was at the end of the paved road, which was still several hundred meters away. The grumbling swelled, turned suddenly into a singing, high-pitched engine sound. Turning her head in terror, Sophie saw the motorbike further down the hill, leaning sharply into a bend.

Her vision blurred. Panting, she raced past the vehicles to the end of the lot. She was wiping the sweat out of her eyes when two shapes blocked her path. A man wearing a bomber jacket and shades, and a woman with rose-tinted glasses—that was all she could take in. "Closed off," she heard the calls. "We're shooting here, you can't..."

The lookouts were determined to keep the running woman from the theater stage, the sight of which now filled Sophie with a sense of relief; its ancient structure appearing timelessly safe and stable in the late afternoon sun. The woman used her fists in a manner that startled the clueless pair. This wasn't an ordinary jostling, but hard, powerful blows that they were forced to endure. They were still rubbing their sore spots when the motorcycle came careening toward them, skidding on its side. The rider had jumped off and was running after the first woman without paying the slightest heed to the amateur guards.

"Holy crap! That was...what a perfect stunt! Did you see that?"

Sophie ran. Not a single fragment of thought was able to take shape. She knew only that she had to run, run, run. The people whom she was running toward were clapping. They were calling out. "Go, go…" she heard, and "they're training for the marathon." What the hell was this? She half-tripped over a role of cable, caught herself and found herself standing almost at the center of the amphitheater's stage, where she had danced only yesterday, without a care in the world…before her stood a hero with blond curls, wearing a jerkin, holding a sword in the hand of his slightly raised arm. Not George!

Suddenly the sword is gone, ripped from his hand. The Greek man starts yelling angrily. Shouts of protest ring out. Sophie now finds herself faced with an even less George-like Lenka Borsk, who is standing in front of her with a sneering grimace on her face, grasping the glinting sword in both hands.

"Stop! That weapon is not a toy," the director yells. "Somebody get these women off my set, damn it!"

Sophie draws back in fright, bumps into a spotlight that falls over and shatters.

Borsk draws back, swings the blade at her foe's head. Gasps of terror are heard. Somebody screams: "That's no stunt! There's going to be a bloodbath!"

"Camera," the astute director yells shrewdly.

Sophie ducks, evading the heavy blow, and instinctively goes for the leg that Borsk's weight is on following the swinging motion. The woman loses her balance and falls. Skillful as the devil's bride is, she manages to swing the sword again mid-fall, nearly making contact with Sophie's throat, but Sophie manages to reflexively roll forward and jump right back to her feet.

Astonishingly, no one intervenes. To the contrary, the spectacle is to the surrounding spectators as blood is to sharks. The rubberneckers still appear to think that this is all a show. It is painfully slow to dawn on Sophie that nobody is going to rectify this misapprehension.

The man warning of a bloodbath was to remain a lone, unheard voice in the wilderness. The director recognized the thrill of the action and did nothing aside from tell the cameraman to continue filming, no matter what. Secretly he fully intended to splice the opportune images of this sensational duel into one of his scenes—if not, there had to be some other use for the material.

His intentions in no way changed, even when the prettier of the two women, having jumped up, cat-like, after her forward role, grabbed his vacant folding chair and hurled it just past his head at her sword-wielding opponent's swinging arm. Then she was gone.

Where is she going? Sophie jumps onto the low wall, runs along it to the stairs that lead to the mosaic platform. Two men, dressed in the same antique garb as the emasculated, formerly sword-wielding hero, are making their way up the stairs at a leisurely pace. One pauses to hold his sword up in front of his face. He is either testing the sharpness of the blade with his thumb, or else showing the other guy, who is turned toward him, something of note.

The two are so taken-aback by the woman pounding toward them, that they remain rooted firmly in place. Sophie effortlessly relieves the first of his weapon, then brusquely shoulders the other aside. Her instincts have led her to this final position, to which there is only one point of access, because she senses that she will have the advantage here, with her back to the wall. It feels like the plane. She can spin, drop; command the tight space, let her foe walk into her trap.

And Borsk does. She descends the stairs agitated, her features contorted with rage, moving frenetically. Uttering obscene curses, sword pointed forward for the final deadly thrust, she leaps off the final step and onto the round platform.

Sophie remains provocatively calm. As Borsk thrusts, she jumps aside lightly and parries, the two blades meeting with a sharp loud clang. The pose is repeated several times. Borsk senses that her opponent is increasingly on the defensive, less controlled in her movements. She catches her under the breast, ripping her T-shirt, a red stain begins to spread. Sophie feels no pain, but far off she hears calls, a male voice, the chopping noise of a helicopter reaches her distantly.

Borsk's face mirrored something akin to satisfaction as Sophie jumped onto the wall separating them from the depths below.

"Now I've got you, you miserable cunt." She draws back wildly, aiming to cut at Sophie's legs and send her over the edge—just as Sophie had anticipated. She has Borsk firmly in her mental crosshairs, her finger on the trigger...As the sword comes swiping across, she jumps, does a somersault in the air—another move she has trained to do hundreds of times—and lands behind her foe. Before Borsk is able to catch her bearings, Sophie spins and stabs the tip of her sword against her neck so firmly that blood immediately begins to spray. Borsk falls back against the wall, arms outstretched. Her weapon is knocked from her hand and skids across the mosaic tiles, out of reach.

Sophie immediately continues her attack. She is not about to leave Borsk any opportunity of a comeback. She presses the sword fiercely under her chin, forcing Borsk to lean far back to avoid the pressure of the blade. Backed over the wall, she waves her legs ineffectively, but with each attempt at a kick, Sophie presses the knife harder against the underside of her chin. Borsk gurgles and groans, her head and shoulders suspended over the drop. In a final, desperate attempt, she tries to pull her leg back to kick Sophie under the chin.

And she succeeds.

As the footage of the talented cameraman, spurred by his director, will later show, Borsk's foot catches Sophie squarely on the throat, throwing her abruptly backward.

She careens, falls, smashes her head against the unforgiving granite to the crowd's shocked screams, lays still.

The spectators of this scene were particularly gripped by the artful, slow-motion sequence showing Borsk as she balanced over the retaining wall on her back, her chin pinned by Sophie's sword. She would, indeed, be able to free herself from this precarious position, but the force of her own thrust against Sophie's neck would send her even further across the edge of the wall and toward the drop that lay beyond it. She fought frantically for balance. She rowed her arms, floundered, tried to jerk her torso up...

The slow, painful sequence leading to the inexorable fall into the abyss resembled a self-inflicted execution. She disappeared over the edge without a sound.

"And *buh-bye*!" the director said mockingly as he finished the scene of the duel to its best dramatic effect in the cutting room later.

…Sophie comes to, blinking and—just like days ago in the snow and ice of the mountains—she finds herself looking into a face. Is the swordsman of yore leaning over her? Has she been vanquished? Then, after a few seconds, she feels an elated rush. "George," she breathes, looking—now adoringly—into his deep, incredibly blue eyes.

"It's alright, darling. You won." He helps her to a sitting position, runs his fingers gingerly through her thick hair. "It's nothing, just a scratch."

The entire film crew has gathered at the top of the stairs. The camera continues to hum. A police helicopter touches down next to the car park.

"Wow," the director's assistant whispers to no one in particular, "would you *believe* this?" All eyes are glued to the spot where they had just witnessed the most breathtaking battle. They hold their collective breaths again. Handsome George Constantinou kneels upon the mosaic image of Eros. His voice resounds through the theater in true heroic fashion. "Sophie Kramer, will you marry me? I want nothing more than to make you happy. You know that we'll be happy together."

She nods, beaming, graciously accepts, flinging her arms around his neck and covering his face with kisses. Her path of destruction has come to an end, the treasure is found, the ruby-red path has led to happiness after all. Up above, the gathered production crew erupts into cheers and applause.

George undoes a thin strap under his shirt, opens a small, leather pouch and produces a sparkling ring. Smiling, he places it on the ring finger of the dainty, blood-smeared hand that his beautiful bride is holding out to him.

EPILOGUE

You will remember Sophie Kramer, who sat in a cabin with Uli Stark on a flight to Yerevan, holding the envelope that Manfred Kleiber had sent her. In it, she was shocked to find the contract originals that meant John Ponter no longer held anything against Baron Suvorov, nor would he be able to legally put his hands on the Rothko painting.

The envelope also contained a CD, which Sophie curiously opened on her laptop, but no longer had the chance to read, since Nachman had called her to the cockpit for landing. Thus she never discovered its contents. Nachman, who had cleared up everything following the shooting, had discovered, much to his surprise, that the data included all of the financial information pertaining to a certain Oleg Borisowich Nedjew, including the names of payment recipients and references to transactions amounting to hundreds of millions of dollars.

Nachman was holding this data on his person when he and his friends confronted John Ponter on the *INS Herev*. The passage back to Israel gave them all the time in the world to bring the obstinate banker to reason. He told them about Garp's plan of exposing the Zurich bank's central role in the scandalous nuclear arms deal between the Russian and the mullahs, all with the intention of subsequently delivering Nedjew's holdings to the mysterious U.S. MADOF Agency.

Nachman conferred with Jack Abramian, who was known to be interested in purchasing a Swiss bank. Threatened with being handed over to U.S. authorities, Ponter ceded on all counts.

He reversed the preparations to transfer Nedjew's fortune with immediate effect. A contract was prepared and signed. And with that, the banker had transferred complete ownership and control of the bank to Abramian.

That same day Cosmo sent Andy to Zurich with a group of financial experts and announced globally that he had taken over the institution.

The fact that Ponter SA was now in the hands of none other than the California tycoon pulled the rug out from under MADOF's feet. All plans to use the Ponter Bank scandal in order to destabilize the Swiss financial market were swiftly and quietly put on ice by the American President personally. Had Cosmo given him a nudge?

The new owner of Ponter SA put the Nedjew monies to a number of uses. First Baron Suvorov's illegitimate daughter was given one hundred million Swiss Francs in reparation for the lost Rothko. Her father's now no longer verifiable debt was waived. Sophie Kramer saw to it that Uli Stark's family was paid ten million Francs in damages for the tragic loss of their son.

Abramian returned one half of the billion dollars that the Iranians had paid for the Sunburns to the Iranian people, who had voted in a new, secular government. He ensured via a contractual agreement that the monies would be used to build a private telecommunications network— in commemoration of Operation Snowdrop. He used the remaining half to compensate for damages that the missile deal had cost him.

Following a heart attack, Shuky Nachman died of a pulmonary embolism at Assuta Hospital in Tel Aviv.

John Ponter was convicted of his crimes in Israel and is currently serving a life sentence. Oleg Nedjew remains untouchable to this day. It is likely that he delivered the Hornbach plans to the Iranians as per the agreement. The Hornbach brothers, who had kept a copy of the plans for the Americans, have never been charged with a crime. Following their iron rule that promises are to be kept, they continue to work with the CIA.

Nico Strom married Sara, the rebel leader Natadschjan's daughter. The festive wedding celebrations in Nagorno-Karabakh lasted three days. Afterward Strom took his bright young bride on a world tour, starting with Europe, the United States and Hawaii, then leading through Asia to south Armenia, where he took over the leadership of the Armenus Corporation as its new CEO.

Sophie Kramer stayed in Cyprus with George and opened a flight school, while her husband continued to officially rent boats.

Armenia's fate developed as Jack Abramian had envisioned. The country experienced a massive economic boom that continues to this day. Thanks to the new, liberal order, Iran grew to become a regional economic power. The new government largely, and wisely, stays out of conflicts in Afghanistan, Lebanon and Palestine. The American president who had placed a call to Jack Abramian after the coup in Tabriz had said it perfectly: "Jack, you stole our show."

Quadrini's heirs were able to claim his Zurich assets. As it turned out, the German had actually paid most of his taxes by the book. Ken Cooper and Marcel Dulliker lent their support to the new management of Ponter SA in setting right any financial transgressions remaining on their books. Both, however, declined Cosmo's generous offer of permanent employment. Chauffeur Petar Ivanovic received a pecuniary reward for valuable services rendered, the exact sum of which remains undisclosed.

Young twin sisters looking for shells on the beach of Kourion found a roll wrapped in plastic. They carried it home and opened it. Liking the pretty shades, they carefully affixed it to their bedroom wall with thumbtacks. The dappled sun shining through their curtains brings out Mark Rothko's subtle, yet resplendent colors each morning, brightening each of their days.

www.ingramcontent.com/pod-product-compliance
Lightning Source LLC
Chambersburg PA
CBHW05090825062
47155CB00001B/147